"A mysterious manuscript in what may be Dumas' own hand, an obscure occult text through which the Devil himself may be summoned, murder, and love dark and dangerous . . . these are the essential ingredients of a . . . dazzlingly allusive, breathlessly exciting novel of adventure and detection"

MICHAEL KERRIGAN, *Scotsman*

"A sophisticated and exciting intellectual game which brilliantly illustrates the sheer delight of fiction"

STEPHANIE MERRITT, *Daily Telegraph*

"Harvill and Sonia Soto (whose translation reads as if it isn't one) are to be congratulated on introducing Pérez-Reverte to English-speaking readers. He deserves to have thousands of them and I, for one, can't wait until his other novels . . . are published" **LEO COLSTON,** *Time Out*

ARTURO PÉREZ-REVERTE was born in Cartagena in 1951. He is a journalist and television reporter specialising in covering the world's trouble-spots. He is the author of two earlier novels, *The Flanders Panel* – a bestseller in Spain and awarded the Grand Prix Annuel de Littérature Policière in France – and *The Fencing Master*. His most recent novel, *The Drumhead*, is to be published by Harvill later this year.

SONIA SOTO is half Spanish and was educated at the French Lycée in London and Newnham College, Cambridge. She works as a freelance translator from Spanish, French and Russian and is the translator of *The Ages of Lulu* by Almudena Grandes.

Arturo Pérez-Reverte

THE DUMAS CLUB

*Translated from the Spanish
by Sonia Soto*

THE HARVILL PRESS
LONDON

First published in with the title *El club Dumas* by Alfaguara S.A., Madrid, 1993

First published in Great Britain in 1996
by The Harvill Press, 84 Thornhill Road, London N1 1RD

1 3 5 7 9 8 6 4 2

A CIP catalogue record for this book is available from the British Library

This translation is published with the financial assistance of the
Spanish Dirección General de Libro y Bibliotecas, Ministerio de Cultura

ISBN 1 86046 152 2

Typeset in Galliard by Libanus Press, Marlborough, Wiltshire

Printed and bound in Great Britain by Mackays of Chatham

Half title illustration: Devil's writing, Newell & Sorrell

To Cala, who set me on the right track

Contents

The flash projected the outline of the hanged man onto the wall. He hung motionless from a light fitting in the centre of the room, and as the photographer moved around him, taking photos, the flash threw the silhouette onto a succession of pictures, glass cabinets full of porcelain, shelves of books, open curtains framing great windows, beyond which the rain was falling.

The examining magistrate was a young man. His thinning hair was untidy and still damp, as was the raincoat he wore while he dictated the formalities to a clerk who sat on the sofa as he typed, his typewriter on a chair. His tapping punctuated the monotonous voice of the magistrate and the whispered comments of the policemen who were moving about the room:

". . . wearing pyjamas and a robe. The cord of this garment was the cause of death by hanging. The deceased has his hands bound in front of him with a tie. On his left foot he is still wearing one of his slippers, the other foot is bare . . ."

The magistrate touched the slippered foot of the dead man and the body turned slightly, slowly, on the end of the taut silk cord which ran from his neck to the light fitting on the ceiling. It moved from left to right, and then back again until it came gradually to a stop in its original position, like the needle of a compass reverting to North. As he moved away, the magistrate turned sideways to avoid a uniformed policeman who was searching for fingerprints beneath the corpse. There was a broken vase on the floor and a book open at a page covered in red pencil marks. The book was an old copy of Bragelonne, The Vicomte de Bragelonne, *a cheap edition bound in cloth. Leaning over the policeman's shoulder, the magistrate glanced at the underlined sentences:*

"They have betrayed me," he murmured, "All is known!"
"All is known at last," answered Porthos, who knew nothing.

He made the clerk note this down, ordering that the book should be included in the report. Then he went to join a tall man who was standing smoking by one of the open windows.

"What do you think?" he asked.

The tall man wore his police badge fastened to a pocket of his leather jacket. Before answering he took time to finish his cigarette, and then threw it over his shoulder and out of the window without looking.

"If it's white and in a bottle, it tends to be milk," he answered cryptically, at last, but not so cryptically that the magistrate didn't smile slightly.

Unlike the policeman he was looking out into the street where it was still raining hard. Somebody opened a door on the other side of the room and a blast of air splashed drops of water against his face.

"Shut the door," he ordered without turning round. Then he spoke to the policeman. "Sometimes homicide disguises itself as suicide."

"And vice versa," the other man pointed out calmly.

"What do you think of the hands and tie?"

"Sometimes they're scared they'll change their minds at the last minute . . . Otherwise he'd have had them tied behind him."

"It makes no difference," objected the magistrate. "It's a strong, thin cord. Once he'd lost his footing he wouldn't have had a chance, even with his hands free."

"Anything's possible. The autopsy will tell us more."

The magistrate glanced once more at the corpse. The policeman searching for fingerprints stood up with the book.

"Strange, that business of the page."

The tall policeman shrugged his shoulders.

"I don't read much," he said, "but Porthos, wasn't he one of those . . . Athos, Porthos, Aramis and d'Artagnan." He was counting with his thumb on the fingers of one hand and when he'd finished he stopped, looking thoughtful. "Funny. I've always wondered why they were called the three musketeers when really there were four of them."

2

I

The Anjou Wine

The reader must be prepared to witness the most sinister scenes.
E. Sue: *The Mysteries of Paris*

My name is Boris Balkan and I once translated *The Charterhouse of Parma*. Apart from that, I've edited a few books on the nineteenth-century popular novel, my reviews and articles appear in supplements and journals throughout Europe and I organize courses on contemporary writers at summer schools. Nothing spectacular, I'm afraid. Particularly these days when suicide disguises itself as homicide, novels are written by Roger Ackroyd's doctor, and far too many people insist on publishing two hundred pages on the fascinating emotions they experience when they look in the mirror.

But let's stick to the story.

I first met Lucas Corso when he came to see me carrying 'The Anjou Wine' under his arm. Corso was a mercenary of the book world, hunting down books for other people. That meant talking fast and getting his hands dirty. He needed good reflexes, patience and a lot of luck – and a prodigious memory to recall the exact dusty corner of an old man's shop where a book now worth a fortune lay forgotten. His clientèle was small and select: a couple of dozen bookdealers in Milan, Paris, London, Barcelona or Lausanne, the kind that sells through catalogues, only makes safe investments, and never handles more than fifty or so titles at any one time. High-class dealers in early printed books for whom thousands of dollars depend on whether something is parchment or vellum, or three centimetres wider in the margin. Jackals on the scent of the Gutenberg Bible, antique fair sharks, auction room leeches, they would sell their grandmothers for a first edition. But they receive their clients in rooms with leather sofas, views of the Duomo or Lake Constance, and they never get their hands – or their consciences – dirty. That's what men like Corso are for.

He took his canvas bag off his shoulder and put it on the floor, down by his scuffed Oxfords. He stared at the framed portrait of Rafael Sabatini that stands on my desk, next to the fountain pen I use for correcting articles and proofs. I was pleased because most visitors paid him little attention, taking him for an aged relative. I waited for his reaction. He was half-smiling as he sat down – a youthful expression, like a cartoon rabbit in a dead-end street. The kind of look that wins over the audience straight away. In time I found out he could also smile like a cruel, hungry wolf, and that he would choose a smile to suit the circumstances. But that was much later. Now he seemed convincing, so I decided to risk a password:

"He was born with the gift of laughter," I quoted, pointing at the portrait, "and with a feeling that the world was mad . . ."

He nodded slowly and deliberately. I felt a friendly complicity with him which, in spite of all that happened later, I still feel. From a hidden packet he brought out an unfiltered cigarette that was as crumpled as his old overcoat and corduroy trousers. He turned it over in his fingers, watching me through steel-rimmed glasses, set crookedly on his nose under his untidy fringe of slightly greying hair. As if holding a hidden gun, he kept his other hand in one of his pockets, huge and deformed by books, catalogues, papers and, as I also found out later, a hip flask full of Bols gin.

". . . and this was his entire inheritance." He completed the quotation effortlessly, before settling himself in the armchair and smiling again. "But if I must be honest, I prefer *Captain Blood*."

With a stern expression I lifted my fountain pen.

"You're mistaken. *Scaramouche* is to Sabatini what *The Three Musketeers* is to Dumas." I bowed briefly to the portrait. "'He was born with the gift of laughter . . .' In the entire history of the adventure serial no two opening lines can compare."

"That may be true," he conceded after a moment's reflection. Then he laid the manuscript on the table, in a protective folder with plastic pockets, one for each page. "It's a coincidence you should mention Dumas."

He pushed the folder towards me, turning it round so I could read its contents. The text was in French, written on one side of the page only. There were two types of paper, both discoloured by age: one white, and the other pale blue with light squares. The handwriting on each was different – on the white pages it was smaller and more spiky. The handwriting on the blue paper, in black ink, also appeared on the white pages but as annotations. There were fifteen pages in all, eleven of them blue.

"Interesting." I looked up at Corso. He was watching me, his calm gaze moving from the folder to me, then back again. "Where did you find it?"

He scratched his eyebrow, no doubt calculating whether he needed to provide such details in exchange for the information he wanted. The result was a third facial expression, this time an innocent rabbit. Corso was a professional.

"Around. Through a client of a client."

"I see."

He paused briefly, cautious. Caution is a sign of prudence and reserve, but also of shrewdness. And we both knew it.

"Of course," he added, "I'll give you names if you request them."

I answered that it wouldn't be necessary, which seemed to reassure him. He adjusted his glasses before asking my opinion of the manuscript. Not answering immediately, I turned the pages until I came to the first. The title was written in capital letters, in thicker strokes: *LE VIN D'ANJOU*.

I read out the first few lines:

Après de nouvelles presque désespérées du roi, le bruit de sa convalescence commençait a se répandre dans le camp . . .

I couldn't help smiling. Corso indicated his approval, inviting me to comment.

"Without the slightest doubt," I said, "this is by Alexandre Dumas père. 'The Anjou Wine': chapter forty-something, I seem to remember, of *The Three Musketeers*."

"Forty-two," confirmed Corso. "Chapter forty-two."

"Is it authentic? Dumas's original manuscript?"

"That's why I'm here. I want you to tell me."

I shrugged slightly, reluctant to assume such a responsibility.

"Why me?"

It was a stupid question, the kind that only serves to gain time. It must have seemed like false modesty, because he suppressed a look of impatience.

"You're an expert," he retorted, somewhat dryly. "As well as being Spain's most influential literary critic, you know all there is to know about the nineteenth-century popular novel."

"You're forgetting Stendhal."

"Not at all. I read your translation of *The Charterhouse of Parma*."

"Indeed. I am honoured."

"Don't be. I preferred Consuelo Berges's version."

We both smiled. I continued to find him likeable, and I was beginning to form an idea of his style.

"Do you know any of my books?" I asked.

"Some. *Lupin, Raffles, Rocambole, Holmes*, for instance. And your studies of Valle-Inclán, Baroja and Galdós. Also *Dumas: the Shadow of a Giant*. And your essay on *The Count of Monte Cristo*."

"Have you read all those?"

"No. I work with books but that doesn't mean I have to read them."

He was lying. Or at least exaggerating. The man was conscientious: before coming to see me he'd looked at everything about me he could lay his hands on. He was one of those compulsive readers who've devoured anything in print since a most tender age – although it was highly unlikely that Corso's childhood had ever merited the term "tender".

"I understand," I answered, just to say something.

He frowned for a moment, wondering whether he'd forgotten anything. He took off his glasses, breathed on the lenses and set about cleaning them with a very crumpled handkerchief which he pulled out from one of the bottomless pockets of his coat. However fragile the over-sized coat made him appear, with his rodent-like incisors and calm expression Corso was as solid as a concrete block. His features were sharp and precise, full of angles. They framed alert eyes always ready to express an innocence which was dangerous for anyone who was taken in by it. At times, particularly when still, he seemed slower and more clumsy than he really was. He looked vulnerable and defenceless: barmen gave him an extra drink on the house, men offered him cigarettes, and women wanted to adopt him on the spot. Later, when you realized what had happened, it was too late to catch him. He was disappearing into the distance, having notched up another victory.

He gestured with his glasses towards the manuscript. "Going back to Dumas. Surely anyone who's written five hundred pages about him ought to sense something familiar when faced with one of his original manuscripts?"

With the reverence of a priest handling holy vestments I laid a hand on the pages protected by the plastic folders.

"I fear I'm going to disappoint you, but I don't feel anything."

We both laughed, Corso in a peculiar way, almost under his breath, like someone who is not sure whether he and his companion are laughing at the same thing. An oblique, distant laugh, with a hint of insolence, the kind that lingers in the air even after it has faded. Even when its owner has been gone for some time.

"Let's take this a step at a time," I went on. "Does the manuscript belong to you?"

"I've already told you that it doesn't. A client of mine has just acquired it, and he finds it strange that no one should have heard of this complete, original chapter of *The Three Musketeers* until now . . . He wants it authenticated by an expert, so that's what I'm working on."

"I'm surprised at you dealing with such a minor matter." This was true. I'd heard of Corso before this meeting. "I mean, after all, nowadays Dumas . . ."

I left the sentence hanging and smiled with the appropriate expression of bitter complicity. But Corso didn't take up my invitation and stayed on the defensive:

"The client's a friend of mine," he said evenly. "It's a personal favour."

"I see, but I'm not sure that I can be any help to you. I have seen some of the original manuscripts, and this one could be authentic. However, certifying it would be another matter. For that you'd need a good graphologist . . . I know an excellent one in Paris, Achille Replinger. He owns a shop which specializes in autographs and historical documents, near Saint-Germain-des-Prés . . . He's an expert on nineteenth-century French writers, a charming man and a good friend of mine." I pointed to one of the frames on the wall. "He sold me that Balzac letter many years ago. For a very high price."

I took out my diary to copy down the address for Corso and gave him a card. He put it in an old worn wallet full of notes and papers. Then he brought out a notepad and pencil from one of his coat pockets. The pencil had a rubber at one end, chewed like a schoolboy's.

"Could I ask you a few questions?"

"Yes, of course."

"Did you know of any complete handwritten chapter of *The Three Musketeers*?"

I shook my head and replaced the cap on my Mont Blanc.

"No. The novel came out in instalments in *Le Siècle* between March and July 1844 . . . Once the text had been typeset by a compositor the original manuscript was thrown away. A few fragments remained, however. You can have a look at them in an appendix to the 1968 Garnier edition."

"Four months isn't very long," Corso was chewing the end of his pencil thoughtfully. "Dumas wrote quickly."

"They all did in those days. Stendhal wrote *The Charterhouse of Parma* in seven weeks. And in any case Dumas used collaborators, ghost writers. The one for *The Three Musketeers* was called Auguste Maquet . . . They worked together on the sequel, *Twenty Years After*, and *The Vicomte de Bragelonne* which completes the cycle. And on *The Count of Monte Cristo* and a few other novels. You will have read those I suppose."

"Of course. Everybody has."

"Everybody had in the old days, you mean." I leafed respectfully through the manuscript. "The times are long gone when Dumas's name increased print runs and made publishers rich. Almost all his novels came out like that – in instalments ending in 'To be continued . . .' The readers would be on tenterhooks until the next episode. But of course you know about all that."

"Don't worry. Go on."

"What more can I tell you? In the classic serial, the recipe for success is simple: the hero, or heroine, has qualities or features that make the reader identify with him or her . . . If it happens nowadays in TV soaps, imagine the effect in those days when there was no television or radio, on a middle class hungry for surprise and entertainment, and undiscriminating when it came to formal quality or taste . . . Dumas was a genius and he understood all this. Like an alchemist in his laboratory he added a dash of this, another dash of that, and, with his talent, combined it all to create a drug which had many addicts." I tapped my chest, not without pride. "Which has them still."

Corso was taking notes. Precise, unscrupulous and deadly as a black mamba, was how one of his acquaintances described him later when his name came up in conversation. He had a singular way of facing people, peering through his crooked glasses and slowly nodding in agreement with a reasonable, well-meaning but doubtful expression, like a whore tolerantly listening to a romantic sonnet. As if he was giving you a chance to correct yourself before it was too late.

After a moment he stopped and looked up.

"But your work doesn't only deal with the popular novel. You're a well-known literary critic of other more –" he hesitated, searching for a word – "more serious works. And Dumas himself described his novels as easy literature . . . Sounds rather patronizing towards his readers."

This device was typical of him. It was one of his trademarks, like Rocambole leaving a playing card instead of a calling card. He'd put something forward casually, as if he himself had no opinion on the matter, slyly goading you into a reaction. Somebody who is annoyed will put forward arguments and justifications, giving out more inform-ation to his opponent. I wasn't a fool and I knew what Corso was doing, but even so, or maybe because of it, I felt annoyed.

"Don't talk in clichés," I said irritably. "The serial genre produced a lot of disposable stuff, but Dumas was way above all that . . . In literature, time is like a shipwreck in which God looks after his own. I challenge you to name any fictional heroes who have survived in as good health as d'Artagnan and his friends, with the possible exception of Sherlock Holmes . . . *The Three Musketeers* was undoubt-edly a swashbuckling novel full of melodrama with all the sins typical of the genre. But it's also a distinguished example of the serial, and of a standard well above the norm. A tale of friendship and adventure that has stayed fresh even though tastes have changed and that there is now an idiotic tendency to despise action in novels. It would seem that since Joyce we have had to make do with Molly Bloom and give up Nausicaa on the beach after the shipwreck . . . Have you read my essay, 'Friday, or the Ship's Compass?' Give me Homer's *Ulysses* any day."

I raised my tone at that point, waiting for Corso's reaction. He smiled slightly and remained silent but I remembered his expression when I had quoted Scaramouche so I felt sure I was on the right track.

"I know what you're referring to," he said at last. "Your views are well known and controversial, Mr Balkan."

"My views are well known because I've made sure of it. And as for patronizing his readers, as you claimed a moment ago, perhaps you didn't know that the author of *The Three Musketeers* fought in the streets during the revolutions of 1830 and 1848. And he supplied arms, paid for out of his own pocket, to Garibaldi . . . Don't forget that

Dumas's father was a famous republican general . . . The man was full of love for the people and liberty."

"Although his respect for the truth was only relative."

"That's not important. Do you know how he answered those who accused him of raping History? 'True, I have raped History, but it has produced some beautiful offspring.'"

I put my pen down and went to the glass cabinets full of books covering the walls of my study. I opened one and took out a volume bound in dark leather.

"Like all great writers of fables," I went on, "Dumas was a liar . . . Countess Dash, who knew him well, says in her memoirs that all he had to do was tell some apocryphal anecdote and it would be taken as the historical truth . . . Take Cardinal Richelieu: he was the greatest man of his time but once the treacherous Dumas had finished with him, the distorted image we've been left with is that of a sinister villain . . ." I turned to Corso, holding the book. "Do you know this? It was written by Gatien de Courtilz de Sandras, a musketeer who lived in the late seventeenth century. They're the memoirs of the real d'Artagnan, Charles de Batz-Castelmore, Comte d'Artagnan. He was a Gascon, born in 1615, and was indeed a musketeer. Although he didn't live in Richelieu's time, but Mazarin's. He died in 1673 during the siege of Maastricht when, like his fictional namesake, he was about to be awarded the marshal's staff . . . So you see, Dumas's raping did indeed breed beautiful offspring . . . An obscure flesh and blood Gascon, forgotten by History, transformed into a legendary giant by the novelist's genius."

Corso sat there and listened. I handed him the book and he leafed through it carefully, with great interest. He turned the pages slowly, barely brushing them with his fingertips, only touching the very edge. From time to time he would pause over a name, or a chapter. Behind his spectacles his eyes worked sure and fast. He stopped once to note the details in his pad: '*Mémoires de M. d'Artagnan*, G. de Courtilz, 1704, P. Rouge, 4 volumes in 12mo, 4th edition'. Then he shut the notebook and looked up at me.

"You said it: he was a trickster."

"Yes," I agreed, sitting down again. "But a genius. While some would simply have plagiarized others' material, he created a fictional world which still endures today . . . 'Man does not steal, he conquers,' he often said. 'Every province he seizes becomes an annexe of his empire: he imposes laws, and fills it with themes and characters, casting his shadow over it . . .' What else is literary creation? For him, the history of France was a rich source of material. His was an extraordinary trick: he'd leave the frame alone but alter the picture, mercilessly plundering the treasure that was offered to him . . . Dumas turned central characters into minor ones, humble secondary characters became protagonists, and he wrote pages about events that only took up two lines in the historical chronicles. The pact of friendship between d'Artagnan and his companions never existed, one of the reasons being that half of them didn't even know each other . . . Nor was there a Comte de la Fère. Or rather there were several of them, though none called Athos. But Athos did exist. He was called Armand de Sillègue, Lord of Athos, and he was killed in a duel before d'Artagnan had even joined the King's musketeers . . . Aramis was Henri d'Aramitz, a squire and lay priest in the seneschalship of Oloron, who enrolled in the musketeers under his uncle's command in 1640. He ended his days on his estate, with a wife and four children. As for Porthos . . ."

"Don't tell me there was a Porthos too."

"Yes. His name was Isaac de Portau and he must have known Aramis because he joined the musketeers just three years after him, in 1643. According to the chronicles he died prematurely, either from a disease, at war, or in a duel like Athos."

Corso drummed his fingers on d'Artagnan's *Mémoires* and shook his head. He was smiling.

"Any minute now you're going to tell me there was a Milady . . ."

"Correct. But her name wasn't Anne de Breuil, and she wasn't the Duchesse de Winter. Nor did she have a fleur-de-lis tattooed on her shoulder. But she was one of Richelieu's secret agents. Her name was the Countess of Carlisle and she stole two diamond tags from the Duke of Buckingham . . . Don't look at me like that. It's all in La Rochefoucauld's memoirs. And La Rochefoucauld was a very reliable man."

Corso was staring at me intently. He didn't seem the type to be easily surprised, particularly when it came to books, but he looked impressed. Later, when I came to know him better, I wondered whether his admiration was sincere, or just another of his professional wiles. Now that it's all over, I think I know: I was one more source of information, and Corso was trying to get as much out of me as possible.

"This is all very interesting," he said.

"If you go to Paris, Replinger can tell you much more than I can."
I looked at the manuscript on the table. "Though I'm not sure it's
worth the price of a trip . . . What would this chapter fetch on the
market?"

He started chewing his pencil again and looked doubtful.

"Not much. I'm really after something else."

I gave a sad conspiratorial smile. Amongst my few possessions I have
an Ibarra edition of *Don Quixote* and a Volkswagen. Of course the car
cost more than the book.

"I know what you mean," I said warmly.

Corso made a resigned gesture. He bared his rodent-like teeth in a
bitter smile:

"Unless the Japanese get fed up with Van Gogh and Picasso," he
suggested, "and start investing in rare books."

I recoiled in horror.

"God help us if that ever happens."

"Speak for yourself." He looked at me sardonically through his
crooked glasses. "I plan to make a fortune."

He put his notebook away and stood up, hanging his canvas bag on
his shoulder. I couldn't help reflecting on his falsely placid appearance,
with his steel-rimmed glasses sitting unsteadily on his nose. I found out
later that he lived alone, surrounded by books, both his own and other
people's, and that as well as being a hired hunter of books he was an
expert on Napoleon's battles. He could set out on a board, from
memory, the exact order of battle on the eve of Waterloo. A family-
related story, slightly strange, and I only found out all about it much
later. I have to admit, described like that, Corso doesn't sound very
attractive. And yet, if I keep to the strict accuracy with which I am
narrating this story, I must add that his awkward appearance, the very
clumsiness which seemed – and I don't know how he managed it – at
once caustic and vulnerable, ingenuous and aggressive, made him both
attractive to women and sympathetic to men. But the positive feeling
suddenly evaporated, as when you feel in your pocket and realize that
you've just had your wallet stolen.

Corso picked up his manuscript and I saw him to the door. He
shook my hand in the hallway, where portraits of Stendhal, Conrad and
Valle-Inclán looked out severely at an atrocious print that the block's
residents' association had decided to hang on the landing a few months
earlier, much against my wishes.

Only then did I dare ask him:

"I confess I'm intrigued as to where you found it."

He hesitated before answering, weighing up the pros and cons. I had received him in a friendly manner so he was in my debt. Also he might need my help again, so he really had no choice.

"Maybe you know him," he answered at last. "My client bought the manuscript from a certain Taillefer."

I allowed myself a look of moderate surprise.

"Enrique Taillefer? The publisher?"

He was gazing absently around the hallway. At last he nodded.

"The very same."

We both fell silent. Corso shrugged, and I very well knew why. The cause could be read about in the pages of any newspaper: Enrique Taillefer had been dead a week. He had been found hanged in his house, the cord of his silk robe around his neck and his feet dangling in empty space, over an open book and a porcelain vase smashed into pieces.

Some time later, when it was all over, Corso agreed to tell me the rest of the story. So I can now give a fairly accurate picture of a chain of events that I didn't witness, leading to the fatal dénouement and the solution to the mystery surrounding the Dumas Club. Thanks to what Corso told me I can now, like Dr Watson, tell you that the following scene took place in Makarova's bar an hour after our meeting. Flavio La Ponte came in shaking off the rain, leant on the bar next to Corso and ordered a beer while he caught his breath. Then he looked back at the street, aggressive but triumphant, as if he had just come through sniper fire. It was raining with biblical force.

"The firm of Armengol & Sons, Antiquarian Books and Biblio-graphical Curiosities, intends to sue you," he said. He had a ring of froth on his curly blond beard, round his mouth. "Their solicitor has just telephoned."

"What are they accusing me of?" asked Corso.

"Cheating a little old lady and plundering her library. They swear the deal was theirs."

"Well, they should have got up early like I did."

"That's what I said but they're still furious. When they went to pick up the books, the *Persiles* and the *Royal Charter of Castille* had disappeared. And you gave a valuation for the rest which was way over the odds. So now the owner won't sell. She wants double what they're prepared to pay . . ." He drank some beer and winked conspiratorially. "That neat manoeuvre is known as nailing a library."

"I know what it's called." Corso smiled malevolently. "And Armengol & Sons know it too."

"You're being unnecessarily cruel," said La Ponte impartially. "But what they're most sore about is the *Royal Charter*. They say that your taking it was a low blow."

"How could I leave it there? Latin glossary by Díaz de Montalvo, no typographical details but printed in Sevilla by Alonso Del Puerto, possibly 1482 . . ." He adjusted his glasses and looked at his friend. "What do you think?"

"Sounds good to me. But they're a bit jumpy."

"They should take a Valium."

It was early evening. There was very little room at the bar and they were pressed shoulder to shoulder, surrounded by cigarette smoke and the murmur of conversation, trying not to dunk their elbows in the puddles of beer on the counter.

"Apparently," added La Ponte, "the *Persiles* is a first edition. The binding's signed by Trautz-Bauzonnet."

Corso shook his head.

"By Hardy. Morocco leather."

"Even better. Anyway I swore I'd had nothing to do with it. You know I have an aversion to lawsuits."

"But not to your thirty per cent."

La Ponte raised his hand with dignity.

"Stop right there. Don't confuse business with pleasure, Corso. One thing is our beautiful friendship. Food for my children is quite another."

"You don't have any children."

La Ponte looked at him mischievously.

"Give me time. I'm still young."

He was short, good-looking, neat and something of a dandy. His hair was thinning on top. He smoothed it down with his hand, checking to see how it looked in the bar's mirror. Then he cast a practised eye around the room, checking out the ladies. He was always on the look-out, just as he always liked to use short sentences in conversation. His father, a very cultured bookseller, had taught him to write by dictating texts by Azorín to him. Hardly anyone reads Azorín any more but La Ponte still constructed his sentences like him. With lots of full stops. It gave him a certain aplomb when it came to seducing female customers in the back room of his bookshop in the Calle Mayor where he kept his erotic classics.

"Anyway," he added, "I've got some business outstanding with Armengol & Sons. Rather delicate, but I could make a quick profit."

"You've got business with me too," said Corso over his beer. "You're the only poor bookseller I work with. And you're going to be the one to sell those books."

"All right, all right," said La Ponte equably. "You know I'm a practical man. A despicable pragmatist."

"Yes."

"Imagine this was a Western. As your friend, I'd take a bullet for you, but only in the shoulder."

"At the very most," said Corso.

"Anyway, it doesn't matter." La Ponte was looking round distractedly. "I've already got a buyer for the *Persiles*."

"Then get me another beer. An advance on your commission."

They were old friends. They both loved frothy beer and Bols gin in its glazed earthenware bottle. But above all they loved antiquarian books and the auctions held in old Madrid auction rooms. They had met many years earlier when Corso was rooting around in bookshops specializing in Spanish authors. A client of his was looking for a bogus copy of *Celestina* which was supposed to pre-date the known 1499 edition. La Ponte didn't have the book and hadn't even heard of it. But he did have an edition of the *Dictionary of Rare and Improbable Books* by Julio Ollero in which it was mentioned. They chatted about books and realized they had a lot in common. La Ponte shut his shop and they sealed their friendship by drinking all there was to drink in Makarova's bar, while swapping anecdotes about Melville. La Ponte had been brought up on tales of the *Pequod* and the escapades of Azorín. "Call me Ishmael," he said as he drained his third Bols straight down. And Corso called him Ishmael, quoting from memory and in his honour, the episode of the forging of Ahab's harpoon:

Three punctures were made in the heathen flesh, and the White Whale's barbs were then tempered.

They duly drank a toast. By then La Ponte was no longer watching the girls coming in and out of the bar. He swore eternal friendship to

Corso. Despite his militant cynicism and his occupation as a rapacious seller of old books, underneath he was a naive man. So he was unaware that his new friend with the crooked glasses was discreetly outflanking him: Corso had glanced over his shelves and spotted a few books he planned to make an offer for. In fact, La Ponte, with his pale, curly beard, the gentle look of seaman Billy Budd with daydreams of a frustrated whale hunter, had awakened Corso's sympathy. He could even recite the names of all the crew of the *Pequod*: Ahab, Stubb, Starbuck, Flask, Perth, Parsee, Queequeg, Tasthego, Daggoo . . . Or the names of all the ships mentioned in *Moby Dick*: the *Goney*, the *Town-Ho*, the *Jeroboam*, the *Jungfrau*, the *Rose Bud,* the *Bachelor,* the *Delight,* the *Rachel* . . . And, proof of proof, he even knew what ambergris was. They had talked of books and whales. And so that night the Brotherhood of Nantucket Harpooneers was founded, with Flavio La Ponte as chairman, Lucas Corso as treasurer. They were the only two members and had Makarova's tolerant patronage. She'd given them their last round on the house and ended up sharing another bottle of gin with them.

"I'm going to Paris," said Corso, watching the reflection of a fat woman putting coin after coin in a fruit machine. It seemed as if the silly little tune and the colours, fruits and bells would keep her there for all eternity, hypnotized and motionless but for her hand pushing the buttons. "To see about your 'Anjou Wine'."

His friend wrinkled his nose and gave him a sideways glance. Paris meant more expense, complications. La Ponte was a stingy, small-time bookseller.

"You know I can't afford it."

Corso slowly emptied his glass.

"Yes, you can." He took out a few coins and paid his round. "I'm going about something else."

"Oh yes?" said La Ponte, intrigued.

Makarova put two more beers on the counter. She was large, blonde, in her forties, and had short hair and a ring in one ear, a souvenir of her time on a Russian trawler. She wore narrow trousers and a shirt with the sleeves rolled up to her shoulders. Her over-developed biceps weren't the only masculine thing about her. She always had a lighted cigarette smouldering in the corner of her mouth. With her Baltic look and her way of moving, she looked like a fitter from a ball-bearing factory in Leningrad.

"I read that book," she told Corso accentuating her r's. As she spoke, ash from her cigarette dropped onto her damp shirt. "That tart Bovary. Poor little fool."

"I'm so glad you grasped the nub of the matter."

Makarova wiped down the counter with a cloth. At the other end of the bar Zizi was watching as she worked the till. She was the complete opposite of Makarova: much younger, slight and terribly jealous. Sometimes, just before closing time, they would quarrel drunkenly and come to blows, with the last few regulars watching. Once, with a black eye after one of these rows, Zizi upped and left, furious and vindictive. Makarova wept copiously into the beer until she returned three days later. That night they closed early and left with their arms around each other's waists, kissing in doorways like two teenagers in love.

"He's off to Paris." La Ponte nodded in Corso's direction. "To see what he can pull out of the hat."

Makarova collected the empty glasses and looked at Corso through the smoke of her cigarette.

"He's always up to something," she said in her flat, guttural tone.

Then she put the glasses in the sink and went to serve some other customers, swinging her broad shoulders. Corso was the only member of the opposite sex who escaped her contempt, and she would proclaim this when she didn't charge him for a drink. Even Zizi looked upon him with a certain neutrality. Once when Makarova was arrested for punching a policeman in the face during a gay rights march, Zizi had waited all night on a bench in the police station. Corso called all his contacts in the police, stayed with her and supplied sandwiches and a bottle of gin. It all made La Ponte absurdly jealous.

"Why Paris?" he asked, though his mind was on other things. His left elbow had just prodded something deliciously soft. He was delighted to find that his neighbour at the bar was a young blonde with enormous breasts.

Corso took another gulp of beer.

"I'm also going to Sintra in Portugal." He was still watching the fat woman at the fruit machine. She'd run out of coins and was now getting change from Zizi. "On some business for Varo Borja."

His friend made a whistling sound. Varo Borja, Spain's leading bookdealer. His catalogue was small and select. He was also well known as a booklover to whom money was no object. Impressed,

La Ponte asked for more beer and more information, with the greedy look that automatically clicked on when he heard the word *book*. Although he admitted to being a miser and a coward, he wasn't an envious man, except when it came to pretty, harpoonable women. In professional matters, he was always glad to get hold of good pieces with little risk, but he also had real respect for his friend's work and clientèle.

"Have you ever heard of *The Nine Doors*?"

The bookseller was searching slowly through his pockets, hoping that Corso would pay for that round too. He was also just about to turn round and take a closer look at his voluptuous neighbour, but Corso's words caused him to forget her instantly. He was open-mouthed.

"Don't tell me Varo Borja's after that book . . ."

Corso put his last few coins on the counter. Makarova brought another two beers.

"He's had it for some time. He paid a fortune for it."

"I'll bet he did. There are only three or four known copies."

"Three," specified Corso. "One in Sintra, in the Fargas collection. Another at the Ungern Foundation in Paris. And the third, from the sale of the Terral-Coy library in Madrid, was bought by Varo Borja."

Fascinated, La Ponte stroked his curly beard. Of course he had heard of Fargas, the Portuguese bookcollector. As for Baroness Ungern, she was a potty old woman who'd become a millionairess from writing books about demonology and the occult. Her recent book, *Naked Isis*, was a runaway bestseller in all the stores.

"What I don't understand," concluded La Ponte, "is what you've got to do with any of it."

"Do you know the book's history?"

"Vaguely," said La Ponte.

Corso dipped a finger in his beer and began to draw pictures on the marble counter.

"Period: mid seventeenth century. Scene: Venice. Central character: a printer by the name of Aristide Torchia, who had the idea of publishing the so-called *Book of the Nine Doors of the Kingdom of Shadows*, a kind of manual for summoning the Devil . . . It wasn't a good time for that sort of thing: the Holy Office managed, without much trouble, to have Torchia handed over to them. He was charged with practising satanic arts and all that goes with them, aggravated by the fact, they said, that he'd reproduced nine prints from the famous *Delomelanicon*, the occult classic which, tradition has it, was written by Lucifer himself . . ."

Makarova had moved closer on the other side of the bar and she was listening with interest, wiping her hands on her shirt. La Ponte, about to take another gulp of beer, stopped and instinctively looking like a greedy bookseller, asked:

"What happened to the book?"

"You can imagine: it all went onto a big bonfire." Corso frowned evilly. He seemed sorry to have missed it. "They also say that as it burned you could hear the Devil screaming."

Her elbows on Corso's beer diagrams, Makarova grunted sceptically amongst the beer handles. With her blonde, manly looks and her cool, Nordic temperament she didn't go in for these murky southern superstitions. La Ponte was more impressionable. Suddenly thirsty, he gulped down his beer.

"It must have been the printer they heard screaming."

"Imagine."

La Ponte shivered at the thought.

Corso went on: "Tortured with the thoroughness the Inquisition reserved for dealing with the Evil Arts, the printer finally confessed, between screams, that there still remained one book, hidden somewhere. Then he shut his mouth and didn't open it again until they burnt him alive. And even then it was only to say *Aagh*."

Makarova smiled contemptuously at the memory of Torchia the printer, or maybe at the executioners who hadn't been able to make him confess. La Ponte was frowning.

"You say that only one of the books was saved," he objected. "But before, you said there were three known copies."

Corso had taken off his glasses and was looking at them against the light to check how clean they were.

"And that's the problem," he said. "The books have appeared and then disappeared through wars, thefts and fires. It's not known which is the authentic one."

"Maybe they're all forgeries," Makarova suggested sensibly.

"Maybe. So I've got to find out whether Varo Borja has been taken for a ride. That's why I'm going to Sintra and Paris." He adjusted his glasses and looked at La Ponte. "While I'm there I'll see about your manuscript as well."

The bookseller agreed thoughtfully, eyeing the girl with the big breasts in the mirror.

"Compared to that, it seems ridiculous to make you waste your time on *The Three Musketeers* . . ."

"What are you talking about?" said Makarova, no longer neutral. She was really offended. "It's the best book I've ever read!"

She slammed her hands down on the bar for emphasis, making the muscles on her bare forearms bulge. Boris Balkan would be happy to hear that, thought Corso. As well as the Dumas novel, Makarova's list of top ten books, for which he was literary adviser, included amongst others *War and Peace, Watership Down,* and *Carol* by Patricia Highsmith.

"Don't worry," he told La Ponte, "I'll charge the expenses to Varo Borja. But I'd say your 'Anjou Wine' is authentic . . . Who would forge something like that?"

"People do all sorts of things," Makarova pointed out sagely.

La Ponte agreed with Corso – forging such a document would be absurd. The late Taillefer had guaranteed its authenticity to him. It was in Dumas's own hand. And Taillefer could be trusted.

"I used to take him old newspaper serials. He'd buy them all." He took a sip and then laughed to himself. "Good excuse to go and get a look at his wife's legs. She's a pretty spectacular blonde. Anyway, one day he opened a drawer and put 'The Anjou Wine' on the table. 'It's yours,' he said straight out, 'as long as you get an expert opinion on it and put it on sale immediately.'"

A customer called Makarova and ordered a tonic water. She told him to go to hell. She stayed where she was, her cigarette burning down in her mouth and her eyes half-closed because of the smoke. Waiting for the rest of the story.

"Is that all?" asked Corso.

La Ponte gestured vaguely.

"Almost. I tried to dissuade him because I knew he was crazy about that sort of thing. He'd have sold his soul for a rare book. But he'd made up his mind. 'If you don't do it I'll give it to someone else,' he said. That touched a nerve, of course. My professional nerve, I mean."

"You don't need to explain," said Corso. "What other kind do you have?"

La Ponte turned to Makarova for support. But one glance at her slate grey eyes and he gave up. They were about as warm as a Scandinavian fjord at three in the morning.

"It's nice to feel loved," he said at last, bitterly.

The man after a tonic water must really have been thirsty, Corso thought, because he was getting insistent. Makarova, looking at him out of the corner of her eye and without moving a muscle, suggested he find another bar before she gave him a black eye. The man thought it over. He seemed to get the message and left.

"Enrique Taillefer was a strange man." La Ponte ran his hand over his thinning hair again, still eyeing the voluptuous blonde in the mirror. "He wanted me to sell the manuscript and get publicity for the whole business." He lowered his voice so as not to worry the blonde. "'Somebody's going to get a surprise,' he told me mysteriously. He winked at me as if he was going to play a joke on someone. Four days later he was dead."

"Dead," repeated Makarova in her guttural way, savouring the word. She was more and more interested.

"Suicide," explained Corso.

But she shrugged, as if to say there wasn't much difference between suicide and murder. There was one doubtful manuscript and a definite corpse: quite enough for a conspiracy theory.

On hearing the word suicide La Ponte nodded lugubriously.

"So they say."

"You don't seem too sure."

"No, I'm not. It's all a bit odd." He frowned again, suddenly looking sombre and forgetting the blonde in the mirror. "Smells very fishy to me."

"Did Taillefer never tell you how he got hold of the manuscript?"

"At the beginning I didn't ask. Then it was too late."

"Did you speak to his widow?"

La Ponte suddenly looked brighter. He grinned from ear to ear.

"I'll save that story for another time." He sounded like someone who has just remembered he has a brilliant trick up his sleeve. "That'll be your payment. I can't afford even a tenth of what you'll get out of Varo Borja for his *Book of the Nine Lies*."

"I'll do the same for you when you find an *Audubon* and become a millionaire. I'll just collect my money later."

La Ponte again looked hurt. For such a cynic, Corso thought, he seemed rather sensitive.

"I thought you were helping me as a friend," protested La Ponte. "You know. The Club of Nantucket Harpooneers. 'There she blows' and all that."

"Friendship," said Corso, looking round as if waiting for someone to explain the word to him. "Bars and cemeteries are full of good friends."

"Whose side are you on, damn it?"

"On his own side," sighed Makarova. "Corso's always on his own side."

La Ponte was disappointed to see the girl with the big breasts leave with a smart young man who looked like a model. Corso was still watching the fat woman at the fruit machine, who'd run out of coins. She was standing next to the machine with a disconcerted, blank look, her hands by her sides. Her place at the machine had been taken by a tall, dark man. He had a thick, black moustache and a scar on his face. For a fleeting moment Corso thought he looked familiar, but the impression vanished before he could grasp it. To the fat woman's despair the machine was now spewing out a noisy stream of coins.

Makarova offered Corso one last beer on the house. La Ponte had to pay for his own this time.

II

The Dead Man's Hand

*Milady smiled, and d'Artagnan felt that he would go to
hell and back for that smile.*
                                        A. Dumas: *The Three Musketeers*

There are inconsolable widows, and then there are widows to whom
any adult male would be delighted to provide the appropriate consolation. Liana Taillefer was undoubtedly the second kind. Tall and blonde,
with pale skin, she moved languorously. The type of woman who takes
an age to light a cigarette, and looks straight into a man's eyes as she
does so. She had the cool composure that was a result of knowing she
looked a little like Kim Novak with a full, almost over-generous figure
and, being the sole beneficiary of the late Enrique Taillefer, Publisher,
Ltd., of having a bank account for which the term *solvent* was a pale
euphemism. It's amazing how much dough you can make, if you'll
excuse the feeble pun, from publishing cookery books, such as *The
Thousand Best Desserts of La Mancha*, or all fifteen bestselling editions
of a classic, *The Secrets of the Barbecue*.

The Taillefers lived in part of what had once been the palace of the
Marques de Los Alumbres, now converted into luxury apartments. In
matters of décor, the owners seemed to have more money than taste.
This could be the only excuse for placing a vulgar Lladro porcelain figure
– a little girl with a duck, noted Lucas Corso dispassionately – in the same
glass cabinet as a group of little Meissen shepherds for which the late
Enrique Taillefer, or his wife, must have paid some sharp antique dealer
a handsome sum. There was a Biedermeier desk, of course, and a
Steinway piano standing on a luxurious, oriental rug. And a comfortable-
looking, white leather sofa on which Liana Taillefer was sitting at that
moment, crossing her extraordinarily shapely legs. She was dressed, as
befits a widow, in a black skirt. It came to just above the knee when she

was sitting, but hinted at the voluptuous curves higher up hidden in mystery and shadow, as Lucas Corso later put it. I would add that Corso's comment should not be ignored. He looked like one of those dubious men one can easily imagine living with an elderly mother who knits and brings him cocoa in bed on a Sunday morning; the kind of son one sees in films, a solitary figure with reddened eyes walking behind the coffin in the rain, and moaning *Mama* inconsolably, like a helpless orphan. But Corso had never been helpless in his life. And when one got to know him slightly better, one wondered if he had ever had a mother.

"I'm sorry to bother you at a time like this," said Corso.

He was sitting facing the widow, still in his coat, his canvas bag on his knees. He held himself straight on the edge of the seat. Liana Taillefer's large ice-blue eyes studied him from top to toe, determined to pigeonhole him in some known category of the male species. He was sure she'd find it difficult. He submitted to her scrutiny, trying not to create any particular impression. He was familiar with the procedure, and he knew that at that moment he didn't rate very highly in the estimation of Enrique Taillefer's widow. This limited the operation to a kind of contemptuous curiosity. She'd kept him waiting for ten minutes, after he'd had a skirmish with a maid who'd taken him for a salesman and was about to slam the door in his face. But now the widow was glancing at the plastic folder that Corso had taken out of his bag, and the situation had changed. As for him, he tried to hold Liana Taillefer's gaze through his crooked glasses, avoiding the thundering reefs – to the South, her legs, and to the North her bust (exuberant was the word, he told himself, having pondered the matter for some time) moulded to devastating effect by her black angora sweater.

"It would be a great help," he added at last, "if you could tell me whether you knew about this document."

He handed her the folder, and as he did so accidentally brushed her hand with its long blood-red fingernails. Or maybe it was her hand that brushed his. Whichever, this slight contact showed that Corso's prospects were looking more favourable. So he adopted a suitably embarrassed expression, just enough to show her that bothering beautiful widows wasn't his speciality. Her ice-blue eyes weren't on the folder now, they were watching Corso with a flicker of interest.

"Why would I know about it?" asked the widow. Her voice was deep, slightly husky. The echo of a heavy night. She hadn't looked inside the folder yet and was still watching Corso, as if she expected something else before examining the document and satisfying her curiosity. He adjusted his glasses on the bridge of his nose and adopted a suitably serious expression. This was the formal stage, so he kept his efficient "honest rabbit" smile for later.

"Until recently it belonged to your husband." He paused a moment. "May his soul rest in peace."

She nodded slowly, as if that explained it, and opened the folder. Corso was looking over her shoulder at the wall. There, between an adequate painting by Tapies and another with a signature he couldn't make out, was a framed piece of child's needlepoint depicting little coloured flowers, signed and dated: *Liana Lasauca, school year 1970–71.* Corso would have found it touching if flowers, embroidered birds and little girls in short socks and blonde pigtails had been the sort of thing that made his heart melt. But they weren't. So he turned to another, smaller picture in a silver frame. It showed the late Enrique Taillefer, Publisher, with a gold wine sampling ladle round his neck, wearing a leather apron that made him look rather like a Mason. He was smiling at the camera and preparing to cut into a roast sucking-pig. He held a plate in one hand and one of his publishing successes in the other. He appeared placid, chubby and paunchy, happy at the sight of the little animal laid out before him on the dish. Corso reflected how Taillefer's premature demise meant that at least he wouldn't have to worry about high cholesterol and gout. He also wondered, with cold technical curiosity, how Liana Taillefer had managed, while her husband was alive, when she needed an orgasm. With that thought he cast another quick glance at the widow's bust and legs, before deciding he'd been right. She was too much of a woman to be satisfied with the sucking-pig.

"This is that Dumas thing," she said, and Corso sat up slightly, alert and clear-headed. Liana Taillefer was tapping one of her red nails on the plastic folders protecting the pages. "The famous chapter. Of course I know about it." As she leaned her head forward, her hair fell over her face. Behind the blonde curtain she observed her visitor suspiciously. "Why have you got it?"

"Your husband sold it. I'm trying to find out if it's authentic."

The widow shrugged her shoulders.

"As far as I know it's not a forgery." She gave a long sigh and handed back the folder. "You say he sold it? That's strange." She thought a moment. "These papers meant a lot to Enrique."

"Perhaps you can recall where he might have bought them."

"I couldn't say. I think somebody gave them to him."

"Did he collect original manuscripts?"

"As far as I know this was the only one he ever had."

"Did he ever mention he was intending to sell it?"

"No. This is the first I've heard about it. Who bought it?"

"A bookseller who's a client of mine. He's going to put it on the market once I give him a report on it."

Liana Taillefer decided to grant him a little more attention. Corso's prospects took another little leap. He took off his glasses and cleaned them with his crumpled handkerchief. Without them he looked more vulnerable, and he knew it. Everybody felt they just had to help him cross the road when he squinted like a short-sighted rabbit.

"Is this your job?" she asked. "Authenticating manuscripts?"

He nodded vaguely. The widow looked slightly blurred and, strangely, closer.

"Sometimes. I also look for rare books, prints, things like that. I get paid for it."

"How much?"

"It depends." He put his glasses back on and her image was sharp again. "Sometimes a lot, others not so much. The market has its ups and downs."

"You're a kind of detective, aren't you?" she said, amused. "A book detective."

This was the moment to smile. He did so, showing his incisors, with a modesty calculated to the millimetre. Adopt me, said his smile.

"Yes. I suppose you could call it that."

"And your client asked you to come and see me . . ."

"That's right." He could now allow himself to look more confident, so he tapped the manuscript with his knuckles. "After all, this came from here. From your house."

She nodded slowly, looking at the folder. She seemed to be thinking something over.

"It's strange," she said. "I can't imagine Enrique selling this Dumas manuscript. Although he was acting strangely those last few days . . . What did you say the name of the bookseller was? The new owner."

"I didn't."

She looked him up and down, with calm surprise. It seemed she was unused to waiting for more than three seconds for any man to do as she said.

"Well, tell me then."

Corso waited a moment, just long enough for Liana Taillefer to start tapping her nails impatiently on the arm of the sofa.

"His name's La Ponte," he said at last. This was another of his tricks: he made only trivial concessions but allowed others to feel they'd won. "Do you know him?"

"Of course I know him. He supplied my husband with books." She frowned. "He'd come round every so often to bring him those stupid serials. I suppose he has a receipt . . . I'd like a copy of it if he doesn't mind."

Corso nodded vaguely and leant towards her slightly.

"Was your husband a great fan of Alexandre Dumas?"

"Of Dumas?" Liana Taillefer smiled. She had shaken back her hair and now her eyes shone, mocking. "Come with me."

She stood up, taking her time, and smoothed down her skirt, glancing round as if she had suddenly forgotten why she had got up. She was much taller than Corso, even though she was only wearing low heels. She led him into the adjoining study. As he followed her he noticed her broad back, like a swimmer's, and her cinched-in waist. He guessed she must be about thirty. She would probably become one of those Nordic matrons, on whose hips the sun never sets, made to give birth effortlessly to blond Eriks and Siegfrieds.

"I wish it had only been Dumas," she said, gesturing towards the contents of the study. "Look at this."

Corso looked. The walls were covered with shelves bowing under the weight of thick, bound volumes. Professional instinct made his mouth water. He took a few steps towards the shelves, adjusting his glasses. *The Countess de Charny*, A. Dumas, eight volumes, the Illustrated Novel collection, editor Vicente Blasco Ibáñez. *The Two Dianas*, A. Dumas, three volumes. *The Musketeers*, A. Dumas, Miguel Guijarro publisher, engravings by Ortega, four volumes. *The Count of Monte Cristo*, A. Dumas, four volumes in the Juan Ros edition, engravings by A. Gil . . . Also forty volumes of *Rocambole*, by Ponson du Terrail. The complete edition of the *Pardellanes* by Zevaco. More Dumas, together with nine volumes of Victor Hugo and the same number by Paul Féval, with an edition of *The Hunchback* luxuriously bound in red morocco and edged with gold. And Dickens's *Pickwick Papers*, translated into Spanish by Benito Pérez Galdós, alongside several volumes by Barbey d'Aurevilly and *The Mysteries of Paris* by

Eugène Sue. And yet more Dumas – *The Forty-Five, The Queen's Necklace, The Companions of Jehu* – and *Corsican Revenge* by Mérimée. Fifteen volumes of Sabatini, several by Ortega y Frías, Conan Doyle, Manuel Fernández y González, Mayne Reid, Patricio de la Escosura . . .

"Very impressive," commented Corso. "How many books are there here?"

"I don't know. Around two thousand. Almost all of them first editions of serials, as they were bound after being published in instalments . . . Some of them are illustrated editions. My husband was an avid collector, he'd pay whatever the asking price."

"A true enthusiast, from what I can see."

"Enthusiast?" Liana Taillefer gave an indefinable smile. "It was a real passion."

"I thought gastronomy . . ."

"The cookery books were just a way of making money. Enrique had the Midas touch: in his hands, any cheap recipe book turned into a bestseller. But this was what he really loved. He liked to shut himself in here and leaf through these old serials. They were often printed on poor quality paper, and he was obsessed with preserving them. Do you see that thermometer and humidity gauge? He could recite whole pages from his favourite books. He'd sometimes even say 'gadzooks', 'ye gods', things like that. He spent his last months writing."

"A historical novel?"

"A serial. Keeping to all the clichés of the genre, of course." She went to a shelf and took down a heavy manuscript with hand-stitched pages. The handwriting was large and round. "What do you think of the title?"

"*The Dead Man's Hand, or Anne of Austria's Page,*" read Corso. "Well, it's certainly – " He ran a finger over his eyebrow, searching for the right word – "suggestive."

"And dull," she added, putting the manuscript back. "And full of anachronisms. And completely idiotic, I can assure you. Believe me, I know what I'm talking about. At the end of each writing session he'd read it to me page by page, from beginning to end." She tapped bitterly on the title, handwritten in capitals. "My God. I really hated that stupid queen and her page."

"Was he intending to publish it?"

"Yes, of course. Under a pseudonym. I assume he would have chosen something like Tristan de Longueville, or Paulo Florentini. It would have been so typical of him."

"What about hanging himself? Was that typical of him?"

Liana Taillefer stared intently at the book-lined walls and said nothing. An uncomfortable silence, Corso thought, even a little forced. She seemed absorbed in her thoughts, like an actress pausing before going on with her speech in a convincing manner.

"I'll never know what happened," she answered at last, her composure once again perfect. "During his last week he was hostile and depressed. He hardly left this study. Then, one afternoon, he went out and slammed the door. He came back in the early hours. I was in bed and I heard the door close. In the morning I was woken by the maid screaming. Enrique had hanged himself from the light fitting."

Now she was looking at Corso, to see the effect of her words. She didn't seem too upset, Corso thought, and remembered the photo with the apron and the sucking-pig. He even saw her blink once, as if to hold back a tear, but her eyes stayed perfectly dry. Of course that didn't mean anything. Centuries of make-up that can be smudged by emotion have taught women to control their feelings. And Liana Taillefer's make-up – light shadow accentuating her eyes – was perfect.

"Did he leave a note?" asked Corso. "People who commit suicide often do."

"He decided to save himself the effort. No explanation, not even a few words. Nothing. Because of his selfishness I've had to answer a lot of questions from an examining magistrate and several policemen. Very unpleasant, believe me."

"I understand."

"Yes. I'm sure you do."

Liana Taillefer made it obvious that their meeting was now at an end. She saw him to the door and held out her hand to him. With the folder under his arm and his bag on his shoulder, Corso held out his hand and felt her firm grip. Inwardly he gave her a good mark for her performance. Not the happy widow, or devastated by grief; not a cold "I'm glad that idiot's gone," or "Alone at last," or "You can come out of the wardrobe now, darling." There probably was someone in the wardrobe, but it was none of Corso's business. Nor was Enrique Taillefer's suicide, however strange – and it was mighty strange, gadzooks, with all that business of the queen's page and the disappearing manuscript.

But neither this nor the beautiful widow were any concern of his. For now.

He looked at Liana Taillefer. I'd love to know who's having you, he thought with cool technical curiosity. He drew a mental picture: handsome, mature, cultured, wealthy. He was almost a hundred per cent sure he must be a friend of her deceased husband. He wondered if the publisher's suicide had anything to do with it, but then stopped himself in disgust. Professional quirk or not, he sometimes had the absurd habit of thinking like a policeman. He shivered in horror at the thought. Who knows what depths of depravity, or stupidity, lie hidden in our souls.

"I must thank you for taking the time to see me," he said, choosing the most touching smile from his repertoire. He resembled a friendly rabbit.

He was met with a blank. She was looking at the Dumas manuscript.

"You don't have to thank me. I'm just naturally interested to know how all this will end."

"I'll let you know how it's going . . . Oh, and there's something else. Do you intend to keep your husband's collection, or are you thinking of selling it?"

She looked at him, disconcerted. Corso knew from experience that when a bookcollector died, the books often followed the body out through the front door twenty-four hours later. He was surprised in fact that none of his predatory colleagues had yet dropped by. After all, as she had admitted herself, Liana Taillefer didn't share her husband's literary tastes.

"The truth is, I haven't had time to think about it . . . Do you mean you'd be interested in those old serials?"

"I could be."

She hesitated a moment. Perhaps a few seconds longer than necessary.

"It's all too recent," she said at last, with a suitable sigh. "Maybe in a few days' time."

Corso put his hand on the banister and started down the stairs. He dragged his feet, taking the first few steps slowly. He felt uneasy, as if he'd left something behind but couldn't remember what. But he was certain he hadn't forgotten anything. When he reached the first landing he looked up and saw that Liana Taillefer was still at the door, watching him. She appeared both worried and curious. Corso carried on down the stairs, and, like a slow film shot, his frame of vision slid down

Liana Taillefer's body. He could no longer see the inquiring look in her ice-blue eyes but instead her bust, hips, and finally her firm, pale legs set slightly apart, strong and suggestive as temple columns.

Corso was still reeling as he crossed the hall and went into the street. He could think of at least five unanswered questions and he needed to put them in order of importance. He stopped at the kerb, opposite the railings of the park of El Retiro, and looked casually to his left, waiting for a taxi. An enormous Jaguar was parked a few metres away. The chauffeur, in a dark grey, almost black, uniform, was leaning on the bonnet reading a newspaper. At that instant, he looked up and his eyes met Corso's. It only lasted for a second and then he went back to reading his paper. He was dark, with a moustache, and his cheek was scored from top to bottom by a pale scar. Corso thought he looked familiar: he definitely reminded him of somebody. It could have been, he remembered, the tall man playing the fruit machine in Makarova's bar. But there was something else. His face stirred some vague, distant memory. But before he could give it any more thought an empty taxi appeared. A man in a Loden coat carrying an executive briefcase hailed it from the other side of the street. But the taxi-driver was looking in Corso's direction. Corso made the most of it and stepped quickly off the kerb to snatch the taxi from under the other man's nose.

He asked the taxi-driver to turn down the radio and then settled himself in the back seat, looking out at the surrounding traffic but not taking it in. He always enjoyed the sense of peace he got inside a taxi. It was the closest he ever came to a truce with the outside world: everything beyond the window was suspended for the duration of the journey. He leant his head on the back of the seat and savoured the prospect.

It was time to think of serious matters. Such as *The Book of the Nine Doors*, and his trip to Portugal, the first step in this job. But Corso couldn't concentrate. His meeting with Enrique Taillefer's widow had raised too many questions and left him strangely uneasy. There was something he couldn't quite put his finger on, like watching a landscape from the wrong angle. And there was something else: it took him several stops at traffic lights to realize that the chauffeur of the Jaguar kept reappearing in his mind's eye. This bothered him. He was sure that he'd never seen him before the time at Makarova's bar. But an irrational memory recurred. I know you, he thought. I'm sure I do.

Once, a long time ago, I bumped into a man like you. And I know you're out there somewhere. On the dark side of my memory.

Grouchy was nowhere to be seen, but it no longer mattered. Bulow's Prussians were retreating from the heights of Chapelle St Lambert, with Sumont and Subervie's light cavalry at their heels. There was no problem on the left flank: the red formations of the Scottish infantry had been overtaken and devastated by the charge of the French cuirassiers. In the centre, the Jérôme division had at last taken Hougoumont. And to the north of Mont St Jean the blue formations of the good Old Guard were gathering slowly but implacably, with Wellington withdrawing in delicious disorder to the little village of Waterloo. It only remained to deal the coup de grâce.

Lucas Corso observed the field. The solution was Ney, of course. The bravest of the brave. He placed him at the front, with Erlon and the Jérôme division, or what remained of it, and made them advance at a charge along the Brussels road. When they made contact with the British troops, Corso leant back slightly in his chair and held his breath, sure of the implications of his action: in a few seconds he had just sealed the fate of 22,000 men. Savouring the feeling, he looked lovingly over the compact blue and red ranks, the pale green of the forest of Soignes, the dun-coloured hills. God, it was a beautiful battle.

The blow struck them hard, poor devils. Erlon's corps was blown to pieces like the three little pigs' hut, but the lines formed by Ney and Jérôme's men held. The Old Guard was advancing, crushing everything in its path. The English formations disappeared one by one from the map. Wellington had no choice but to withdraw, and Corso used the French cavalry's reserves to block his path to Brussels. Then, slowly and deliberately, he dealt the final blow. Holding Ney between his thumb and forefinger, he made him advance three hexagons. He compared forces, consulting his tables: the British were outnumbered by eight to three. Wellington was finished. But there was still one small opening left to chance. He consulted his conversion table and saw that all he needed was a three. He felt one more stab of anxiety as he threw the dice to decide what the small factor of chance would be. Even with the battle won, losing Ney in the final minute was only for real enthusiasts. In the end he got a factor of five. He smiled broadly as he gave an affectionate little tap to the blue counter representing Napoleon. I know how you feel, friend. Wellington and his remaining five thousand wretches were all either dead or taken prisoner, and the Emperor had just won the Battle of Waterloo. *Allons, enfants de la Patrie!* The history books could go to hell.

He yawned. On the table, next to the board which represented the battlefield on a scale of 1:5,000, amongst reference books, charts, a cup of coffee and an ashtray full of cigarette ends, his wristwatch showed it was three in the morning. To one side, on the drinks cabinet, from his red label the colour of a hunting jacket, Johnnie Walker looked mischievous as he took a step. Rosy-cheeked little so-and-so, thought Corso. He didn't give a damn that several thousand of his fellow countrymen had just bitten the dust in Flanders.

He turned his back on the Englishman and addressed an unopened bottle of Bols on a shelf between the *Memoirs of Saint-Helena* in two volumes, and a French edition of *Scarlet and Black* which he laid before him on the table. He tore the seal off the bottle and leafed casually through the book as he poured himself a glass of gin:

. . . Rousseau's *Confessions* was the only book through which his imagination pictured the world. The collection of Grande Armée reports and the *Memoirs of Saint-Helena* completed his Bible. He would have died for those three books. He never believed in any others.

He stood there sipping his gin and stretching his stiff limbs. He gave a last glance to the battlefield, where the sounds of the fighting were dying down after the slaughter. He emptied his glass, feeling like a drunken god playing with real lives as if they were little tin soldiers. He pictured Lord Arthur Wellesley, Duke of Wellington, handing over his sword to Ney. Dead young soldiers lay in the mud, horses cantered by without riders, and an officer of the Scots Greys lay dying beneath a shattered cannon, holding a gold locket with the portrait of a woman and a lock of blonde hair in his bloody fingers. On the other side of the shadows into which he was sinking he could hear the beat of the last waltz. And the little dancer watched him from her shelf, with the sequin on her forehead reflecting the flames in the fireplace, ready to fall into the hands of the spirit of the tobacco pouch. Or the shopkeeper on the corner.

Waterloo. The bones of his great-great-grandfather, the old Grenadier, could rest in peace. He pictured him in any one of the blue formations on the board along the brown line of the Brussels road. His face blackened, his moustache singed by the explosions of gunpowder, he advanced, hoarse and feverish from three days of fighting with his bayonet. He had the same absent expression that Corso had a thousand times imagined that all men in all wars had had. Exhausted, he and his comrades raised their bearskin caps, riddled with holes, on the end of their rifles. Long live the Emperor! Bonaparte's solitary, squat, cancerous ghost was avenged. May he rest in peace. Hip, hip, hurray.

He poured himself another glass of Bols and, facing the sabre hanging on the wall, drank a toast to the faithful ghost of Grenadier Jean-Pax Corso, 1770–1851, Legion of Honour, knight of the Order of Saint Helena, staunch Bonapartist to the end of his days, and French consul in the Mediterranean town where his great-great-grandson was born a century later. With the taste of gin still lingering in his mouth he recited under his breath the only inheritance left him by his great-great-grandfather, transmitted down the century by the line of Corsos that would die with him:

> . . . And the Emperor, at the head of
> his impatient army
> will ride amidst the clamour.
> And armed I will leave this land,
> and once more I will follow
> the Emperor to war.

He was laughing to himself as he picked up the phone and dialled La Ponte's number. In the quiet of the room you could hear the record spinning on the turntable. There were books on the walls, rain-soaked roofs through the dark window. The view wasn't great, except on winter afternoons when the sunset filtered through the blasts of centrally-heated air and pollution from the street, and the sky turned red and ochre, like a thick curtain catching fire. His desk, his computer and the board with the battle of Waterloo sat facing the view, in front of the window against which the rain was falling that night. There were no mementoes, pictures or photos on the wall. Only the sabre of the Old Guard in its brass and leather sheath. Visitors were surprised to find no signs there of his personal life, none of the ties with their memories and their past that people instinctively preserve, only his books and the sabre. Just as there were objects lacking from his house, Lucas Corso came from a world that was long since dead and gone. None of the grave faces which sometimes stood out in his memory would have recognized him had they come back to life. And maybe it was better that way. It was as if he had never owned anything, or left anything behind. As if he had always been completely self-contained, needing nothing but the clothes he stood up in, an erudite, urban itinerant carrying all his worldly possessions in his pockets. And yet, the few people he had allowed to see him on one of those crimson evenings, sitting at his window, dazzled by the sunset, his eyes bleary with gin, say that his expression – that of a clumsy, helpless rabbit – seemed sincere.

La Ponte's sleepy voice answered.

"I've just crushed Wellington," announced Corso.

After a stunned silence, La Ponte said that he was very happy for him. Perfidious Albion – steak and kidney pie and gas meters in dingy hotel rooms. Kipling. Balaclava, Trafalgar, the Falklands and all that. And he'd like to remind Corso – the line went silent while La Ponte fumbled for his watch – that it was three in the morning. Then he mumbled something incoherent, the only intelligible words being "damn you" and "bastard", in that order.

Corso was still laughing to himself as he hung up. Once he had made a reverse-charge call to La Ponte from an auction in Buenos Aires, just to tell him a joke, about a whore who was so ugly she died a virgin. Ha, ha, very funny. And I'll make you swallow the phone bill when you get back, you bloody idiot. And then there was the time, years earlier, when he'd woken up in Nikon's arms. The first thing he'd done was phone La Ponte and tell him he'd met a beautiful woman and it was very much like being in love. Any time he wanted to, Corso could shut his eyes and see Nikon waking slowly, her hair flowing all over the pillow. He had described her to La Ponte over the phone, feeling a strange emotion, an inexplicable, unfamiliar tenderness while he spoke, and she listened, watching him silently. And he knew that at the other end of the line – I'm happy for you Corso, it was about time, I'm really happy for you, my friend – La Ponte was sincerely happy to share in his awakening, his triumph, his happiness. That morning he had loved La Ponte as much as he loved her. Or maybe it was the other way round.

But that was all a long time ago. Corso turned out the light. Outside it was still raining. In his bedroom he lit one last cigarette. He sat motionless on the edge of the bed in the dark, listening for an echo of her absent breathing. Then he put out his hand to stroke her hair, no longer spilling over the pillow. Nikon was his only regret. The rain was coming down harder now, and the droplets on the window broke the faint light outside up into minute reflections, sprinkling the sheets with moving dots, black trails, tiny shadows plunging in no particular direction, like the shreds of a life.

"Lucas."

He said his own name out loud like she used to. She was the only one who'd always called him that. That name was a symbol of the common homeland, now destroyed, that they had once wanted to share. Corso focused his attention on the tip of his cigarette glowing red in the darkness. Once he'd thought he really loved Nikon. When he found her beautiful and intelligent, infallible as a papal encyclical, and passionate, like her black-and-white photos: wide-eyed children, old people, dogs with faithful expressions. When he watched her defending the freedom of peoples and signing petitions for the release of imprisoned intellectuals, oppressed ethnic minorities, things like that. And seals. Once she'd even managed to get him to sign something about seals.

He got up slowly from the bed so as not to wake the ghost sleeping by his side, listening out for the sound of her breathing. Sometimes he believed he could hear it. "You're as dead as your books, Corso. You've never loved anyone." That was the first and last time she'd ever called him by his surname. The first and last time she'd refused him her body, before leaving him for good. In search of the child he'd never wanted.

He opened the window and felt the cold damp night as rain splashed against his face. He took one last puff of his cigarette and then dropped it into the shadows, a red dot fading into the darkness, the curve of its fall broken, or hidden.

That night it was raining on other landscapes too. On the footprints Nikon left behind. On the fields of Waterloo, great-great-grandfather Corso and his comrades. On the scarlet and black tomb of Julien Sorel, guillotined for believing that, with Bonaparte's death, the bronze statues lay dying on old forgotten paths. A stupid mistake. Lucas Corso knew better than anyone that an itinerant, clear-headed soldier could still choose his battlefield and get his pay, standing guard alongside ghosts of paper and leather, amidst the hangover from a thousand failures.

III

Men of Words and Men of Action

"The dead do not speak."
"They speak if God wishes it," retorted Lagardère.
P. Féval: The Hunchback

The secretary's heels clicked loudly on the polished wood floor. Lucas Corso followed her down the long corridor – pale cream walls, hidden lighting, ambient music – until they came to a heavy oak door. He obeyed her sign to wait there a moment. Then, when she moved aside with a perfunctory smile, he went into the office. Varo Borja was sitting in a black leather reclining chair, between half a ton of mahogany and a window with a magnificent panoramic view of Toledo: ancient ochre rooftops, the gothic spire of the cathedral silhouetted against a clean blue sky, and in the background the large grey mass of the Alcázar palace.

"Do sit down, Corso. How are you?"

"Fine."

"You've had to wait."

It wasn't an apology but a statement of fact. Corso frowned.

"Don't worry. Only forty-five minutes this time."

Varo Borja didn't even bother to smile as Corso sat down in the armchair reserved for visitors. The desk was completely clear except for a complicated, high-tech telephone and intercom system. The book-dealer's face was reflected in the desk surface together with the view from the window as a backdrop. Varo Borja was about fifty. He was bald, with a tan acquired on a sunbed, and he looked respectable, which was very far from being the truth. He had sharp, darting little eyes. He hid his excessive girth beneath tight-fitting, exuberantly patterned waistcoats and bespoke jackets. He was some sort of marquis and his stormy past as a rake included a police record, a scandal over fraud and four prudent years of self-imposed exile in Brazil and Paraguay.

"I have something to show you."

He had a deliberately abrupt manner, bordering on rudeness, which he cultivated carefully. Corso watched him walk over to a small glass cabinet. He opened it with a tiny key on a gold chain pulled from his pocket. He had no public premises, apart from a stand reserved at the major international fairs. Varo Borja's catalogue never included more than a few dozen select titles. He would follow the trail of rare books to any corner of the world, fight hard and dirty to get hold of them, and then speculate on the vagaries of the market. On his payroll at any one time he had collectors, curators, engravers, printers and suppliers, like Lucas Corso.

"What do you think?"

Corso took the book as carefully as if he were being handed a newborn baby. It was an old volume bound in brown leather, decorated in gold and in excellent condition.

"*La Hypnerotomachia di Poliphilo* by Colonna," he said. "You managed to get hold of it at last."

"Three days ago. Venice, 1545. *In casa di figlivoli di Aldo*. One hundred and seventy woodcuts. Do you think that Swiss you mentioned would still be interested?"

"I suppose so. Is the book complete?"

"Of course. All but four of the woodcuts in this edition are reprints from the 1499 edition."

"My client really wanted a first edition, but I'll try to convince him a second edition is good enough . . . Five years ago a copy just slipped through his fingers at the Monaco auction."

"Well, you have the option on this one."

"Give me a couple of weeks to get in touch with him."

"I'd prefer to deal directly." Varo Borja smiled like a shark after a swimmer. "Of course you'd still get your commission, at the usual rate."

"No way. The Swiss is *my* client."

Varo Borja smiled sarcastically.

"You don't trust anyone, do you? I can picture you as a baby, testing your mother's milk before you'd breastfeed."

"And you'd sell your mother's milk, wouldn't you?"

Varo Borja stared pointedly at Corso, who at that instant didn't look in the least bit like a friendly rabbit. More like a wolf baring his fangs.

"You know what I like about you, Corso? The easy way you fall into the part of a mercenary, with all the demagogues and charlatans out there . . . You're like one of those thin, dangerous men Julius Caesar was so afraid of . . . Do you sleep well at night?"

"Like a log."

"I'm sure you don't. I'd wager a couple of Gothic manuscripts that you're the type who spends a long time staring into the darkness . . . Can I tell you something? I instinctively distrust thin men who are willing and enthusiastic. I only use well-paid mercenaries, rootless, straightforward types. I'm suspicious of anyone who's tied to a homeland, family or cause."

The bookdealer put the *Poliphilo* back in the cabinet and gave a dry, humourless laugh:

"Sometimes I wonder if someone like you can have friends. Do you have any, Corso?"

"Go to hell."

He had said it with an impeccably cold tone. Varo Borja smiled slowly and deliberately. He didn't seem offended.

"You're right. Your friendship doesn't interest me in the least. I buy your loyalty instead. It's more solid and lasting. Isn't that right? The professional pride of a man meeting his contract even though the king who employed him has fled, the battle is lost and there is no hope of salvation . . ."

His expression was teasing, provocative, as he waited for Corso's reaction. But Corso just gestured impatiently, tapping his watch.

"You can write down the rest and send it to me," he said. "I don't get paid to laugh at your little jokes."

Varo Borja seemed to think this over. Then he agreed, though still mocking.

"Once again, you're right, Corso. Let's get back to business . . ." He looked round before getting to the point. "Do you remember the *Treatise on the Art of Fencing* by Astarloa?"

"Yes. A very rare 1870 edition. I got hold of a copy for you a couple of months ago."

"I've now been asked for *Académie de l'épée* by the same client. Maybe one you're acquainted with?"

"I'm not sure if you mean the client or the book . . . You're so convoluted, sometimes I get in a muddle."

Judging by his hostile look, Varo Borja had been stung by this remark.

"We don't all possess your clear, concise prose, Corso. I was referring to the book."

"It's a seventeenth-century Elzevir. Large format, with engravings. Considered the most beautiful treatise on fencing. And the most valuable."

"The buyer is prepared to pay any price."

"Then I'll have to find it."

Varo Borja sat down again in his armchair in front of the window with the panoramic view of the ancient city. He crossed his legs, looking pleased with himself, his thumbs hooked in his waistcoat pockets. Business was obviously going well. Only very few of his most high-powered European colleagues could afford such a view from their desks. But Corso wasn't impressed. Men like that depended on men like him, and they both knew it.

He adjusted his crooked glasses and stared at the bookdealer.

"What shall we do about the *Poliphilo*, then?"

Varo Borja hesitated between antagonism and curiosity. He glanced at the cabinet and then at Corso.

"All right," he said half-heartedly, "you make the deal with the Swiss."

Corso nodded without showing any satisfaction at his small victory. The Swiss didn't exist, but that was his business. It wouldn't be hard to find a buyer for a book like that.

"Let's talk about *The Nine Doors*," he said. The dealer's face grew more animated.

"Yes. Will you take the job?"

Corso was biting a hangnail on his thumb. He gently spat it out onto the spotless table.

"Let's suppose for a moment that your copy is a forgery. And that either of the others is the authentic one. Or none of them is."

Varo Borja, irritated, seemed to be looking to see where Corso's tiny hangnail had landed. At last he gave up.

"In that case," he said, "you'll take good note and follow my instructions."

"Which are?"

"All in good time."

"No. I think you should give me your instructions now." He saw the bookdealer hesitate for a second. In a corner of his brain, where his hunter's instinct lay, something didn't feel quite right. An almost imperceptible jarring sound like a badly tuned machine.

"We'll decide things," said Varo Borja, "as we go along."

"What's there to decide?" Corso was beginning to feel irritated. "One of the books is in a private collection and the other is in a public foundation. Neither is for sale. That's as far as things can go. My part in this and your ambitions end there. As I said: one or other is a forgery, or isn't. Either way, once I've done my job you pay me and that's it."

Much too simple, said the bookdealer's half-smile.

"That depends."

"That's what worries me . . . You've got something up your sleeve, haven't you?"

Varo Borja raised his hand slightly, contemplating its reflection in the polished surface of his desk. Then he slowly lowered it, until the hand came down to meet its reflection. Corso watched the wide, hairy hand, with a huge gold signet ring on the little finger. He was all too familiar with it. He'd seen it sign cheques on non-existent accounts, add emphasis to complete lies, shake the hands of people he would soon be betraying. He could still hear the jarring sound, warning him. Suddenly he felt strangely tired. He was no longer sure if he wanted the job.

"I'm not sure I want this job," he said aloud.

Varo Borja must have realized he meant it because his manner changed. He sat motionless, his chin resting on his hands, the light from the window burnishing his perfectly tanned bald head. He seemed to be weighing things up as he stared intently at Corso.

"Have I ever told you why I became a bookdealer?"

"No. And I really don't give a damn."

Borja laughed theatrically to show he was prepared to be magnanimous and take Corso's rudeness. Corso could safely vent his bad temper, for the moment.

"I pay you to listen to whatever I want to tell you."

"You haven't paid me yet, this time."

Borja took a cheque-book from one of the drawers and put it on the desk, while Corso looked round, resigned and defenceless. This was the moment to say, "So long," or stay put and wait. It was also the moment to be offered a drink, but Borja wasn't that kind of host. So Corso shrugged, feeling the flask of gin in his pocket. It was absurd. He knew perfectly well he wouldn't leave, whether or not he liked what Borja was about to propose. And Borja knew it. He wrote out a figure, signed and tore out the cheque, then pushed it towards Corso.

Without touching it, Corso glanced at it.

"You've convinced me," he sighed. "I'm listening."

The bookdealer didn't even allow himself a look of triumph. Just a brief nod, cold and confident, as if he had just made some insignificant deal.

"I got into this business by chance," he began. "One day I found myself penniless, with my great-uncle's library as my only inheritance . . . About two thousand books. Only about a hundred were of any value. But amongst them there was a first edition *Don Quixote*, a couple of eighteenth-century Psalters and one of the only four known copies of *Champfleuri* by Geoffroy Tory . . . What do you think?"

"You were too lucky."

"You can say that again," agreed Varo Borja in an even, confident tone. He didn't have the smugness of so many successful people when they talk about themselves. "In those days I knew nothing about collectors of rare books, but I grasped the essential fact: they're willing to pay a lot of money for scarce products . . . I learnt terms I'd never heard of before, like colophon, dented chisel, golden mean or fanfare binding. And while I was becoming interested in the business I discovered something else: some books are for selling and others are for keeping. Becoming a bookcollector is like joining a religion: it's for life."

"Very moving. So now tell me what I and your *Nine Doors* have got to do with your taking vows."

"You asked me what I'd do if you discovered my copy was a forgery . . . Well, let me make this clear: it is a forgery."

"How do you know?"

"I am absolutely certain of it."

Corso grimaced, showing what he thought of absolute certainty in matters of rare books.

"Well, in Mateu's *Universal Bibliography* and in the Terral-Coy catalogue it's listed as authentic . . ."

"Yes," said Varo Borja. "Though there's a small error in Mateu: it states that there are eight illustrations when there are nine of them . . . But its *formal* authenticity means very little. According to the bibliographies, the Fargas and Ungern copies are also authentic."

"Maybe all three of them are."

Borja shook his head.

"That's not possible. The records of Torchia's trial leave no doubt: only one copy was saved." He smiled mysteriously. "I have other proof."

"Such as?"

"It doesn't concern you."

"Then why do you need me?"

Varo Borja pushed back his chair and stood up.

"Come with me."

"I've already told you – " Corso was shaking his head – "I'm not remotely interested in all of this."

"You're lying. You're burning with curiosity. You'd do the job for free."

He took the cheque and put it in his waistcoat pocket. Then he led Corso up a spiral staircase to the floor above. Borja's office was at the back of his house. It was a huge, medieval building in the old part of the city, and he'd paid a fortune for it. He took Corso along a corridor leading to the hall and main entrance, up to a door which opened with a modern security keypad. It was a large room, with a black marble floor, a beamed ceiling and ancient iron bars at the windows. There was a desk, leather armchairs and a large stone fireplace. All the walls were covered with glass cabinets full of books, and prints in beautiful frames. Some of them by Holbein and Dürer, Corso noted.

"Nice room," he said. He'd never been in there before. "But I thought you kept your books in the storeroom in the basement . . ."

Varo Borja stopped at his side.

"These are mine. They're not for sale. Some people collect chivalric or romantic novels. Some search for *Don Quixotes* or uncut volumes . . . All those you see here have the same central character: the Devil."

"Can I take a look?"

"That's why I brought you here."

Corso took a few steps forward. The books all had ancient bindings from the leather-covered boards of the incunabula to the morocco leather decorated with plaques and rosettes. His scuffed shoes squeaked on the marble floor as he stopped in front of one of the cabinets and leaned over to examine the contents: *De spectris et apparitionibus* by Juan Rivio. *Summa diabolica* by Benedicto Casiano. *La haine de Satan* by Pierre Crespet. The *Steganography* by Abbot Tritemius. *De Consummatione sæculi* by St Pontius . . . They were all extremely rare and valuable books, most of which Corso knew only from bibliographical references.

"Have you ever seen anything more beautiful?" said Varo Borja, watching Corso closely. "There's nothing like that sheen, the gold on leather, behind glass . . . Not to mention the treasures they contain: centuries of study, of wisdom. Answers to the secrets of the universe and the heart of man." He raised his arms slightly and let them drop, giving up his attempt to express in words his pride at owning them all. "I know people who would kill for a collection like this."

Corso nodded without taking his eyes off the books.

"You, for instance," he said. "Although you wouldn't do it yourself. You'd get somebody else to do the killing for you."

Varo Borja laughed contemptuously.

"That's one of the advantages of having money – you can hire henchmen to do your dirty work. And remain pure yourself."

Corso looked at the bookdealer.

"That's a matter of opinion," he said after a few moments' thought. He seemed to ponder the matter. "I despise people who don't get their hands dirty. The pure ones."

"I don't care what you despise, so let's get down to serious matters."

Varo Borja took a few steps past the cabinets, each containing about a hundred volumes.

"*Ars Diavoli* . . ." He opened the one nearest to him and ran his finger over the spines of the books, almost in a caress. "You'll never see such a collection anywhere else. These are the rarest, most choice books. It took me years to build up this collection, but I was still lacking the prize piece."

He took out one of the books, a folio bound in black leather in the Venetian style, with no title on the outside but with five raised bands on the spine and a golden pentacle on the front cover. Corso took it and opened it carefully. The first printed page, the original title page, was in Latin: *De umbrarum regni novem portis*: the book of the nine doors of the kingdom of shadows. Then came the printer's mark, place, name and date: '*Venetiæ, apud Aristidem Torchiam. M.DC.LX.VI. Cum superiorum privilegio veniaque.*' With the privilege and permission of the superiors.

Varo Borja was watching to see his reaction.

"One can always tell a booklover," he said, "by the way he handles a book."

"I'm not a booklover."

"True. But sometimes you make one forgive that you have the manners of a mercenary. When it comes to books, certain gestures can be reassuring. The way some people touch them is criminal."

Corso turned more pages. All the text was in Latin, printed in a handsome type on thick, good quality paper which had withstood the passage of time. There were nine splendid full-page engravings, showing scenes of a medieval appearance. He paused over one of them, at random. It was numbered with a Latin V, together with one Hebrew and one Greek letter or numeral. At the foot, one word which was incomplete or in code: *"FR.ST.A"*. A man who looked like a merchant was counting out a sack of gold in front of a closed door, unaware of the skeleton behind him holding an hourglass in one hand and a pitchfork in the other.

"What do you think?" asked Borja.

"You told me it was a forgery, but this doesn't look like one. Have you examined it thoroughly?"

"I've gone over the whole thing, down to the last comma, with a magnifying glass. I've had plenty of time. I bought it six months ago, when the heirs of Gualterio Terral decided to sell his collection."

The bookhunter turned more pages. The engravings were beautiful, of a simple, mysterious elegance. In another one, a young girl was about to be beheaded by an executioner in armour with his sword raised.

"I doubt if the heirs would have put a forgery on sale," said Corso when he'd finished examining it. "They've got too much money, and they don't give a damn about books. The catalogue for the collection even had to be drawn up by Claymore's auctioneers . . . And I knew old Terral. He would never have accepted a book that had been tampered with or forged."

"I agree," said Borja. "And Terral inherited *The Nine Doors* from his father-in-law, Don Lisardo Coy, a bookcollector with impeccable credentials."

"And he," said Corso as he put the book down on the desk and pulled out his notebook from his coat pocket, "bought it from an Italian, Domenico Chiara, whose family, according to the Weiss catalogue, had owned it since 1817 . . ."

Borja nodded, obviously pleased.

"I see you've gone into the matter in some depth."

"Of course I have." Corso looked at him as if he'd just said something very stupid. "It's my job."

Varo Borja made a placatory gesture.

"I don't doubt Terral and his heirs' good faith," he clarified. "Nor did I say that the book wasn't old."

"You said it was a forgery."

"Maybe forgery isn't the right word."

"Well, what is it then? It all belongs to the right era." Corso picked up the book again, then with his thumb against the edge of the pages he flicked them, listening to the sound they made. "Even the paper sounds right."

"There's something in it that doesn't sound right. And I don't mean the paper."

"Maybe the prints."

"What's the matter with them?"

"They're not quite right. I would have expected copperplates. By 1666 nobody used woodcuts any more."

"Don't forget this was an unusual edition. The engravings are reproductions of other older ones, supposedly discovered or seen by the printer."

"The *Delomelanicon* . . . Do you really believe it?"

"You don't care what I believe. But the book's nine original engravings aren't attributed to just anybody . . . Legend has it that Lucifer, after being defeated and thrown out of Heaven, drew up the magic formula to be used by his followers: the authoritative handbook of the shadows. A terrible book kept in secret, burnt many times, sold for huge sums by the few privileged to own it . . . These illustrations are really satanic hieroglyphs. Interpreted with the aid of the text and the appropriate knowledge, they can be used to summon the prince of darkness."

Corso nodded with exaggerated gravity.

"I can think of better ways to sell one's soul."

"Please don't joke, it's more serious than it seems . . . Do you know what *Delomelanicon* means?"

"I think so. It comes from the Greek: *Delo*, meaning to summon. And *Melas*: black, dark."

Varo Borja's high-pitched laugh rang out. He said in a tone of approval:

"I was forgetting that you're an educated mercenary. You're right: to summon the shadows, or illuminate them . . . The prophet Daniel, Hippocrates, Flavius Josephus, Albertus Magnus and Leo III all mention this wonderful book. Men have only been writing for the last six thousand years, but the *Delomelanicon* is reputed to be three times as old . . . The first direct mention of it is in the Turis papyrus, written thirty-three centuries ago. Then, between I BC and the second year of our era, it is quoted several times in the *Corpus Hermeticum*. According to the *Asclemandres*, the book enables one to 'face the Light' . . . And in an incomplete inventory of the library at Alexandria, before it was destroyed for the third and last time in the year 646, there is a specific reference to the nine magic enigmas it contains . . . We don't know if there was only one copy or several, or if any survived the burning of the library . . . Since then its trail has disappeared and reappeared throughout history, through fires, wars and disasters."

Corso looked doubtful.

"That's always the case. All magic books have the same legend: from Thoth to Nicholas Flamel . . . Once a client of mine who was fascinated by alchemy asked me to find him the bibliography quoted by Fulcanelli and his followers. I couldn't convince him that half the books didn't exist."

"Well, this one did exist. It must have done for the Holy Office to list it in its Index. Don't you think?"

"It doesn't matter what I think. Some lawyers don't believe their clients are innocent and they still get them acquitted."

"That's the case here. I'm not hiring you because you believe in it but because you're good at your job."

Corso turned more pages of the book. Another engraving, number I, showed a walled city on a hill. A strange unarmed horseman was riding towards it, his finger to his lips requesting complicity or silence. The caption to the engraving read: "*Nem. perv.t qui n.n leg. cert.rit.*"

"It's in an abbreviated but decipherable code," explained Varo Borja watching him. '*Nemo pervenit qui non legitime certaverit.*'"

"'Only he who has fought according to the rules will succeed'?"

"That's about it. For the moment it's the only one of the nine captions that we can decipher with any certainty. An almost identical one appears in the works of Roger Bacon, a specialist in demonology, cryptography and magic . . . Bacon claimed to own a *Delomelanicon* which had belonged to King Solomon, containing the key to terrible mysteries. The book was made of rolls of parchment with illustrations. It was burned in 1350 by personal order of Pope Innocent VI who declared: 'It contains a method to summon devils.' In Venice, three centuries later, Aristide Torchia decided to print it with the original illustrations."

"They're too perfect," objected Corso. "They can't be the originals: they'd be in an older style."

"I agree. Torchia must have updated them."

Another engraving, number III, showed a bridge with gate towers spanning a river. Corso looked up and saw that Varo Borja was smiling mysteriously, like an alchemist confident of what's cooking in his crucible.

"There's one last connection," said the bookdealer. "Giordano Bruno, martyr of rationalism, mathematician and champion of the theory that the Earth rotates round the sun . . ." He waved his hand contemptuously, as if all this was trivial. "But that was only part of his work. He wrote sixty-one books, and magic played an important part in them. And how about this: Bruno makes specific reference to the *Delomelanicon*, even using the Greek words *Delo* and *Melas*, and he adds: 'On the path of men who want to know, there are nine secret doors.' He then goes on to describe the methods for making the Light shine once more . . . *'Sic luceat Lux,'* he writes, which is actually the same motto – " he showed Corso the printer's mark: a tree split by lightning, a snake and a motto – "that Aristide Torchia used on the frontispiece of *The Nine Doors* . . . What do you think of that?"

"It's all well and good. But it all comes to the same. You can make a text mean anything, especially if it's old and full of ambiguities."

"Or precautions. Although Giordano Bruno forgot the golden rule for survival: *'Scire, tacere.'* To know and keep silent. Apparently he knew the right things but he talked too much. And there are more coincidences: Giordano Bruno was arrested in Venice, declared an obdurate heretic and burned alive in Rome at Campo dei Fiori in February 1600. The same journey, the same places and the same dates that marked Aristide Torchia's path to execution sixty-seven years later: he was arrested in Venice, tortured in Rome and burned at Campo dei Fiori in February 1667. By then very few people were still being burned at the stake and yet he was."

"I'm impressed," said Corso, who wasn't in the least.

Varo Borja tutted reprovingly.

"Sometimes I wonder if you believe in anything."

Corso seemed to think about it for a moment, then shrugged.

"A long time ago I did believe in something. But I was young and cruel then. Now I'm forty-five: I'm old and cruel."

"I am too. But there are things I still believe in. Things that make my heart beat faster."

"Like money?"

"Don't make fun of me. Money is the key that opens the door to man's dark secrets. And it pays for your services. And grants me the only thing in the world I respect: these books." He took a few steps along the cabinets full of books. "They're mirrors in the image of those who wrote them. They reflect their concerns, questions, desires, life, death . . . They're living beings: you have to know how to feed them, protect them . . ."

"And use them."

"Sometimes."

"But this one doesn't work."

"No."

"You've tried it."

It was a statement, not a question. Varo Borja looked at Corso with hostility.

"Don't be absurd. Let's just say I'm certain that it's a forgery, and leave it at that. That's why I need to compare it to the other copies."

"I still say it doesn't have to be a forgery. Books often differ, even if they're part of the same edition. No two books are the same really. From birth they all have distinguishing details. And each book lives a different life: it can lose pages, or have them added or replaced, or have a new binding . . . Over the years two books printed on the same press can end up looking entirely different. That's what might have happened to this one."

"Well, find out. Investigate *The Nine Doors* as if were a crime. Follow trails, check each page, each engraving, the paper, the binding . . . Work your way backwards and find out where my copy comes from. Then do the same with the other two, in Sintra and in Paris."

"It would help me if I knew how you found out yours was a forgery."

"I can't tell you. Trust my intuition."

"Your intuition is going to cost you a lot of money."

"All you have to do is spend it."

He pulled the cheque out of his pocket and gave it to Corso, who turned it over in his fingers, undecided.

"Why are you paying me in advance? You've never done that before."

"You'll have a lot of expenses to cover. This is so you can start getting on with things." He handed him a thick bound file. "Everything I know about the book is in there. You may find it useful."

Corso was still looking at the cheque.

"This is too much for an advance."

"You may encounter certain complications . . ."

"You don't say."

As he said this he heard Borja clear his throat. They were getting to the crux of the matter at last.

"If you find out that the three copies are forgeries or are incomplete," Borja said, "then you'll have done your job and we'll settle up . . ." He paused briefly and ran his hand over his tanned head. He smiled awkwardly at Corso. "But one of the books may turn out to be authentic, so then you'll have more money at your disposal. Because if that's the case I want it by whatever means, and without regard to expense."

"You're joking, aren't you?"

"Do I look as if I'm joking, Corso?"

"It's against the law."

"You've done illegal things before."

"Not this kind of thing."

"Nobody's ever paid you what I'll pay you."

"How can I be sure of that?"

"I'm letting you take the book with you. You'll need the original for your work. Isn't that enough of a guarantee?"

The jarring sound again, warning him. Corso was still holding *The Nine Doors*. He put the cheque in between the pages like a bookmark and blew some imaginary dust off the book before returning it to Varo Borja.

"A moment ago you said that you can buy anything with money, so now you can test that out yourself. Go and see the owners of the books and do the dirty work yourself."

He turned and walked towards the door, wondering how many steps he'd take before the bookdealer said anything. Three.

"This isn't a matter for men of words," said Varo Borja. "It's a matter for men of action."

His tone had changed. Gone was the arrogant composure and the disdain for the mercenary he was hiring. On the wall, an engraving of an angel by Dürer gently beat its wings behind the glass of a picture frame, while Corso's shoes turned on the black marble floor. Next to his cabinets full of books and the barred window with the cathedral in the background, next to everything that his money could buy, Varo Borja stood blinking, disconcerted. His expression was still arrogant.

He was even tapping on the book cover with mechanical disdain. But even before that glorious moment, Lucas Corso had learnt to recognize defeat in a man's eyes. And fear.

His heart was beating with calm satisfaction as, without a word, he retraced his steps. As he came up to Varo Borja he took the cheque poking out from between the pages of *The Nine Doors*. He folded it carefully and put it in his pocket. Then he took the file and the book.

"I'll be in touch," he said.

He realized he'd thrown the dice. That he'd moved on to the first square in a dangerous game of Snakes and Ladders and it was too late to turn back. But he felt like playing. He went down the stairs followed by the echo of his own dry laughter. Varo Borja was wrong. There were certain things money couldn't buy.

The stairs from the main entrance led to an interior courtyard, with a well and two Venetian marble lions, fenced off from the street by railings. An unpleasant dankness rose from the Tagus and Corso stopped beneath the Moorish arch at the entrance to turn up his collar. He walked along the silent, narrow, cobbled streets with uneven paving, until he came to a small square. There was a bar with metal tables, and chestnut trees with bare branches beneath the bell tower of a church. He sat down in a patch of tepid sun on the terrace and tried to warm his stiff limbs. Two glasses of neat gin helped things along. Only then did he open the file on *The Nine Doors* and look through it properly for the first time.

There was a forty-two-page typed report giving the book's historical background, both for the supposed original version, the *Delomelanicon* or *Invocation of Darkness*, and for Torchia's version, *The Nine Doors of the Kingdom of Shadows*, printed in Venice in 1666. There were various appendices providing a bibliography, photocopies of citations in classical texts and information on the other two known copies – their owners, any restoration work, purchase dates, present locations. There was also a transcription of the records of Aristide Torchia's trial, with the account of an eyewitness, one Gennaro Galeazzo, describing the unfortunate printer's last moments:

* * *

. . . He mounted the scaffold without agreeing to be reconciled with God and maintained an obstinate silence. When the fire was lit smoke began to suffocate him. He opened his eyes wide and uttered a terrible cry, commending himself to the Father. Many of those present crossed themselves, for in death he requested God's mercy. Others say that he shouted at the ground, in other words towards the depths of the earth . . .

A car drove past on the other side of the square and turned down one of the corner streets leading to the cathedral. The engine paused for a moment beyond the corner, as if the driver had stopped before driving on down the street. Corso paid little attention, engrossed as he was in the book. The first page was the title page and the second was blank. The third, which began with a handsome capital N, was the first real page of text and began with a cryptic introduction:

Nos p.tens L.f.r, juv.te Stn. Blz.b, Lvtn, Elm, atq Ast.rot. ali.q, h.die ha.ems ace.t pct fo.de.is c.m t. qui no.st; et h.ic pol.icem am.rem mul. flo.em virg.num de.us mon. hon v.lup et op. for.icab tr.d.o,.os.ta int. nos ma.et eb.iet i.li c.ra er. No.is of.ret se.el in ano sag. sig. s.b ped. cocul.ab sa Ecl.e et no.s r.gat i.sius er.t; p.ct v.v.t an v.q fe.ix in t.a hom. et ven D:
    Fa.t in inf int co.s daem.
    Satanas. Belzebub, Lcfr, Elimi, Leviathan, Astaroth
    Siq pos mag. diab. et daem. pri.cp dom.

After the introduction, whose supposed authorship was obvious, came the text. Corso read the first lines:

D.mine mag.que L.fr, te D.um m. et.pr ag.sco. et pol.c.or t ser.ire. a.ob.re quam.d p. vvre; et rn.io al.rum d. et js.ch.st. et a.s sn.ts tq.e s.ctas e. ec.les. apstl. et rom. et om. i sc.am. et o.nia ips. s.cramen. et o.nes.atio et r.g. q.ib fid. pos.nt int.rcd. p.o me; et

.t.bi po.lceor q. fac. qu.tqu.t m.lum pot., et atra. ad mala p. omn.
Et ab.rncio chrsm. et b.ptm et omn . . .

He looked up at the church portico. The arches were carved with images of the Final Judgement worn down by the elements. Beneath them, dividing the door in two, a niche sheltered an angry-looking Pantocrator. His raised right hand suggested punishment rather than mercy. In his left hand he held an open book, and Corso could not help drawing parallels. He looked round at the church tower and the surrounding buildings. The façades still wore bishops' coats of arms, and he reflected that this square too had once watched the bonfires of the Inquisition burn. After all, this was Toledo. A crucible for underground cults, initiation mysteries, false converts. And heretics.

He drank some gin before going back to the book. The text, in an abbreviated Latin code, took up another hundred and fifty-seven pages, the final one being blank. The other nine contained the famous engravings inspired, according to legend, by Lucifer himself. Each print had a Latin, Hebrew and Greek numeral at the top, including a Latin phrase in the same abbreviated code as the rest. Corso ordered a third gin and went over them. They looked like the figures of the Tarot, or old medieval engravings: the king and the beggar, the hermit, the hangman, death, the executioner. In the last engraving a beautiful woman was riding a dragon. Too beautiful, he thought, for the religious morality of the time.

He found an identical illustration on a photocopy of a page in Mateu's *Universal Bibliography*. But it wasn't the same. Corso was holding the Terral-Coy copy, whereas the engraving reproduced came, as recorded by the scholarly Mateu in 1929, from another one of the books:

Torchia (Aristide). *De Umbrarum Regni Novem Portis. Venetiæ, apud Aristidem Torchiam. MDCLXVI*. Folio. 160 pages incl. title page. 9 full-page woodcuts. Of exceptional rarity. Only 3 known copies. Fargas Library, Sintra, Port. (see illustration). Coy Library, Madrid, Sp. (engraving 9 missing). Morel Library, Paris, Fr.

por ti solo ser causada
siente agora el gran dolor
que me das en tu partida
agradesce el gran amor
que te puse con fauor
reparando tu venida.

S. l. ni a. *(hácia* 1525*).* 4.° let. gót. 4 *hojas sin foliacion con la sign.* a.

HOMERO. La Vlyxea de Homero. Repartida en XIII. Libros. Tradvzida de Griego en Romance castellano por el Señor Gonçalo Perez. Venetia, en casa de Gabriel Giolito de Ferrariis, y svs hermanos, MDLIII. 12.° let. curs. 209 *hojas foliadas, inclusos los prels. y una al fin, en cuyo reverso se repiten las señas de la impresion.*

He visto la primera edicion, con el siguiente titulo: *De la Ulyxea de Homero. XIII. libros, traduzidos de Griego en Romance Castellano por Gonçalo Perez. Anvers, en casa de Iuan Stelsio,* 1550. 8.° let. cursiva. 4 hojas prels. y 293 fols.
Nic. Antonio menciona otra tambien de *Anvers,* 1553. 12.°

Poema en ciento treinta y cinco octavas. Hal al fin una disertacion en prosa, intitulada: *Prueba, que huuo Cigantes, y que oy los ay,* y por cierto para mi solo prueba que el autor era sumamente cándido ó tenia mui grandes tragaderas: sea esto dicho con perdon de los varios testos bíblicos y de Santos Padres que aduce en confirmacion de sus ideas gigantescas.

OVIDIO NASON. Metamorphoseos del excelente poeta Ouidio Nasson. Traduzidos en verso suelto y octaua rima: con sus allegorias al fin de cada libro. Por el Doctor Antonio Perez Sigler. Nueuamente agora enmēdados, y añadido por el mismo autor vn Diccionario Poetico copiosissimo. Bvrgos, Iuan Baptista Varesio, 1609. 1 t.° let. curs. 21 *hojas prels.* y 584 *fols.*

Este tomito por ser tan grueso suele hallarse dividido en dos volúmenes. No estoi cierto si mi ejemplar está perfectamente completo con las 21 hojas de preliminares.

N.NC SC.O TEN.BR. LVX

Sedano, en el tom. VII. del *Autores* llama á esta primera edicion; sin embargo me pone en duda el ver lleva la Aprobacion, la Censura, el Privilegio, la Fe de erratas y la Tasa fechadas en 1464. Por otra parte tambien puede ser cierto lo sentado por dicho Sedano, pues D. José Pellicer, al principio de su introduccion biográfico-literaria, observa que *salen ya á luz pública, despues de*

He found an identical illustration in
Mateu's *Universal Bibliography* . . .

Engraving 9 missing. Corso checked and saw this was wrong. Engraving number nine was there in the copy he was holding, originally from the Coy, later the Terral-Coy Library, and now the property of Varo Borja. It must have been a printing error, or a mistake by Mateu himself. In 1929, when the *Universal Bibliography* was published, printing techniques and distribution methods weren't as efficient. Many scholars mentioned books that they only knew of through third parties. Maybe the engraving was missing from one of the other copies. Corso made a note in the margin. He needed to check it.

A clock somewhere struck three and pigeons flew up off the tower and roofs. Corso shuddered gently, as if slowly coming to. He felt in his pocket and took out some money. He left it on the table and then stood up. The gin made him feel pleasantly detached, blurring external sounds and images. He put the book and file in his canvas bag, slung it over his shoulder and then stood for a few seconds looking at the angry Pantocrator in the portico. He wasn't in a hurry and he wanted to clear his head so he decided to walk to the railway station.

When he reached the cathedral he took a short cut through the cloisters. He passed the closed souvenir kiosk, and stood for a moment looking at the empty scaffolding over the murals undergoing restoration. The place was deserted, and his steps echoed beneath the vault. For a moment he thought he heard something behind him. A priest late to confession.

He came out through an iron gate into a dark, narrow street, where passing cars had taken chunks out of the walls. As he turned to the right he heard a car coming from somewhere to the left. There was a traffic sign, a triangle warning that the street narrowed, and when he came to it the car accelerated unexpectedly. He could hear it behind him moving closer. Too fast, he thought as he turned to look round. But he only had time to half-turn, just enough to see a dark shape bearing down on him. His reflexes were dulled by the gin, but by chance his attention was still on the traffic sign. Instinct pushed him towards it, seeking the narrow area of protection between the metal post and the wall. He slid into the small gap like a bullfighter hiding from the bull behind the barrier. The car only managed to strike his hand as it passed him. The blow was sharp and the pain made his knees buckle. He fell onto the uneven cobbles, and saw the car disappear down the street with a screeching of tyres.

Corso walked on to the station, rubbing his bruised hand. But now he turned every so often to look behind him, and his bag, with *The Nine Doors* inside, was burning his shoulder. For three seconds he'd caught a fleeting glimpse, but it had been enough: this time he was driving a black Mercedes, not a Jaguar, but the man who'd nearly run him down was dark, with a moustache and a scar on his face. The man from Makarova's bar. The same man he'd seen in a chauffeur's uniform, reading a newspaper outside Liana Taillefer's house.

IV

The Man with the Scar

*I know not where he comes from. But I know where he is
going: he is going to Hell.*

A. Dumas: *The Count of Monte Cristo*

Night was falling when Corso got home. Inside his coat pocket his
bruised hand was throbbing painfully. He went to the bathroom,
picked up his crumpled pyjamas and a towel from the floor, and held
the hand under a stream of cold water for five minutes. Then he
opened a couple of tins and ate them standing up in the kitchen.

It had been a strange and dangerous day. As he thought about it, he
felt confused, though he was less worried than curious. For some time,
he had treated the unexpected with the detached fatalism of one who
waits for life to make the next move. His detachment, his neutrality,
meant that he could never be the prime mover. Until that morning in
the narrow street in Toledo, his role had been merely to carry out
orders. Other people were the victims. Every time he lied or made a
deal with someone, he remained objective. He formed no relationships
with the persons or things involved – they were simply tools of the
trade. Lucas Corso remained on the edge, a mercenary with no cause
other than financial gain. The indifferent third man. Perhaps this atti-
tude had always made him feel safe, just as, when he took off his
glasses, people and distant objects became blurred, indistinct; he could
ignore them by removing their sharp outline. Now, though, the pain
from his injured hand, the sense of imminent danger, of violence aimed
directly at him alone, implied frightening changes in his world. Lucas
Corso, who had acted as executioner so many times, wasn't used to
being a victim. And he found it highly disconcerting.

In addition to the pain in his hand, he felt that his muscles were rigid
with tension and his mouth was dry. So he opened a bottle of Bols and

searched for aspirin in his canvas bag. He always carried a good supply, together with books, pencils, pens, half-filled notepads, a many-bladed Swiss Army knife, passport, money, a bulging address book, and books belonging to him and to others. He could, at any time, disappear without a trace like a snail with its shell. With his bag he could make himself at home wherever chance, or his clients, might lead him – airports, railway stations, dusty European libraries, hotel rooms which merged in his memory into a single room with fluid dimensions, where he would wake with a start, disorientated and confused in the darkness, searching for the light switch only to stumble upon the phone. Blank moments torn from his life and his consciousness. He was never very sure of himself, or anything, for the first thirty seconds after he opened his eyes, when his body woke up more quickly than his mind or his memory.

He sat at his computer and put his notepads and several reference books on his desk to his left. On his right he put *The Nine Doors* and Varo Borja's file. Then he leaned back in his chair, letting his cigarette burn down in his hand for five minutes, only rarely bringing it to his lips. During that time all he did was sip the rest of his gin and stare at the blank computer screen and the pentacle on the book's cover. At last he seemed to wake up. He stubbed out the cigarette in the ashtray and, adjusting his crooked glasses, set to work. Varo Borja's file agreed with Crozet's *Encyclopedia of Printers and Rare and Curious Books*.

TORCHIA, Aristide. Venetian printer, engraver and bookbinder. (1620–67). Printer's mark: a snake and a tree split by lightning. Trained as an apprentice in Leyden (Holland), at the workshop of the Elzevirs. On his return to Venice he completed a series of works on philosophical and esoteric themes in small formats (12mo, 16mo), which were highly esteemed. Among these stand out *The Secrets of Wisdom* by Nicholas Tamisso (3 vols, 12mo, Venice 1650) and a strange *Key to Captive Thoughts* (1 vol, 132 x 75 mm, Venice 1653). *The Three Books of the Art* by Paolo d'Este (6 vols, 8vo, Venice 1658), *Curious Explanation of Mysteries and Hieroglyphs* (1 vol, 8vo, Venice 1659), a reprint of *The Lost Word* by Bernardo Trevisano (1 vol, 8vo, Venice 1661) and *The Nine Doors of the Kingdom of Shadows* (1 vol, folio, Venice 1666). Owing to the printing of the latter he fell into the hands of the Inquisition. His workshop was destroyed, together with all the printed matter and texts yet to be printed that it contained. Torchia suffered the same fate. Condemned for magic and witchcraft, he was burned at the stake on 17 February 1667.

Corso looked away from the computer and examined the first page of the book that had cost the Venetian printer his life. The title was *De Umbrarum Regni Novem Portis*. Beneath it came the printer's mark, the stamp acting as the printer's signature which might be anything from a simple monogram to an elaborate illustration. In Aristide Torchia's case, as mentioned in Crozet, the mark was a tree with one branch snapped off by lightning and a snake coiled round the trunk, devouring its own tail. The picture was accompanied by the motto *Sic luceat Lux*: 'Thus shines the light'. At the foot of the page, there was the location, name and date: '*Venetia, apud Aristidem Torchiam*'. Printed in Venice, at the establishment of Aristide Torchia. Underneath, separated by a decoration: '*MDCLXVI. Cum superiorum privilegio veniaque.*' By authority and permission of the superiors.

Corso typed in:

Copy has no bookplates or handwritten notes. Complete according to catalogue for Terral-Coy collection auction (Claymore, Madrid). Error in Mateu (states 8, not 9, engravings in this copy). Folio. 299 x 215 mm. 2 blank flyleaves, 160 pages and 9 full-page prints, numbered I to VIIII. Pages: 1 title page with printer's mark. 157 pages of text. Last one blank, no colophon. Full-page engravings on right-hand page. Reverse blank.

DE VMBRARVM REGNI
NOVEM PORTIS

Sic   *Luceat*

Lux

Venetiae, apud Aristidem Torchiam

M. DC. LX. VI.

Cum superiorum privilegio veniaque

NEM. PERV.T QVI N.N LEG. CERT.RIT

CLAVS. PAT.T

VERB. D.SVM C.S.T ARCAN.

FOR. N.N OMN. A.QVE

FR. ST. A

DIT.SCO M.R.

DIS.S P.TI.R M.

VIC. I.T VIR.

N.NC SC.O TEN.BR. LVX

He examined the illustrations one by one. According to Varo Borja, legend attributed the original drawings to the hand of Lucifer himself. Each print was accompanied by a Roman ordinal, its Hebrew and Greek equivalent, and a Latin phrase in abbreviated code. He started writing again:

I NEM. PERV.T QUI N.N LEG. CERT.RIT: A horseman rides towards a walled city. He has a finger to his lips advising caution or silence.

II CLAUS. PAT.T: A hermit in front of a locked door holding 2 keys. A lantern on the ground. He is accompanied by a dog. At his side a sign resembling the Hebrew letter Teth.

III VERB. D.SUM C.S.T ARCAN.: A vagabond, or pilgrim, heads towards a bridge over a river. At both ends of the bridge, gate towers with closed doors bar the way. An archer on a cloud aims at the path leading to the bridge.

IIII (The Latin numeral appears in this form, not the more usual IV). FOR. N.N OMN. A.QUE: A jester stands in front of a stone labyrinth. The entrance is also closed. Three dice on the ground all showing the numbers 1, 2 and 3.

V FR.ST.A. A miser, or merchant, is counting out a sack of gold pieces. Behind him, Death holds an hourglass in one hand and a pitchfork in the other.

VI DIT.SCO M.R.: A hanged man, like the one in the Tarot, hands tied behind his back, is hanging by his foot from the battlements of a castle, next to a closed postern. A hand in a gauntlet is sticking out of a slot window holding a flaming sword.

VII DIS.S P.TI.R M.: A king and a beggar are playing chess on a board with only white squares. The Moon can be seen through the window. Beneath the window next to a closed door two dogs are fighting.

VIII VIC. I.T VIR.: Next to the wall of a city a woman is kneeling on the ground offering up her bare neck to the executioner.

In the background there is a wheel of fortune with three human figures: one at the top, one going up and one going down.

VIIII (Also in this form, not the usual numeral IX). N.NC SC.O TEN.BR. LUX: A naked woman riding a seven-headed dragon. She is holding an open book, and a half-moon hides her sex. On a hill in the background there is a castle in flames. The door is closed as in the other engravings.

He stopped typing, stretched his stiffened limbs, and yawned. The room was in darkness beyond the cone of light from his work lamp and his computer screen. Through the window there was the pale glow of street lights. He went up to it and looked out, not quite knowing what he hoped to see. A car waiting at the kerb perhaps, its headlights off and a dark figure inside. But nothing attracted his attention except, for a moment, the siren of an ambulance fading amongst the dark masses of buildings. He looked at the clock on the nearby church tower: it was five minutes past midnight.

He sat down again at the computer and the book. He examined the first illustration – the printer's mark on the title page, the snake with its tail in its mouth which Aristide Torchia had chosen as the symbol of his work. '*Sic luceat Lux*'. Snakes and devils, invocations and hidden meanings. He lifted his glass to drink a sarcastic toast to Torchia's memory. He must have been very brave, or very stupid. You paid a high price for that kind of thing in seventeenth century Italy, even if it was printed '*cum superiorum privilegio veniaque*'.

But then Corso stopped and cursed out loud, looking into the dark corners of the room, for not having noticed before. 'With the privilege and licence of the superiors.' That wasn't possible.

Without taking his eyes from the page, he sat back in his chair and lit another of his crushed cigarettes. Spirals of smoke rose in the lamp light, a translucent grey curtain behind which the lines of print rippled.

'*Cum superiorum privilegio veniaque*' didn't make sense. Or else it was brilliantly subtle. The reference to the *imprimatur* couldn't possibly apply to a conventional authorization. The Catholic Church would never have allowed such a book in 1666 because its direct predecessor, the *Delomelanicon,* had been listed in the index of forbidden books for the previous hundred and fifty years. So Aristide Torchia wasn't referring to the permission to print granted by the

Church censors. Nor to a civil authority, the government of the republic of Venice. He must have had other superiors.

The telephone interrupted his thought. It was Flavio La Ponte. He wanted to tell Corso how he'd found, in with some books (he'd had to buy the whole lot, that was the deal), a collection of European tram tickets, 5,775 of them to be exact. All of them palindromic numbers, sorted by country in shoe boxes. He wasn't joking. The collector had just died and the family wanted to get rid of them. Maybe Corso knew someone who'd be interested. Naturally. La Ponte knew that apart from the tireless, and pathological, activity of collecting 5,775 palindromic tickets, it was completely pointless. Who would buy such a stupid collection? Yes, perhaps it was a good idea: the Transport Museum in London. The English and their perversions . . . Would Corso deal with the matter?

La Ponte was also worried about the Dumas chapter. He'd received two telephone calls, from a man and a woman who didn't identify themselves, asking about 'The Anjou Wine'. And it was strange because he hadn't mentioned the chapter to anyone and wasn't intending to until he had Corso's report. Corso told him of his conversation with Liana Taillefer, to whom he had revealed the identity of the new owner.

"She knew you because you used to go and see her late husband. Oh, and by the way," he remembered, "she wants a copy of the receipt."

La Ponte laughed at the other end of the line. There was no bloody receipt. Taillefer had sold it to him, and that was that. But if the lovely widow wanted to discuss the matter, he added laughing lewdly, he'd be delighted. Corso mentioned the possibility that before he died Taillefer might have told someone about the manuscript. But La Ponte didn't think so. Taillefer had been very insistent that the matter should be kept secret until he himself gave a sign. In the end he never gave any sign, unless hanging himself from the light fitting could be seen as one.

"It's as good a sign as any," said Corso.

La Ponte agreed, chuckling cynically. Then he asked about Corso's visit to Liana Taillefer. After a couple more lecherous comments La Ponte said goodbye. Corso hadn't mentioned the skirmish in Toledo. They agreed to meet the following day.

After he hung up, Corso went back to *The Nine Doors*. But his mind was on other things. He was drawn back to the Dumas manuscript.

Finally he went and got the file with the white and blue pages. He rubbed his painful hand and typed in the name of the DUMAS files. The computer screen began to flicker. He stopped at a file called BIO:

DUMAS DAVY DE LA PAILLETERIE, Alexandre. Born 24.7.1802. Died 5.12.1870. Son of Thomas Alexandre Dumas, general of the Republic. Author of 257 volumes of novels, memoirs and other stories. 25 volumes of plays. Mulatto on his father's side. His black blood gave him certain exotic features. Appearance: tall, powerful neck, curly hair, fleshy lips, long legs, physically strong. Character: bon viveur, fickle, overpowering, liar, unreliable, popular. He had 27 known mistresses, 2 legitimate children and 4 illegitimate. He earned several fortunes and squandered them on parties, travel, expensive wines and bunches of flowers. As he earned money from his writing he lost it all through his extravagant spending on his mistresses, friends and hangers-on who besieged his castle home on Montecristo. When he was forced to flee Paris it was to escape his creditors, not for political reasons like his friend Victor Hugo. Friends: Hugo, Lamartine, Michelet, Gérard de Nerval, Nodier, George Sand, Berlioz, Théophile Gautier, Alfred de Vigny and others. Enemies: Balzac, Badère and others.

None of this really got him anywhere. He felt he was stumbling around in the dark, surrounded by countless false, or useless clues. And yet, there had to be a link somewhere. With his good hand he typed DUMAS.NOV:

Novels by Alexandre Dumas that appeared in instalments:
1831: *Historical Scenes* (*Revue des Deux Mondes*). 1834: *Jacques I et Jacques II* (*Journal des Enfants*). 1835: *Elizabeth of Bavaria* (*Dumont*). 1836: *Murat* (*La Presse*). 1837: *Pascal Bruno* (*La Presse*). Story of a Tenor (*Gazette Musicale*). 1838: *Count Horatio* (*La Presse*). *Nero's Night* (*La Presse*). *The Arms Hall* (*Dumont*). *Captain Paul* (*Le Siècle*). 1839: *Jacques Ortis* (*Dumont*). *The Life and Adventures of John Davys* (*Revue de Paris*). *Captain Panphile* (*Dumont*). 1840: *The Fencing Master* (*Revue de Paris*). 1841: *Le Chevalier d'Harmental* (*Le Siècle*). 1843: *Sylvandire* (*La Presse*). *The Wedding Dress* (*La Mode*). *Albine* (*Revue de Paris*). *Ascanio* (*Le Siècle*). *Fernande* (*Revue de Paris*). *Amaury* (*La Presse*). 1844:

The Three Musketeers (Le Siècle). Gabriel Lambert (La Chronique). The Regent's Daughter (Le Commerce). The Corsican Brothers (Démocratie Pacifique). The Count of Monte Cristo (Journal des Débats). Countess Bertha (Hetzel). Story of a Nutcracker (Hetzel). Queen Margot (La Presse). 1845: Nanon (La Patrie). Twenty Years After (Le Siècle). Le Chevalier de la Maison Rouge (Démocratie Pacifique). The Lady of Monsoreau (Le Constitutionnel). Madame de Condé (La Patrie). 1846: The Viscountess of Cambes (La Patrie). The Half-Brothers (Le Commerce). Joseph Balsam (La Presse). Pessac Abbey (La Patrie). 1847: The Forty-Five (Le Constitutionnel). Le Vicomte de Bragelonne (Le Siècle). 1848: The Queen's Necklace (La Presse). 1849: The Weddings of Father Olifus (Le Constitutionnel). 1850: God's Will (Evènement). The Black Tulip (Le Siècle). The Dove (Le Siècle). Angel Pitou (La Presse). 1851: Olympe de Clèves (Le Siècle). 1852: God and the Devil (Le Pays). The Comtesse de Charny (Cadot). Isaac Laquedem (Le Constitutionnel). 1853: The Shepherd of Ashbourn (Le Pays). Catherine Blum (Le Pays). 1854: The Life and Adventures of Catherine-Charlotte (Le Mousquetaire). The Brigand (Le Mousquetaire). The Mohicans of Paris (Le Mousquetaire). Captain Richard (Le Siècle). The Page of the Duke of Savoy (Le Constitutionnel). 1856: The Companions of Jehu (Journal pour Tous). 1857: The Last Saxon King (Le Monte-Cristo). The Wolf Leader (Le Siècle). The Wild Duck Shooter (Cadot). Black (Le Constitutionnel). 1858: The She-Wolves of Machecoul (Journal pour Tous). Memoirs of a Policeman (Le Siècle). The Palace of Ice (Le Monte-Cristo). 1859: The Frigate (Le Monte-Cristo). Ammalat-Beg (Moniteur Universel). Story of a Dungeon and a Little House (Revue Européenne). A Love Story (Le Monte-Cristo). 1860: Memoirs of Horatio (Le Siècle). Father La Ruine (Le Siècle). The Marchioness of Escoman (Le Constitutionnel). The Doctor of Java (Le Siècle). Jane (Le Siècle). 1861: A Night in Florence (Lévy-Hetzel). 1862: The Volunteer of '92 (Le Monte-Cristo). 1863: The Saint Félice (La Presse). 1864: The Two Dianas (Lévy). Ivanhoe (Pub. du Siècle). 1865: Memoirs of a Favourite (Avenir National). The Count of Moret (Les Nouvelles). 1866: A Case of Conscience (Le Soleil). Parisians and Provincials (La Presse). The Count of Mazarra (Le Mousquetaire). 1867: The Whites and the Blues (Le Mousquetaire). The Prussian Terror (La Situation). 1869: Hector de Sainte-Hermine (Moniteur Universel).

The Mysterious Physician (*Le Siècle*). *The Marquis's Daughter* (*Le Siècle*).

He smiled, wondering how much the late Enrique Taillefer would have paid to obtain all those titles. His glasses were misted, so he took them off and carefully cleaned the lenses. The lines on the computer were now blurred, as were other strange images he couldn't identify. With his glasses back on, the words on the screen became sharp again, but the images were still floating around, indistinct, in his mind, and without a key to give them any meaning. And yet Corso felt he was on the right path. The screen began to flicker again:

BAUDRY, editor of *Le Siècle*. Publishes *The Three Musketeers* between 14 March and 11 July 1844.

He took a look at the other files. According to his information, Dumas had had, at different periods of his literary life, fifty-two collaborators. Relations with a large number of them had ended stormily. But Corso was only interested in one of the names:

MAQUET, AUGUSTE-JULES. 1813–86. Collaborated with Alexandre Dumas on several plays and on 19 novels, including the most famous ones (*The Count of Monte Cristo, Le Chevalier de la Maison Rouge, The Black Tulip, The Queen's Necklace*) and, in particular, the cycle of *The Musketeers*. His collaboration with Dumas made him famous and wealthy. While Dumas died penniless, Maquet died a rich man at his castle in Saint-Mesme. None of his own works written without Dumas survives.

He looked at his biographical notes. There were some paragraphs taken from Dumas's *Memoirs*:

"We were the inventors, Hugo, Balzac, Soulie, De Musset and myself, of popular literature. We managed, for better or worse, to make a reputation for ourselves with that kind of writing, even though it was popular . . ."

". . . My imagination, confronted with reality, resembles a man who, visiting the ruins of an old building, must walk over the rubble, follow the passageways, bend down to go through doorways so as to reconstruct an approximate picture of the original building when it was full of life, when joy filled it with laughter and song, or when it echoed with sobs of sorrow."

Exasperated, Corso looked away from the screen. He was losing the feeling, it was disappearing into the corners of his memory before he could identify it. He stood up and paced the darkened room. Then he angled his lamp at a pile of books on the floor against the wall. He picked up two thick volumes: a modern edition of the *Memoirs* of Alexandre Dumas père. He went back to his desk and began to leaf through them until three photos caught his eye. In one of them, his African blood clearly visible in his curly hair and mulatto looks, Dumas was sitting smiling at Isabelle Constant who, Corso gathered from the caption, was fifteen when she became the novelist's mistress. The second photo showed an older Dumas, posing with his daughter Marie. Here, at the height of his fame, the father of the adventure serial sat, good-natured and placid, before the photographer. The third photo, Corso decided, was definitely the most amusing and significant. Dumas aged sixty-five, grey-haired but still tall and strong, his frock coat open to reveal a contented paunch, was embracing Adah Menken, one of his last mistresses. According to the text, "after the seances and sessions of black magic of which she was such a devotee, she liked to be photographed, scantily clad, with the great men in her life." In the photograph La Menken's legs, arms and neck were all bare which was scandalous for the time. The young woman, paying more attention to the camera than to the object of her embrace, was leaning her head on the old man's powerful right shoulder. As for him, his face showed the signs of a long life of dissipation, pleasure and parties. His smile, between the bloated cheeks of a bon viveur, was contented, ironic. And his expression for the photographer was teasing, crafty, seeking complicity. The fat old man with the shameless, passionate young girl who showed him off like a rare trophy: he, whose characters and stories had made so many women dream. It was as if old Dumas was asking for understanding, having given in to the girl's capricious wish to be photographed. After all, she was young and pretty, her skin soft and her mouth passionate, this girl that life had kept for him on the last lap of his journey, only three years before his death. The old devil.

Corso shut the book and yawned. His watch, an old chronometer that he often forgot to wind up, had stopped at a quarter past midnight. He went and opened the window and breathed in the cold night air. The street was still deserted.

It was all very strange, he thought, as he went back to his desk and turned off the computer. His eyes came to rest on the folder with

Dumas embraced by Adah Menken, one of his last lovers

the manuscript. He opened it mechanically and took another look at the fifteen pages covered in two different types of handwriting, eleven of them blue, four of them white. "*Après de nouvelles presque désespérées du roi* . . ." Upon almost desperate news from the king . . . In the pile of books he found a huge red tome, a facsimile edition – J. C. Lattès 1988 – containing the entire cycle of *The Musketeers* and *Monte Cristo* in the Le Vasseur edition with engravings, published shortly after Dumas's death. He found the chapter called 'The Anjou Wine' on page 144 and started to read, comparing it to the original manuscript. Except for a small error here or there, both texts were identical. In the book, the chapter was illustrated with two drawings by Maurice Leloir, engraved by Huyot. King Louis XIII arriving at the siege of La Rochelle with ten thousand men, with four horsemen at the head of his escort, holding their muskets, wearing the wide-brimmed hat and jacket of de Treville's company. Three of them are without doubt Athos, Porthos and Aramis. A moment later they will be meeting their friend d'Artagnan, still a simple cadet in Monsieur des Essarts's company of guards. The Gascon still doesn't know that the bottles of Anjou wine, a gift from his mortal enemy Milady, Richelieu's agent, are poisoned. She wants to avenge the insult done to her by d'Artagnan. He has passed himself off as the Comte de Wardes, slipped into her bed, and enjoyed a night of love that should have been the Count's. To make matters worse, d'Artagnan has by chance discovered Milady's terrible secret, the fleur-de-lis on her shoulder, the shameful mark branded on her by the executioner's iron. With such preliminaries, and given Milady's disposition, the contents of the second illustration are easy to guess: as d'Artagnan and his companions watch in astonishment, the manservant Fourreau expires in terrible agony after drinking the wine intended for his master. Sensitive to the magic of a text he hadn't read in twenty years, Corso came to the passage where the Musketeers and d'Artagnan are speaking about Milady:

" . . . Well," said d'Artagnan to Athos. "So you see, dear friend. It is a fight to the death."

Athos nodded.

"Yes, yes," he said. "I know. But do you think it's really her?"

"I am sure of it."

"Nevertheless, I confess I still have doubts."

"And the fleur-de-lis on her shoulder?"

"She is an Englishwoman who must have committed some crime in France, and who has been marked for her crime."

"Athos, that woman is your wife, I tell you," repeated d'Artagnan. "Do you not recall that both marks are identical?"

"Nevertheless, I would have sworn that the woman was dead, I hanged her very well."

This time it was d'Artagnan who shook his head.

"Well? What are we to do?" said the young man.

"We certainly can't go on like this, with a sword hanging eternally over our heads," said Athos. "We must find a way out of this situation."

"But how?"

"Listen, try to have a meeting with her and explain everything. Tell her: 'Peace or war! My word as a gentleman that I will never say or do anything against you. For your part, give me your solemn word to do nothing against me. Otherwise I will go to the Chancellor, the King, the executioner, I will incite the Court against you, I will denounce you as a marked woman, I will have you put on trial, and should you be acquitted, then upon my word as a gentleman, I will kill you myself, in any corner, as I would a rabid dog.'"

"I am delighted with this plan," said d'Artagnan.

Memories bring other memories in their wake. Corso tried to hold a fleeting, familiar image that had suddenly crossed his mind. He managed to capture it just before it faded, and once again it was the man in the black suit, the chauffeur of the Jaguar outside Liana Taillefer's house, at the wheel of the Mercedes in Toledo . . . The man with the scar. And it was Milady who had stirred his memory.

He thought it over, disconcerted. And suddenly the image became perfectly sharp. Milady, of course. Milady de Winter as d'Artagnan first sees her at the window of her carriage in the opening chapter of the novel, outside the inn at Meung. Milady in conversation with a stranger . . . Corso quickly turned the pages, searching for the passage. He found it easily:

. . . A man around forty to forty-five years of age, with black, piercing eyes, a pale complexion, a strongly pronounced nose, and a perfectly trimmed, black moustache . . .

Rochefort. The Cardinal's sinister agent and d'Artagnan's enemy, who has him beaten in the first chapter, steals the letter of recommendation to Monsieur de Treville and is indirectly responsible for the Gascon almost fighting duels with Athos, Porthos and Aramis . . . Following this somersault of his memory, Corso scratched his head, disconcerted by the unusual association of ideas and characters. What link was there between Milady's companion and the driver who tried to run him down in Toledo? And then there was the scar. The paragraph didn't mention a scar but he remembered clearly that Rochefort had always had a mark on his face. He turned more pages until he found the confirmation of this in chapter three, where d'Artagnan is recounting his adventure to Treville:

"Tell me," he replied, "did this gentleman have a faint scar on his temple?"

"Yes, the sort of mark that might have been made by a bullet grazing it . . ."

A faint scar on his temple. There was his confirmation, but as Corso remembered it the scar was *bigger*, and not on his temple, but on his cheek, like that of the chauffeur dressed in black. He went over it all until at last he let out a laugh. The picture was now complete, and in full colour: Lana Turner in *The Three Musketeers*, at her carriage window, beside a suitably sinister Rochefort, not pale as in Dumas's novel, but dark, with a plumed hat and a long scar – it was definite this time – cutting his right cheek from top to bottom. He remembered it as a film not a novel, and his exasperation at this both amused and irritated him. Bloody Hollywood.

Film scenes apart, he had at last managed to find some order to all of it, a common, if secret, thread, a tune composed of disparate, mysterious notes. Through the vague uneasiness that Corso had experienced since his visit to Taillefer's widow, he could now glimpse outlines, faces, an atmosphere and characters, half way between reality and fiction, and all linked in strange, as yet unclear manner. Dumas and a seventeenth-century book. The Devil and *The Three Musketeers*. Milady and the bonfires of the Inquisition . . . Although it was all more absurd than definite, more like a novel than real life.

He turned out the light and went to bed. But it took him some time to fall asleep because one image wouldn't leave his mind. It floated in the darkness before his open eyes. A distant landscape, that of his reading as a boy, filled with shadows which reappeared now twenty years later, materialized as ghosts that were so close he could almost feel them. The scar. Rochefort. The man from Meung. His Eminence's mercenary.

V

Remember

He was sitting just as he had left him, in front of the fireplace.

A. Christie. *The Murder of Roger Ackroyd*

This is the point at which I enter the stage for the second time. Corso came to me again, and he did so, I seem to remember, a few days before leaving for Portugal. As he told me later, by then he already suspected that the Dumas manuscript and Varo Borja's *Nine Doors* were only the tip of the iceberg. To understand it all he first needed to find out the other stories, all knotted together like the cord Enrique Taillefer used to hang himself. It wouldn't be easy, I told him, because in literature there are never any clear boundaries. Everything is dependent on everything else and one thing is superimposed on top of another. It all ends up as a complicated intertextual game, like a hall of mirrors or those Russian dolls. Establishing a specific fact or the precise source involves risks that only some of my very stupid or very confident colleagues would dare take. It would be like saying that you can see the influence of *Quo Vadis*, but not Suetonius or Apollonius of Rhodes, on Robert Graves. As for me, all I know is that I know nothing. And when I want to know something, I look it up in books – their memory never fails.

"Count Rochefort is one of the most important secondary characters in *The Three Musketeers*," I explained to Corso when he came to see me for the second time. "He is the Cardinal's agent and a friend of Milady's, and the first enemy that d'Artagnan makes. And I can pinpoint the exact date: the first Monday of April 1625, in Meung-sur-Loire . . . I refer to the fictional Rochefort, of course, although a similar character did exist. Gatien de Courtilz described him, in the supposed *Memoirs* of the real d'Artagnan, with the name of

Rosnas . . . But the Rochefort with the scar didn't exist in real life. Dumas took the character from another book, the *Mémoires de MLCDR (Monsieur le Comte de Rochefort)*, possibly apocryphal and also attributed to Courtilz . . . Some say that they could refer to Henri Louis d'Aloigny, Marquis de Rochefort, born around 1625, but that would be stretching things."

I looked out at the lights of the evening traffic in the avenues beyond the window of the café where I meet up with my literary friends. A few of them were sitting with us round a table covered in newspapers, cups and smoking ashtrays – a couple of writers, a painter down on his luck, a lady journalist on the up, a stage actor and four or five students, the kind who sit in a corner and don't open their mouths, watching you as if you were God. Corso was sitting amongst them, still in his coat. He leant against the window, drank gin and occasionally took notes.

"To be sure," I added, "the reader who goes through the sixty-seven chapters of *The Three Musketeers* waiting for a duel between Rochefort and d'Artagnan, is in for a disappointment. Dumas settles the matter in three lines, and is rather underhand about it. Because when we next meet the character in *Twenty Years After*, he and d'Artagnan have fought three times, and Rochefort bears as many scars as a result. Nevertheless, there no longer remains any hatred between them. Instead they have the twisted respect for each other that is only possible between two old enemies. Once again fate has decreed that they fight on different sides, but now friendly, complicit; two gentlemen who have known each other for twenty years. Rochefort falls out of favour with Mazarin, breaks out of the Bastille and helps the Duke of Beaufort to escape. He conspires in the Fronde rebellion and dies in the arms of d'Artagnan, who has stabbed him with his sword, failing to recognize him in all the confusion . . . 'You were my fate,' he more or less says to the Gascon. 'I recovered from three of your sword wounds, but I will not recover from the fourth.' And he dies. 'I have just killed an old friend,' d'Artagnan later tells Porthos . . . This is the only epitaph Richelieu's former agent is given."

My words provoked a lively discussion with several factions. The actor hadn't taken his eyes off the lady journalist all afternoon. He was an old heart-throb who'd played Monte Cristo in a television series and, encouraged by the painter and the two writers, he launched into a brilliant account of his recollections of the characters. In this way we moved from Dumas to Zevaco and Paul Féval, and ended by once again confirming Sabatini's indisputable influence on Salgari. I seem to recall that somebody timidly mentioned Jules Verne, but was shouted down by all those present. Verne's cold, soulless heroes had no place in a discussion of passionate tales of cloak and dagger.

As for the journalist, one of those fashionable young ladies with a column in a leading Sunday newspaper, her literary memory began with Milan Kundera. So she remained in a state of cautious expectation and agreed with relief whenever a title, anecdote or character (the Black Swan, Yañez, Nevers's sword wound) stirred some memory of a film glimpsed on TV. Meanwhile, Corso, with a hunter's calm patience, looked steadily at me over his glass of gin, waiting for a chance to return the conversation to the original subject. And he succeeded, making the most of an awkward silence that fell when the journalist said that, anyway, she found these adventure stories rather lightweight, I mean kind of superficial, don't you think?

Corso chewed the end of his pencil.

"And how do you see Rochefort's role in history, Mr Balkan?" he asked.

They all looked at me, in particular the students, two of them girls. I don't know why, but in certain circles I'm considered a high priest of letters and every time I open my mouth people expect to hear principles of faith. An article of mine, in the appropriate literary reviews, can make or break a writer who's starting out. Absurd, certainly, but that's life. Think of the last Nobel Prize-winner, the author of *I, Onan. In Search of Myself* and the ultra-successful *Oui, c'est moi*. It was I who made him a household name fifteen years ago, with a page and a half in *Le Monde* on April Fools Day. I'll never forgive myself, but that's how things work.

"At first, Rochefort is the enemy," I said. "He symbolizes the hidden forces, darkness . . . He is the agent of the satanic conspiracy surrounding d'Artagnan and his friends, the Cardinal's plot growing in the shadows, threatening their lives . . ."

I saw one of the students smile, but I couldn't tell if her absorbed, slightly mocking expression, was a result of my comments or of private thoughts which had nothing to do with the discussion. I was surprised because, as I've said, students tend to listen to me with the awe of an editor of the *Osservatore Romano* getting the exclusive rights to one of the Pope's encyclicals. So it made me look at her with interest. Although she'd already caught my eye at the beginning, when she joined us, because of her unsettling green eyes. She was wearing a blue duffle coat and carried a pile of books under her arm. Her chestnut hair was cut very short like a boy's. Now she sat at a slight distance, not quite part of the group. There are always a few young people at our table, literature students that I invite for a coffee. But this girl had never attended before. It was impossible to forget her eyes. In contrast to her tanned face their colour was so light it was almost transparent. A slender, supple girl, one could tell she spent a lot of time outdoors. Under her jeans her long legs were no doubt also tanned. And I retained one other thing about her: she wore neither rings, watch nor earrings. Her ears weren't pierced.

" . . . Rochefort is also the man glimpsed, never caught," I went on, getting back to the subject. "A mysterious mask with a scar. He stands for paradox and d'Artagnan's powerlessness. D'Artagnan is always in pursuit but he never quite catches up with him. He tries to kill him but only manages to do so by mistake twenty years later. By then he is no longer an adversary but a friend."

"Your d'Artagnan's a bit jinxed," said one of my circle, the older of the two writers. He'd only sold five hundred copies of his last novel, but he earned a fortune writing crime stories under the perverse pseudonym of Emilia Forster. I looked at him gratefully, pleased by his opportune remark.

"Absolutely. The love of his life gets poisoned. Despite all his exploits and services to the crown of France, he spends twenty years as an obscure lieutenant in the musketeers. And in the last lines of *The Vicomte de Bragelonne*, when he is finally awarded the marshal's baton, which has taken him four volumes and four hundred and twenty-five chapters to achieve, he is killed by a Dutch bullet."

"Like the real d'Artagnan," said the actor, who had managed to place his hand on the fashionable lady columnist's thigh.

I took a sip of coffee before agreeing. Corso was staring at me intently.

"There are three d'Artagnans," I explained. "Of the first, Charles de Batz Castlemore, we know that he died on 23 June 1673, from a shot in the throat during the siege of Maastricht, as reported in the *Gazette de France* at the time. Half his men fell with him . . . Apart from this posthumous detail, in life he was only slightly more fortunate than his fictional namesake."

"Was he a Gascon too?"

"Yes, from Lupiac. The village still exists, and he is commemorated by a stone plaque there: 'D'Artagnan, whose real name was Charles de Batz, was born here around 1615. He died in the siege of Maastricht in 1673.'"

"It doesn't quite fit historically," said Corso, looking at his notes. "According to Dumas, d'Artagnan was eighteen at the start of the novel, around 1625. But at that time the real d'Artagnan would only have been ten years old." He smiled like a clever, sceptical little rabbit. "Too young to handle a sword."

I agreed. "Yes. Dumas altered things so d'Artagnan could take part in the adventure of the diamond tags under Richelieu and Louis XIII. Charles de Batz must have arrived in Paris very young: he was listed amongst the guards of Monsieur des Essarts's company in documents on the siege of Arras in 1640, and two years later in the Roussillon campaign. But he never served as a musketeer under Richelieu because he only joined the elite regiment after Louis XIII's death. His real protector was Cardinal Jules Mazarin. There is indeed a jump of ten or fifteen years between the two d'Artagnans. But following the success of *The Three Musketeers*, Dumas extended the action to cover almost forty years of France's history. In later volumes he adjusted his story to coincide better with real events."

"Which events have been verified? I mean historical events in which the real d'Artagnan was involved?"

"Quite a few. His name appears in Mazarin's letters and in the correspondence of the Ministry of War. Like the fictional hero, he was the Cardinal's agent during the Fronde rebellion, with important responsibilities at the court of Louis XIV. He was even entrusted with the delicate matter of detaining and escorting the finance minister Fouquet. All these events were confirmed in the letters of Madame de Sévigné. And he could even have met the painter Velázquez on the Isle of Pheasants when he accompanied Louis XIV on his journey to meet his bride-to-be, Maria Theresa of Austria . . ."

"He was quite a man of the Court, then. Very different from Dumas's swashbuckling d'Artagnan."

I raised my hand, in defence of Dumas's respect for the facts.

"Don't be fooled. Charles de Batz, or d'Artagnan, went on fighting to the end of his life. He served under Turenne in Flanders, and in 1657 was appointed lieutenant in the grey musketeers, which was equivalent to commander. Ten years later he became a captain in the musketeers and fought in Flanders, a post equivalent to cavalry general . . ."

Corso was squinting behind his glasses.

"Excuse me." He leant across the table towards me, pencil in hand. He'd been writing down a name or date. "In which year did this happen?"

"His promotion to general? 1667. Why did that draw your attention?"

He was showing his incisors as he bit his lower lip. But only for an instant.

"No reason." As he spoke his face regained its impassivity. "That same year a certain person was burned at the stake in Rome. A strange coincidence . . ." Now he was staring at me blankly. "Does the name Aristide Torchia mean anything to you?"

I tried to remember. I had no idea.

"Not a thing," I answered. "Does he have anything to do with Dumas?"

He hesitated.

"No," he said at last, although he didn't seem very convinced. "I don't think so. But please go on. You were talking about the real d'Artagnan in Flanders."

"He died at Maastricht, as I've said, at the head of his men. A heroic death. The English and the French were besieging the town. They needed to cross a dangerous pass and d'Artagnan offered to go first out of courtesy to his allies . . . A musket bullet tore through his jugular."

"He never got to be marshal, then."

"No. Alexandre Dumas deserves exclusive credit for giving the fictional d'Artagnan what a miserly Louis XIV refused his flesh and blood predecessor . . . There are a couple of interesting books on the subject. You can take down the titles if you want. One is by Charles Samaran, *D'Artagnan, capitaine des mousquetaires du roi, histoire véridique d'un héros de roman*, published in 1912. The other one is *Le vrai d'Artagnan*, written by the Duke of Montesquieu-Fezensac, a direct descendant of the real d'Artagnan. Published in 1963, I think."

None of this information was obviously related to the Dumas manuscript, but Corso noted it down as if his life depended on it. Occasionally he looked up from his notepad and glanced at me inquisitively through his crooked glasses. Or he put his head to one side as if he were no longer listening and was absorbed in his own thoughts. At that time, I myself knew all the details regarding 'The Anjou Wine', even certain keys to the mystery of which Corso was unaware. But

I had no idea of the complex implications that *The Nine Doors* would have for this story. Despite his logical turn of mind, Corso was already beginning to glimpse sinister links between the facts at his disposal, and – how shall I put it – the literary source of those facts. It may all appear rather confused, but we must remember that this was how it seemed to Corso at the time. And although I am narrating this story after the resolution of the momentous events to come, the very nature of the loop – think of Escher's paintings, or the work of that old joker, Bach – forces us to return continually to the beginning and limit ourselves to the narrow confines of Corso's knowledge. The rule is to know and keep silent. Even if there is foul play, without rules there is no game.

"OK," said Corso once he'd written down the recommended titles. "That's the first d'Artagnan, the real one. And Dumas's fictional character is the third one. I'm assuming the link between them is the book by Gatien de Courtilz you showed me the other day, the *Mémoires de M. d'Artagnan*."

"Correct. We can call him the missing link, the least famous of the three. A Gascon who is an intermediary, a literary and a real character all at the same time. The very same one that Dumas used to create his character . . . The writer Gatien de Courtilz de Sandras was a contemporary of d'Artagnan's. He recognized the novelesque potential of the character and set to work. A century and a half later, Dumas found out about the book during a trip to Marseilles. His landlord had a brother who ran the municipal library. Apparently the brother showed him the book, edited in Cologne in 1700. Dumas saw that he could make use of the story and asked to borrow the book. He never returned it."

"What do we know about this predecessor of Dumas, Gatien de Courtilz?"

"Quite a lot. Partly because he had a sizeable police file. He was born in 1644 or 1647 and was a musketeer, a bugler in the Royal-Etranger, which was a type of foreign legion of the time, and captain of the cavalry regiment of Beaupré-Choiseul. At the end of the war against Holland, in which d'Artagnan was killed, Courtilz remained in Holland and traded his sword for a pen. He wrote biographies, historical monographs, more or less apocryphal memoirs, shocking tales of gossip and intrigue at the French Court . . . This got him into trouble. The *Mémoires de M. d'Artagnan* was astonishingly successful: five editions in ten years. But they displeased Louis XIV. He disliked the irreverent tone used to recount certain details regarding the royal family and its entourage. As a result Courtilz was arrested on his return to France and held in the Bastille at His Majesty's pleasure until shortly before his death."

The actor made the most of my pause to slip in, quite irrelevantly, a quotation from "The sun has set in Flanders" by Marquina: "Our captain," he recited, "/gravely wounded led us/ sparing no effort though in his final agony./Sirs, what a captain/he was indeed that day . . ." Or something like that. It was a shameless attempt to shine in front of the lady journalist, whose thigh he now held with a proprietorial air. The others, in particular the novelist who wrote under the pseudonym of Emilia Forster, were looking at him with envy or barely concealed resentment.

After a polite silence, Corso decided to hand control of the situation back to me.

"How much does Dumas's d'Artagnan owe to Courtilz?"

"A great deal. Although in *Twenty Years After* and in *Bragelonne* he used other sources, the basic story of *The Three Musketeers* is to be found in Courtilz. Dumas applied his genius to it and gave it breadth, but it contained a rough outline of all the elements of the story: d'Artagnan's father granting his blessing, the letter to Treville, the challenge to the musketeers, who incidentally were brothers in the first draft . . . Milady also appears. And the two d'Artagnans were like two peas in a pod. Courtilz's character was rather more cynical, more miserly and less trustworthy. But they're one and the same."

Corso leaned forward slightly.

"Earlier you said that Rochefort stands for the evil plot surrounding d'Artagnan and his friends . . . But Rochefort is just a henchman."

"Indeed. In the pay of His Eminence Armand Jean du Plessis, Cardinal Richelieu . . ."

"The evil one," said Corso.

"The spirit of evil," commented the actor, determined to butt in. Impressed by our foray into the subject of serials that afternoon, the students were taking notes or listening open-mouthed. Only the girl with the green eyes remained impassive, slightly apart, as if she had only dropped in by chance.

"For Dumas," I went on, returning to the subject, "at least in the first part of *The Musketeers* cycle, Richelieu provided the character essential to all romantic adventure and mystery stories: the powerful enemy lurking in the shadows, the embodiment of Evil. For the history of France, Richelieu was a great man. But in *The Musketeers* he is only rehabilitated twenty years later. Shrewd Dumas fitted in with reality without diminishing the novel's interest. He'd already found another villain: Mazarin. This correction, even as voiced by d'Artagnan and his companions when they praise the nobility of their former enemy, is morally questionable. For Dumas it was a convenient act of contrition . . . Nevertheless, in the first volume of the cycle, whether plotting Buckingham's murder, Anne of Austria's downfall, or giving carte blanche to the sinister Milady, Cardinal Richelieu is the embodiment of the perfect villain. His Eminence is to d'Artagnan what Prince Gonzaga was to Lagardère, or Professor Moriarty to Sherlock Holmes. A mysterious, demonic presence . . ."

Corso seemed about to interrupt me, which I thought odd. I was getting to know him and typically he wouldn't interrupt until the other person had given up all his information, when every last detail had been squeezed out.

"You've used the word *demonic* twice," he said looking over his notes. "And both times referring to Richelieu . . . Was the Cardinal a devotee of the occult?"

His words had a strange effect. The young girl had turned to look curiously at Corso. He was looking at me, and I was watching the girl. He was waiting for my answer, unaware of this strange triangle.

"Richelieu was keenly interested in many things," I explained. "In addition to turning France into a great power, he had time to collect pictures, carpets, porcelain and statues. He was also an important bookcollector. He bound his books in calf skin and red morocco leather . . ."

" . . . And had weapons of silver and three red angles on his coat of arms." Corso gestured impatiently. All this information was trivial and he didn't need me to tell him about it. "There's a very well-known Richelieu catalogue."

"The catalogue is incomplete because the collection was broken up. Parts of it are now kept in the national library of France, the Mazarin library and the Sorbonne, while other books are in private hands. He owned Hebrew and Syrian manuscripts, notable works on mathematics, medicine, theology, law and history . . . And you were right. Scholars were most surprised to find many ancient texts on the occult, from the Cabbala to black magic."

Corso swallowed without taking his eyes off mine. He seemed tense – a bowstring about to snap.

"Any book in particular?"

I shook my head before I answered. His insistence intrigued me. The girl was listening attentively, but it was apparent that she was no longer directing her attention at me.

I excused myself. "My information on Richelieu as a character in a serial doesn't go that far."

"What about Dumas? Was he interested in the occult too?"

Here I was emphatic:

"No. Dumas was a bon viveur who did everything out in the open, to the great enjoyment and shock of all those around him. He was also somewhat superstitious. He believed in the evil eye, he wore an amulet on his watch chain and he'd have his fortune told by Madame Desbarolles. But I don't see him practising black magic in the back room. He wasn't even a Mason, as he confesses in *The Century of Louis XV* . . . He had debts and he was hounded by his publishers and his creditors – he was too busy to go round wasting his time on such things. Perhaps at one time, when researching one of his characters, he studied the subject, but never in much depth. I believe he drew all the Masonic practices described in *Joseph Balsam* and in *The Mohicans of Paris* directly from Clavel's *Picturesque History of Freemasonry*."

"What about Adah Menken?"

I looked at Corso with genuine respect. This was a real expert's question.

"That was different. Adah-Isaacs Menken, his last lover, was an American actress. During the Exhibition of 1867, while attending a performance of *The Pirates of the Savannah*, Dumas noticed a pretty young woman on stage who had to grab hold of a galloping horse. The girl embraced the novelist as he left the theatre and told him bluntly that she had read all his books and was prepared to go to bed with him straight away. Old Dumas needed a great deal less than that to become infatuated with a woman, so he accepted her tribute. She claimed to have been the wife of a millionaire, a king's lover, the general of a republic . . . Really she was a Portuguese Jew born in America and the mistress of a strange man, a mixture of pimp and boxer. Her relationship with Dumas caused a great deal of scandal because Menken liked to be photographed scantily clad and she frequented number 107 Rue Malesherbes, Dumas's last house in Paris. She died from peritonitis after falling from a horse, aged thirty-one."

"Was she keen on black magic?"

"So they say. She liked strange ceremonies where she'd dress up in a tunic, burn incense and make offerings to the Prince of Darkness . . . Sometimes she'd claim to be possessed by Satan, with various connotations that today we might describe as pornographic. I'm sure old Dumas never believed a word of it, but he must have enjoyed the whole performance. It seems that when Menken was possessed by the Devil she was very hot in bed."

There was laughter round the table. I even allowed myself a slight smile, but the girl and Corso remained serious. She seemed to be thinking, her light-coloured eyes intent on Corso while he nodded slowly, though he now looked distracted and distant. He was looking through the window at the streets and he seemed to be searching in the night, in the silent flow of car lights reflected in his glasses, for the lost word, the key to uniting all these different stories which floated like dead leaves on the dark waters of time.

I must now once more move into the background, as the near-omniscient narrator of Lucas Corso's adventures. In this way, with the information Corso later confided to me, the subsequent tragic events can be put into some sort of order. So we now come to the moment when, returning home, he sees that the concierge has just swept the hallway and is about to leave. He passes him as he is bringing the dustbins up from the basement.

"They came to fix your TV this afternoon, Mr Corso."

Corso had read enough books and seen enough films to know what that meant. So he couldn't help laughing, much to the concierge's astonishment.

"I haven't had a television for ages."

The concierge let out a stream of confused apologies but Corso barely paid attention. It was all beginning to seem wonderfully predictable. Since this was a question of books, he had to approach the problem as a lucid, critical reader not as the hero of a cheap novelette, which was what somebody was trying to make of him. Nor did he have another option. And, after all, he was naturally cool and sceptical. He wasn't likely to break out into a sweat and moan, "Woe is me!"

"I hope I haven't done anything wrong, Mr Corso."

"Not at all. The repair man was dark, wasn't he? With a moustache and a scar on his face?"

"Exactly."

"Don't worry. He's a friend of mine. A bit of a joker."

The concierge sighed with relief.

"That's a weight off my mind, Mr Corso."

Corso wasn't worried about *The Nine Doors* or the Dumas manuscript. When he wasn't carrying them with him in his canvas bag he left them for safekeeping at Makarova's bar. This was the safest place for any of his things. So he climbed the stairs calmly, trying to picture the coming scene. By now he had become what some refer to as a second-level reader, and he would have been disappointed had he been met by too stereotypical a scene. He was relieved when he opened the door. There were no papers strewn on the floor, no turned-out drawers. Not even any armchairs slashed with knives. It was all tidy, just as he'd left it in the early afternoon.

He went to his desk. The boxes of floppy disks were in their place, the papers and documents in their trays just as he remembered them. The man with the scar, Rochefort or whoever the hell he was, was certainly efficient. But there are limits to everything. When he switched on the computer Corso smiled triumphantly.

```
DAGMAR PC 555 K (S1) ELECTRONIC PLC
LAST USED AT 19.35/THU/21/3
A>ECHO OFF
A>
```

Last used at 19.35 that day, the screen stated. But he hadn't touched the computer in the last twenty-four hours. At 19.35 he was with us round the table at the café, while the man with the scar was lying his way into Corso's flat.

He found something else, which he hadn't noticed at first, by the telephone. It hadn't been left there by chance, or due to carelessness on the part of the mysterious visitor. In the ashtray, amongst the butts left by Corso himself, he found a fresh one which wasn't his. It was a Havana cigar almost completely burnt down, but the band was intact. He held it up by the tip. He couldn't believe it. Then, gradually, as he understood its meaning, he laughed, showing his eye-teeth like a malicious, angry wolf.

The brand was Montecristo. Naturally.

Flavio La Ponte had had a visitor too. The plumber in his case.

"It's not bloody funny," he said by way of a greeting. He waited for Makarova to serve the gin and then emptied the contents of a small Cellophane packet on to the counter. The cigar end was identical, and the band was also intact.

"Edmundo Dantés strikes again," said Corso.

La Ponte couldn't get into the spirit of the thing.

"Well, he smokes expensive cigars, the bastard." His hand was trembling and he spilt some gin down his curly blond beard. "I found it on my bedside table."

Corso teased him.

"You should take things more calmly, Flavio. You've got to be hard." He patted him on the shoulder. "Remember the Nantucket Harpooneers' Club."

La Ponte shook his hand, frowning.

"I was hard, until I was exactly eight years old. Then I came to understand the benefits of survival. After that I got a bit softer."

Between gulps of gin Corso quoted Shakespeare. A coward dies a thousand deaths but the brave man and so on . . . But La Ponte wasn't about to be reassured by quotations. At least not by that type.

"I'm not scared really," he said thoughtfully, looking down. "What worries me is losing things . . . like money. Or my incredible sexual powers. Or my life."

These were weighty arguments and Corso had to admit that any possible developments might turn out to be slightly uncomfortable. La Ponte added that there had been other clues: strange clients wanting to purchase the Dumas manuscript at any price, mysterious phone calls during the night . . .

Corso sat up, interested.

"You're getting calls in the middle of the night?"

"Yes, but they don't say anything. They just stay quiet for a bit and then hang up."

While La Ponte was recounting his misfortunes, Corso felt the canvas bag he had retrieved moments earlier. Makarova had kept it there all day, under the counter, between boxes of bottles and barrels of beer.

"I don't know what to do," ended La Ponte tragically.

"Why don't you sell the manuscript and have done with it? Things are getting out of hand."

La Ponte shook his head and ordered another gin. A double.

"I promised Enrique Taillefer that the manuscript would go on public sale."

"Taillefer's dead. And anyway you've never kept a promise in your life."

La Ponte agreed gloomily, as if he didn't want to be reminded. But then he suddenly brightened. A slightly dazed expression showed through his beard. If one really tried one could take it for a smile.

"By the way, guess who called."

"Milady."

"Almost. Liana Taillefer."

Corso looked at his friend wearily. Then he picked up his glass of gin and emptied it in one long gulp.

"You know what, Flavio?" he said at last, wiping his mouth with the back of his hand. "Sometimes it seems that I've read this book before."

La Ponte was frowning again.

"She wants 'The Anjou Wine' back," he explained. "Just as it is, without authentication or anything . . ." He took a drink and then smiled uncertainly at Corso. "Strange, isn't it, this sudden interest?"

"What did you tell her?"

La Ponte raised his eyebrows.

"That it wasn't in my control. You have the manuscript and I've signed a contract with you."

"That's a lie. We haven't signed anything."

"Of course it's a lie. But this way I lumber you with everything if things get nasty. And it doesn't mean I can't consider any offers. I'm going to have dinner with the lovely widow one evening. To discuss business. I'm the daring harpooneer."

"You're not a harpooneer. You're a dirty, lying bastard."

"Yes. England made me, as that pious old goody-goody Graham Greene would have said. At school my nickname was *Wasn't-me* . . . Haven't I ever told you how I passed maths?" He raised his eyebrows again, tenderly nostalgic at the memory. "I'm a born liar."

"Well, be careful with Liana Taillefer."

"Why?" La Ponte was admiring himself in the bar mirror. He smiled lewdly. "I've had the hots for that woman ever since I started taking serials over to her husband. She's got a lot of class."

"Yes," admitted Corso, "a lot of middle class."

"What have you got against her?"

"There's something funny going on."

"That's fine by me, if it involves a beautiful blonde."

Corso was tapping his finger against the knot of his tie.

"Listen, idiot. In mystery stories the friend always dies. Don't you see? This is a mystery story and you're my friend." He winked at him for emphasis. "So you're going to get it."

Obstinately clinging to his dreams of the widow, La Ponte wouldn't be intimidated.

"Oh come on. I've never hit the jackpot before. Anyway I told you where I intend to take the bullet: in the shoulder."

"I'm serious. Taillefer's dead."

"He committed suicide."

"Who knows? More people could die."

"Well, you go and die, you bastard, ruining my fun."

The rest of the evening consisted of variations on the same theme. They left after five or six more drinks and agreed to speak on the phone once Corso got to Portugal. La Ponte, rather unsteady on his feet, left without paying, but he did give Corso Rochefort's cigar butt. Now you've got a pair, he told him.

VI

Of Apocrypha and Interpolations

Chance? Permit me to laugh, by God. That is an explanation that would only satisfy an imbecile.

M. Zevaco: *Los Pardellanes*

CENIZA BROS.
BOOKBINDING
AND RESTORATION

The wooden sign hung in a window thick with dust. It was cracked and faded with age and damp. The Ceniza brothers' workshop was on the mezzanine floor of an old four-storey building, shored up at the back, in a shady street in the old quarter of Madrid.

Lucas Corso rang the bell twice, but nobody answered. He looked at his watch, and leant against the wall, preparing himself for a wait. He knew the habits of Pedro and Pablo Ceniza well. At that hour they would be a few streets away, at the marble counter of the bar La Taurina, draining half a litre of wine for their breakfast and discussing books and bullfighting. Both grumpy bachelors and fond of their drink, they were inseparable.

They arrived ten minutes later, side by side, their grey overalls floating like shrouds on their skinny frames. Stooping from a lifetime spent hunched over their press and stamping tools, stitching pages together and gilding leather. They were both under fifty, but one could easily have believed they were ten years older. Their cheeks were sunken, their hands and eyes were worn out by their painstaking craft, and their skin was faded, as if the parchment they worked with had transmitted its pale, cold quality to them. The resemblance between the two brothers was extraordinary. They had the same large nose, identical ears stuck to their skulls and sparse hair combed straight back. The only noticeable differences between them were that Pablo, the younger of the two, was taller and quieter. His brother Pedro was frequently racked by the

97

hoarse rattling cough of a heavy smoker and his hands shook as he lit one cigarette after another.

"It's been a long time, Mr Corso. How nice to see you."

They led him up stairs that were worn with use, to a door that creaked as it opened, and switched on the light to reveal their motley workshop. An ancient printing press presided. Next to this a zinc-topped table was covered with tools, half-stitched or already backed gatherings, guillotines, dyed skins, bottles of glue, tooled designs and other equipment. There were books everywhere: large piles of them, bound in morocco, shagreen or vellum, packets of them ready for dispatch or only half-prepared, books without boards or with limp covers. Ancient tomes damaged by worms or damp sat waiting to be restored on benches and shelves. It smelt of paper, glue and new leather. Corso breathed it in with pleasure. Then he took the book out of his bag and laid it on the table.

"I'd like your opinion on this."

This wasn't the first time. Slowly, even cautiously, Pedro and Pablo Ceniza moved closer. As usual, the older of the two brothers spoke first.

"*The Nine Doors . . .*" He touched the book without moving it. His bony, nicotine-stained fingers seemed to be stroking living skin. "Beautiful. A very valuable book."

His eyes were grey, like a mouse. Grey overalls, grey hair, grey eyes, just like his surname.* He looked at it greedily.

"Have you ever seen it before?"

"Yes. Less than a year ago when Claymore asked us to clean twenty books from the library of Mr Gualterio Terral."

"What condition was it in when you got it?"

"Excellent. Mr Terral knew how to look after his books. Almost all of them came to us in good condition, except for a Teixeira which we had to do quite a bit of work on. The rest, including this one, only needed some cleaning."

"It's a forgery," said Corso bluntly. "Or so I'm told."

The two brothers looked at each other.

"Forgeries . . ." muttered the older of the two grumpily. "People speak too lightly of forged books."

"Much too lightly," echoed his brother.

"Even you, Mr Corso. And that comes as a surprise. It isn't

*In Spanish *ceniza* means 'ash'.

98

worth forging a book, it's too much effort to be profitable: I mean a high-quality forgery, not a facsimile for fooling gullible ignoramuses."

Corso made a gesture as if pleading for clemency.

"I didn't say that the *entire* book was a forgery, only part of it. Pages from complete copies can be interpolated into books that have one or several pages missing."

"Of course, that's a basic trick of the trade. But adding a photocopy or facsimile doesn't give the same results as completing a book with missing pages following . . ." He half-turned towards his brother, but still looked at Corso. "Tell him, Pablo."

"Following all the rules of our art," added the younger Ceniza.

Corso gave them a conspiratorial look. A rabbit sharing half a carrot.

"That could be the case with this book."

"Who says so?"

"The owner. Who isn't a gullible ignoramus, by the way."

Pedro Ceniza shrugged his narrow shoulders and lit a cigarette with the previous one. As he took his first drag he was shaken by a dry cough. But he carried on smoking, unperturbed.

"Have you had access to an authentic copy, to compare them?"

"No, but I soon will. That's why I want your opinion first."

"It's a valuable book, and ours is not an exact science." He turned again towards his brother. "Isn't that so, Pablo?"

"It's an art," insisted his brother.

"Yes. We wouldn't want to disappoint you, Mr Corso."

"I'm sure you won't. You know what you're talking about. After all, you were able to forge a *Speculum Vitæ* from the only known copy, and have it listed as an original in one of the best catalogues in Europe."

They both smiled sourly at exactly the same time. Si and Am, thought Corso, a cunning pair of cats who've just been stroked.

"It was never proved to be our work," said Pedro Ceniza at last. He was rubbing his hands, looking at the book out of the corner of his eye.

"No, never," repeated his brother sadly. They seemed sorry not to have gone to prison in return for public recognition.

"True," admitted Corso. "Nor was there any proof in the case of the Chaucer, allegedly bound by Marius Michel, listed in the catalogue for the Manoukian collection. Or for that copy of Baron Bielke's *Polyglot Bible* with three missing pages you replaced so perfectly that even today experts don't dispute its authenticity . . ."

Pedro Ceniza lifted his yellowed hand, with its long nails.

"I'd like to deal with a couple of points in greater detail, Mr Corso. It's one thing to forge books for profit, and quite another to do it out of love for one's art, creating something for the satisfaction provided by that very act of creation, or, as in most cases, of re-creation . . ." The bookbinder blinked a few times and then smiled mischievously. His small, mouse-like eyes shone as he looked at *The Nine Doors* again. "Although I don't recall having had a hand in the works you've just described as admirable, and I'm sure my brother doesn't either."

"I called them perfect."

"Did you? Well, never mind." He put his cigarette in his mouth and sucked in his cheeks as he took a long drag. "But whoever the person, or persons, responsible, you can be sure that he, or they, obtained a great deal of enjoyment out of it, a degree of personal satisfaction that money can't buy . . ."

"*Sine pecunia*," added his brother.

Pedro Ceniza blew cigarette smoke through his nose and half-open mouth and recalled:

"Let's take the *Speculum*, for instance, which the Sorbonne bought in the belief that it was authentic. The paper, typography, printing and binding alone must have cost those you call forgers five times more than any profit they might have made. People just don't understand . . . What would be more satisfying to a painter with as much talent as Velázquez and the skill to imitate his works: making money or seeing one of his own paintings hanging in the Prado, between *Las Meninas* and *Vulcan's Forge*?"

Corso agreed. For eight years, the Ceniza brothers' *Speculum* had been one of the most valuable books owned by the University of Paris. It was discovered to be a forgery not by experts, but due to a chance indiscretion by a go-between.

"Do the police still bother you?"

"Rarely. You must remember that the business of the Sorbonne erupted in France between the buyer and the intermediaries. True, our name was linked to the affair but nothing was ever proved." Pedro Ceniza smiled his crooked smile again, and sounded sorry that there had been no proof. "We have a good relationship with the police. They even come to see us sometimes when they need to identify a stolen book." He waved his cigarette in his brother's direction. "There's no one as good as Pablo when it comes to erasing traces of library stamps, or removing bookplates and marks of origin. But sometimes they want him to work his way backwards through the process. You know how it is: live and let live."

"What do you think of *The Nine Doors*?"

The older Ceniza looked at his brother, then at the book. He shook his head.

"Nothing drew our attention while we were working on it. The paper and ink are as they should be. Even at first glance, you notice that sort of thing."

"We notice them," specified his brother.

"What's your opinion now?"

Pedro Ceniza took a last puff of his cigarette, now reduced to a tiny stub between his fingers. Then he dropped it on the floor, between his feet, where it burnt itself out. The linoleum was covered in similar burns.

"Seventeenth-century Venetian binding, in good condition . . ." The brothers leant over the book, but only the elder of the two touched the pages with his pale, cold hands. They looked like a pair of taxidermists working out the best way to stuff a corpse with straw. "The leather is black morocco, with gold rosettes imitating flowers . . ."

"Somewhat sober for Venice," added Pablo Ceniza.

His elder brother agreed with another coughing fit.

"The artist kept it restrained. No doubt the subject matter . . ." He looked at Corso. "Have you tested the core of the binding? Sixteenth- or seventeenth-century books bound in leather or hide sometimes contain surprises. The board inside was made of separate sheets, assembled with paste and pressed. Sometimes they used proofs of the same book, or earlier editions . . . Some discoveries are now more valuable than the copies they bind." He pointed to some papers on the table. "There's an example there. Tell him about it, Pablo."

"Papal bulls of the Holy Crusade, dated 1483." The brother was smiling equivocally. He might have been talking about pornographic material rather than a pile of old papers. "Bound using the boards of some sixteenth-century memorials of no value."

Pedro Ceniza was still examining *The Nine Doors*.

"The binding seems to be in order," he said. "It all fits. Odd book, isn't it? The five raised bands on the spine, no title, and this strange pentacle on the cover. Torchia, Venice 1666. He might have bound it himself. A beautiful piece of work."

"What about the paper?"

"That's just like you, Mr Corso. A good question." The bookbinder licked his lips as if he was trying to warm them. Then he listened carefully to the sound of the pages as he flicked them, just as Corso had done at Varo Borja's. "Excellent paper. Nothing like the cellulose they use nowadays. Do you know the average lifespan of a book printed today? Tell him, Pablo."

"Sixty years," said the brother bitterly as if it were Corso's fault. "Sixty miserable years."

His elder brother was searching amongst the tools on the table. At last he found a special high magnification lens and held it up to the book.

"In a century's time," he murmured as he lifted a page and examined it against the light, closing one eye, "almost all the contents of today's libraries will have disappeared. But these books, printed two hundred or even five hundred years ago will remain intact . . . We have the books, and the world, that we deserve . . . Isn't that so, Pablo?"

"Lousy books printed on lousy paper."

Pedro Ceniza nodded in agreement. He was still examining the book through the lens.

"That's right. Cellulose paper turns yellow and brittle as a wafer, and cracks irreparably. It just ages and dies."

"Not the case here," said Corso, pointing at the book.

The bookbinder was still examining the pages against the light.

"Rag content paper, which is as it should be. Good paper handmade from rags, it'll withstand the passage of time, and human stupidity . . . No, I tell a lie. It's linen. Authentic linen paper." He put down the lens and looked at his brother. "How strange, it's not Venetian paper. It's thick, spongy, fibrous . . . Could it be Spanish?"

"From Valencia," said his brother. "Jativa linen."

"That's right. One of the best in Europe at the time. The printer could have got hold of an imported batch . . . He really set out to do things properly."

"He was very conscientious," said Corso, "and it cost him his life."

"Risks of the trade." Pedro Ceniza accepted the crushed cigarette Corso offered him. He lit it immediately, coughing indifferently. "As you know yourself, it's difficult to fool anyone about the paper. The ream used would have had to be blank, from the same time, and even then there would be differences: the sheets go brown, the inks fade and change over time . . . Of course, added pages can be stained, or washed in tea to darken them . . . Any restoration work, or addition of missing pages, should leave the book all of a piece. It's these small details that count. Don't they, Pablo? Always the damned details."

"What's your diagnosis?"

"So far, considering only the impossible, the probable, and the convincing, we have established that the binding could be seventeenth-century . . . That doesn't mean that the pages match this binding and not another. But let's assume they do. As for the paper, it seems similar to other batches whose origin has been authenticated. And it does seem to be of the time."

"Right. The binding and paper are authentic. Let's look at the text and illustrations."

"Now that's more complicated. We can approach the typography from two different angles. One: we can assume that the book is authentic. The owner, however, denies this, and according to you he has powerful motives for knowing. So it's possible but not very probable. Let's consider the other theory, that it's a forgery, and work out the possibilities. On the one hand the entire text might be a forgery, a fabrication, printed on paper dating from the time and bound using earlier boards. This might be the case, but it's unlikely. Or, to be more precise, not very convincing. The cost of the book would be disproportionately high . . . There's a second reasonable alternative: the forgery might have been made very soon after the first edition of the book. I mean that it was reprinted with alterations, disguised to resemble the first edition, some ten or twenty years after this date of 1666 which appears in the frontispiece. But to what end?"

"It was a banned book," pointed out Pablo Ceniza.

"It's possible," agreed Corso. "Somebody who had access to the equipment – the plates and types – used by Aristide Torchia might have been able to print it again . . ."

The elder of the two brothers had picked up a pencil and was scribbling on the back of a printed sheet.

"That would be one explanation. But the other alternatives, or theories, seem more plausible . . . Imagine, for instance, that most of the book's pages are authentic, but that some were missing, either torn out or lost . . . And that somebody has replaced those missing pages using paper dating from the time, good printing techniques and a lot of patience. In that case there are two further possibilities: one is that the added pages are reproductions of those from another complete copy . . . Another is that, in the absence of the original to reproduce or

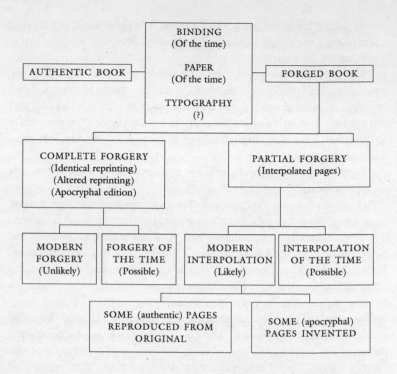

copy, the contents of the pages were invented." The bookbinder then showed Corso what he had been writing. "It would be a true case of forgery, as illustrated by this diagram."

While Corso and the younger of the two brothers were looking at the paper, Pedro Ceniza again leafed through *The Nine Doors*.

"I am inclined to think," he added after a moment, once he had their attention again, "that if some pages were interpolated it was either done around the time of the original edition, or now, in our time. We can discount the time between the two because such a perfect reproduction of an ancient work has only very recently been possible."

Corso handed back the diagram.

"Imagine you were faced with a book that had pages missing. And you wanted to complete it using modern techniques. How would you go about it?"

The Ceniza brothers sighed deeply in unison, professionally relishing the prospect. They were now both staring intently at *The Nine Doors*.

"Let us suppose," the elder one said, "that this 168-page book has page 100 missing . . . Page 100 and page 99, since it's one sheet, with two sides or pages. And we want to complete it. The trick is to locate a twin."

"A twin?"

"As we say in the trade," said Pablo Ceniza. "Another complete copy."

"Or at least, one in which the two pages we need to copy are intact. If possible, it would also be advisable to compare the twin with our incomplete copy, to see if the pressures are different or if the types are more worn in one or the other . . . As you know yourself, at that time types were movable and could easily wear out or alter. So with manual printing, the first and last copy of a same print run could vary greatly. They might have crooked or broken letters, differing ink shades, things like that. Examining such variations means that on the interpolated page imperfections can later be added or removed so that it matches the rest of the book. We would then proceed with photomechanical reproduction and produce a plastic photolith. And from that we would obtain a polymer or a zinc."

"A plate in relief," said Corso, "made of resin or metal."

"Exactly. However perfect the reproduction technique, we would never get the relief, the mark on paper typical of ancient printing techniques using inked wood or metal. So the entire page has to be reproduced using a mouldable material – resin or metal. These create very similar effects to printing with movable lead types as would have been the case in 1666. Then we put the plate on the press and print the page manually as it would have been done four centuries ago. Using paper dating from the same time, of course, treated both before and after with artificial ageing methods . . . The composition of the ink has to be thoroughly researched. It has to be treated with chemical agents so that it matches the other pages. And there you are, the crime is carried out."

"But suppose the original sheet doesn't exist. That there's no model from which to copy the two missing pages."

The Ceniza brothers both smiled confidently.

"That," said the older of the two, "makes it even more interesting."

"Research and imagination," added his brother.

"And daring, of course, Mr Corso. Suppose Pablo and I have that copy of *The Nine Doors* with pages missing. The remaining 166 pages would then provide us with a catalogue of all the letters and symbols used by the printer. So we would take samples until we had obtained an entire alphabet. We'd reproduce the alphabet on photographic paper, which is easier to handle, and then multiply each letter by the number of times needed to compose the entire page . . . The ideal, the artistic flourish, would be to reproduce the types in molten lead as ancient printers used to do . . . Unfortunately this is too complicated and expensive. So we'd make do with modern techniques. We'd divide up the letters with a blade into loose types, and Pablo, who has a steadier hand for the job, would compose the two pages on a template, line by line, just as a compositor would have done in the seventeenth century. From that we would produce another proof on paper and eliminate any joins or imperfections in the letters, or add faults similar to those found in other letters, lines or pages of the original text . . . After that all we would have to do is make a negative. From that you get a reproduction in relief and there you have your printing plate."

"What if the missing pages are illustrations?"

"It makes no difference. If we had access to the original engraving, the technique for making a copy would be even easier. In this case, the fact that the engravings are all woodcuts, which have lighter lines than copperplate or dry point, means that we can produce an almost perfect piece of work."

"Suppose the original engraving no longer exists."

"That's not a problem either. If we know of it from references, we can imitate it. If not, we can invent it. After studying the technique used for the other known engravings, of course. Any good draughtsman could do it."

"What about printing it?"

"As you know, a woodcut is an engraving in relief. A cube of wood is cut with the grain and covered with a white background. The picture is drawn on top. Then it has to be carved, and the ink applied on the crests, or ridges, so that it can be transferred onto paper. When reproducing woodcuts there are two options. One is to make a copy of the drawing, in this case preferably in resin. But the alternative, if you have a good engraver, is to make another real woodcut, with the same techniques used to produce the original engravings, and to print directly from that. In my case, as I have a good engraver in my brother, I would hand-print it from a woodcut. Wherever possible, art should imitate art."

"You get better results," added Pablo.

Corso looked at him conspiratorially.

"As was the case of the Sorbonne's *Speculum*."

"Maybe. The creator, or creators, of that piece of work may have thought like us . . . Don't you think, Pablo?"

"They must have been romantics," agreed his brother, not quite managing a smile.

"Yes, they must." Corso pointed at the book. "So, what's your verdict?"

"I would say that it's original," answered Pedro Ceniza without hesitation. "Even we wouldn't be able to produce such perfect results. Look, the quality of the paper, stains on the pages, identical tones and variations in the ink, and typography . . . It's possible that some forged pages may have been inserted, but I think it improbable. If it is a forgery, the only explanation is that it must have been done around the same time. How many known copies are there? Three? I assume you have considered the possibility that all three are forgeries."

"Yes, I have. What about the woodcuts?"

"They're definitely very strange. With all those symbols . . . But they do date from the time. The degree of pressure on the plates is identical. The ink, the shades of the paper . . . Maybe the key lies not in how and when they were printed, but in their contents. We're sorry we haven't got any further."

"You're wrong." Corso prepared to close the book. "In fact we've come a long way."

Pedro Ceniza stopped him.

"There's one more thing . . . I'm sure you've noticed them yourself. The printer's marks."

Corso looked at him, confused.

"I don't know what you mean."

"The microscopic signatures at the foot of each illustration. Show him, Pablo."

The younger of the two brothers made as if to wipe his hands on his overall, as if to dry off imaginary sweat. Then, moving closer to *The Nine Doors,* he showed Corso some of the pages through a magnifying glass.

"Each engraving," he explained, "has the usual abbreviations: *Inv.* for *invenit,* with the signature of the original artist, and *Sculp.* for *sculpsit,* the engraver . . . Look. In seven of the nine woodcuts the abbreviation A.TORCH appears as both the *sculp.* and the *inv.* Obviously the printer himself drew and engraved seven of the illustrations. But in the other two he is only named as the *sculp.* That means that he only engraved them. And that someone else created the original drawings, someone else was the *inv.* Somebody with the initials L.F."

Pedro Ceniza, who had briefly nodded in approval during his brother's explanation, lit his umpteenth cigarette.

"Not bad, eh?" He started to cough amidst the smoke. He watched for Corso's reaction, a malicious little glint in his astute mouse-like eyes. "He might have been the one burnt at the stake, but that printer wasn't the only one involved."

"No," agreed his brother, "somebody helped him to light the fire at his feet."

That same afternoon, Corso had a visit from Liana Taillefer. The widow arrived unannounced, at that hour which is neither one thing nor the other when Corso, dressed in a faded cotton shirt and old corduroys, was standing by the west-facing window, watching the sunset turn the city rooftops red and ochre. Maybe it wasn't a good moment, and much of what happened later might have been avoided had she turned up at a different time of day. But we'll never know. What we do know is that Corso was looking out of the window, his eyes growing mistier as he emptied his glass of gin. The doorbell rang and Liana Taillefer – blonde, impressively tall, in an English raincoat, tailored suit and black stockings – appeared on the doorstep. Her hair was gathered into a bun beneath a tobacco-coloured, wide-brimmed hat elegantly tilted to one side that suited her very well. She was a beautiful woman. She knew it and she expected everyone to notice.

"To what do I owe the honour?" asked Corso. It was a stupid question, but at that hour and having drunk all that Bols he couldn't be expected to shine in conversation. Liana Taillefer had already stepped into the room. She was standing at the desk where the folder with the Dumas manuscript was lying, next to his computer and box of diskettes.

"Are you still working on this?"

"Of course."

She lifted her gaze from 'The Anjou Wine' and glanced round calmly at the books covering the walls and piled up all over the room. Corso knew she was looking for photographs, mementoes, clues to the personality of the occupant. Arrogantly, she arched an eyebrow, irritated at not finding any. At last she saw the sabre of the Old Guard.

"Do you collect swords?"

This was a logical inference. Of an inductive nature. At least, Corso thought with relief, Liana Taillefer's ability to smooth over embarrassing situations didn't match her appearance. Unless she was teasing him. He smiled warily, feeling cornered.

"I collect that one. It's called a sabre."

She nodded, expressionless. Impossible to tell if she was simple, or a good actress.

"A family heirloom?"

"An acquisition," lied Corso. "I thought it would look nice on the wall. Books on their own can get a bit boring."

"How come you don't have any pictures or photos?"

"There's no one I particularly want to remember." He thought of the photo in the silver frame, the late Taillefer in an apron carving the sucking-pig. "In your case it's different, of course."

She looked at him intently, possibly trying to weigh up how rude his comment had been. There was a glint of steel in her blue eyes, so icy they made one feel chilled. She paced around the room, stopping to look at some of his books, at the view from the window, and then back at the desk. She slid a finger with its blood-red nail over the folder with the Dumas manuscript. Maybe she was expecting Corso to say something but he remained silent. He just waited patiently. If she was after something – and it was pretty obvious she was – he'd let her do all the work. He wasn't going to make it easier for her.

"May I sit down?"

The slightly husky voice. The echo of a heavy night, thought Corso again. He stood in the middle of the room, his hands in his pockets, waiting. Liana Taillefer took off her hat and raincoat. She looked around with one of her interminably slow gestures and chose an old sofa. She went over to it and sat down slowly, her skirt riding up very high. She crossed her legs with an effect that anyone, even Corso with half a gin less in him, would have found devastating.

"I've come on business."

That was obvious. She must be after something, to put on such a display. Corso had as much self-esteem as the next person, but he was no fool.

"Fine," he said. "Have you had dinner with Flavio La Ponte yet?"

No reaction. For a few seconds she carried on looking at him unperturbed, with the same air of contemptuous confidence.

"Not yet," she answered at last, without anger. "I wanted to see you first."

"Well, here I am."

Liana Taillefer leant back slightly farther into the sofa. One hand was resting on a split in the shabby leather upholstery where the horsehair stuffing was poking through.

"You work for money," she said.

"I do."

"You sell yourself to the highest bidder."

"Sometimes." Corso showed one of his eye teeth. He was on his own territory so he could allow himself his friendly rabbit expression. "Generally what I do is hire myself out. Like Humphrey Bogart in the movies. Or like a whore."

For a widow who'd spent her schooldays doing needlework, Liana Taillefer didn't seem shocked by his language.

"I want to offer you a job."

"How nice. Everybody's offering me jobs these days."

"I'll pay you very well."

"Wonderful. They all want to pay me lots of money too."

She pulled at some of the horsehair poking out of the sofa arm and twisted it absent-mindedly round her index finger.

"What are you charging your friend La Ponte?"

"Flavio? Nothing. You couldn't get a penny out of him."

"Why are you working for him, then?"

"As you put it yourself, he's my friend."

She repeated the word thoughtfully.

"It sounds strange to hear you say that word," she then said. She was smiling almost imperceptibly, with curious disdain. "Do you have girlfriends as well?"

Corso looked at her legs unhurriedly, from her ankles to her thighs. Shamelessly.

"I have memories of some. The memory of you might be useful tonight."

She took his crudeness stoically. Or maybe, Corso wondered, she hadn't caught his subtle reference.

"Name a price," she said coldly. "I want my husband's manuscript."

Things were looking good. Corso went and sat in an armchair opposite Liana Taillefer. From there he could get a better view of her legs. She had taken off her shoes and was resting her bare feet on the rug.

"You didn't seem very interested last time."

"I've thought it over. That manuscript has . . ."

"Sentimental value?" mocked Corso.

"Something like that." Her voice now sounded defiant. "But not in the sense you'd suppose."

"What would you be prepared to do to get it?"

"I've told you. Pay you."

Corso smiled leeringly.

"You offend me. I'm a professional."

"You're a professional mercenary, Mr Corso. And mercenaries change sides. I've read books too, you know."

"I've got as much money as I need."

"I'm not talking of money now."

She was lying right back on the sofa, and with one of her bare feet she was stroking the instep of the other. Corso pictured her toenails painted red under the black stockings. As she moved, her skirt rode up giving a glimpse of white flesh above her black garters where all mysteries are reduced to a single one, as old as Time itself. Corso looked up with difficulty. Her ice-blue eyes were still fixed intently on him.

He took off his glasses before standing up and moving towards the sofa. Liana Taillefer followed him impassively with her eyes, even when he was right in front of her, so close that their knees were touching. Then she lifted her hand and placed her fingers with their red lacquered nails precisely on the zipper of Corso's corduroy trousers. She was smiling again almost imperceptibly, contemptuous and self-assured, when at last Corso leant over her and lifted her skirt up to her waist.

It was a mutual assault, rather than an exchange. A settling of scores there on the sofa. A crude, hard struggle between adults, with the appropriate moans at the right moment, a few muttered curses and the woman's nails digging mercilessly into Corso's back. And it happened in barely any space, without them taking their clothes off. Her skirt was up over her strong, wide hips which he gripped as the studs on her suspender belt pressed into his groin. He never even saw her breasts, although he did manage to touch them a couple of times, dense, warm, abundant flesh beneath the bra, silk shirt and jacket. In the heat of the fray, Liana Taillefer hadn't had time to remove them. And now there they were, the two of them, still tangled up in each other, amongst a mess of crumpled clothes, and breathless, like two exhausted wrestlers. Corso was wondering how to extricate himself from this mess.

"Who's Rochefort?" he asked, prepared to precipitate the crisis.

Liana Taillefer looked at him from a few inches away. The setting sun threw reddish glints onto her face. The hairpins had fallen out of her bun, and her blonde hair was spread untidily over the leather sofa. She looked relaxed for the first time.

"It doesn't matter," she answered, "now that I'm getting the manuscript back."

Corso kissed her disordered cleavage, bidding farewell to its contents. He had a feeling it would be some time before he kissed it again.

"What manuscript?" he said, for the sake of it, and he saw her expression harden instantly. Her body went rigid under his.

"'The Anjou Wine'." For the first time there was a hint of anxiety in her voice. "You're going to return it to me, aren't you, Mr Corso?"

Corso didn't like the sound of the return to a formal mode of address. He vaguely remembered having been on first name terms during the skirmish.

"I never said that."

"I thought . . ."

"You thought wrong."

Her steely blue eyes flashed with anger. She sat up, furious, pushing him away abruptly with her hips.

"Bastard!"

Corso, who was about to laugh the whole thing off with a couple of cynical jokes, felt himself pushed back violently. He fell to his knees. As he struggled to his feet, fastening his belt, he saw Liana Taillefer stand up, pale and terrifying, unconcerned by her dishevelled clothes, her magnificent thighs still exposed. She slapped him so hard his left ear vibrated like a drum.

"Pig!"

Corso staggered from the blow. Stunned, he looked round like a boxer searching for a fixed point to stop him falling into the ropes. Liana Taillefer crossed his field of vision but he didn't pay her too much attention because of the agonizing pain in his ear. He was staring stupidly at the sabre from Waterloo when he heard the sound of breaking glass. He saw her again against the reddish light from the window. She had pulled her skirt down. In one hand she was holding the manuscript, and in the other the neck of a broken bottle. Its edge was pointed at Corso's throat.

. . . Keeping her at bay with the tip of his sword

Instinctively he raised his arm and stepped back. The danger had brought him back to his senses and made the adrenaline pump. He pushed aside the hand with the bottle and punched her in the neck. It left her winded, stopping her dead. The following scene was somewhat calmer. Corso picked the manuscript and broken bottle off the floor. Liana Taillefer was once again sitting on the sofa, her tousled hair hanging over her face. She was holding a hand to her aching neck, breathing with difficulty between sobs of fury.

"They'll kill you for this, Corso," she said at last. The sun had now set beyond the city, and the corners of the room were filling with shadow. Ashamed, he switched on the light and held out her coat and hat before ringing for a taxi. He avoided her eyes. Then, as he listened to her steps receding down the stairs, he stood for a moment by the window, watching the dark roofs against the brightness of the rising moon.

"They'll kill you for this, Corso."

He poured himself a large glass of gin. He couldn't rid himself of Liana Taillefer's expression once she realized she'd been tricked. Eyes as deadly as a dagger, a rictus of vengeful fury. And she meant it, she really had wanted to kill him. Once again the memories stirred, gradually filling his mind. This time, though, he needed no effort to relive them. The image was sharp and he knew exactly where it came from. The facsimile edition of *The Three Musketeers* was on his desk. He opened it and searched for the scene. Page 129. There, amongst overturned furniture, leaping from the bed, dagger in hand like a furious demon, Milady throws herself at d'Artagnan who retreats, terrified, in his shirt, keeping her at bay with the tip of his sword.

VII
Book Number One and Book Number Two

*The truth is that the Devil is very cunning. The truth is
that he is not always as ugly as they say.*

J. Cazotte: *The Devil in Love*

With only a few minutes to go before the departure of the express train
to Lisbon, he saw the girl. Corso was on the platform, about to mount
the steps to his carriage – *Companhia Internacional de Carruagems-
Camas*–when he bumped into her in a group of other passengers, heading
towards the first-class carriages. She was carrying a small rucksack and
wearing the same blue duffle coat, but he didn't recognize her at first.
He only felt there was something familiar about her green eyes, so light
they seemed transparent, and her very short hair. He continued to watch
her for a moment, until she disappeared two carriages further down.
The whistle blew. As he climbed aboard the train and the guard shut the
door behind him, Corso remembered the scene: the girl sitting at one end
of the table at the gathering of Boris Balkan and his circle in the café.

He walked along the corridor to his compartment. The station lights
streamed past increasingly quickly beyond the windows and the train
clattered rhythmically. Moving around the cramped compartment with
difficulty, he hung up his coat and jacket before sitting down on the
bunk, his canvas bag beside him. In it, together with *The Nine Doors*
and the folder with the Dumas manuscript, was a book by Las Cases,
the *Memorial of Saint-Helena*:

Friday 14 July 1816. The Emperor has been unwell all night . . .

He lit a cigarette. Occasionally, when lights from the window
strobed across his face, Corso would glance out before returning to the
tale of Napoleon's slow agony and the wiliness of his English gaoler,
Sir Hudson Lowe. He frowned as he read and adjusted his glasses on

the bridge of his nose. From time to time he stopped and stared for a moment at his own reflection in the window, and pulled a funny face. Even now, he still felt indignant at the victors condemning the fallen titan to a miserable end, clinging to a rock in the middle of the Atlantic. Strange, going over the historical events and his earlier feelings about them from his present clear-headed perspective. How far away he seemed, that other Lucas Corso who reverently admired the Waterloo veteran's sabre; the boy absorbing the family myths with aggressive enthusiasm, the precocious bonapartist and avid reader of books with engravings of the glorious campaigns, names that echoed like drumrolls for a charge: Wagram, Jena, Smolensk, Marengo . . . The boy wide-eyed with wonder who had long since ceased to exist; a hazy ghost sometimes appearing in his memory, between the pages of a book, in a smell or a sound, or through a dark window with the rain from Another Country beating against it, outside in the night.

The guard passed the door ringing his bell. Half an hour till the restaurant car closed. Corso shut the book. He put on his jacket, slung the canvas bag over his shoulder and left the compartment. At the end of the corridor, beyond the door, a cold draught blew through the passageway leading to the next sleeper. He felt the thundering beneath his feet as he crossed into the section of first-class carriages. He let a couple of passengers pass and then looked into the nearest compartment, which was only half-full. The girl was there, by the door, wearing a jumper and jeans, her bare feet resting on the seat opposite. As Corso passed she looked up from her book and their eyes met. He was about to nod briefly in her direction, but when she showed no sign of recognition, he stopped himself. She must have sensed something because she looked up at him with curiosity. But by then Corso had already moved on down the corridor.

He ate his dinner, rocked by the swaying of the train, and had time for a coffee and a gin before they closed for the evening. The moon, in shades of raw silk, was rising in the night. Telephone poles rushed past in the darkened plain, fleeting frames for a sequence of stills from a badly-adjusted movie projector.

He was on his way back to his compartment when he saw the girl in the corridor of the first-class carriage. She had opened the window and the cold night air was blowing against her face. As he came up to her, Corso turned sideways so he could get past. Then she turned towards him.

"I know you," she said.

Close up, her green eyes seemed even lighter, like liquid crystal, and luminous against her suntanned skin. It was only March, and with her hair parted like a boy's, her tan made her look unusual, sporty, pleasantly ambiguous. She was tall, slim and supple. And very young.

"Yes," said Corso, pausing a moment. "A few days ago, at the café."

She smiled. Another contrast, this time of white teeth against brown skin. Her mouth was big and well defined. A pretty girl, Flavio La Ponte would have said, stroking his curly beard.

"You were the one asking about d'Artagnan."

The cold air from the window was blowing her hair. She was still barefoot. Her white plimsolls were on the floor by her empty seat. He instinctively glanced at the book lying there: *The Adventures of Sherlock Holmes*. A cheap paperback, he noticed. The Mexican edition from the publishers Porrua.

"You'll catch cold," he said.

Still smiling, the girl shook her head, but she turned the handle and shut the window. Corso, about to go on his way, paused to find a cigarette. He did it as he always did, taking one directly from his pocket and putting it in his mouth, when he realized she was watching him.

"Do you smoke?" he asked hesitantly, stopping his hand halfway.

"Sometimes."

He put the cigarette in his mouth and took out another one. It was dark tobacco, without a filter, and as crushed as all the packets he usually carried with him. The girl took it. She looked to see the make. Then she leant over for Corso to light it, after his own, with the last match in the box.

"It's strong," she said, breathing out her first mouthful of smoke, but then made none of the fuss he expected. She held the cigarette in an unusual way, between forefinger and thumb, with the ember outward. "Are you in this carriage?"

"No, in the next one."

"You're lucky to have a sleeper." She tapped her jeans pocket, indicating a non-existent wallet. "I wish I could. Luckily the compartment's half-empty."

"Are you a student?"

"Sort of."

The train thundered into a tunnel. The girl turned then as if the darkness outside drew her attention. Tense and alert, she leant against her own reflection in the window. She seemed to be expecting something in the noisy rush of air. Then, when the train came out into the open and small lights again punctuated the night like brush strokes as the train passed, she smiled, distant.

"I like trains," she said.

"Me too."

The girl was still facing the window, touching it with the fingertips of one hand.

"Imagine," she said. She was smiling nostalgically, obviously remembering something. "Leaving Paris in the evening to wake up on the lagoon in Venice, en route to Istanbul . . ."

Corso made a face. How old could she be? Eighteen, maybe twenty at most.

"Playing poker," he suggested, "between Calais and Brindisi."

She looked at him more attentively.

"Not bad." She thought a moment. "How about a champagne breakfast between Vienna and Nice?"

"Interesting. Like spying on Basil Zaharoff."

"Or getting drunk with Nijinsky."

"Stealing Coco Chanel's pearls."

"Flirting with Paul Morand . . . Or Mr Barnabooth."

They both laughed, Corso under his breath. She laughed openly, leaning her forehead against the cold window. Her laugh was loud, frank and boyish, matching her hair and her luminous green eyes.

"Trains aren't like that any more," he said.

"I know."

The lights of a signal post passed like a flash of lightning. Then a dimly-lit, deserted platform, with a sign made illegible by their speed. The moon was rising and now and then clarified the confused outline of trees and roofs. It seemed to be flying alongside the train in a mad, purposeless race.

"What's your name?"

"Corso. And yours?"

"Irene Adler."

He looked at her intently and she held his gaze, calmly.

"That's not a proper name."

"Neither is Corso."

"You're wrong. I am Corso. The man who courses after things."

"You don't look like a man who runs anywhere. You seem like the calm type."

He bowed his head slightly, looking at the girl's bare feet on the floor of the corridor. He could tell she was staring at him, examining him. Unusually, it made him feel slightly uncomfortable. She was too young, he told himself. And too attractive. He automatically adjusted his crooked glasses and was about to go on his way.

"Have a good journey."

"Thanks."

He took a few steps, knowing that she was watching him.

"Maybe we'll see each other around," she said, behind him.

"Maybe."

Impossible. That was another Corso returning home, uneasy, the Grande Armée about to melt in the snow. The fire of Moscow was crackling in his wake. He couldn't leave like that, so he stopped and turned round. As he did so he was smiling like a hungry wolf.

"Irene Adler," he repeated, as if trying to remember. "*A Study in Scarlet?*"

"No," she answered calmly. "*A Scandal in Bohemia.*" Now she was smiling too and her gaze shone emerald green in the dimly-lit corridor. "*The Woman*, my dear Watson."

Corso gave himself a slap on the forehead as if he'd just remembered.

"Elementary," he said. And he was sure they'd meet again.

Corso spent just under fifty minutes in Lisbon. Just enough time to get from Santa Apolonia Station to Rossio Station. An hour and a half later he stepped onto the platform in Sintra, beneath a sky full of low clouds blurring the tops of the melancholy grey towers of the castle of Da Pena further up the hill. There was no taxi in sight so he walked to the small hotel opposite the National Palace with its two large chimneys. It was ten o'clock on a Wednesday morning and the esplanade was empty of tourists and coaches. He had no trouble getting a room. It looked out onto the uneven landscape, where the roofs and towers of old houses peered above the thick greenery, their ruined gardens suffocating in ivy.

After a shower and a coffee he asked for the Quinta da Soledade, and the hotel receptionist told him the way, up the road. There weren't any taxis on the esplanade either, although there were a couple of horse-drawn carriages. Corso negotiated a price and a few minutes later he was passing under the lacy baroque stonework of the Regaleira Tower.

The sound of the horse's hooves echoed against the dark walls, the drains and fountains running with water, the ivy-covered walls, railings and tree trunks, the stone steps carpeted with moss and the ancient tiles on the abandoned manor houses.

The Quinta da Soledade was a rectangular, eighteenth-century house, with four chimneys and an ochre plaster façade covered in trails and stains. Corso got out of the carriage and stood looking at the place for a moment before opening the iron gate. Two mossy, grey-green stone statues on granite columns stood at either end of the wall. One was a bust of a woman. The other seemed to be identical but the features were hidden by the ivy climbing up it, about to take over the sculpted face beneath and merge with it.

As he walked towards the house the dead leaves crackled beneath his steps. The path was lined with marble statues, almost all of them lying broken next to their empty pedestals. The garden was completely wild. Vegetation had taken over, climbing up benches and into alcoves. The wrought iron left rusty trails on the moss-covered stone. To his left, in a pond full of aquatic plants, a fountain with cracked tiles sheltered a chubby angel with empty eyes and mutilated hands. It slept with its head resting on a book, and a thread of water trickled from its mouth. Everything seemed suffused with infinite sadness and Corso couldn't help being affected. Quinta da Soledade, he repeated. House of Solitude. The name suited it.

He climbed the stone steps leading to the door and looked up. Beneath the grey sky no time was indicated on the Roman numerals of the ancient sundial on the wall. Above it ran the legend: '*Omnes vulnerant, postuma necat.*'

They all wound, he read. The last one kills.

"You've arrived just in time," said Fargas, "for the ceremony."

Corso held out his hand, slightly disconcerted. Victor Fargas was as tall and thin as an El Greco figure. He seemed to move around inside his loose, thick woollen jumper and baggy trousers like a tortoise in its shell. His moustache was trimmed with geometrical precision, and his old-fashioned, worn-out shoes gleamed. Corso noticed this much at first glance, before his attention was drawn to the huge, empty house, with its bare walls, and the paintings on the ceilings falling into mildewed shreds, eaten by damp.

Fargas examined his visitor closely.

"I assume you'll accept a brandy," he said at last after some thought. He set off down the corridor, limping slightly, without bothering to check whether Corso was following or not. They passed other rooms, which were empty or contained the remains of broken furniture thrown in a corner. Bare light fittings and dusty light bulbs hung from the ceilings.

The only rooms that seemed to be in use were two interconnecting reception rooms. There was a sliding door between them with coats of arms etched into the glass. It was open, revealing more bare walls, with their ancient wallpaper marked by long-gone pictures and furniture, rusty nails, and fittings for non-existent lamps. Above this gloomy scene hung a ceiling painted to resemble a vault of clouds with the sacrifice of Abraham in the centre. The cracked figure of the old patriarch was holding a dagger, about to strike a blond young man. His hand was held back by an angel with huge wings. Beneath the trompe l'œil sky, dusty French windows, some of the panes replaced with cardboard, led to the terrace and, beyond that, to the garden.

"Home sweet home," said Fargas.

His irony was unconvincing. He seemed to have made the remark too often and was no longer sure of its effect. He spoke Spanish with a heavy, distinguished Portuguese accent. And he moved very slowly, perhaps because of his bad leg, like someone who has all the time in the world.

"Brandy," he said again, as if he didn't quite remember how they'd reached that point.

Corso nodded vaguely but Fargas didn't notice. At one end of the vast room was an enormous fireplace with logs piled up in it. There was a pair of unmatched armchairs, a table and a sideboard, an oil lamp, two big candlesticks, a violin in its case, and little else. But on the floor, lined up perfectly neatly on old, faded, threadbare rugs, as far away as possible from the windows and the leaden light coming through them, there were a great many books; five hundred or more, Corso calculated, maybe even a thousand. Many codices and incunables amongst them. Wonderful old books bound in leather or parchment. Ancient tomes with studs in the covers, folios, Elzevirs, their bindings decorated with gophering, bosses, rosettes, locks, their spines and fore-edges covered in gilding and calligraphy done by medieval monks in the scriptoria of their monasteries. He also noticed a dozen or so rusty mousetraps in various corners.

Fargas, who had been searching through the sideboard, turned round holding a glass and a bottle of Rémy Martin. He held it up to the light to look at the contents.

"Nectar of the gods," he said triumphantly. "Or the Devil." He smiled only with his mouth, twisting his moustache like an old-fashioned movie star. His eyes remained fixed and expressionless, with bags beneath them as if from chronic insomnia. Corso noticed his delicate hands – a sign of good breeding – as he took the glass of brandy. The glass vibrated gently as he raised it to his lips.

"Nice glass," he said to make conversation.

Fargas agreed, and made a gesture halfway between resignation and self-mockery, suggesting a different reading of it all: the glass, the tiny amount of brandy in the bottle, the bare house, his own presence. An elegant, pale, worn ghost.

"I only have one more left," he confided in a calm, neutral tone. "That's why I take care of them."

Corso nodded. He glanced at the bare walls and then again at the books.

"This must have been a beautiful house," he said.

Fargas shrugged.

"Yes, it was. But old families are like civilizations. One day they just wither and die." He looked around without seeing. All the missing objects seemed to be reflected in his eyes. "At first one resorts to the barbarians to guard the *limes* of the Danube but it makes them rich and they end up as one's creditors . . . Then one day they rebel and invade, looting everything." He suddenly peered at his visitor suspiciously. "I hope you understand what I mean."

Corso nodded. By now he was smiling his best conspiratorial smile.

"Perfectly," he said. "Hobnail boots crushing Meissen porcelain. Isn't that it? Skivvies in evening dress. Working-class parvenus who wipe their arses on illuminated manuscripts."

Fargas nodded approvingly. He was smiling. Then he limped over to the sideboard in search of the other glass.

"I think I'll have a brandy too," he said.

They drank a toast in silence, looking at each other like two members of a secret fraternity who have just agreed the signs of recognition. Then, moving closer to the books, Fargas gestured towards them with the hand holding the glass, as if Corso had just passed his initiation test and he were inviting him to go through an invisible barrier.

"There they are. Eight hundred and thirty-four volumes. Less than half of them are worth anything." He drank some more and then ran his finger over his damp moustache, looking around. "It's a shame that you didn't know them in better days, lined up on their cedarwood shelves . . . I managed to collect five thousand of them. These are the survivors."

Corso put his canvas bag down on the floor and went over to the books. His fingers were itching instinctively. It was a magnificent sight. He adjusted his glasses and immediately saw a 1588 first edition Vasari in quarto, and a sixteenth-century *Tractatus* by Berengario de Carpi bound in parchment.

"I would never have dreamt that the Fargas collection listed in all the bibliographies was kept like this. Piled up on the floor against the wall, in an empty house . . ."

"That's life, my friend. But I have to say, in my defence, that they are all in immaculate condition. I clean them and make sure they're aired. I check that insects or rodents don't get at them, and that they're protected against light, heat and damp. In fact I do nothing else all day."

"What happened to the rest?"

Fargas looked towards the window, asking himself the same question. He was frowning.

"You can imagine," he answered, and he looked a very unhappy man when he turned back to look at Corso. "Apart from the house, a few pieces of furniture and my father's library, I inherited nothing but debts. Whenever I got any money I invested it in books. And when my income dwindled I got rid of what was left – pictures, furniture and china. I think you understand what it is to be a passionate collector of books. But I'm pathologically obsessed. I suffered atrociously just thinking about breaking up my collection."

"I've known people like that."

"Really?" Fargas looked at him interested. "I still doubt you can really imagine what it's like. I used to get up at night and wander about like a lost soul looking at my books. I'd talk to them, and stroke their spines, swearing I'd always take care of them . . . But none of it was any use. One day I took my decision: to sacrifice most of the books, and keep only the most cherished, valuable ones. Neither you nor anyone can ever understand how that felt, letting the vultures pick over my collection."

"I can imagine," said Corso, who wouldn't have minded in the least joining in the feast.

"Can you? I don't think so. Not in a million years. Separating the ones from the others took me two months. Sixty-one days of agony, and an attack of fever that almost killed me. At last, they took them away, and I thought I would go mad . . . I remember it as if it were yesterday, although it was twelve years ago."

"And now?"

Fargas held up the empty glass, as if it were symbolic.

"For some time now I've had to resort to selling my books again. Not that I need very much. Once a week someone comes in to clean, and I get my food brought from the village . . . Almost all the money goes in tax paid to the State for keeping on the house."

He pronounced the word *State* as if he'd said vermin. Corso looked sympathetic, glancing again at the bare walls.

"You could sell it."

"Yes," Fargas agreed indifferently. "There are things you can't understand."

Corso bent down to pick up a folio bound in parchment and leafed through it with interest. *De Symmetria* by Dürer, Paris 1557, reprinting of the first Nuremberg edition in Latin. In good condition, with wide margins. Flavio La Ponte would have gone wild over it. Anybody would have gone wild over it.

"How often do you have to sell books?"

"Two or three a year is enough. After going over and over it, I choose one book to sell. That's the ceremony I was referring to when I answered the door. I have a buyer, a compatriot of yours. He comes here a couple of times a year."

"Do I know him?" asked Corso.

"I've no idea," answered Fargas, without supplying a name. "In fact, I'm expecting him any day now. When you arrived I was getting ready to choose a victim . . ." He made a guillotine movement with one of his slender hands, still smiling wearily. "The one that has to die in order for the others to stay together."

Corso looked up at the ceiling, drawing the inevitable parallel. Abraham, a deep crack across his face, was making visible efforts to free the hand in which he held the dagger. The angel was holding on to it firmly with one hand and severely reprimanding the patriarch with the other. Beneath the blade, his head resting on a stone, Isaac waited, resigned to his fate. He was blond with pink cheeks, like an ancient Greek youth who never said no. Beyond him a sheep was tangled up in brambles, and Corso mentally voted for the sheep to be spared.

"I suppose you have no other choice," he said, looking at Fargas.

"If there was one I would have found it . . ." Fargas smiled bitterly. "But the lion demands his share, the sharks smell the bait. Unfortunately there aren't any people left like the Comte d'Artois, who was king of France. Do you know the story? The old Marquis de Paulmy, who owned sixty thousand books, went bankrupt. To escape his creditors he sold his collection to the Comte d'Artois. But the Count stipulated that the old man should keep them until his death. In that way Paulmy used the money to buy more books and extend the collection even though it was no longer his . . ."

He had put his hands in his pockets and was limping up and down alongside the books examining each one, like a shabby, gaunt Montgomery inspecting his troops at El Alamein.

"Sometimes I don't even touch them or open them." He stopped and leant over to straighten up a book in its row, on the old rug. "All I do is dust them and stare at them for hours. I know what lies inside each binding down to the last detail . . . Look at this one: *De revolutionis celestium*, Nicholas Copernicus. Second edition, Basle, 1566. A mere trifle, don't you think? Like the *Vulgata Clementina* to your right, between the six volumes of the *Polyglot* by your compatriot Cisneros, and the Nuremberg *Cronicarum*. And look at the strange folio over there: *Praxis criminis persequendi* by Simon de Colines, 1541. Or that monastic binding with four raised bands and bosses that you see there. Do you know what's inside? *The Golden Legend* by Jacopo de Voragine, Basle 1493, printed by Nicholas Kesler."

Corso leafed through the book. It was a magnificent edition, also with very wide margins. He put it back carefully. Then he stood up, wiping his glasses with his handkerchief. It would have made the coolest of men break out in a sweat.

"You must be crazy. If you sold all this you wouldn't have any money problems."

"I know." Fargas was leaning over to adjust the position of the book imperceptibly. "But if I sold them all I'd have no reason to go on living. So I wouldn't care if I had problems or not."

Corso pointed at a row of books in very bad condition. There were several incunables and manuscripts. Judging from the bindings, none dated from later than the seventeenth-century.

"You've got a great many ancient editions of chivalric novels . . ."

"Yes. Inherited from my father. His obsession was acquiring the ninety-five books of Don Quixote's collection, in particular those mentioned in the priest's expurgation . . . He also left me that strange *Quixote* that you see there, next to the first edition of *Os Lusiadas*. It's a 1789 Ibarra in four volumes. In addition to the corresponding illustrations, it is enriched with others printed in England in the first half of the eighteenth century, six wash drawings and a facsimile of Cervantes' birth certificate printed on vellum. To each his own obsessions. My father's, a diplomat who lived for many years in Spain, was Cervantes. In some people it's a mania. They won't accept restoration work, even if it's invisible, or won't buy a book numbered over fifty . . . My passion, as you must have noticed, was uncut books. I scoured auctions and bookshops, ruler in hand, and I went weak at the knees if I found one that was intact or hadn't been ploughed. Have you read Nodier's burlesque tale about the bookcollector? The same happened to me. I'd have happily shot any bookbinder who'd been too free with the guillotine. I was in ecstasy if I discovered an edition with margins two millimetres wider than those described in the canonical bibliographies."

"Me too."

"Congratulations, then. Welcome to the brotherhood."

"Not so fast. My interest is financial rather than aesthetic in nature."

"Never mind. I like you. I believe that when it comes to books, conventional morality doesn't exist." He was at the other end of the room but leaned slightly towards Corso, confidingly. "Do you know something? You Spaniards have a story about a bookseller in Barcelona who committed murder. Well, I'd be capable of killing for a book too."

"I wouldn't recommend it. That's how it all starts. It doesn't seem like a big deal but then you end up lying, voting in elections, things like that."

"Even selling one's own books."

"Even that."

Fargas was shaking his head sadly. Then he stood still a moment, frowning. When he came to, he studied Corso closely for some time.

"Which brings us," he said at last, "to the business I was engaged in when you rang at the door . . . Every time I have to address the problem I feel like a priest renouncing his beliefs. Are you surprised that I should think of this as a sacrilege?"

"Not at all. I suppose that's exactly what it is."

Fargas wrung his hands tormentedly. He looked round at the bare room and the books on the floor, and then back at Corso. His smile seemed false, painted on.

"Yes. Sacrilege can only be justified in faith . . . Only a believer can sense the terrible enormity of the action. We'd feel no horror at profaning a religion to which we were indifferent. It would be like an atheist blaspheming. Absurd."

Corso agreed.

"I know what you mean. It's Julian the Apostate crying, 'You have defeated me, Galileo.'"

"I'm not familiar with that quotation."

"It may be apocryphal. One of the Marist brothers used to quote it when I was at school. He was warning us not to go off at a tangent. Julian ends up shot through with arrows on the battlefield, spitting blood at a heaven without God."

Fargas assented, as if it were all terribly close to him. There was something disturbing in the strange rictus contracting his mouth, in the obsessive intensity of his eyes.

"That's how I feel now," he said. "I get up because I can't sleep and stand here, resolved to commit another desecration." He had moved so close to Corso as he spoke that Corso wanted to take a step back. "To sin against myself and against them . . . I touch one book, then change my mind, choose another one but end up putting it back in its place . . . I must sacrifice one so that the others can stay together, snap off a branch to continue enjoying the rest . . ." He held up his right hand. "I would rather cut off one of my fingers."

As he made the gesture his hand trembled. Corso nodded. He knew how to listen. It was part of the job. He could even understand. But he wasn't prepared to join in. It was none of his business. As Varo Borja would have said, he was a mercenary, and he was paying a visit. What Fargas needed was a confessor, or a psychiatrist.

"Nobody would pay a penny for an old bookcollector's finger," Corso said lightly.

The joke became lost in the immense void filling Fargas's eyes. He was looking through Corso. In his dilated pupils and absent eyes there were only books.

"So which should I choose?" Fargas went on. Corso had taken a cigarette from his coat pocket and was now offering it to the old man, but he didn't notice Corso's gesture. Absorbed, obsessed, he was listening only to himself. He was aware of nothing but the hallucinations of his tortured mind. "After much thought I have chosen two candidates." He took two books from the floor and put them on the table. "Tell me what you think."

Corso leaned over the books. He opened one of them at a page with an engraving, a woodcut of three men and a woman working in a mine. It was a second edition of *De re metallica* by Georgius Agricola, in Latin, printed by Froben and Episcopius in Basle only five years after its first edition in 1556. He gave a grunt of approval as he lit his cigarette.

"As you can see, making a choice isn't easy." Fargas was following Corso's movements intently. Anxiously he watched him turn the pages, just brushing them with his fingertips. "I have to sell one book each time. And not just any one. The sacrifice has to ensure that the rest are safe for another six months . . . It's my tribute to the Minotaur." He tapped his temple. "We all have one at the centre of the labyrinth . . . Our reason creates him, and he imposes his own horror."

"Why don't you sell several less valuable books at one time? Then you'd raise the money you need and still keep the rarer ones. Or your favourites."

"And reject some for the benefit of the others?" Fargas shuddered. "I simply couldn't do it. They all have the same immortal soul. To me they all have the same rights. I do have my favourites, of course. How could I not? But I never distinguish between them by a gesture, a word which might raise them above their less favoured companions. Rather the opposite. Remember that God designated his own son to be sacrificed. For the redemption of mankind. And Abraham . . ." He seemed to be referring to the painting on the ceiling because he looked up and smiled sadly at the empty space, leaving the sentence unfinished.

Corso had opened the second book, a folio with an Italian parchment binding from the seventeen hundreds. Inside was a magnificent Virgil. Giunta's Venetian edition, printed in 1544. This revived Fargas.

"Beautiful, isn't it?" He stepped in front of Corso and snatched it from him impatiently. "Look at the title page, at the architectural border . . . One hundred and thirteen woodcuts, all perfect except for page 345, which has a small, ancient restoration, almost imperceptible, in one of the bottom corners. As it happens, this is my favourite. Look: Aeneas in Hell, next to the Sibyl. Have you ever seen anything like it? Look at these flames behind the triple wall, the cauldron of the damned, the bird devouring their entrails . . ." The old bookcollector's pulse was almost visible, throbbing in his wrists and temples. His voice became deeper as he held the book up to his eyes so he could read more clearly. His expression was radiant. "*Mœnia amnlata videt, triplici circundata muro, quae rapidus flamnis ambit torrentibus amnis . . .*" He paused, ecstatic. "The engraver had a beautiful, violent, medieval view of Virgil's Hades."

"A magnificent book," confirmed Corso, dragging on his cigarette.

"It's more than that. Feel the paper. '*Esemplare buono e genuino con le figure assai ben impresse,*' assure the old catalogues . . ." After this feverish outburst, Fargas once more gazed into empty space, absorbed, engrossed in the dark corners of his nightmare. "I think I'll sell this one."

Corso exhaled impatiently.

"I don't understand. This is obviously one of your favourites. So is the Agricola. Your hands tremble as you touch them."

"My hands? What you mean is my soul burns in the torments of hell. I thought I'd explained . . . The book to be sacrificed can never be one to which I am indifferent. What meaning would this painful act have otherwise? A sordid transaction determined by market forces, several cheap ones instead of a single expensive one . . ." Scornful, he shook his head violently. He looked round grimly, searching for someone on whom to vent his anger. "These are the ones I love most. They shine above the rest for their beauty, for the love they have inspired. These are the ones I walk hand in hand with to the very brink of the abyss . . . Life may strip me of all I have. But it won't turn me into a miserable wretch."

He paced aimlessly about the room. The sad scene, his bad leg, his shabby clothes, all added to his weary, fragile appearance.

"That's why I remain in this house," he went on. "The ghosts of my lost books roam within its walls." He had stopped in front of the fireplace and was looking at the wretched pile of logs in the hearth. "Sometimes I feel they come back to demand that I make amends . . . So, to placate them, I take up the violin that you see there and I play for hours, wandering through the house in darkness, like one of the damned . . ." He had turned round to look at Corso and was silhouetted against the dirty window. "The wandering bookcollector."

He walked slowly to the table and laid a hand on each book, as if he had delayed making his decision until that moment. Now he was smiling, inquiringly.

"Which one would you choose, if you were in my place?"

Corso fidgeted uneasily.

"Please, leave me out of this. I'm lucky enough not to be in your place."

"That's right. Very lucky. How clever of you to realize. A stupid man would envy me I suppose. All this treasure in my house . . . But you haven't told me which one to sell. Which son to sacrifice." His face suddenly became distorted with anguish, as if both his mind and body were in pain. "May his blood taint me and mine," he added in a very low, intense voice, "down to the seventh generation."

He returned the Agricola to its place on the rug and stroked the parchment of the Virgil, muttering "his blood". His eyes were moist and his hands were shaking uncontrollably.

"I think I'll sell this one," he insisted.

Fargas might not be out of his mind yet, but he soon would be. Corso looked at the bare walls, the marks left by pictures on the damp-stained wallpaper. The highly unlikely seventh generation didn't give a damn about any of it. Like Lucas Corso's own, the Fargas line would end here. And find peace at last. Corso's cigarette smoke rose up to the decrepit paintings on the ceiling, straight upwards like the smoke from a sacrifice in the calm of dawn. He looked out of the window, at the garden overrun with weeds, searching for a way out like the sheep tangled in the brambles. But there was nothing but books. The angel let go of the hand holding up the knife and went away, weeping. And left Abraham alone, the poor fool.

Corso finished his cigarette and threw it into the fireplace. He was tired and cold. He had heard too many words within those bare walls. He was glad there were no mirrors for him to see the expression on his face. He looked at his watch, without noticing the time. With a fortune sitting there on the old rugs and carpets, Victor Fargas had more than paid their price in suffering. For Corso it was now time to talk about business.

"What about *The Nine Doors*?"

"What about it?"

"That's what brought me here. I assume you got my letter."

"Your letter? Yes, of course. I remember. It's just that with all of this . . . Forgive me. *The Nine Doors*. Of course."

He looked round, bewildered, like a sleepwalker who had just been jolted awake. He suddenly seemed infinitely tired, after a long ordeal.

He lifted a finger, requesting a minute to think, then limped over to a corner of the room. Some fifty or so books were lined up there on the floor on a faded French rug. Corso could just make out that it depicted Alexander's victory over Darius.

"Did you know," asked Fargas, pointing at the scene on the Gobelin, "that Alexander used his rival's treasure chest to store Homer's books?" He nodded, pleased, looking at the Macedonian's threadbare profile. "He was a fellow bookcollector. A good man."

Corso didn't give a damn about Alexander the Great's literary tastes. He had knelt down and was reading the titles printed on some of the spines and fore-edges. They were all ancient treatises on magic, alchemy and demonology. *Les trois livres de l'Art, Destructor omnium rerum, Dissertazioni sopra le apparizioni de' spiriti e diavoli, De origine, moribus et rebus gestis Satanæ* . . .

"What do you think?" asked Fargas.

"Not bad."

The bookcollector laughed wearily. He knelt down on the rug next to Corso and went over the books mechanically, making sure that none of them had moved by a millimetre since he last checked them.

"Not bad at all. You're right. At least ten of them are extremely rare . . . I inherited all this part of the collection from my grandfather. He was a devotee of the hermetic arts and astrology, and he was a Mason. Look. This is a classic, the *Infernal Dictionary* by Collin de Plancy, a first edition dating from 1842. And this is the 1571 printing of the *Compendi dei secreti*, by Leonardo Fioravanti . . . That strange duodecimo there is the second edition of the *Book of Wonders*." He opened another book and showed Corso an engraving. "Look at Isis . . . And do you know what this is?"

"Yes, of course. The *Œdipus Ægiptiacus* by Atanasius Kircher."

"Correct. The 1652 Rome edition." Fargas put the book back and picked up another one. Corso recognized the Venetian binding: the black leather with five raised bands, and a pentacle but no title on the cover. "Here's the one you're looking for, *De umbrarum regni novem portis* . . . The nine doors of the kingdom of shadows."

Corso shivered in spite of himself. On the outside at least the book was identical to the one he had in his canvas bag. Fargas handed him the book and Corso stood up as he leafed through it. They looked absolutely identical, or almost. The leather on the back of Fargas's copy was slightly worn, and there was an old mark left by a label that had been added and then removed. The rest was in the same immaculate condition as Varo Borja's copy, even engraving number VIIII which was intact.

"It's complete and in good condition," said Fargas, correctly interpreting the look on Corso's face. "It's been out in the world for three centuries and a half, but when you open it, it looks as fresh as the day it came off the press . . . As if the printer made a pact with the Devil."

"Maybe he did," said Corso.

"I wouldn't mind knowing the magic formula. My soul in exchange for keeping all this." The bookcollector made a sweeping gesture which took in the desolate room, the rows of books on the floor.

"You could try it," said Corso, pointing at *The Nine Doors.* "They say the formula is in there."

"I never believed all that nonsense. Although maybe now would be a good time to start. Don't you think? You have a saying in Spain: If all is lost we may as well jump in the river."*

"Is the book in order? Have you noticed anything strange about it?"

"Nothing whatsoever. There are no pages missing. And the engravings are all there, nine of them, plus the title page. Just as it was when my grandfather bought it at the turn of the century. It matches the description in the catalogues and it's identical to the other two copies, the Ungern in Paris, and the Terral-Coy."

"It's no longer Terral-Coy. Now it's in the Varo Borja collection in Toledo."

Corso saw that Fargas's expression had become suspicious, alert.

"Varo Borja, you say?" He'd been about to add something, but changed his mind at the last moment. "His collection is remarkable. And very well known." He paced around aimlessly and then looked at the books lined up on the rug again. "Varo Borja . . ." he repeated thoughtfully. "He's a specialist in demonology, isn't he? A very rich bookcollector. He's been after that *Nine Doors* you've got there for years. He's always been prepared to pay any price . . . I didn't know that he'd managed to find a copy. And you work for him."

"Occasionally," admitted Corso.

Fargas nodded a couple of times, looking puzzled, and then turned his attention to the books on the floor again.

"Strange that he should send you. After all . . ."

*equivalent to "In for a penny, in for a pound".

He broke off and let his sentence hang in mid-air. He was looking at Corso's bag.

"Have you brought the book with you? Could I see it?"

They went up to the table and Corso laid his copy next to Fargas's. As he did so he could hear the old man's agitated breathing. His face looked ecstatic again.

"Look at them closely," he whispered as if he was afraid of waking something sleeping between their pages. "They're perfect, beautiful. And identical . . . Two of the only three copies which escaped the flames, brought together for the first time since they were parted three hundred and fifty years ago . . ." His hands were trembling again. He rubbed his wrists to slow down the blood coursing violently through them. "Look at the errata on page 72. The split *s* here, in the fourth line of page 87 . . . The same paper, identical printing . . . Isn't it a wonder?"

"Yes." Corso cleared his throat. "I'd like to stay for a while. Have a thorough look at them."

Fargas gave him a piercing look. He seemed to hesitate.

"As you wish," he said at last. "But if you have the Terral-Coy copy, there's no doubt as to its authenticity." He looked at Corso with curiosity, trying to read his mind. "Varo Borja must know that."

"I suppose he must." Corso gave his best neutral smile. "But I'm getting paid to make sure." He kept smiling. They were getting to the difficult part. "By the way, talking of money, I've been told to make you an offer."

The bookcollector's curiosity turned to suspicion.

"What kind of offer?"

"Financial. And substantial." Corso laid his hand on the second copy. "You could solve your money problems for some time."

"Would it be Varo Borja paying?"

"It could be."

Fargas stroked his chin.

"He already has one of the books," he concluded. "Does he want all three of them?"

The man might have been slightly insane but he was no fool. Corso gestured vaguely, not wanting to commit himself. Perhaps. One of those things collectors get into their heads. But if he sold it Fargas would then be able to keep the Virgil.

"You don't understand," said Fargas. But Corso understood only too well. He wasn't going to get anywhere with the old man.

"Forget it," he said. "It was just a thought."

"I don't sell at random. I choose the books. I thought I'd made that clear."

The veins on the back of his tensed hands were knotted. He was beginning to get irritated, so Corso spent the next few minutes in placatory mode. The offer was a secondary matter, a mere formality. What he really wanted, he concluded, was to make a comparative study of both books. At last, to his relief, Fargas nodded in agreement.

"I don't see any problem with that," he said. His mistrust was receding slightly. It was obvious he liked Corso or things would have gone quite differently. "Although I can't offer you many creature comforts here . . ."

He led him down a bare passage to another, smaller room which had a dilapidated piano in one corner. There was a table with an old bronze candelabrum covered in wax drips and a couple of rickety chairs.

"At least it's quiet here," said Fargas. "And all the window-panes are intact."

He clicked his fingers as if he'd forgotten something. He disappeared for a moment and returned holding the rest of the bottle of brandy.

"So Varo Borja finally managed to get hold of it . . ." he repeated. He smiled to himself, as if at some thought that obviously caused him great satisfaction. Then he put the bottle and glass on the floor, at a safe distance from the two copies of *The Nine Doors.* Like an attentive host, he looked round to make sure that everything was in order, and then made a final, ironic comment before leaving.

"Make yourself at home."

Corso poured the rest of the brandy into the glass. Then he took out his notes and set to work. He had drawn three boxes on a sheet of paper. Each one contained a number and name:

COPY ONE (Varo Borja) Toledo
COPY TWO (Fargas) Sintra
COPY THREE (Von Ungern) Paris

Page after page he noted down any difference between Book Number One and Number Two, however slight: a stain on the paper, the ink slightly darker in one copy or another. When he came to the first engraving – 'NEM. PERV.T QUI N.N LEG. CERT.RIT', the horseman advising the reader to keep silent – he took out a magnifying glass with a magnification of seven from his bag and examined both woodcuts, line by line. They were identical. He noticed that even the pressure of the engravings on the paper, like that of the typography, was the same. The lines and characters looked worn, broken or crooked in exactly the same places in both copies. This meant that Number One and Number Two had been printed one after the other, or almost, and on the same press. As the Ceniza brothers would have put it, Corso was looking at a pair of twins.

He went on making notes. An imperfection in line six of page nineteen in Book Number Two made him stop a moment, but then he realized it was just an ink stain. He turned more pages. Both books had the same structure: two flyleaves and one hundred and sixty pages stitched into twenty signatures of eight. All nine illustrations in both books occupied a full page. They had been printed separately on the same type of paper, blank on the reverse, and inserted into the book during the binding process. They were positioned identically in both books:

NEM. PERV.T QVI N.N LEG. CERT.RIT

CLAVS. PAT.T

VERB. D.SVM C.S.T ARCAN.

FOR. N.N OMN. A.QVE

FR.ST.A

DIT.SCO M.R.

DIS.S P.TI.R M.

VIC. I.T VIR.

N.NC SC.O TEN.BR. LVX

Either Varo Borja was raving, or this was a very strange job he'd been sent on. There was no way that they were forgeries. At the most they might have both come from an apocryphal edition, but which still dated from the seventeenth century. Number One and Number Two were the embodiment of honesty on printed paper.

He drank the rest of the brandy and then examined illustration II with his magnifying glass. "*CLAUS. PAT.T.*", the bearded hermit holding two keys, the closed door, a lantern on the ground. He had the illustrations side by side and he suddenly felt rather silly. It was like playing "spot the difference". He grimaced. Life as a game. And books as a reflection of life.

Then he saw it. It happened suddenly, just as from the correct angle something that has previously seemed meaningless all at once appears ordered and precise. Corso breathed out as if he were about to laugh, astounded. But all that emerged was a dry sound, like a laugh of disbelief but without the humour. It wasn't possible. One didn't joke with that kind of thing. He shook his head, confused. This wasn't a cheap book of puzzles bought at a railway station. These books were three and a half centuries old. Their printer had lost his life over them. They had been included amongst the books banned by the Inquisition. And they were listed in all the serious bibliographies. "Illustration II. Caption in Latin. Old man with two keys and a lantern, standing in front of a closed door". . . But nobody had compared two of the three known copies until then. It wasn't easy bringing them together. Or necessary. Old man with two keys. That was enough.

Corso got up and went to the window. He stood there for a while, looking through the panes misted by his own breath. Varo Borja was right after all. Aristide Torchia must have been laughing to himself on his pyre at Campo dei Fiori, before the flames took away his sense of humour forever. As a posthumous joke it was brilliant.

VIII

Postuma necat

"Is anybody there?"
"No."
"Too bad. He must be dead."

M. Leblanc: *Arsène Lupin*

Lucas Corso knew better than anyone one of the main problems of his profession: bibliographies are drawn up by scholars who have never actually seen the books they're citing, relying instead on second-hand accounts and information recorded by others. An error or incomplete description might circulate for generations without being noticed. Then, by chance it comes to light. This was the case with *The Nine Doors*. Apart from its obligatory mention in the canonical bibliographies, even the most precise references had only ever included summary descriptions of the nine engravings, without minor details. In the case of the book's second illustration, all the known texts referred to an old man who looked like a sage or a hermit, standing before a door with two keys in his hand. But nobody had ever bothered to specify in which hand he was holding the keys. Now Corso had the answer: in the *left* in the engraving in Book Number One, and in the *right* in Number Two.

He still had to find out what Number Three was like. But this wasn't possible yet. Corso stayed at the Quinta da Soledade until dark. He worked solidly in the light of the candelabra, taking copious notes, checking both books over and over again. He examined each engraving until he had confirmed his theory. More proof emerged. At last he sat looking at his booty in the form of notes on a sheet of paper, tables and diagrams with strange links with each other. Five of the engravings were not identical in both books. In addition to the old man in engraving II holding the keys in different hands, the labyrinth in IIII had an exit in one of the books but not in the other. In illustration V of Book One, Death was brandishing an hourglass with the sand in the lower half, while in Book Two the sand was in the upper half. As for the chessboard in number VII, in Varo Borja's copy the squares were all white while in Fargas's copy they were black. And in engraving number VIII, the executioner poised to behead the young girl in one of the books became an avenging angel in the other through the addition of an aureole above his head.

And there were yet more differences. Close examination through the magnifying glass yielded unexpected results. The printer's marks hidden in the woodcuts contained another subtle clue. *A.T.* – Aristide Torchia – was named as the *sculptor* in the engraving of the old man, but as the *inventor* only in the same engraving in Book Number Two. As the Ceniza brothers had pointed out, the signature in Book One was *L.F.* The same occurred in four more of the illustrations. This could mean that all the woodcuts were carved by the printer himself, but that the original drawings from which he copied some of his engravings were created by somebody else. So this wasn't a matter of a forgery dating from the same era as the books, nor of apocryphal reprintings. It was the printer, Torchia himself, "by authority and permission of the superiors," who had altered his own work in accordance with a pre-established plan. He had signed the engravings he had changed so as to make sure it was clear that L.F. had created the others. Only one copy remains, he told his executioners. Whereas in actual fact he had left three copies behind, and a key which might possibly turn them into a single one. The rest of his secret he took with him to the grave.

He resorted to an ancient collating system: the comparative tables used by Umberto Eco in his study of the Hanau. Having set out in order on paper the illustrations which contained differences, he obtained the following table:

	I	II	III	IIII	V	VI	VII	VIII	VIIII
ONE	–	left hand	–	no exit	sand down	–	white board	no aureole	–
TWO	–	right hand	–	exit	sand up	–	black board	aureole	–

As for the engraver's marks, the variations in the signatures *A.T.* (the printer, Torchia) and *L.F.* (unknown? Lucifer?) corresponding to the *sculptor* and the *inventor*, they were set out as follows:

	I	II	III	IIII	V	VI	VII	VIII	VIIII
ONE	AT(s) AT(i)	AT(s) LF(i)	AT(s) AT(i)	AT(s) AT(i)	AT(s) LF(i)	AT(s) AT(i)	AT(s) AT(i)	AT(s) AT(i)	AT(s) AT(i)
TWO	AT(s) AT(i)	AT(s) AT(i)	AT(s) AT(i)	AT(s) LF(i)	AT(s) AT(i)	AT(s) AT(i)	AT(s) LF(i)	AT(s) LF(i)	AT(s) AT(i)

Strange code. But Corso at last had something definite. He now knew there was a key of some sort. He stood up slowly, as if he were afraid that all the links would vanish before his eyes. But he was calm, like a hunter who is sure that he will catch his prey at the end of the trail, however confusing.

Hand. Exit. Sand. Board. Aureole.

He glanced out of the window. Beyond the dirty panes, a remnant of reddish light silhouetting a branch refused to disappear into the night.

Books One and Two. Differences in numbers 2, 4, 5, 7 and 8.

He had to go to Paris. Book Number Three was there, together with the possible solution to the mystery. But he was now preoccupied with another matter, something he had to deal with urgently. Varo Borja had been categorical. Now that Corso was sure he wouldn't be able to obtain Book Number Two by conventional methods, he had to devise a plan to acquire it by more unorthodox means. With the minimum chance of risk to Fargas, and to Corso himself, of course. Something gentle and discreet. He took out his diary from his coat pocket and searched for the phone number he needed. It was the perfect job for Amilcar Pinto.

One of the candles had burnt right down and went out with a small spiral of smoke. Corso could hear the violin being played somewhere in the house. He laughed drily again as the flames of the candelabra made shadows dance on his face when he leant over to light a cigarette. Then he straightened up and listened. The music sounded like a lament floating through the dark empty rooms with their remains of dusty, worm-eaten furniture, painted ceilings, stained walls covered in spiders' webs and shadows; echoes of footsteps, voices extinguished long ago. And outside, above the rusty railings, the two statues, one with its eyes open in the darkness, the other covered by a mask of ivy, listened motionless, as time stood still, to the music that Victor Fargas played on his violin to summon the ghosts of his lost books.

He returned to the village on foot, his hands in his coat pockets and his collar turned up. It took him twenty minutes on the deserted road. There was no moon and Corso walked into large patches of darkness beneath the black canopy of trees. There was almost total silence, broken only by the sound of his shoes crunching on the gravel at the side of the road, and channels of water coursing down the hill between rockrose and ivy, invisible in the darkness.

A car came from behind and overtook him. Corso saw his own shadow, with its enlarged, ghostly outline, glide undulating across the nearby tree-trunks and dense woods. Only once he was again enveloped in shadow did he breathe out and feel his tense muscles relax. He wasn't one who saw ghosts around every corner. Instead he viewed things, however extraordinary, with the southern fatalism of an old soldier, no doubt inherited from this great-great-grandfather Corso. However much one spurred one's horse in the opposite direction, the inevitable was always lurking at the gate of the nearest Samarkand, picking its nails with a Venetian dagger, or a Scottish bayonet. Even so, since the incident in the street in Toledo, Corso felt understandably apprehensive every time he heard a car behind him.

Maybe because of this, when the lights of another car pulled up beside him, Corso turned round sharply and changed his canvas bag over to his other shoulder. He found his bunch of keys inside his coat pocket. It was a weapon of fortune but with it he could poke the eye out of anybody who got too close. But now there seemed no reason to worry. He saw a large, dark shape, like that of an old berlin, and inside, lit by the faint glow from the dashboard, the profile of a man. His voice was friendly, well-educated.

"Good evening . . ." The accent was indefinable, neither Portuguese nor Spanish. "Do you have a match?"

The request could be genuine, or just a pretext, he couldn't be sure. But he didn't need to run away or brandish his sharpest key just because he'd been asked for a light. So Corso let go of his keyring. He took out his matches and lit one, shielding the flame with his hand.

"Thanks."

There was the scar, of course. It was an old one, long and vertical, from his temple to halfway down his left cheek. He was able to see it closely as the man leant forward to light his Montecristo cigar. Corso held up the light long enough to glimpse the thick, black moustache and dark eyes watching him intently from the gloom. Then the match went out and it seemed as if a black mask had covered the stranger's face. He had become a shadow again, his outline only just distinguishable in the faint light from the dashboard.

"Who the bloody hell are you?"

His tone wasn't calm. Nor was it a particularly brilliant question. Anyway it was too late. The question was drowned out by the sound of the engine accelerating. The twin red points of the car's rear lights were already heading off into the distance, leaving a fleeting trail against the dark ribbon of road. It shone more intensely for an instant as the car turned the first corner, and then disappeared as if it had never been there.

The bookhunter stood motionless by the side of the road, trying to piece the picture together. Madrid, outside Liana Taillefer's house. Toledo, his visit to Varo Borja. And Sintra, after an afternoon at Victor Fargas's house. There were also Dumas's serials, a publisher hanged in his study, a printer burnt at the stake with his strange manual . . . And among all of this, shadowing Corso: Rochefort, a fictional, seventeenth-century swordsman reincarnated as a uniformed chauffeur of luxury cars. Responsible for an attempted hit-and-run incident, and breaking and entering. A smoker of Montecristo cigars. A smoker without a lighter.

He swore gently under his breath. He'd have given a rare incunabulum – in good condition – to punch the face of whoever was writing this ridiculous script.

As soon as he got back to the hotel he made several telephone calls. The first was to the Lisbon number in his diary. He was lucky, Amilcar Pinto was at home. He ascertained as much in a conversation with his bad-tempered wife, the sound of a television blaring in the background, the high-pitched crying of children and adult voices arguing violently coming through the black Bakelite earpiece. Finally Pinto came to the phone. They agreed to meet an hour and a half later, the time it would take the Portuguese to travel the fifty kilometres to

Sintra. Having arranged this, Corso looked at his watch and dialled Varo Borja's number. But the bookdealer wasn't at his house in Toledo. He left a message on the answerphone and dialled Flavio La Ponte's number in Madrid. He wasn't at home either, so Corso hid his canvas bag on top of the wardrobe and went out for a drink.

The first thing he saw as he pushed open the door of the small hotel lounge was the girl. It couldn't be anyone else: her cropped hair giving her a boyish look, her skin as tanned as if it were August. She was sitting in an armchair reading in the cone of light from a lamp, her legs stretched out and crossed on the seat opposite. She was barefoot, in jeans and a white cotton T-shirt, her sweater around her shoulders. Corso stopped, his hand on the door handle, an absurd feeling hammering at his brain. Coincidence or deliberate occurrence, this was too much.

At last, still incredulous, he went up to the girl. He was almost by her side when she looked up from her book and fixed her green eyes on him with their deep, liquid clarity which he remembered so well from their meeting on the train. He stopped, not knowing what to say. He had the strange feeling he was going to fall into her eyes.

"You didn't tell me you were coming to Sintra," he said.

"Nor did you."

She smiled calmly as she said it, looking neither surprised nor embarrassed. She seemed sincerely pleased to see him.

"What are you doing here?" asked Corso.

She took her feet down from the armchair and gestured for him to sit down. But the bookhunter remained standing.

"Travelling," said the girl, and she showed him her book. It wasn't the same one as on the train. *Melmoth the Wanderer* by Charles Maturin. "Reading. And bumping into people unexpectedly."

"Unexpectedly," repeated Corso like an echo.

He'd bumped into too many people for one evening, whether unexpectedly or not. He found himself trying to find a link between her presence at the hotel and Rochefort's appearance on the road. From a certain angle all these things must have fitted together, but he was nowhere near finding it. He didn't even know where to start.

"Won't you sit down?"

He did so, vaguely anxious. The girl had shut her book and was looking at him curiously.

"You don't look like a tourist," she said.

"I'm not."

"Are you working?"

"Yes."

"Any job in Sintra must be interesting."

That's all I need, thought Corso, adjusting his glasses. Being interrogated after all I've been through, even if it was by an extremely young, beautiful girl. Maybe that was the problem. She was too young to be a threat. Or maybe that was where the danger lay. He picked up the girl's book from the table and flicked through it. It was a modern, English edition, some of the paragraphs underlined in pencil. He read one:

His eyes remained fixed in the diminishing light and growing darkness. That preternatural blackness which seems to be saying to God's most luminous and sublime creation: "Give me space. Stop shining."

"Do you enjoy Gothic novels?"

"I enjoy reading." She had bowed her head slightly and the light made a foreshortened outline of her bare neck. "And touching books. I always carry several in my rucksack when I travel."

"Do you travel a lot?"

"Yes. I've been travelling for ages."

Corso winced when he heard her answer. She had said it very seriously, frowning slightly like a little girl talking about serious matters.

"I thought you were a student."

"I am sometimes."

Corso put the *Melmoth* back on the table.

"You're a strange young lady. How old are you? Eighteen? Nineteen? Sometimes your expression changes, as if you were much older."

"Maybe I am. One's gestures are influenced by what one has experienced and read. Look at you."

"What's the matter with me?"

"Have you ever seen yourself smile? You look like an old soldier." He shifted slightly in his seat, embarrassed.

"I don't know how an old soldier smiles."

"Well, I do." The girl's eyes darkened. She was searching in her memory. "Once I knew ten thousand men who were looking for the sea."

Corso lifted an eyebrow in mock-interest.

"Really. Is that something you read or experienced?"

"Guess." She stopped and looked at him intently before adding, "You seem like a clever man, Mr Corso."

She stood up, taking the book from the table and her white tennis shoes off the floor. Her eyes brightened, and Corso recognized the reflections in them. He glimpsed something familiar in her gaze.

"Maybe we'll see each other around," she said as she left.

Corso had no doubt that they would. He wasn't very sure whether he wanted to or not. One way or another, the thought only lasted an instant. As she left, the girl passed Amilcar Pinto at the door.

He was a short, greasy little man. His skin was dark and shiny, as if it had just been varnished, and he had a thick, wiry moustache, roughly trimmed. He would have been an honest policeman, even a good policeman, if he hadn't had to feed five children, a wife and a retired father who secretly stole his cigarettes. His wife was a mulatto and had been very beautiful twenty years ago. He brought her back from Mozambique at the time of Independence, when Maputo was called Lourenço Marques and he himself was a decorated sergeant in the paratroops, a slight, brave man. During the course of some of the deals they did from time to time he had caught sight of Pinto's wife, eyes ringed with fatigue, large, flaccid breasts, in old slippers and her hair tied with a red scarf, in the hallway to their house which smelt of dirty kids and boiled vegetables.

The policeman came straight into the lounge, looking at the girl out of the corner of his eye as he passed her, and sank into the armchair opposite Corso. He was out of breath, as if he'd just walked all the way from Lisbon.

"Who was the girl?"

"Nobody important," answered Corso. "She's Spanish. A tourist."

Pinto nodded, having caught his breath. He wiped his sweaty palms on his trouser legs. It was something he often did. He sweated abundantly, and his shirt collars always had a dark ring where they touched his skin.

"I've got a bit of a problem," said Corso.

Pinto's grin widened. No problem is insoluble, his expression seemed to say. Not as long as you and I still get along.

"I'm sure we'll be able to solve it together," he answered.

Now it was Corso's turn to smile. He'd met Amilcar Pinto four years before. Some stolen books had appeared on stands at the Ladra Book Fair – a bad business. Corso came to Lisbon to identify them, Pinto made a couple of arrests, and en route back to their owner a few very valuable books disappeared forever. To celebrate the beginning of a fruitful friendship, they got drunk together in the fados bars of the Barrio Alto. The ex-paratroop sergeant reminisced about his time in the colonies with tales of how he'd nearly had his balls blown off at the battle of Gorongosa. They ended up singing '*Grandola vila morena*' at the tops of their voices up on Santa Luzia. Illuminated by the moon, the district of Alfama lay at their feet with the Tagus beyond it, wide and gleaming like a sheet of silver. The dark shapes of boats, moving very slowly, headed out towards the Belém tower and the Atlantic.

A waiter brought Pinto the coffee he had ordered. Corso waited for him to leave before continuing.

"It's about a book."

The policeman leant over the little low table and put sugar in his coffee.

"It's always about a book," he said gravely.

"This one's special."

"Which one isn't?"

Corso smiled again. A sharp, metallic smile.

"The owner doesn't want to sell."

"That's bad." Pinto drank some coffee, savouring it. "Trade's a good thing. Things moving, coming and going. It generates wealth, makes money for the go-betweens . . ." He put the cup down and wiped his hands on his trousers. "Products have to circulate. It's the law of the market, of life. Not selling should be banned: it's almost a crime."

"I agree," said Corso. "You should do something about it."

Pinto leaned back in his chair. Calm and confident, he looked at Corso expectantly. Once, after an ambush in the *mato* in Mozambique, he had fled, carrying a dying officer for ten kilometres through the jungle. At dawn he felt the lieutenant die, but didn't want to leave him behind. So he went on, with the corpse over his shoulders, until he reached the base. The officer was very young, and Pinto thought that his mother would like to have him buried back in Portugal. They gave him a medal for it. Now Pinto's children played about the house with his old tarnished medals.

"Maybe you know the man: Victor Fargas."

The policeman nodded.

"The Fargases are a very old, very respectable family," he said. "In the past they had a lot of influence, but not any more."

Corso handed him a sealed envelope.

"This is all the information you need: owner, book and location."

"I know the house." Pinto licked his upper lip, wetting his moustache. "Very unwise, keeping valuable books there. Any unscrupulous individual might get in." He looked at Corso sadly, as if he really thought Victor Fargas was being irresponsible. "I can think of one, a petty thief from Chiado who owes me a favour."

Corso shook some invisible dust from his clothes. It had nothing to do with him. Not in the operational phase anyway.

"I don't want to be in the area when it happens."

"Don't worry. You'll get your book and Mr Fargas will be disturbed as little as possible. A broken window-pane at the most. It'll be a clean job. About payment . . ."

Corso pointed at the envelope that Pinto was holding, still unopened.

"That's an advance of a quarter of the total. The rest on delivery."

"That's fine. When are you leaving?"

"First thing tomorrow morning. I'll get in touch with you from Paris." Pinto was about to get up, but Corso stopped him. "There's something else. I need an identification. Tall man, about six feet, with a moustache and a scar on his face. Black hair, dark eyes. Slim. He's not Spanish or Portuguese. And he was lurking around here tonight."

"Is he dangerous?"

"I don't know. He's followed me from Madrid."

Pinto was taking notes on the back of the envelope.

"Does this have anything to do with our business?"

"I'm assuming it does. But I don't have any more information."

"I'll do what I can. I've got friends at the police station here in Sintra. And I'll take a look at the files at central headquarters in Lisbon."

He stood up and put the envelope in the inside pocket of his jacket. Corso caught a fleeting glimpse of a revolver in the holster under his left arm.

"Why don't you stay for a drink?"

Pinto sighed and shook his head.

"I'd like to, but three of the kids have got measles. They catch it off each other, the little swine."

He said this with a tired smile. All the heroes in Corso's world were tired.

They went to the hotel entrance where Pinto had parked his old Citroën 2CV. As they shook hands, Corso mentioned Victor Fargas again.

"Make sure that Fargas is disturbed as little as possible. This is just a burglary."

Pinto switched on the engine and turned on the lights. He looked at Corso reproachfully through the open window. He looked offended.

"Please. You don't need to tell me again. I know what I'm doing."

After Pinto had left, Corso went up to his room to sort out his notes. He worked on late into the night, his bed covered in papers and *The Nine Doors* open on his pillow. He felt extremely tired and thought a hot shower might help him relax. He was on his way to the bathroom when the phone rang. It was Varo Borja, wanting to know how he had got on with Fargas. He gave him a general idea of how things were going, including the discrepancies he had found in five of the nine engravings.

"By the way," he added, "our friend Fargas won't sell."

There was a silence at the other end of the line. Borja seemed to be thinking, although there was no way of telling whether it was about the engravings or Fargas's refusal to sell. When he spoke again his tone was extremely cautious.

"That seemed likely," he said. Corso still couldn't tell exactly what he was referring to. "Is there any way of getting round the problem?"

"There might be."

Borja was silent again. Corso counted five seconds by his watch.

"I'll leave it in your hands."

They didn't say much else after that. Corso didn't mention his conversation with Pinto, and Borja didn't enquire how Corso was going to solve the "problem", as he had euphemistically put it. He only asked if Corso needed more money, and Corso said no. They agreed to talk again when Corso reached Paris.

Corso then dialled La Ponte's number, but there was still no answer. The blue pages of the Dumas manuscript remained in their folder. He gathered up his notes and the black leather-bound book with the pentacle on the cover. He put them back in his canvas bag and slipped it under the bed, tying the strap to one of the legs. In that way, if anybody got into the room and tried to take it, they'd have to wake him however soundly he was sleeping. Rather an awkward piece of luggage to carry around, he thought as he went to the bathroom to turn on the shower. And, for some reason, dangerous too.

He brushed his teeth. Then he undressed and dropped his clothes on the floor. The mirror was almost completely steamed over but he could see his reflection, thin and hard like an emaciated wolf. Once again he felt a burst of anxiety from the distant past, swamping his mind in a painful wave. Like a string vibrating in his flesh and his memory. Nikon. He remembered her every time he undid his belt. She'd always insisted on undoing it for him as if it were a strange ritual. He shut his eyes and saw her in front of him, sitting on the edge of the bed, slipping his trousers and then his underpants down very slowly, savouring the moment with a conspiratorial, tender smile. Relax, Lucas Corso. Once she had taken a photo of him secretly, while he was sleeping. He was face down with a vertical crease on his brow and his cheek was darkened by stubble. It made his face look thinner and emphasized the tense, bitter lines at the corners of his half-open mouth. He looked like an exhausted wolf, suspicious and tormented in the deserted snow plain of the pillow. He didn't like the photo. He found it by chance, in the fixing tray in the bathroom that Nikon used as a dark room. He'd torn it, and the negative, into little pieces. She'd never mentioned it.

When he stepped into the shower the hot water scalded him. He let it run over his face, burning his eyelids. He put up with the pain, his jaw clenched and his muscles tensed, suppressing the urge to howl with loneliness in the suffocating steam. For four years, one month and twelve days, Nikon always got into the shower with him after they had made love and soaped his back slowly, interminably. And often she put her arms round him, like a little girl in the rain. One day I'll leave without ever really knowing you. You'll remember my big, dark eyes. The reproachful silences. The moans of anxiety as I slept. The nightmares you couldn't save me from. You'll remember all this once I'm gone.

He leant his head against the dripping white tiles, in a damp steaming desert which seemed like a kind of hell. Nobody had ever soaped his back before or since Nikon. Nobody. Ever.

After his shower he got into bed with the *Memoirs of Saint-Helena* but only managed to read a couple of lines:

Returning to the subject of war, the Emperor continued: "The Spaniards en masse acted as a man of honour."

He frowned at Napoleon's praise, two centuries old. He remembered words he'd heard as a child, perhaps from one of his grandparents, or his father. "There's one thing we Spaniards do better than anyone else: appear in Goya's pictures." Men of honour, Bonaparte had said. Corso thought of Varo Borja and his cheque-book. Of Flavio La Ponte and widows' libraries plundered for a pittance. Of Nikon's ghost wandering in a lonely, white desert. Of himself, a hunter who worked for the highest bidder. These were different times.

He was still smiling, desperate and bitter, when he fell asleep.

When he woke the first thing he saw was the grey light of dawn through the window. Too early. Confused, he tried to find his watch on the bedside table when he realized that the phone was ringing. He dropped the receiver twice before managing to lodge it between his ear and the pillow.

"Hello?"

"This is your friend from last night. Remember? Irene Adler. I'm in the lobby. We have to talk. Now."

"What the hell . . ."

But she'd already hung up. Cursing, Corso searched for his glasses. He threw back the sheets and put on his trousers, drowsy and disconcerted. With sudden panic, he looked under the bed. The bag was still there, intact. With an effort he managed to focus on the things around him. Everything in the room was in order. It was outside that things were happening. He had time to go to the bathroom and splash water on his face before she knocked at the door.

"Do you know what the bloody time is?"

The girl was standing there in her blue duffle coat with her rucksack on her back. Her eyes were even more green than Corso remembered.

"It's half past six in the morning," she announced calmly. "And you've got to get dressed right now."

"Have you gone crazy?"

"No." She came into the room without being asked and looked round critically. "We've got very little time."

"We?"

"You and I. Things have got rather complicated."

Corso snorted, irritated.

"It's too early for jokes."

"Don't be stupid." She wrinkled her nose with an expression of concentration. Despite her youth and boyishness, she looked different, older and more self-assured. "I'm serious."

She put her rucksack on the unmade bed. Corso gave it back to her and showed her the door.

"Go to hell."

She didn't move, just looked at him intently.

"Listen." Her light eyes were very near, like liquid ice, so luminous against her tanned skin. "Do you know who Victor Fargas is?"

Corso caught sight of his own face in the mirror above the chest of drawers, beyond the girl's shoulder. He was open-mouthed, like a complete idiot.

"Of course I do."

He'd taken several seconds to react and was still blinking, confused. She waited, not entirely satisfied with his reaction to her words. It was obvious her mind was on other things.

"He's dead," she said.

She said it neutrally as if she'd just told him Fargas had coffee for breakfast, or had gone to the dentist. Corso took a deep breath, trying to take in what she'd just said.

"That's not possible. I was with him last night. He was fine."

"Well, now he's not. He's not fine at all."

"How do you know?"

"I just do."

Corso shook his head, suspicious, before going to get a cigarette. En route he saw the flask of Bols, so he took a swig. The gin hitting his empty stomach made his hair stand on end. Then he waited, forcing himself not to look at the girl until he'd inhaled his first puff of smoke. He wasn't at all happy with the part he was being forced to play this morning. He needed time to think.

"The café in Madrid, the train, last night and now this morning here in Sintra . . ." He counted on the fingers of his left hand, with his cigarette in his mouth, his eyes half-closed because of the smoke. "That's a lot of coincidences, don't you think?"

She shook her head impatiently.

"I thought you were smarter than that. Who said anything about coincidences?"

"Why are you following me?"

"I like you."

Corso didn't feel like laughing. He just twisted his mouth slightly. "That's ridiculous."

She looked at him for a time, thoughtfully.

"I suppose it is," she said at last. "You don't exactly look breathtaking, always in that old coat and those glasses."

"What is it, then?"

"Find another answer. Anything would do. But now get dressed, will you? We've got to go to Victor Fargas's house."

"We?"

"You and I. Before the police get there."

The dead leaves crackled beneath their feet as they pushed the iron gate and walked up the path lined with broken statues and empty pedestals. The grey morning light cast no shadows and above the stone staircase the sundial still showed no time. '*Postuma necat.*' The last one kills, Corso read again. The girl had followed his gaze.

"Absolutely true," she said coldly and pushed the door. It was locked.

"Let's try the back," suggested Corso.

They went round the house, past the tiled fountain with the chubby stone angel, eyes empty and hands cut off, water still trickling from its mouth into the pond. Surprisingly composed, the girl – Irene Adler or whatever her name was – went ahead of Corso in her blue duffle coat with the small rucksack on her back. She walked, her long supple legs in jeans, her stubborn head leaning forward with the determined air of someone who knew exactly where she was going. Unlike Corso. He had overcome his doubt and let the girl lead him. He was leaving the questions till later. Clear-headed after a quick shower, carrying all he was most concerned about in his canvas bag, he could think of nothing else now but Victor Fargas's *Nine Doors*, Book Number Two.

They got in without difficulty through the French window leading from the garden into the drawing-room. On the ceiling, dagger aloft, Abraham was still watching over the books lined up on the floor. The house seemed deserted.

"Where's Fargas?" asked Corso.

The girl shrugged.

"I've no idea."

"You said he was dead."

"He is." After glancing at her surroundings, at the bare walls and the books, she picked up the violin from the sideboard and looked at it curiously. "What I don't know is where he is."

"You're pulling my leg."

She placed the violin under her chin and plucked at the strings before putting it back in its case, unhappy with the sound. Then she looked at Corso.

"Oh ye of little faith."

She was smiling again, absently. To Corso her composure seemed both deep and frivolous, incongruously mature. This young lady behaved according to a strange code of conduct, determined by thoughts that were more complex than her age and appearance let one suppose.

Suddenly, these thoughts – the girl, the strange events, even the supposed corpse of Victor Fargas – all left Corso's mind. On the threadbare rug depicting the battle of Arbelas, between books on satanic arts and the occult, there was a gap. *The Nine Doors* was no longer there.

"Shit," he said.

He muttered it again as he leant over the row of books and knelt beside them. His expert glance, accustomed to finding a book instantly, wandered from one side to another without success. Black morocco, five raised bands, no title on the exterior, a pentacle on the cover. *Umbrarum regni*, etc. He wasn't mistaken. A third of the mystery, exactly 33.33 recurring per cent, had vanished.

"Damn."

It couldn't have been Pinto, he wouldn't have had time to organize anything. The girl was watching him as if waiting for him to do something interesting. Corso stood up.

"Who are you?"

It was the second time in less than twelve hours that he'd asked the question, but of two different people. Things were getting complicated far too quickly. For her part, the girl didn't react to the question and held his gaze. After a time she looked away from Corso into empty space. Or possibly at the books lined up on the floor.

"It doesn't matter," she answered at last. "You'd be better off wondering where the book has gone."

"What book?"

She looked at him again but didn't answer. He felt incredibly stupid.

"You know too much," he said to the girl. "Even more than me."

Again she shrugged. She was looking at Corso's watch.

"You don't have much time."

"I don't give a damn how much time I've got."

"That's up to you. But there's a flight from Lisbon to Paris in five hours' time, from Portela airport. We have just enough time to get there."

God. Corso shivered under his coat, horrified. She sounded like an efficient secretary, diary in hand, listing her boss's appointments for the day. He opened his mouth to complain. And so young with those disturbing eyes. Damned little witch.

"Why should I leave now?"

"Because the police might arrive."

"I don't have anything to hide."

The girl smiled indefinably, as if she had just heard a funny but very old joke. Then she put her rucksack on her back and waved goodbye.

"I'll bring you cigarettes in prison. Though they don't sell your brand here in Portugal."

She went out into the garden without a backward glance at the room. Corso was about to go after her and stop her. But then he saw something on the mantelpiece.

After an initial moment of disbelief he went over to it. Very slowly, so that things might return to normal. But when he reached the fireplace and leant on the mantelpiece he saw that the situation was irreversible. In the brief time lapse between the previous night and this morning, a minute period of time compared to their centuries-old contents, the antiquarian bibliographies had just gone out of date. There now remained not three known copies of *The Nine Doors*, but only two. The third, or what was left of it, was still smouldering among the embers.

He knelt, taking care not to touch anything. The binding, no doubt because of the leather covering, was less damaged than the pages inside. Two of the five raised bands on the spine were intact, and the pentacle was only half-burnt. But the pages had been almost entirely consumed by the flames. There only remained a few charred edges, with fragments of writing. Corso held his hand over the still warm remains.

He took out a cigarette and put it in his mouth, but didn't light it. He remembered how the logs had been piled up in the fireplace the night before. Judging by the ashes – the burnt logs were underneath those of the book, nobody had raked over the embers – the fire had burnt until it had gone out with the book on top. He remembered seeing enough logs piled there to last about four or five hours. And the still warm ashes indicated that the fire had gone out about the same number of hours ago. This added up to a total of eight to ten hours. Somebody must have lit it between ten o'clock and midnight, and then put the book into the fire. And whoever had done so hadn't hung around afterwards to rake over the embers.

Corso wrapped any remains that he could save from the fireplace in some old newspaper. The page fragments were stiff and brittle, so it took him some time. As he did so he noticed that the pages and cover had burnt separately. Whoever had thrown them into the fire had torn them apart so they should burn more efficiently.

Once he had retrieved all the pieces, he paused to glance round the room. The Virgil and the Agricola were where Fargas had put them. The *De re metalica* lined up with the others on the rug, and the Virgil on the table, just as Fargas had left it when, with the tone of a priest performing a ritual sacrifice, he had uttered the words, "I think I'll sell this one" . . .There was a sheet of paper between its pages. Corso opened the book. It was a handwritten receipt, unfinished.

Victor Coutinho Fargas, Identity Card No. 3554712, address: Quinta da Soledade, Carretera de Colares, km.4, Sintra.
Received with thanks the sum of 800,000 escudos for the work in my possession, "Virgil. Opera nunc recens accuratissime castigata . . . Venezia, Giunta, 1544". (Essling 61. Sander 7671). Folio, 10.587, 1c, 113 woodcuts. Complete and in good condition. The buyer . . .

There was no name or signature. The receipt had never been completed. Corso put the paper back and shut the book. Then he went to the room where he'd spent the previous afternoon, to make sure he'd left no trace, papers with his handwriting or anything like that. He also removed his cigarette butts from the ashtray, and put them in his pocket wrapped in another piece of newspaper. He looked around for a little while longer. His steps echoed through the empty house. No sign of the owner.

As he again passed the books lined up on the floor, he stopped, tempted. It was too easy – a couple of conveniently small Elzevirs attracted his attention. But Corso was a sensible man. It would only complicate matters if things became nasty. So, with a sigh, he bade farewell to the Fargas collection.

He went out through the French window into the garden to look for the girl, dragging his feet on the leaves on the ground. He found her sitting on a short flight of steps leading to the pond. He could hear the water trickling from the chubby angel's mouth onto the greenish surface, covered in floating plants. She was staring engrossed, at the pond. Only the sound of his steps interrupted her contemplation and made her turn her head.

Corso put his canvas bag on the bottom step and sat down next to her. Then he lit the cigarette he'd had in his mouth for some time. He inhaled, his head to one side, and threw away the match. Then he turned to the girl.

"Now tell me everything."

Still staring at the pond, she gently shook her head. Not abruptly, or unpleasantly. On the contrary, the movement of her head, her chin and the corners of her mouth was sweet and thoughtful, as if Corso's presence, the sad, neglected garden, the sound of the water, were all peculiarly moving. With her duffle coat and her rucksack still on her back she looked incredibly young. Almost defenceless. And very tired.

"We have to go," she said so low that Corso scarcely heard her. "To Paris."

"First tell me what's your link with Fargas. With all of this."

She shook her head again, in silence. Corso blew out some smoke. The air was so damp that it floated in front of him for a moment and condensed, before gradually disappearing. He looked at the girl.

"Do you know Rochefort?"

"Rochefort?"

"Or whatever his name is. He's dark, with a scar. He was lurking round here last night." As he spoke, Corso was aware of how silly it all was. He ended with an incredulous grimace, doubting his own memories. "I even spoke to him."

The girl again shook her head, still staring at the pond.

"I don't know him."

"What are you doing here, then?"

"I'm looking after you."

Corso stared at the tips of his shoes, rubbing his numb hands. The tinkle of the water in the pond was beginning to get on his nerves. He took a last drag on his cigarette. It was about to burn his lips and tasted bitter.

"You're mad, girl."

He threw away the cigarette end, staring at the smoke fading before his eyes.

"Completely mad," he added.

She still said nothing. After a moment, Corso brought out his flask of gin and took a long swig, without offering her any. Then he looked at her again.

"Where's Fargas?"

She took a moment to answer, still absorbed, lost. At last she indicated with her chin.

"Over there."

Corso followed the direction of her gaze. In the pond, beneath the thread of water from the mouth of the mutilated angel with empty eyes, he saw the vague outline of a man floating face down among the water lilies and dead leaves.

IX

The Bookseller in the Rue Bonaparte

*"My friend," Athos said gravely, "remember that the
dead are the only ones whom one does not risk meeting
again on this earth."*

A. Dumas: *The Three Musketeers*

Lucas Corso ordered a second gin and leant back comfortably in the
wicker chair. It was pleasant in the sun. He was sitting on the terrace of
the Café Atlas in the Rue de Buci, in the rectangle of light framing the
tables. It was one of the cold luminous mornings when the left bank of
the Seine crawls with people: disorientated Japanese, Anglo-Saxons in
trainers with metro tickets marking their place in a Hemingway novel,
ladies with baskets full of lettuces and baguettes, and slender gallery
owners who've had their noses fixed, heading for a café during their lunch
break. A very attractive young woman was looking in the window of a
luxury charcuterie, on the arm of a mature, well-dressed man who might
have been an antique dealer, or a scoundrel, or both. There was also a
Harley Davidson with all its shiny chrome, a bad-tempered fox terrier tied
up at the door of an expensive wine shop, a young man with plaits playing
the flute outside a boutique. And at the table next to Corso's, a couple
of very elegant Africans kissing on the mouth in a leisurely way, as if they
had all the time in the world and the arms race, AIDS, the hole in the
ozone layer were all trivial anecdotes on that sunny Parisian morning.

He saw her at the end of the Rue Mazarin, turning the corner
towards the café where he waited. With her boyish looks, her duffle
coat open over her jeans, her eyes like two points of light against her
suntan, visible from a distance in the crowd, in the street overflowing
with dazzling sunlight. Devilishly pretty, Flavio La Ponte would no
doubt have said, clearing his throat and turning his best side – where
his beard was slightly thicker and more curly – towards her. But Corso
wasn't La Ponte, so he didn't say or think anything. He just gave

a hostile glance at the waiter who was putting a glass of gin on his table – "*Pas d'Bols, m'sieu*" – and handed him the exact amount on the bill – "*Service compris*, young man" – before looking back at the girl approaching. As far as that stuff went, Nikon had left him a hole in the stomach the size of a clipful of bullets. That was enough. Nor was Corso very sure whether he had, now or ever, a better profile than anyone else. And he was damned if he cared anyway.

He took off his glasses and cleaned them with his handkerchief. The street became a series of vague outlines, of shapes with blurred faces. One stood out, and became clearer as it got nearer, although it never grew completely sharp: short hair, long legs, white tennis shoes acquired definition as he focused on her with difficulty and partial success when she reached him and sat down in the empty chair.

"I've found the shop. It's a couple of blocks away."

He put his glasses back on and looked at her without answering. They had travelled together from Lisbon. They left Sintra for the airport posthaste, as old Dumas would have described it. Twenty minutes before the plane's departure Corso phoned Amilcar Pinto to tell him that Victor Fargas's torment as a bookcollector was over and that the plan was cancelled. Pinto would still be paid the sum agreed, on account of his trouble. Apart from being surprised – the call had woken him – Pinto reacted fairly well. All he answered was, "I don't know what you're on about, Corso, you and I never saw each other last night in Sintra." Nevertheless, he promised he'd make some discreet enquiries into Victor Fargas's death. But only once he'd heard about it officially. For the time being he knew nothing about it, nor did he want to, and as for the autopsy, Corso could only hope that the forensic report would give the cause of death as suicide. Just in case, Pinto would pass the description of the individual with the scar on to the relevant departments as a possible suspect. He'd keep in touch by phone and he strongly urged Corso not to come back to Portugal for some time. "Oh, and one last thing," added Pinto as the departure of the Paris flight was being announced. Next time, before he thought of involving a friend in possible murders, Corso could go to hell. Corso hurriedly protested his innocence as the phone swallowed his last escudo. "Yeah, yeah," said Pinto, "that's what they all say."

The girl was waiting in the departure lounge. Corso, who was still dazed and not up to tying all the loose ends appearing all over the place, was surprised to see she had been extremely efficient and managed to get them two plane tickets without any difficulty. "I've just inherited some money," was her answer when, on seeing her pay for both tickets, he made some snide remarks about the limited funds he'd assumed her to have up till then. Afterwards, during the two-hour flight from Lisbon to Paris, she refused to answer any of his questions. All in good time, was all she would say, looking at Corso out of the corner of her eye, almost sneaking a glance at him, before she became absorbed in the trails of condensation left by the plane in the cold air. Then she fell asleep, or rather pretended to, resting her head on his shoulder. Corso could tell from her breathing that she was still awake. Feigning sleep was merely a convenient way of avoiding questions that she wasn't prepared, or allowed, to answer.

Anyone else in his situation would have insisted on answers, shaking her abruptly out of her pretence. But he was a well-trained, patient wolf, with the instincts and reflexes of a hunter. After all, the girl was his only real link in this unreal, novelesque, unjustifiable situation. In addition, by that stage in the script he had fully assumed the part of qualified reader and protagonist that someone, whoever was tying the knots on the back of the rug, on the underside of the plot, seemed to be offering him with a wink that could either be contemptuous, or conspiratorial, he couldn't tell which.

"Somebody's setting me up," Corso said out loud, nine thousand metres above the Bay of Biscay. Then he glanced at the girl out of the corner of his eye, waiting for a reaction, but she didn't move. Her breathing was slow, and either she really was asleep or she hadn't heard. Annoyed by her silence, he moved his shoulder away. Her head lolled for a moment. Then she sighed and made herself comfortable again, this time leaning against the window.

"Of course they are," she said at last sleepily and scornfully, her eyes still closed. "Any idiot could see that."

"What happened to Fargas?"

She didn't answer immediately. Out of the corner of his eye he could see her blinking, looking intently at the seat in front of her.

"You saw yourself," she said after a moment. "He drowned."

"Who did it?"

She turned her head slowly, from one side to the other, and ended up looking out. She slid her hand, slender and tanned with short unvarnished nails, slowly across the armrest. She stopped at the edge as if her fingers had come up against some invisible object.

"It doesn't matter."

Corso grimaced. He looked as if he were about to laugh, but didn't. He just showed his teeth.

"It does to me. It matters a lot."

The girl shrugged. They weren't concerned about the same things, she seemed to imply. Or at least didn't have the same priorities.

Corso persisted.

"What's your part in all this?"

"I've already told you. To take care of you."

She turned towards him and looked at him as firmly as she had been evasive a moment ago. She slid her hand over the armrest again, as if trying to bridge the distance between her and Corso. She was altogether too near, so Corso moved away instinctively, embarrassed and slightly disconcerted. In the pit of his stomach, in Nikon's wake, obscure, disturbing emotions were stirring. With the emptiness the pain was gently returning. In the girl's eyes, silent and without memory, Corso could see the reflection of ghosts from the past and he could feel them brush his skin.

"Who sent you?"

She lowered her eyelashes over her luminous irises, and it was as if she had turned a page. There was nothing there any more, just emptiness. The girl wrinkled her nose, irritated.

"You're boring me, Corso."

She turned to the window and looked at the view. The great expanse of blue flecked with tiny white threads seemed to be split in the distance by a yellow and ochre line. Land ahoy. France. Next stop, Paris. Or next chapter. To be continued in next week's issue. Ending, sword aloft, a cliffhanger typical of all romantic serials. He thought of the Quinta da Soledade, the water trickling from the fountain, Fargas's body among the water lilies and dead leaves in the pond. He flushed and shifted uncomfortably in his seat. With good reason, he felt like a man on the run. Absurd. Rather than fleeing by choice he was being forced to.

He looked at the girl and then tried to see his own situation with the necessary objectivity. Maybe he wasn't running away but towards something instead. Or maybe the mystery he was trying to escape was hidden in his own suitcase. 'The Anjou Wine'. *The Nine Doors*. Irene Adler. The stewardess, with a trained, fatuous smile, said something as she passed. Corso looked at her without seeing her, absorbed in his own thoughts. If only he knew whether the end of the story was already written, or whether he himself was writing it as he went along, chapter by chapter.

He didn't say another word to the girl that day. When they arrived at Orly he ignored her, although he was aware of her walking behind him along the airport corridors. At passport control, after showing his identity card, he turned round to see what kind of document she had, but he couldn't see clearly. All he saw was a passport bound in black leather without any markings. It must be European because she had gone through the gate for EC citizens. Outside, while Corso was climbing into a taxi, giving his usual address, the Louvre Concorde, she slipped into the seat next to him. They drove to the hotel in silence. There she got out of the taxi first and let him pay the fare. The taxi-driver didn't have any change so Corso was slightly delayed. By the time he at last crossed the lobby she had already checked in and was walking away behind a porter carrying her rucksack. She waved at him before she entered the elevator.

"It's a very nice shop. Replinger, Booksellers, it says. Autographs and historical documents. And it's open."

She indicated a sign to the waiter that she didn't want to order and leant slightly towards Corso across the table, in the café on the Rue de Buci. Like a mirror, the liquid transparency of her eyes reflected the street scenes which were themselves reflections in the café window.

"We could go there now."

They had met again at breakfast, as Corso was reading the papers at one of the windows overlooking the Place du Palais Royal. She said good morning and sat down at the table. She devoured toast and croissants with a healthy appetite. Then she looked at Corso. She had a rim of milky coffee on her upper lip, like a little girl.

"Where do we start?"

So now there they were, two blocks from Achille Replinger's book-shop. The girl had offered to go and find it while Corso drank his first gin of the day. He had a feeling it wouldn't be the last.

"We could go there now," she said again.

Corso still hesitated. He'd seen her tanned skin in his dreams. He was holding her hand, crossing a deserted plain in the shadow of dusk. Columns of smoke rose on the horizon, volcanoes about to erupt.

Occasionally they passed a soldier with a grave face, his armour covered in dust, who stared at them in silence, distant and cold like the sullen Trojans of Hades. The plain was darkening on the horizon and the columns of smoke grew thicker. The impassive, ghostly faces of the dead warriors contained a warning. Corso wanted to get away. He pulled the girl along by the hand anxious not to leave her behind, but the air was becoming thick and hot, stifling, dark. Their flight ended in an interminable fall, an agony in slow motion. The darkness burnt like an oven. The only link with the outside was Corso's hand, holding on to hers in an effort to go on. The last thing he felt was her hand, its grip fading, finally turn to ash. And in front of him, in the darkness closing in on the burning plain and on his mind, white marks, traces as fleeting as lightning, picked out the ghostly contour of a skull. It wasn't pleasant to recall. To try to remove the taste of ash from his mouth and erase these horrors, Corso finished his glass of gin and looked at the girl. She was watching him, a disciplined collaborator waiting calmly for instructions. Serene, she simply accepted her strange part in the story. Her loyal expression was inexplicable and disconcerting.

She stood up at the same time as Corso. He put the canvas bag over his shoulder and they made their way slowly towards the river. The girl walked along the inside of the pavement and occasionally stopped in front of a shop window, calling his attention to a picture, an engraving, a book. She looked at everything with wide eyes and intense curiosity, seeming slightly nostalgic as she smiled thoughtfully. She seemed to be searching for traces of herself in those old things. As if, in some corner of her memory, she shared a common past with the few survivors washed up by the tide after each of history's inexorable shipwrecks.

There were two bookshops facing each other on either side of the street. Achille Replinger's had a very old, elegant shopfront, of varnished wood, with a sign saying "*Livres anciens, autographes et documents historiques*". Corso told the girl to wait outside and she didn't object. As he headed towards the door he looked in the window and saw her reflection over his shoulder. She was standing on the other side of the road, watching him.

A bell rang as he pushed the door. There was an oak table, shelves full of old books, stands with folders of prints and a dozen old wooden filing cabinets. These had letters in alphabetical order, carefully written in brass slots. On the wall there was a framed autograph with the caption, "Fragment of *Tartuffe*. Molière". Also three good prints, Victor Hugo and Flaubert, and Dumas in the centre.

Achille Replinger was standing by the table. He was thick-set with a reddish complexion. Porthos with a bushy grey moustache and thick double chin overlapping the collar of his shirt worn with a knitted tie. He was expensively but carelessly dressed. His jacket was straining to contain his girth and his flannel trousers were creased and sagging.

"Corso . . . Lucas Corso," he said holding Boris Balkan's letter of introduction in his thick, strong fingers and frowning. "Yes, he called me the other day. Something about Dumas."

Corso put his bag on the table and took out the folder with the fifteen manuscript pages of 'The Anjou Wine'. The bookseller spread them out in front of him, arching his brow.

"Interesting," he said quietly. "Very interesting."

He wheezed as he spoke, breathing with difficulty like an asthmatic. He took his glasses from one of his jacket pockets and put them on after a brief glance at his visitor. Then he leant over the pages. When he looked up he was smiling ecstatically.

"Extraordinary," he said, "I'll buy it from you here and now."

"It's not for sale."

Replinger seemed surprised. He pursed his lips, nearly pouting.

"I thought . . ."

"I just need an expert opinion. You'll be paid for your time, of course."

Achille Replinger shook his head. He didn't care about the money. He looked confused and a couple of times he stopped to look at Corso mistrustfully over his glasses. Then he leant over the manuscript again.

"A pity," he said at last, and cast a curious glance at Corso. He looked as if he was wondering how on earth it had fallen into his hands. "How did you get hold of it?"

"I inherited it from an old aunt. Have you ever seen it before?"

Still suspicious, Replinger looked over Corso's shoulder, through the window at the street, as if someone out there might be able to give him some information about his visitor. Or maybe he was considering how to answer Corso's question. He pulled at his moustache, as if it were false and he was checking it was still in place, and smiled evasively.

"Here in the *quartier* you can never be sure if you've seen something before . . . This has always been a good area for people dealing in books and prints. People come here to buy and sell, and everything has passed several times through the same hands." He paused to catch his breath and then looked at Corso uneasily. "I don't think so . . . No, I've never seen this manuscript before," he said. He looked out at the street again, flushed. "I'd be sure if I had."

"Do I take it that it's authentic?" asked Corso.

"Well . . . In fact, yes." Replinger wheezed as he stroked the blue pages. He seemed to be trying to stop himself touching them. Finally he held one up between his thumb and forefinger. "Semi-rounded, medium weight handwriting, no annotations or erasures . . . Almost no punctuation marks, and unexpected capital letters. This is definitely Dumas at his peak, towards the middle of his life, when he wrote *The Musketeers* . . ." He'd become more animated as he spoke. Now he suddenly fell silent and lifted a finger. Corso could see him smiling beneath his moustache. He seemed to have reached a decision. "Wait just one moment."

He went over to one of the filing cabinets marked "D" and took out some buff-coloured folders.

"All of this is by Alexandre Dumas père. The handwriting is identical."

There were about a dozen documents, some unsigned or else initialled A.D. Some had the full signature. Most of them were short notes to publishers, letters to friends, or invitations.

"This is one of his American autographs," explained Replinger. "Lincoln requested one, and Dumas sent him ten dollars and a hundred autographs. They were sold in Pittsburgh for charity . . ." He showed Corso all the documents with a restrained but obvious professional pride. "Look at this one. An invitation to dine with him on Montecristo, at the house he had built in Port-Marly. Sometimes he only signed his initials, at others he used pseudonyms. But not all the autographs that are in circulation are authentic. At the newspaper *The Musketeer*, which he owned, there was a man called Viellot who could imitate his handwriting and signature. And during the last three years of his life, Dumas's hands trembled so much he had to dictate his work."

"Why blue paper?"

"He would have it sent from Lille. It was made for him specially by a printer who was a great admirer. He almost always used this colour, especially for the novels. Occasionally he used pale pink for his articles, or yellow for poetry. He used several different pens, according to what kind of thing he was writing. And he couldn't stand blue ink."

Corso pointed to the four white pages of the manuscript, with notes and corrections.

"What about these?"

Replinger frowned.

"Maquet. His collaborator Auguste Maquet. These are corrections made by Dumas to the original text." He stroked his moustache. Then he leant over and read aloud in a theatrical voice. "'Horrifying! Horrifying!' murmured Athos, as Porthos shattered the bottles and Aramis gave somewhat belated orders to send for a confessor . . .'" Replinger broke off with a sigh. He nodded, satisfied, and then showed Corso the page. "Look: all Maquet wrote was: 'And he expired before d'Artagnan's terrified companions.' Dumas crossed out that line and added others above it, fleshing out the passage with more dialogue."

"What can you tell me about Maquet?"

Replinger shrugged his powerful shoulders, hesitating.

"Not a great deal." Once again he sounded evasive. "He was ten years younger than Dumas. A mutual friend, Gérard de Nerval, recommended him. He wrote historical novels without success. He showed Dumas the original version of one, *Buvat the Good, or the Conspiracy of Cellamare*. Dumas turned the story into *The Chevalier d'Harmental* and had it published under his name. In return Maquet was paid 1,200 francs."

"Can you tell from the handwriting and the style of writing when 'The Anjou Wine' was written?"

"Of course I can. It's similar to other documents from 1844, the year of *The Three Musketeers* . . . These white and blue pages fit in with his way of working. Dumas and his associate would piece the story together. From Courtilz's *D'Artagnan* they took the names of their heroes, the journey to Paris, the intrigue with Milady, and the character of the innkeeper's wife – Dumas created Madame Bonacieux, giving her the features of his mistress, Belle Krebsamer. Constance's kidnap came from the *Memoirs* of De la Porte, a man in the confidence of Anne of Austria. And they obtained the famous story of the diamond tags from La Rochefoucauld and from a book by Roederer, *Political and Romantic Intrigues from the Court of France*. At that time, in addition to *The Three Musketeers*, they were also writing *Queen Margot* and *The Chevalier de la Maison Rouge*."

Replinger paused again for breath. He was becoming more and more flushed and animated as he spoke. He mentioned the last few titles in a rush, stumbling slightly over the words. He was afraid of boring Corso but, at the same time, he wanted to give him all the information he could.

"There's an amusing anecdote about *The Chevalier de la Maison Rouge*," he went on once he'd caught his breath. "When the serial was announced with its original title, *The Knight of Rougeville*, Dumas received a letter of complaint from a marquis of the same name. This made him change the title, but soon afterwards he received another letter. 'My dear Sir," wrote the marquis, "Please give your novel whatever title you wish. I am the last of my family and am going to blow my brains out in an hour." And the Marquis de Rougeville did indeed commit suicide, over some woman."

He gasped for air again. Large and pink-cheeked, he smiled almost apologetically. He leant one of his strong hands on the table next to the blue pages. He looked like an exhausted giant, thought Corso. Porthos in the cave at Locmaria.

"Boris Balkan didn't do you justice. You're an expert on Dumas. I'm not surprised you're friends."

"We respect each other. But I'm only doing my job." Replinger looked down, slightly embarrassed. "I'm a conscientious Frenchman who works with annotated books and documents and handwritten dedications. Always by nineteenth-century French authors. I couldn't give a valuation of the things that come to me if I wasn't sure who they were written by, and how. Do you understand?"

"Perfectly," answered Corso. "It's the difference between a professional, and a vulgar salesman."

Replinger looked at him with gratitude.

"You're in the profession. It's very obvious."

"Yes," Corso grimaced. "The oldest profession."

Replinger's laugh ended in another asthmatic wheeze. Corso made the most of the pause to direct the conversation towards Maquet again.

"Tell me how they did it," he said.

"Their technique was complicated." Replinger gestured towards the chairs and table, as if the scene had taken place there. "Dumas drew up a plan for each novel and discussed it with his collaborator, who then did the research and made an outline of the story, or a first draft. These were the white pages. Then Dumas would rewrite it on the blue paper. He worked in his shirt sleeves, and only in the morning or at night, almost never in the afternoon. He didn't drink coffee or spirits, only seltzer water. Also he hardly smoked. He wrote page after page under pressure from his publishers who always demanded more. Maquet sent him the material in bulk by post, and Dumas would complain about the delays." He took a sheet from the folder and put it on the table in front of Corso. "Here's proof, in one of the notes they exchanged during the writing of *Queen Margot*. As you can see, Dumas was complaining slightly. 'All is going perfectly, despite the six or seven pages of politics we'll have to endure so as to revive interest . . . If we're not going faster, dear friend, it is your fault. I've been hard at work since nine o'clock yesterday.'" He paused to take a breath and pointed at 'The Anjou Wine'. "These four pages in Maquet's handwriting with annotations by Dumas were probably only received by Dumas moments before *Le Siècle* went to press. So he had to make do with rewriting a few of them and hurriedly correcting some of the other pages on the original itself."

He put the papers back in their folders and returned them to the filing cabinet, under "D". Corso had time to cast a final glance at Dumas's note demanding more pages from his collaborator. In addition to the handwriting, which was similar in every way, the paper was identical – blue with faint squaring – to that of the *Anjou Wine* manuscript. One folio cut in two – the bottom part was more uneven than the others. Maybe all the pages had been part of the same ream lying on the novelist's desk.

"Who really wrote *The Three Musketeers*?"

Replinger, busy shutting the filing cabinet, took some time to answer.

"I can't give you a definite answer. Maquet was a resourceful man, he was well-versed in history, he had read a lot . . . But he didn't have the master's touch."

"They fell out with each other in the end, didn't they?"

"Yes. A pity. Did you know they travelled to Spain together at the time of Isabel II's wedding? Dumas even published a serial, *From Madrid to Cadiz*, in the form of letters. As for Maquet, he later went to court to demand that he should be declared the author of eighteen of Dumas's novels, but the judges ruled that his work had only been preparatory. Today he is considered a mediocre writer, who made the most of Dumas's fame to make money. Although there are some who believe he was exploited – the great man's ghost writer . . ."

"What do you think?"

Replinger glanced furtively at Dumas's portrait above the door.

"I've already told you that I'm not an expert like my friend Mr Balkan . . . Just a trader, a bookseller." He seemed to reflect, weighing up where his professional opinion ended and his personal taste began. "But I'd like to draw your attention to something. In France between 1870 and 1894 three million books and eight million serials were sold with the name of Alexandre Dumas on the title page. Novels written before, during and after his collaboration with Maquet. I think that has some significance."

"Fame in his lifetime, at least," said Corso.

"Definitely. For half a century he was the voice of Europe. Boats were sent over from the Americas for the sole purpose of bringing back consignments of his novels. They were read just as much in Cairo, Moscow, Istanbul or Chandernagore. Dumas lived life to the full, enjoying all his pleasures and his fame. He lived and enjoyed himself, stood on the barricades, fought in duels, was taken to court, chartered boats, paid pensions out of his own pocket, loved, ate, drank, earned ten million and squandered twenty, and died gently in his sleep like a child . . ." Replinger pointed at the corrections to Maquet's pages. "It could be called many things: talent, genius . . . But whatever it was, he didn't improvise, or steal from others." He thumped his chest like Porthos. "It's something you have in here. No other writer has ever known such glory in his lifetime. Dumas rose from nothing to have it all. As if he'd made a pact with God."

"Yes," said Corso. "Or with the Devil."

He crossed the road to the other bookshop. Outside, under an awning, stacks of books were piled up on trestle tables. The girl was still there, rummaging about amongst the books and bunches of old pictures and postcards. She was standing against the light. The sun was on her shoulders, turning the hair on the back of her head and her temples golden. She didn't stop what she was doing when he arrived.

"Which one would you choose?" she asked. She was hesitating between a sepia postcard of Tristan and Isolde embracing, and another of Daumier's *The Picture Hunter*. Undecided, she held them both out in front of her.

"Take both of them," suggested Corso. Out of the corner of his eye he caught sight of a man who had stopped at the stall and was about to pick up a thick bundle of cards held together by a rubber band. Corso shot out his arm with the reflex of a hunter, almost grabbing the packet from the man's hand. The man left, muttering. Corso looked through the cards and chose several with a Napoleonic theme: Empress Marie-Louise, the Bonaparte family, the death of the Emperor, and his final victory: a Polish lancer and two hussars on horseback in front of Reims cathedral, during the French campaign of 1814, waving flags snatched from the enemy. After hesitating a moment he added one of Marshal Ney in dress uniform and another of an elderly Wellington posing for posterity. Lucky old devil.

The girl's long tanned hands moved deftly amongst the cards and yellowed printed paper. She chose a few more postcards: Robespierre and Saint-Just, and an elegant portrait of Richelieu in his cardinal's habit and wearing the insignia of the Order of the Holy Spirit.

"How appropriate," remarked Corso acidly.

She didn't answer. She headed towards a pile of books and the sun slid across her shoulders, enveloping Corso in a golden haze. Dazzled, he closed his eyes. When he opened them again the girl was showing him a thick volume in quarto that was over to one side.

"What do you think?"

He glanced at it: *The Three Musketeers*, with the original illustrations by Leloir, bound in cloth and leather, in good condition. When he looked at her again he saw that she had a lopsided smile and was waiting, looking at him intently.

"Nice edition," was all he said. "Are you intending to read it?"

"Of course. Don't tell me the ending."

Corso laughed quietly, half-heartedly.

"As if I could tell you the ending," he said, sorting the bundles of cards.

"I've got a present for you," said the girl.

They were walking along the Left Bank, past the stalls of the *bouquinistes* with their prints hanging up in plastic and Cellophane covers and second-hand books lined up along the parapet. A *bateau-mouche* was heading slowly up-river, straining under the weight of what Corso estimated must have been about five thousand Japanese, and as many Sony camcorders. Across the street, behind exclusive shop windows covered in Visa and American Express stickers, snooty antique dealers scanned the horizon for a Kuwaiti, a black marketeer or an African minister of state to whom they might sell Eugénie Grandet's Sèvres porcelain bidet. Their sales patter delivered in the most proper accent, of course.

"I don't like presents," muttered Corso sullenly. "Some guys once accepted a wooden horse. Handcrafted by the Achaeans, it said on the label. The fools."

"Weren't there any dissenters?"

"One, with his sons. But some beasts came out of the sea, and made a lovely sculpture out of them. Hellenistic, I seem to remember. Rhodes school. In those days the gods were too biased."

"They always have been." The girl was staring at the muddy river as if it were sweeping away her memories. Corso saw her smile, thoughtfully, absently. "I never knew an impartial god. Or devil." She turned to him suddenly – her earlier thoughts seemed to have been washed downstream. "Do you believe in the Devil, Corso?"

He looked at her intently, but the river had also swept away the images that had filled her eyes seconds before. All he could see there now was liquid green, and light.

"I believe in stupidity and ignorance." He smiled wearily at the girl. "And I think that the best cut of all is the one you get here. See?" He pointed at his groin. "In the femoral artery. While you're in somebody's arms."

"What are you so afraid of, Corso? That I'll put my arms around you? That the sky'll fall in on you?"

"I'm scared of wooden horses, cheap gin and pretty girls. Especially when they give me presents. And when they go by the name of the woman who defeated Sherlock Holmes."

They had continued walking and were now on the wooden boards of the Pont des Arts. The girl stopped and leaned on the metal rail, by a street artist selling tiny watercolours.

"I like this bridge," she said. "No cars. Only lovers, and old ladies in hats. People with nothing to do. This bridge has absolutely no common sense."

Corso said nothing. He was watching the barges, masts down, pass between the pillars supporting the iron structure. Nikon's steps had once echoed alongside his on that bridge. He remembered that she too stopped at a stall selling watercolours. Maybe it was the same one. She wrinkled up her nose because her light meter couldn't deal with the dazzling sunshine slanting across the spire and towers of Notre-Dame. They bought *foie gras* and a bottle of Burgundy. Later they ate it for dinner in their hotel room, sitting on their bed watching one of those wordy discussions on TV with huge studio audiences that the French like so much. Earlier, on the bridge, Nikon had taken a photo of him without him knowing. She confessed this, her mouth full of bread and *foie gras*, her lips moistened with Burgundy, as she stroked his side with her bare foot. I know you hate it, Lucas Corso, you'll just have to put up with it. I got you in profile on the bridge watching the barges pass underneath, you almost look handsome this time, you bastard. Nikon was Ashkenazi, with large eyes. Her father had been number 77,843 in Treblinka, saved by the bell in the last round. If Israeli soldiers ever appeared on TV, invading places in huge tanks, she jumped off the bed, naked, and kissed the screen, her eyes wet with tears, whispering "Shalom, Shalom" in a caressing tone. The same tone she used when she called Corso by his first name, until the day she stopped. Nikon. He never got to see the photo of him leaning on the Pont des Arts, watching the barges pass under the arches. In profile, almost looking handsome, you bastard.

When he looked up Nikon had gone. Another girl was by his side. Tall, with tanned skin, short boyish haircut and eyes the colour of freshly washed grapes, almost colourless. For a second, he blinked, confused, until everything fell back into place. The present cut a line cleanly like a scalpel. Corso, in profile, in black and white (Nikon always worked in black and white) fluttered down into the river and was swept downstream with the dead leaves and the rubbish discharged by the barges and the drains. Now, the girl who wasn't Nikon was holding a small, leather-bound book. She was holding it out to him.

"I hope you like it."

The Devil in Love by Jacques Cazotte, the 1878 edition. When he opened it, Corso recognized the prints from the first edition in a facsimile appendix: Alvaro in the magic circle before the Devil, who asks, *"Che vuoi?"*; Biondetta untangling her hair with her fingers; the handsome pageboy sitting at the harpsichord . . . He chose a page at random:

. . . man emerged from a handful of earth and water. Why should a woman not be made of dew, earthly vapours and rays of light, of the condensed residues of a rainbow? Where does the possible lie? And where the impossible?

He closed the book and looked up. His eyes met the smiling eyes of the girl. Below, in the water, the sun sparkled in the wake of a boat, and lights moved over her skin like the reflections from the facets of a diamond.

" 'Residues of a rainbow,'" quoted Corso. "What do you know of any of that?"

The girl ran her hand through her hair and turned her face to the sun, closing her eyes against the glare. Everything about her was light: the reflection of the river, the brightness of the morning, the two green slits between her dark eyelashes.

"I know what I was told a long time ago. The rainbow is the bridge between heaven and earth. It will shatter at the end of the world, once the Devil has crossed it on horseback."

"Not bad. Did your grandmother tell you that?"

She shook her head. She looked at Corso again, absorbed and serious.

"I heard it told to a friend, Bileto." As she said his name she stopped a moment and frowned tenderly, like a little girl revealing a secret. "He likes horses and wine, and he's the most optimistic person I know. He's still hoping to get back to Heaven."

They crossed to the other side of the bridge. Strangely, Corso felt that the gargoyles of Notre-Dame were watching him from a distance. They were forgeries, of course, like so many other things. They, and their infernal grimaces, horns and goatee beards, hadn't been there when honest master builders had looked up, sweaty and proud, and drunk a glass of *eau de vie*. Or when Quasimodo brooded in the bell towers over his unrequited love for the gypsy Esmeralda. But since Charles Laughton, as the hideous hunchback who resembled them, and Gina Lollobrigida in the remake – Technicolor, as Nikon would have specified – was executed in their shadow, it was impossible to think of Notre-Dame without the sinister neo-medieval sentinels. Corso imagined the bird's eye view: the Pont Neuf, and beyond it, narrow and dark in the luminous morning, the Pont des Arts over the grey-green band of river, with two tiny figures moving imperceptibly towards the Right Bank. Bridges and rainbows with black Caronte barges gliding slowly beneath the pillars and vaults of stone. The world is full of banks, and rivers running between them, of men and women crossing bridges and fords, unaware of the consequences, not looking back or beneath their feet, and with no loose change for the boatman.

They emerged opposite the Louvre and stopped at traffic lights before crossing. Corso shifted the strap of his canvas bag on his shoulder and glanced absently to right and left. The traffic was heavy, and he happened to notice one of the passing cars. He froze, turned to stone like one of the gargoyles on the cathedral.

"What's the matter?" asked the girl when the lights turned green and she saw that Corso wasn't moving. "You look like you've seen a ghost!"

He had. Not just one but two. They were in the back of a taxi already moving off in the distance, engaged in animated conversation, and they didn't notice Corso. The woman was blonde and very attractive. He recognized her immediately despite her hat and the veil covering her eyes. Liana Taillefer. Next to her, his arm round her shoulders, showing his best side and stroking his curly beard vainly, was Flavio La Ponte.

X

Number Three

They suspected that he had no heart.
R. Sabatini: *Scaramouche*

Corso had a rare knack: he could make a loyal ally of a stranger instantly, in return for a tip or even a smile. As we've seen, there was something about him – the half-calculated clumsiness, his customary, friendly rabbit expression, his air of absent-minded helplessness which was nothing of the sort – that won people over. This had happened to some of us. And it had happened to Gruber, the concierge of the Louvre Concorde, with whom Corso had had dealings for fifteen years. Gruber was dry and imperturbable, with a crew-cut and a permanent poker player's expression round the corners of his mouth. During the retreat of 1944, when he was sixteen years old, a Croat volunteer in the *Horst Wessel* 18th Panzergrenadier division, a Russian bullet had hit him in the spine. It left him with an Iron Cross second class and three fused vertebrae for life. This was why he was so stiff and upright behind the reception desk, as if he was wearing a steel corset.

"I need a favour, Gruber."

"Yes, sir."

He almost clicked his heels as he stood to attention. His impeccable burgundy jacket with the gold keys on the lapels gave the old exile a military air, very much to the taste of the Central Europeans who stayed at the hotel. After the fall of communism and the fragmenting of the Slav hordes, they arrived in Paris to glance at the Champs-Elysées out of the corners of their eyes and dream of a Fourth Reich.

"La Ponte, Flavio. Spanish nationality. Also Herrero, Liana, though she may be going by the name of Taillefer or De Taillefer. I want to know if they're at a hotel in the city."

He wrote the names down on a card and handed it to Gruber,

together with five hundred francs. Corso always gave tips or bribes with a shrug of the shoulders, as if to say, "I'll do the same for you sometime." It made it a friendly, almost conspiratorial, exchange and it was difficult to tell who was doing who a favour. Gruber, who murmured a polite *"Merci, m'sieu"* to Spaniards on package tours, Italians in loud ties and Americans with airline bags and baseball caps for a miserable ten-franc tip, took Corso's banknote without a word or even a nod. He just slipped it in his pocket with an elegant, semi-circular movement of his hand and a croupier's impassive gravity, reserved for the few, like Corso, who still knew how to play the game. Gruber had learnt the job in the days when a guest just had to raise an eyebrow for hotel employees to come running. The dear old Europe of international hotels was now reduced to a few cognoscenti.

"Are the lady and gentleman staying together?"

"I don't know." Corso frowned. He pictured La Ponte emerging from the bathroom in an embroidered dressing-gown and Taillefer's widow lying on the bed in a silk nightdress. "I'd like to know that too."

Gruber bowed imperceptibly.

"It'll take a few hours, Mr Corso."

"I know." He glanced down the corridor leading from the lobby to the dining-room. The girl was there, her duffle coat under her arm and her hands in her pockets, staring at a display of perfumes and silk scarves. "What about her?"

The concierge took a card from under the desk.

"Irene Adler," he read. "British passport, issued two months ago. Nineteen years old. Address: 223b Baker Street, London."

"Don't joke with me, Gruber."

"I'd never take such a liberty, Mr Corso. That's what it says here."

There was the hint, the faintest suggestion of a smile on the face of the old SS Waffen. Corso had only seen him smile once: the day the Berlin Wall came down. He observed Gruber's white crew-cut, stiff neck, hands arranged symmetrically, his wrists resting exactly on the edge of the desk. Old Europe, or what was left of it. He was too old to go back home and risk finding that nothing was as he remembered; neither the bell tower in Zagreb, nor the warm, blonde peasant girls smelling of fresh bread, nor the green plains with rivers and bridges that he had seen blown up twice: once in his youth, in the retreat from Tito's guerrillas, and then on TV, autumn '91, in the faces of the Serbian *Chetniks*. Corso could picture him in his room standing in front of a dusty portrait of the Emperor Franz Joseph, taking off the maroon jacket with little golden keys on the lapels as if it were his Austro-Hungarian army jacket. He probably played the Radetsky March on the record-player, drank a toast with a glass of Montenegrin liqueur and masturbated to videos of the Empress Sissy.

The girl was no longer staring at the display but was now looking at Corso. 223b Baker Street, he repeated to himself and he felt the urge to laugh uncontrollably. He wouldn't have been in the least surprised had a bellboy appeared with an invitation from Milady de Winter to take tea at If Castle or at the palace in Ruritania with Richelieu, Professor Moriarty and Rupert of Hentzau. Since this was a literary matter, it would have seemed the most natural thing in the world.

He asked for a phone book and looked up Baroness Ungern's number. Then, ignoring the girl's stare, he went to the phone booth in the lobby and made an appointment for the following day. He also rang Varo Borja's number in Toledo but there was no answer.

He was watching the television with the sound down: a film with Gregory Peck surrounded by seals, a fight in a hotel ballroom, two schooners side by side, with the waves crashing against the bow, heading north in full sail, towards true freedom which only begins ten miles away from the nearest coast. On Corso's side of the TV screen, a bottle of Bols with the level below the Plimsoll line stood guard on the bedside table, like the old, alcoholic grenadier on the eve of battle, between *The Nine Doors* and the folder with the Dumas manuscript.

Lucas Corso took off his glasses and rubbed his eyes, red from cigarette smoke and gin. On the bed, with the precision of an archaeologist, he had laid out the fragments of Book Number Two rescued from the fireplace in Victor Fargas's house. There wasn't much left: the boards, protected by the covering of leather, were less damaged than the rest, of which there remained no more than the charred margins and a few barely legible paragraphs. He picked up one of the pieces, made yellow and brittle by the fire. '. . . *si non obig.nem me. ips.s fecere, f.r q.qe die, tib. do vitam m.m sicut t.m . . .*'. This came from one of the bottom corners. He examined it for a few moments and then searched for the same page in Book Number One. It was page 89, and the two paragraphs were identical. He did the same with as many paragraphs as he could and managed to identify sixteen. It was impossible to tell where another twenty-two of the fragments came from as they were too small or too damaged. Eleven more fragments were blank and he managed to identify only one, thanks to a crooked "7" which was the third and only legible digit in the page number, page 107.

The cigarette had burnt right down and was burning his lips. He stubbed it out in the ashtray. Then he grabbed the Bols and took a swig directly from the bottle. He was wearing an old cotton khaki shirt with big pockets, sleeves rolled up, and a crumpled tie. On the TV the man from Boston standing by the helm was embracing a Russian princess. They were both moving their lips soundlessly, happy and in love under a Technicolor sky. The only noise in the room was the gentle rattling of the window-panes caused by the traffic rumbling by, two floors below, heading for the Louvre.

Nikon loved that kind of thing. Corso remembered how she would be moved, like a sentimental little girl, by a couple kissing against a cloudy sky, to the sound of violins and "The End" across the screen. Sometimes, munching on crisps at the cinema or in front of the TV, she'd lean on Corso's shoulder and cry quietly, gently for a long time, her eyes fixed on the screen. It might be Paul Henreid singing the Marseillaise in Rick's café; Rutger Hauer dying, head bowed, in the final shots of *Blade Runner*; John Wayne and Maureen O'Hara in front of the fireplace in Innisfree; Custer and Arthur Kennedy on the eve of Little Big Horn; O'Toole as Jim deceived by gentleman Brown; Henry Fonda on his way to the OK Corral; or Marcello Mastroianni up to his waist in a pond at a spa retrieving a woman's hat, waving to right and left, elegant, imperturbable, and in love with a pair of black eyes. Nikon was happy crying over it all and she was proud of her tears. It's because I'm alive, she'd say afterwards, laughing, her eyes still wet. Because I'm part of the rest of the world and I'm glad I am. Films are for everyone, collective, generous, with children cheering when the Cavalry arrives. They're even better on TV: two of you can watch and comment. But your books are selfish. Solitary. Some of them can't even be read, they fall to bits if you open them. Somebody who's only interested in books doesn't need anyone else, and that frightens me. Nikon was eating the last crisp and watching him intently, her lips parted, searching his face for signs of an illness that would soon manifest itself. Sometimes you frighten me.

Happy endings. Corso pressed a button on the remote control and the image disappeared from the screen. Now he was in Paris and Nikon was photographing children with tragic eyes somewhere in Africa, or in the Balkans. Once, in a bar, he thought he caught sight of her on the news, in the chaotic shots of a bombardment. She was surrounded by terrified fleeing refugees, her hair in a plait, cameras round her neck and one at her eye, backed by smoke and flames. Nikon. Of all the universal lies she accepted unquestioningly, the happy ending was the most absurd. They lived happily ever after, and the ending seemed indisputable, definitive. No questions asked about how long does love, or happiness, last, in that "forever" that could be divided into lifetimes, years, months. Even days. Until the very end, their inevitable end, Nikon refused to accept that the hero might have drowned two weeks later when his boat struck a reef in the Southern Hebrides. Or that the heroine was run over by a car three months later. Or that maybe everything turned out differently, in a thousand different ways: one of them had an affair, one of them became bitter or bored, one of them wanted to back out. Maybe nights full of tears, silence, loneliness followed that screen kiss. Maybe cancer killed him before he was forty. Maybe she lived on and died in an old people's home aged ninety. Maybe the handsome officer turned into a pathetic ruin, his wounds become hideous scars and his glorious battles forgotten by all. And maybe, old and defenceless, they suffered ordeals without the strength to fight or defend themselves, tossed this way and that by the storms of life, by stupidity, by cruelty, by the miserable human condition.

Sometimes you frighten me, Lucas Corso.

Five minutes before eleven that night he solved the mystery of the fire at Victor Fargas's house. Although it still didn't make things any clearer. He looked at his watch as he stretched and yawned. Then, after glancing again at the fragments spread out on the bedcover, he caught sight of his reflection in the mirror next to the old postcard of the hussars outside Reims Cathedral stuck into the wooden frame. He was dishevelled, unshaven, and his glasses sat crookedly on his nose. He started to laugh quietly. One of his slightly bad-tempered, wolf-like, twisted laughs reserved for special occasions. And this was one. All the fragments of *The Nine Doors* that he had managed to identify came from pages with text. No trace remained of the nine engravings and the frontispiece on the title page. There were two possibilities: either they had burnt in the fire, or, the more likely option hinted at by the torn-off cover, somebody had taken them before throwing the rest of the book into the flames. Whoever it was must have thought himself, or herself, very clever. Or themselves. Maybe, after the unexpected sighting of La Ponte and Liana Taillefer at the traffic lights, he should get used to the third person plural. The question was knowing whether the clues Corso was following were his opponent's mistakes, or tricks. At any rate they were very elaborate.

Talking of tricks. The door bell rang and Corso opened it to find the girl standing there. He had just had enough time to hide Book Number One and the Dumas manuscript carefully under the cover. She was barefoot and wearing her usual jeans and white T-shirt.

"Hello, Corso. I hope you're not intending to go out tonight."

She didn't come in but stood at the door with her thumbs in her pockets. She was frowning, as if expecting bad news.

"You can relax your guard," he reassured her. She smiled, relieved.

"I'm exhausted."

Corso turned his back on her and went to the bedside table. The bottle of gin was empty so he started searching the drinks cabinet until he stood up triumphantly holding a miniature bottle of gin. He emptied it in to a glass and took a sip. The girl was still at the door.

"They took the engravings. All nine of them." Corso waved his glass at the fragments of Book Number Two. "They burnt the rest so that it wouldn't show. That's why not all of it was burnt. They made sure some pieces were left intact . . . Like that, the book would be recorded as officially destroyed."

She leant her head to one side, looking at him intently.

"You're clever."

"Of course I am. That's why they got me involved."

The girl took a few steps around the room. Corso looked at her bare feet on the carpet, next to the bed. She was looking closely at the charred bits of paper.

"Fargas didn't burn the book," he added. "He wasn't capable of something like that . . . What did they do to him? Was it suicide, like Enrique Taillefer?"

She didn't answer straight away. She picked up a piece of paper and examined the words.

"Find your own answers," she said, not looking at him. "That's why they got you involved."

"What about you?"

She was reading silently, moving her lips as if she knew the words. When she put the fragment down on the bedcover, her smile was nostalgic, unsuited to her young face.

"You already know why I'm here: I've got to look after you. You need me."

"What I need is more gin."

He cursed to himself and finished his drink, trying to hide his impatience, or his confusion. Damn everything. Emerald green, luminous white – her eyes and her smile against her tanned skin, her bare, straight neck, warm and alive. Can you believe it, Corso? Even now, with all you've got to deal with, and you're thinking about her tanned arms, fine wrists, long fingers. Thinking about things like that. He noticed that her breasts, under her tight-fitting T-shirt, were magnificent. He hadn't been able to get a good look at them before. He imagined them tanned and heavy under the white cotton, flesh of clarity and shadow. Once again he was struck by her height. She was as tall as he was. Maybe taller.

"Who are you?"

"The Devil," she said. "The Devil in love."

And she laughed. The book by Cazotte was on the sideboard, next to the *Memoirs of Saint-Helena* and some papers. The girl looked at it but didn't touch it. Then she laid one finger on it and looked at Corso.

"Do you believe in the Devil?"

"I'm paid to believe in him. On this job anyway."

She nodded slowly, as if she already knew what he was going to say. She stared at Corso with curiosity, her lips parted, waiting for a sign or gesture which only she would understand.

"Do you know why I like this book, Corso?"

"No. Tell me."

"Because the protagonist is sincere. His love isn't just a trick to damn a soul. Biondetta is tender and faithful. She admires in Alvaro the same things the Devil loves in mankind: his courage, his independence . . ." Her eyelashes came down over her light irises for a moment. "His desire for knowledge and his lucidity."

"You seem very well informed. What do you know of all this?"

"Much more than you imagine."

"I don't imagine anything. Everything I know about the Devil and his loves and hates comes from literature: *Paradise Lost, The Divine Comedy*, passing through *Faust* and *The Brothers Karamazov* . . ."

He made a vague, evasive gesture. "I only know Lucifer second-hand."

Now she was looking at him mockingly.

"And which Devil do you prefer? Dante's?"

"No way. Much too terrifying. Excessively medieval for my taste."

"Mephistopheles?"

"No, not him either. He's too pleased with himself. Too much of a trickster, like a crooked lawyer . . . And anyway I never trust people who smile too much."

"What about the one in *The Karamazovs*?"

Corso made a face.

"Petty. A vulgar civil servant with dirty nails." He paused. "I suppose the one I prefer is Milton's fallen angel." He looked at her with interest. "That's what you were hoping I would say."

She smiled enigmatically. She still had her thumbs in her pockets. He'd never seen anyone wear jeans like that. It needed her long legs, of course. The legs of a young girl hitchhiking at the roadside, her rucksack at her feet and all the light in the world in those damned green eyes.

"How do you see Lucifer?" asked the girl.

"No idea." Corso thought a moment and then grimaced, indifferent. "Taciturn and silent, I suppose. Boring." His expression became acid. "On the throne in a deserted hall. At the centre of a cold, desolate, monotonous kingdom where nothing ever happens."

She looked at him in silence.

"You surprise me, Corso," she said at last.

"I don't know why. Anyone can read Milton. Even me."

She moved slowly round the bed, in a semi-circle, keeping the same distance, until she was standing between him and the lamp. Whether casual or premeditated, it meant that her shadow fell over the fragments of *The Nine Doors* spread out on the bedcover.

"You've just mentioned the price to be paid." Her face was now in darkness, against the light. "Pride, freedom . . . Knowledge. Whether at the beginning or at the end you've got to pay for everything. Even courage, don't you think? Don't you think you need a lot of courage to face God?"

Her words were a soft murmur in the silence filling the room, slipping under the door and through the gaps around the window. Even the noise of the traffic outside in the street seemed to fade. Corso looked at one silhouette, then the other. First the shadow, stylized against the bedcover and the fragments of the book. Then the body standing against the light. At that moment he wondered which was the more real.

"With all those archangels," she, or her shadow, added. There was bitterness in her words, even a contemptuous breath, a sigh of defeat. "Beautiful and perfect. As disciplined as Nazis."

At that instant she didn't seem so young. She seemed to be carrying the weariness of the ages: an obscure inheritance, the guilt of others which he, in his confusion and surprise, couldn't identify. After all, he thought, maybe neither the shadow across the bed nor the outline against the light was real.

"There's a painting in the Prado. Do you remember it, Corso? Men with knives facing horsemen with their swords. I've always been certain: the fallen angel looked like that as he rebelled. With the same lost expression as those poor bastards with the knives. The courage of desperation."

She moved slightly as she spoke, only a few inches, but as she did so her shadow moved nearer to Corso's, as if it had a will of its own.

"What do you know about any of that?" he asked.

"More than I want to."

Her shadow was lying across all the fragments of the book and almost touching Corso's. He moved back instinctively, leaving a section of light between them, on the bed.

"Imagine him," she said in the same absorbed tone. "The most beautiful of the fallen angels plotting, alone in his empty palace . . . He clings desperately to a routine he despises, but which at least allows him to hide his grief. His failure." The girl laughed gently, joylessly, as if from a great distance. "He misses Heaven."

The shadows had now come together and almost merged amongst the fragments snatched from the fireplace at the Quinta da Soledade. The girl and Corso, on the bed, with the nine doors of the kingdom of other shadows, or maybe the same ones. Singed paper, incomplete clues, a mystery shrouded in several veils, by the printer, by time and by fire. Enrique Taillefer swinging, his feet dangling in empty space, on the end of a silk cord; Victor Fargas floating face down in the murky waters of the pond. Aristide Torchia burning at Campo dei Fiori, shouting the name of the father, not looking at Heaven but down at the ground beneath his feet. And old Dumas writing, sitting at the top of the world, while there in Paris, very near where Corso was at that very moment, another shadow, of a cardinal whose library contained too many books on the Devil, held all the threads of the plot.

The girl, or her outline against the light, moved towards Corso. Only slightly, a single step. Enough for his shadow to disappear under hers.

"It was worse for those who followed him." Corso took a moment to understand who she meant. "Those he dragged down with him: soldiers, messengers, servants by trade and by calling. Some mercenaries, like you . . . Many didn't even realize that they were choosing between submission and freedom, between God and mankind. Out of habit, with the absurd loyalty of faithful soldiers, they followed their leader in rebellion and defeat."

"Like Xenophon's Ten Thousand," teased Corso.

She was silent a moment, surprised by his accuracy.

"Maybe," she said at last. "Out in the world alone, they still hope that their leader will one day take them home."

Corso bent down to look for a cigarette, and as he did so his shadow reappeared. Then he switched on the other lamp, on the bedside table, and the dark outline of the girl disappeared as her face was lit up. Her light eyes were fixed on him. She seemed very young again.

"Very moving," said Corso. "All those old soldiers searching for the sea."

She blinked as if now, with her face illuminated, she didn't understand what he was saying. There was no longer a shadow on the bed. The fragments of the book were merely pieces of charred paper. All he had to do was open the window and a gust of air would blow them all over the room.

She smiled. Irene Adler, 223b Baker Street. The café in Madrid, the train, that morning in Sintra . . . The battle lost, the retreat of the defeated legions: she was very young to remember such things. She smiled like a little girl both mischievous and innocent, and there were faint traces of tiredness under her eyes. She was sleepy and warm.

Corso swallowed. A part of him went up to her and pulled her T-shirt up over her tanned skin, undid her jeans and laid her on the bed, among the remains of the book that could summon the forces of darkness. And sank into her warm flesh, settling scores with God and Lucifer, with the inexorable flow of time, with his own ghosts, with life and death. But he just lit a cigarette and breathed out smoke in silence. She stared at him for a long time, waiting for something, a gesture, a word. Then she said good night and went to the door. But in the doorway she turned and slowly raised her hand, palm inwards, index and middle fingers joined and pointing upwards. And her smile was both tender and conspiratorial, ingenuous and knowing. Like a lost angel pointing nostalgically up to Heaven.

Baroness Frieda Ungern had two sweet little dimples when she smiled. She looked as if she had smiled continuously for the past seventy years and it had left a permanently benevolent expression around her eyes and mouth. Corso, a precocious reader, had known since childhood that there are many different types of witch: wicked stepmothers, bad fairies, beautiful, evil queens, and even nasty old witches with warts on their noses. But despite all he'd heard about the septuagenarian baroness, he didn't know to which category she belonged. She might have been one of those elderly ladies who live, as if cushioned by a dream, outside real life where no unpleasantness ever intrudes upon their existence, had it not been for the depth of her quick, intelligent, suspicious eyes cancelling that first impression. And if the right-hand sleeve of her cardigan hadn't hung empty, her arm amputated above the elbow. Otherwise she was small and plump, and looked like a French teacher at a boarding school for young ladies. In the days when "young ladies" still existed, that is. Or so Corso thought as he looked at her grey hair tied into a bun at the nape of her neck, and her rather masculine shoes worn with white ankle socks.

"Mr Corso. Pleased to meet you."

She held out her only hand – small like the rest of her – with unusual energy, and showed her dimples. She had a slight accent which was German rather than French. A certain von Ungern, Corso remembered reading somewhere, had become notorious in Manchuria, or Mongolia, in the early twenties. A warlord of sorts, he had made a last stand against the Red Army at the head of a ragged army of White Russians, Cossacks, Chinese, deserters and bandits. With armoured trains, looting, killing, that sort of thing, concluding with the epilogue at dawn before a firing squad. Maybe he was a relation.

"He was my husband's great-uncle. His family was Russian and emigrated to France with a fair amount of money before the Revolution." There was neither nostalgia nor pride in her tone. It had all happened in the past, to other people, to another family, she seemed to imply. Strangers who disappeared before she even existed. "I was born in Germany. My family lost everything under the Nazis.

I was married here in France after the war." She carefully removed a dead leaf from a plant by the window and smiled slightly. "I never could stand my in-laws' obsession with the past: their nostalgia for St Petersburg, the Tsar's birthday. It was like a wake."

Corso looked at the desk covered in books, the packed shelves. He calculated there must be a thousand volumes in that room alone. The most rare and valuable ones seemed to be there, from modern editions to more ancient, leather-bound tomes.

"And what about all this?"

"That's different. It's material for research, not worship. I use it for my work."

Times are bad, thought Corso, when witches, or whatever they are, talk about their in-laws and exchange their cauldron for a library, filing cabinets and a place in the bestseller list. Through the open door he could see more books in the other rooms and in the corridor. Books and plants. There were pots of them all over the place: on the window-sills, on the floor, on the wooden shelves. It was a large, expensive apartment with views of the river and, in another time, the bonfires of the Inquisition. There were several reading tables occupied by young people who looked like students, and all the walls were covered in books. Ancient, gilded bindings shone from between the plants. The Ungern Foundation contained the largest collection of books on the occult in Europe. Corso glanced at the books closest to him. *Dæmonolatriæ Libri* by Nicholas Rémy. *Compendium Maleficarum* by Francesco Maria Guazzo. *De Dæmonialitate et Incubus et Succubus* by Ludovico Sinistrari . . . In addition to one of the best catalogues of demonology, and the foundation named after her late husband, the baron, Baroness Ungern had a solid reputation as a writer of books on magic and witchcraft. Her last book, *Isis, the Naked Virgin*, had been on the bestseller list for three years. The Vatican had boosted sales by publicly condemning the work which drew worrying parallels between the pagan deity and the mother of Christ. There had been eight editions in France, twelve in Spain, and seventeen in Catholic Italy.

"What are you working on at the moment?"

"It's called *The Devil, History and Legend*. An irreverent biography. It'll be ready by the beginning of next year."

Corso stopped by a row of books. His attention had been drawn by the *Disquisitionum Magicarum* by Martin del Rio, the three volumes of the Lovaina first edition, 1599–1600: a classic on demonic magic.

"Where did you get hold of this?"

Frieda Ungern must have been considering how much information to provide, because she took a moment to answer.

"At an auction in Madrid in '89. I had a great deal of trouble preventing your compatriot, Varo Borja, getting hold of it." She sighed as if still recovering from the effort. "And money. I would never have managed it without help from Paco Montegrifo. Do you know him? A delightful man."

Corso smiled crookedly. Not only did he know Montegrifo, the head of the Spanish branch of Claymore's Auctioneers, but he had worked with him on several unorthodox and highly profitable deals. Such as the sale, to a certain Swiss collector, of a *Cosmography* by Ptolemy, a gothic manuscript dating from 1456, which had mysteriously disappeared from the University of Salamanca not long before. Montegrifo had found himself in possession of the book and used Corso as an intermediary. The entire operation had been clean and discreet, and had included a visit to the Ceniza brothers' workshop where a compromising stamp had been removed. Corso had delivered the book himself to Lausanne. All inclusive for a thirty per cent commission.

"Yes, I know him." He stroked the spines of the several volumes of the *Disquisitionum Magicarum* and wondered how much Montegrifo must have charged the Baroness for rigging the auction in her favour. "As for the Martin del Rio, I've only seen a copy once before, in the collection of the Jesuits in Bilbao . . . Bound in a single piece of leather. But it's the same edition."

As he spoke he moved his hand along the row of books, touching some. There were many interesting volumes, with good-quality bindings in vellum, shagreen, parchment. Many others were only mediocre, or in poor condition, and looked much-used. Nearly all of them had page-markers, strips of white card covered in a small, spiky hand, written in pencil. Material for her research. He stopped in front of a book which looked very familiar: black, no title, five raised bands on the spine. Book Number Three.

"How long have you had this?"

Now, Corso was a steady character. Especially at this stage in the story. But he'd spent the night sorting through the ashes of Number Two, and he couldn't prevent the Baroness from noticing something peculiar in his tone of voice. He saw that she was looking at him suspiciously despite the friendly dimples in her youthful old face.

"*The Nine Doors?* I'm not sure. A long time." Her only hand moved quickly and deftly. She took the book from the shelf effortlessly and, supporting the spine in her palm, she opened it at the first page, decorated with several bookplates, some very old. The last one was an arabesque design with the name von Ungern, and the date written in ink. As she saw it she nodded nostalgically. "A present from my husband. I married very young. He was twice my age. He bought the book in 1949."

That was the problem with modern-day witches, thought Corso: they didn't have any secrets. Everything was out in the open, you could read all about them in any *Who's Who* or gossip column. Baronesses or not, they'd become predictable. Vulgar. Torquemada would have been bored to death by it all.

"Did your husband share your interest in this sort of thing?"

"Not in the slightest. He never read a single book. He just made all my wishes come true like the genie of the lamp." Her amputated arm seemed to shudder for a moment in the empty sleeve of her cardigan. "An expensive book or a perfect pearl necklace, it was all the same to him." She paused and smiled with gentle melancholy. "But he was an amusing man, capable of seducing his best friends' wives. And he made excellent champagne cocktails."

She was silent for a moment and looked round as if her husband had left a glass behind.

"I collected all this myself," she added, waving at her library, "One by one, down to the last book. I even chose *The Nine Doors*, after discovering it in the catalogue of a bankrupt, former Pétain supporter. All my husband did was sign the cheque."

"Why are you so interested in the Devil?"

"I saw him once. I was fifteen and I saw him as clearly as I'm seeing you. He had a hard collar, a hat and a walking stick. He was very handsome. He looked like John Barrymore as Baron Gaigern in *Grand Hotel*. So, like a fool, I fell in love." She became thoughtful again, her only hand in her cardigan pocket, as if remembering something distant, familiar. "I suppose that's why I was never really troubled by my husband's infidelities."

Corso looked around as if there might be someone else in the room and then leaned over confidentially.

"Only three centuries ago you would have burnt at the stake for telling me this."

She made a guttural sound of amusement, stifling her laughter, and almost stood on tiptoes to whisper in the same tone:

"Three centuries ago I wouldn't have mentioned it to anyone. But I know a lot of people who would gladly burn me at the stake." She smiled again, showing her dimples. She was always smiling, Corso decided. But her bright, intelligent eyes remained alert, studying him. "Even now, in this day and age."

She handed him *The Nine Doors* and watched him as he leafed through the book slowly, although he could barely contain his impatience to check if there were any differences in the nine engravings. Sighing with relief to himself, he found them intact. In fact, Mateu's *Bibliography* was wrong: none of the three books had the final engraving missing. Book Number Three was in worse condition than Varo Borja's, and Victor Fargas's before it was thrown into the fire. The lower half had been exposed to damp and almost all the pages were stained. The binding also needed a thorough clean, but the book seemed complete.

"Would you like a drink?" asked the Baroness. "I've got tea or coffee."

No potions or magic herbs, Corso thought with disappointment. Not even a tisane.

"Coffee."

It was a sunny day and the sky over the nearby towers of Notre Dame was blue. Corso went over to a window and parted the net curtains so he could see the book in better light. Two floors down, between the bare trees on the banks of the Seine, the girl was sitting on a stone bench in her duffle coat, reading a book. He knew it was *The Three Musketeers* because he'd seen it on the table when they met at breakfast. Afterwards Corso walked along the Rue de Rivoli knowing that the girl was following fifteen or twenty paces behind. He deliberately ignored her, and she kept her distance. Now he saw her look up. She must have seen him clearly from down there, but she made no sign of recognition. Expressionless and still, she continued to watch him until he moved away from the window. When he looked out again she had gone back to her book, her head bowed.

There was a secretary, a middle-aged woman with thick glasses, moving amongst the tables and books, but Frieda Ungern brought the coffee herself, two cups on a silver tray which she carried with ease. One glance from her told him not to offer help, and they sat down at the desk, the tray amongst all the books, plant pots, papers and note cards.

"What gave you the idea of setting up this foundation?"

"I can claim against tax. Also it means that people come here, I can find collaborators . . ." She smiled melancholically. "I'm the last of the witches and I felt lonely."

"You don't look anything like a witch." Corso made the appropriate face, like an ingenuous, friendly rabbit. "I read your *Isis.*"

She was holding her coffee cup in her one hand and slightly raised the stump of her other arm, at the same time tilting her head as if to rearrange her hair. Although incomplete, it was an unconsciously coquettish gesture, as old as the world itself and yet ageless.

"Did you like it?"

He looked her in the eyes, as he raised his cup to his mouth.

"Very much."

"Not everyone did. Do you know what *L'Osservatore Romano* said? It regretted the demise of the Index of the Holy Office. And you're right." She indicated *The Nine Doors* that Corso had put by her on the table. "In the past I would have been burnt at the stake, like the poor wretch who wrote the gospel according to Satan."

"Do you really believe in the Devil, Baroness?"

"Don't call me Baroness. It's ridiculous."

"What would you like me to call you?"

"I don't know. Mrs Ungern. Or Frieda."

"Do you believe in the Devil, Mrs Ungern?"

"Sufficiently to dedicate my life, my collection, this foundation, many years of work and the five hundred pages of my new book all to him . . ." She looked at him with interest. Corso had taken off his glasses to clean them. His helpless smile completed the effect. "What about you?"

"Everybody's asking me that lately."

"Of course. You've been going round asking questions about a book that has to be read with a certain kind of faith."

"My faith is limited," Corso said, risking a hint of sincerity. This kind of frankness often proved profitable. "Really I work for money."

The dimples appeared again. She must have been very pretty about half a century ago, thought Corso. With both arms intact, casting spells, or whatever they were, slender and mischievous. She still had something of that.

"Pity," remarked Frieda Ungern. "Others, who worked for nothing, had blind faith in the book's protagonist . . . Albertus Magnus,

Raymund Lully, Roger Bacon, none of them ever disputed the Devil's existence, only his nature."

Corso adjusted his glasses, and gave a hint of a sceptical smile.

"Things were different a long time ago."

"You don't have to go that far back. 'The Devil does exist, not only as a symbol of evil, but as a physical reality.' How do you like that? Well, it was written by a pope, Paul VI. In 1974."

"He was a professional," said Corso equably. "He must have had his reasons."

"In fact all he was doing was confirming a point of doctrine: the existence of the Devil was established by the fourth Lateran Council. I mean in 1215 . . ." She paused and looked at him doubtfully. "Are you interested in erudite facts? I can be unbearably scholarly if I try . . ." The dimples appeared. "I always wanted to be top of the class. The smart aleck."

"I'm sure you were. Did you win all the prizes?"

"Of course. And the other girls hated me."

They both laughed. Corso sensed that Frieda Ungern was now on his side. So he took two cigarettes from his coat pocket and offered her one. She refused, glancing at him slightly apprehensively. Corso ignored this and lit his cigarette.

"Two centuries later," continued the Baroness as Corso craned over the lighted match, "Innocent VIII's papal bull *Sumnis Desiderantes Affectibus* confirmed that Western Europe was plagued by demons and witches. So two Dominican monks, Kramer and Sprenger, drew up the *Malleus Malleficarum*, a manual for inquisitors . . ."

Corso raised his index finger.

"Lyon, 1519. An octavo in the Gothic style, with no author's name. At least, not the copy I know."

"Not bad." She looked at him, surprised. "Mine is a later one." She pointed at a shelf. "It's over there. Published in 1668, also in Lyon. But the very first edition dated from 1486 . . ." She shuddered, half-closing her eyes. "Kramer and Sprenger were fanatical and stupid. Their *Malleus* was a load of nonsense. It might even seem funny, if thousands of poor wretches hadn't been tortured and burnt in its name."

"Like Aristide Torchia."

"Yes, like him. Although he wasn't remotely innocent."

"What do you know about him?"

The Baroness shook her head, drank the last of her coffee and then shook her head again.

"The Torchias were a Venetian family of well-to-do merchants who imported vat paper from Spain and France . . . As a young man he travelled to Holland and was an apprentice of the Elzevirs, who had corresponded with his father. He stayed there for a time and then went to Prague."

"I didn't know that."

"Well, there you are. Prague was Europe's capital of magic and the occult, just as Toledo had been four centuries earlier . . . Can you see the links? Torchia chose to live in Saint Mary of the Snows, the district of magic, near Jungmannove Square where there is a statue of Jan Hus . . . Do you remember Hus at the stake?"

"'From my ashes a swan will rise that you will not be able to burn . . .'"

"Exactly. You're easy to talk to. I expect you already know that. It must help you in your work." The Baroness involuntarily inhaled some of Corso's cigarette smoke. She looked slightly reproachful but he remained unperturbed. "Now, where were we? Ah yes. Prague, act two. Torchia moves to a house in the Jewish quarter nearby, next to the synagogue. A district where the windows are lit up every night and the Cabbalists are searching for the magic formula of the Golem. After a while he moves again, this time to the district of Mala Strana . . ." She smiled at him conspiratorially. "What does all this sound like to you?"

"Like a pilgrimage. Or a study trip, as we'd say nowadays."

"That's what I think," the Baroness agreed with satisfaction. Corso, now well and truly adopted, was moving quickly to the top of the class. "It must be more than coincidence that Aristide Torchia went to the three districts in which all the esoteric knowledge of the time was concentrated. And in a Prague whose streets still echoed with the steps of Agrippa and Paracelsus, where the last manuscripts of Chaldean magic and the Pythagorean keys lost or dispersed after the murder of Metapontius were to be found . . ." She leaned over towards him and lowered her voice. Miss Marple about to confide in her best friend that she's found cyanide in the teacakes. "In that Prague, Mr Corso, in those dark studies, there were men who practised the *carmina*, the art of magic words, and necromancy, or the art of communicating with the dead." She paused, holding her breath, before whispering, "And goety . . ."

"The art of communicating with the Devil."

"Yes." The Baroness leaned back in her armchair, deliciously shocked by it all. She was in her element. Her eyes shone and she was speaking quickly as if she had much to say and too little time. "At that time, Torchia lived in the place where the pages and engravings that had survived wars, fires and persecution were hidden . . . The remains of the magic book which opens the doors to knowledge and power: the *Delomelanicon,* the word that summons the darkness."

She said it in a conspiratorial, almost theatrical tone, but she was also smiling, as if she didn't quite take it seriously herself, or was suggesting that Corso maintain a healthy distance.

"Once he had completed his apprenticeship, Torchia returned to Venice," she went on. "Take note of this because it's important: in spite of the risks he would run in Italy, the printer left the relative safety of Prague to return to his home town. There he published a series of compromising books which led to his being burnt at the stake. Isn't that strange?"

"Seems as if he had a mission to accomplish."

"Yes. But entrusted by whom?" The Baroness opened *The Nine Doors* at the title page. "'By authority and permission of the superiors.' Makes one think, doesn't it? It's very likely that Torchia became a member of a secret brotherhood in Prague that entrusted him with spreading a message. A kind of preaching."

"You said it yourself earlier: the gospel according to Satan."

"Maybe. The fact is that Torchia published *The Nine Doors* at the worst time. Between 1550 and 1666, humanist neo-platonism and the hermetic and Cabbalist movements were losing the battle amid rumours of demonism . . . Men like Giordano Bruno and John Dee were burnt at the stake, or died persecuted and destitute. With the triumph of the Counter-Reformation, the Inquisition grew unhindered. Created to fight heresy, it specialized in witches, wizards and sorcery to justify its shadowy existence. And here they were offered a printer who had dealings with the Devil . . . Torchia made things easy for them, it must be said. Listen." She turned several pages of the book at random. "'*Pot. m.vere im.go* . . .'" She looked at Corso. "I've translated numerous passages. The code is quite simple. 'I will bring wax images to life,' it says. 'And unhinge the moon, and put flesh back on dead bodies . . .' What do you think of that?"

"Rather childish. It seems stupid to die for that."

"Maybe. One never knows . . . Do you like Shakespeare?"

"Sometimes."

"'There are more things in heaven and earth, Horatio,/ Than are dreamt of in your philosophy.'"

"Hamlet. A very insecure man."

"Not everyone is able, or deserves, to gain access to these occult things, Mr Corso. As the old saying goes, one must know and keep silent."

"But Torchia didn't."

"As you know, according to the Cabbala, God has a terrible and secret name . . ."

"The Tetragrammaton."

"That's right. The harmony and balance of the Universe rests upon its four letters . . . As the Archangel Gabriel warned Mohammed: 'God is hidden by seventy thousand veils of light and darkness. And were those veils to be lifted, even I would be annihilated . . .' But God isn't the only one to have such a name. The Devil has one too. A terrible, evil combination of letters which summons him when spoken . . . And unleashes terrifying consequences."

"That's nothing new. It had a name long before Christianity and Judaism: Pandora's box."

She looked at him with satisfaction, as if awarding top marks.

"Very good, Mr Corso. In fact, down the centuries, we've always talked about the same things, but with different names. Isis and the Virgin Mary, Mithras and Jesus Christ, the 25th of December as Christmas or the festival of the winter solstice, the anniversary of the unconquered sun . . . Think of St Gregory. Even in the seventh century he was recommending that missionaries use the pagan festivals and adapt them to Christianity."

"Sound business sense. In essence it was a marketing operation: they were trying to attract somebody else's customers . . . Could you tell me what you know about Pandora's boxes and such like? Including pacts with the Devil."

"The art of locking devils inside bottles or books is very ancient . . . Gervase of Tilbury and Gerson both mentioned it in the thirteenth and fourteenth centuries. As for pacts with the Devil, the tradition goes back even further: from the Book of Enoch to St Jeronimus, through the Cabbala and the Fathers of the Church. Not forgetting Bishop Theophilus, who was actually a 'lover of knowledge', the historical Faust and Roger Bacon . . . Or Pope Sylvester II, of whom it was said that he robbed the Saracens of a book which 'contained all one needs to know'."

"So it was a question of obtaining knowledge."

"Of course. Nobody would take so much trouble, wandering to the very edge of the abyss just to pass the time. Scholarly demonology identifies Lucifer with knowledge. In *Genesis*, the Devil in the form of a serpent succeeds in getting man to stop being a stupid simpleton and gain awareness, free will, lucidity, knowledge, with all the pain and uncertainty that they entail."

The evening conversation was too fresh so, inevitably, Corso thought of the girl. He picked up *The Nine Doors* and with the excuse of looking at it in better light again, he went to the window. But she was no longer there. Surprised, he looked up and down the street, along the embankment and the stone benches under the trees, but couldn't see her. He was intrigued but didn't have time to think about it. Frieda Ungern was speaking again.

"Do you like guessing games? Puzzles with hidden keys? In a way the book you're holding is exactly that. Like any intelligent being, the Devil likes games, riddles. Obstacle races where the weak and incapable fall by the wayside and only superior spirits – the initiates – win." Corso moved closer to the desk and put down the book, open at the frontispiece. The serpent with the tail in its mouth wound round the tree. "He who sees nothing but a serpent in the figure devouring its tail, deserves to go no further."

"What is this book for?" asked Corso.

The Baroness put a finger to her lips like the knight in the first engraving. She was smiling.

"St John of Patmos says that in the reign of the Second Beast, before the final, decisive battle of Armageddon, 'only he who has the mark, the name of the Beast or the number of his name will be able to buy and sell' . . . Waiting for the hour to come, Luke (iv, 13) tells us at the end of his story of the Temptation that the Devil, repudiated three times, 'withdrew until another time'. But he left several paths for the impatient, including the way to reach him, to make a pact with him."

"To sell him one's soul."

Frieda Ungern giggled confidentially. Miss Marple with her cronies, engaged in gossip about the Devil. You'll never guess the latest about Satan. This, that and the other. I don't know where to start, Peggy my dear.

"The Devil learnt his lesson," she said. "He was young and naïve, and he made mistakes. Souls escaped at the last minute through the false door, saving themselves for the sake of love, God's mercy and other specious promises. So he ended up including a non-negotiable clause for the handing over of body and soul once the deadline had expired 'without reserve of any right to redemption, or future recourse to God's mercy . . .' The clause is in fact to be found in this book."

"What a lousy world," said Corso. "Even Lucifer has to resort to the small print."

"You must understand. Nowadays people will swindle you out of anything. Even their soul. His clients slip away and don't comply with their contractual obligations. The Devil's fed up and he has every reason to be."

"What else is in the book? What do the nine engravings mean?"

"In principle they're puzzles that have to be solved. Used in conjunction with the text they confer power. And provide the formula for constructing the magic name to make Satan appear."

"Does it work?"

"No. It's a forgery."

"Have you tried it yourself?"

Frieda Ungern looked shocked.

"Can you see me at my age, standing in a magic circle, invoking Beelzebub? Please! However much he looked like John Barrymore fifty years ago, heart throb too. Can you imagine the disappointment at my age? I prefer to be faithful to the memories of my youth."

Corso looked at her in mock surprise.

"But surely you and the Devil . . . Your readers take you for a committed witch."

"Well, they're mistaken. What I look for in the Devil is money, not emotion." She looked round, towards the window. "I spent my husband's fortune building up this collection, so I have to live off my royalties."

"Which are considerable, I'm sure. You're the queen of the bookshops . . ."

"But life is expensive, Mr Corso. Very expensive, especially when one has to make deals with people like our friend Mr Montegrifo to get the rare books one wants . . . Satan serves as a good source of income nowadays, but that's all. I'm seventy years old. I don't have time for gratuitous, silly fantasies, spinsters' dreams . . . Do you understand?"

It was Corso's turn to smile.

"Perfectly."

"When I say that this book is a forgery," continued the Baroness, "it's because I've studied it in depth . . . There's something in it that doesn't work. There are gaps in it, blanks. I mean this figuratively, because my copy is in fact complete. It belonged to Madame de Montespan, Louis XIV's mistress. She was a high priestess of Satanism and she managed to have the ritual of the Black Mass included in the palace routine. There is a letter from Madame de Montespan to Madame de Peyrolles, her friend and confidante, in which she complains of the inefficacy of a book which, she states 'has all that which the sages specify and yet, there is something incorrect in it, a play on words which never falls into the correct sequence'."

"Who else owned it?"

"The Count of Saint-Germain, who sold it to Cazotte."

"Jacques Cazotte?"

"Yes. The author of *The Devil in Love*, who was guillotined in 1792. Do you know the book?"

Corso nodded cautiously. The links were so obvious that they were impossible.

"I read it once."

Somewhere in the apartment a phone rang, and the secretary's steps could be heard along the corridor. The ringing stopped.

"As for *The Nine Doors*," the Baroness continued, "the trail went cold here in Paris, at the time of the Terror after the Revolution. There are a couple of subsequent references but they're very vague. Gérard de Nerval mentions it in passing in one of his articles, assuring us that he's seen it at a friend's house."

Corso blinked imperceptibly behind his glasses.

"Dumas was a friend of his," he said, alert.

"Yes. But Nerval doesn't say at whose house. The fact is nobody saw the book again until the Pétain collaborator's collection was auctioned, which is when I got hold of it . . ."

Corso was no longer listening. According to the legend, Gérard de Nerval hanged himself with the cord from a bodice, Madame de Montespan's. Or was it Madame de Maintenon's? Whoever it belonged to, he couldn't help drawing worrying parallels with the cord from Enrique Taillefer's dressing-gown.

The secretary came to the door, interrupting his thoughts. Somebody wanted Corso on the telephone. He excused himself and walked past the tables of readers out into the corridor, full of yet more books and plants. On a walnut corner table there was an antique metal phone with the earpiece off the hook.

"Hello."

"Corso? It's Irene Adler."

"So I gather." He looked behind him down the empty corridor. The secretary had disappeared. "I was surprised you weren't still keeping a lookout. Where are you calling from?"

"The bar on the corner. There's a man watching the house. That's why I came here."

For a moment Corso just breathed slowly. Then he bit off a hangnail with his teeth. It was bound to happen sooner or later, he thought with twisted resignation. He was part of the landscape, or the furniture. Then, although he knew it was pointless, he said:

"Describe him."

"Dark, with a moustache and a big scar on his face." The girl's voice was calm, without a trace of emotion or awareness of danger. "He's sitting in a grey BMW across the street."

"Has he seen you?"

"I don't know. But I can see him. He's been there an hour. He's got out of the car twice: first to look at the names at the door, and then to buy a newspaper."

Corso spat the hangnail out of his mouth and sucked his thumb. It smarted.

"Listen. I don't know what the man's up to. I don't even know if the two of you are part of the same set-up. But I don't like him being near you. Not at all. So go back to the hotel."

"Don't be an idiot, Corso. I'll go where I have to."

Then she added, "Regards to Treville," and hung up. Corso made a gesture halfway between exasperation and sarcasm because he was thinking the same thing and he didn't like the coincidence. So he stood for a moment looking at the earpiece before hanging up. Of course, she was reading *The Three Musketeers*. She'd even had the book open when he saw her from the window. In chapter three, having just arrived in Paris, and during an audience with Monsieur de Treville, commander of the King's musketeers, d'Artagnan sees Rochefort from the window. He runs after him, bumps into Athos's shoulder, Porthos's shoulder-belt and Aramis's handkerchief. Regards to Treville. It was a clever joke, if it was spontaneous. But Corso didn't find it at all funny.

After he'd hung up he stood thinking for a moment in the darkness of the corridor. Maybe that's exactly what they were expecting him to do: rush downstairs after Rochefort, sword in hand, taking the bait. The girl's call might even have been part of the plan. Or maybe – and this was really getting convoluted – it had been a warning about the plan, if there was one. That's if she was playing fair – Corso was too experienced to put his hand in the fire for anybody.

Bad times, he said to himself again. Absurd times. After so many books, films and TV shows, after reading on so many different possible levels, it was difficult to tell if one was seeing the original or a copy; to know when one was seeing a real image, an inverted image, or both, in a hall of mirrors. And what were the authors' intentions. It was as easy to fall short of the truth as to go over the top with one's interpretations. Here was one more reason to feel envious of his great-great-grandfather with his grenadier's moustache, the smell of gunpowder floating over the muddy fields of Flanders. In those days a flag was still a flag, the Emperor was the Emperor, a rose was a rose was a rose. But now at least, here in Paris, something was clear to Corso: even as a second-level reader he was only prepared to play the game up to a certain point. And he no longer had the youth, the innocence or the desire to go and fight at a place chosen by his opponents, three duels arranged in ten minutes, in the grounds of the Carmelite convent or wherever the hell it might be. When the time came to say hello, he'd make sure he approached Rochefort with everything in his favour, if possible from behind, with a steel bar in his hand. He owed it to him since that narrow street in Toledo, not forgetting the interest accrued in Sintra. Corso would settle his debts calmly. Biding his time.

XI

The Banks of the Seine

This mystery is considered insoluble for the very same
reasons that should lead one to consider it solvable.
E. A. Poe: *The Murders in the Rue Morgue*

"The code is simple," said Frieda Ungern, "consisting of abbreviations similar to those used in ancient Latin manuscripts. This may be because Aristide Torchia took the major part of the text word for word from another manuscript, possibly the legendary *Delomelanicon*. In the first engraving, the meaning is obvious to anyone slightly familiar with esoteric language: '*Nem. perv.t qui n.n leg. cert.rit*' is obviously '*Nemo pervenit qui non legitime certaverit.*'"

"'Only he who has fought according to the rules will succeed.'"

They were on their third cup of coffee, and it was obvious, at least on a formal level, that Corso had been adopted. He saw the Baroness nod, gratified.

"Very good. Can you interpret any part of this engraving?"

"No," Corso lied calmly. He had just noticed that in the Baroness's copy there were only three, instead of four towers to the walled city with the horseman riding towards it. "Except for the character's gesture, which seems eloquent."

"And so it is: he is turned towards any follower with a finger to his lips, advising silence ... It's the *tacere* of the philosophers of the Occult. In the background the city walls surround the towers, the secret. Notice that the door is closed. It has to be opened."

Tense and very alert, Corso turned more pages until he came to the second engraving, the hermit in front of another door, holding the keys in his *right* hand. The legend read "*Claus. pat.t.*"

"'*Clausæ patent*,'" the Baroness deciphered. "'They open that which is closed,' the closed doors ... The hermit symbolizes knowledge, study, wisdom. And look, at his side there's the same black dog that, according to legend, accompanied Agrippa. The faithful dog . . . From Plutarch to Bram Stoker and his *Dracula*, not forgetting Goethe's *Faust*, the black dog is one of the animals the Devil most often chose to embody him. As for the lantern, it belongs to the philosopher Diogenes who so despised worldly powers. All he requested of powerful Alexander was that he should not overshadow him, that he move because he was standing in front of the sun, the light."

"And this letter Teth?"

"I'm not sure." She tapped the engraving lightly. "The Hermit in the Tarot, very similar to this one, is sometimes accompanied by a serpent, or by the stick which symbolizes it. In occult philosophy, the serpent and the dragon are the guardians of the wonderful enclosure, garden or Fleece, and they sleep with their eyes open. They are the Mirror of the Art."

"'*Ars diavoli*,'" said Corso casually, and the Baroness half smiled, nodding mysteriously. But he knew, from Fulcanelli and other ancient texts, that the term 'Mirror of the Art' didn't come from demonology, but from alchemy. He wondered how much charlatanism lay beneath the Baroness's display of erudition. He sighed to himself. He felt like a gold prospector standing up to his waist in the river, sieve in hand. After all, he thought, she had to find something to fill her five-hundred-page bestsellers.

But Frieda Ungern had already moved on to the third engraving. "The motto is '*Verb. d.sum c.s.t. arcan.*' This stands for '*Verbum dimissum custodiat arcanum.*' It can be translated as 'The lost word keeps the secret.' And the engraving is significant: a bridge, the union between the light and the dark banks. From classical mythology to Snakes and Ladders, its meaning is clear. Like the rainbow, it links earth with heaven or hell . . . To cross this one, of course, one has to open the fortified gates."

"What about the archer hiding in the clouds?"

This time his voice shook as he asked the question. In Books One and Two, the quiver hanging from the archer's shoulder was empty. But in Book Three it contained an arrow. Frieda Ungern was resting her finger on it.

"The bow is the weapon of Apollo and Diana, the light of the supreme power. The wrath of the god, or God. It's the enemy lying in wait for anyone crossing the bridge." She leaned forward and said quietly and confidentially, "Here it represents a terrible warning. It's not advisable to trifle with this sort of thing."

Corso nodded and moved on to the fourth engraving. He could sense the fog lifting in his mind. Doors opening with a sinister creak. Now he was looking at the joker and his stone labyrinth, with the caption: "*For. n.n omn. a.que.*" Frieda Ungern translated it as "*fortuna non omnibus æque*": "Fate is not the same for all."

"The character is similar to the madman in the Tarot," she explained. "God's madman in Islam. And, of course, he's also holding a stick or symbolic serpent . . . He's the medieval fool, the Joker in a pack of cards, the jester. He symbolizes Destiny, chance, the end of everything, the expected or unexpected conclusion. Look at the dice. In the Middle Ages, jesters were privileged beings. They were permitted to do things forbidden to others. Their purpose was to remind their masters that they were mortal, that their end was as inevitable as other men's . . ."

"Here he's stating the opposite," objected Corso. "'Fate is not the same for all.'"

"Of course. He who rebels, exercises his freedom and takes the risk, can earn a different fate. That's what this book is about, hence the joker, paradigm of freedom. The only truly free man, and also the most wise. In occult philosophy the joker is identified with the mercury of the alchemists. Emissary of the gods, he guides souls through the kingdom of shadows . . ."

"The labyrinth."

"Yes. There it is." She pointed at the engraving. "And as you can see, the entry door is closed."

So is the exit, thought Corso with an involuntary shudder. Then he turned more pages to the next engraving.

"This legend is simpler," he said. "'*Fr.st.a.*' It's the only one I dare take a guess at. I'd say there's a 'u' and an 'r' missing: '*Frustra.*' Which means 'In vain.'"

"Very good. That's exactly what it says, and the picture matches the caption. The miser is counting his gold pieces, unaware of Death who is holding two clear symbols: an hourglass and a pitchfork."

"Why a pitchfork and not a scythe?"

"Because Death reaps, but the Devil harvests."

They stopped at the sixth engraving, the man hanging from the battlements by his foot. Frieda Ungern pretended to yawn with boredom, as if it were too obvious.

"'*Dit.sco m.r*' stands for '*Ditesco mori*': 'I am enriched by death,' a sentence the Devil can utter with his head held high. Don't you think?"

"I suppose so. It's his trade, after all." Corso ran a finger over the engraving. "What does the hanged man symbolize?"

"Firstly, arcanum number twelve in the Tarot. But there are other possible interpretations. I believe it symbolizes change through sacrifice . . . Are you familiar with the saga of Odin?

"'Wounded, I hung from a scaffold
swept by the winds,
for nine long nights . . .'

"You can make the following associations," continued the Baroness. "Lucifer, champion of freedom, suffers from love of mankind. And he provides him with knowledge through sacrifice, thus damning himself."

"What can you tell me about the seventh engraving?"

"'*Dis.s p.ti.r m.*' doesn't seem very clear at first. But I would infer that it's a traditional saying, much liked by occult philosophers: '*Discipulus potior magistro.*'"

"'The disciple surpasses the master'?"

"More or less. The king and the beggar play chess on a strange board where all the squares are the same colour, while the black dog and the white dog, Good and Evil, viciously tear each other to pieces. The moon, representing both darkness and the mother, can be seen through the window. Think of the mythical belief that, after death, souls take refuge on the Moon. You read my *Isis*, didn't you? Black is the symbolic colour of darkness and Cimmerian shadows, sable in heraldry, earth, night, death . . . The black of Isis corresponds with the colour of the Virgin, who is robed in blue and dwells on the Moon. When we die we return to her, to the darkness from which we came. That darkness is ambiguous as it is both protective and threatening . . . The dogs and the Moon can also be interpreted another way. The goddess of hunting, Artemis, the Roman Diana, was known to take revenge on those who fell in love with her or tried to take advantage of her femininity . . . I assume you know the story."

Corso, who was thinking about Irene Adler, nodded slowly.

"Yes. She would let her dogs loose on gawkers after turning them into stags." He swallowed, in spite of himself. The two dogs in the engraving, locked in mortal combat, now seemed ominous. Himself and Rochefort? "So they'd be torn to pieces."

The Baroness glanced at him, expressionless. It was Corso who was providing the context, not her.

"The basic meaning of the eighth engraving," she continued, "is not difficult to grasp. '*Vic. i.t Vir.*' stands for a rather nice motto, '*Victa iacet Virtus.*' Which means: 'Virtue lies defeated.' The damsel about to have her throat slit by the handsome young man in armour carrying a sword, represents Virtue. Meanwhile, the wheel of Fortune or Fate, turns inexorably in the background, moving slowly but always making a complete turn. The three figures on it symbolize the three stages which, in the Middle Ages, were referred to as '*regno*' (I reign), '*regnavi*' (I have reigned) and '*regnabo*' (I shall reign)."

"There's one more engraving."

"Yes. The last one, and also the most the significant picture. '*N.nc sc.o ten.br. lux*' stands without doubt for '*Nunc scio tenebris lux*': 'Now I know that from darkness comes light'. . . What we have here is in fact a scene from the Revelation of St John. The final seal has been broken, the secret city is in flames. The time of the Whore of Babylon has come and, having pronounced the terrible name or the number of the Beast, she rides, triumphant, on the dragon with seven heads . . ."

"Doesn't seem very profitable," said Corso, "taking all that trouble only to find this horror."

"That's not what it's about. All the allegories are kinds of compositions in code, rebuses . . . Just as on a puzzle page the word 'in' followed by the pictures of a fan and a tree make up the word 'infantry', these engravings and their captions combined, together with the book's text, enable one to determine a sequence, a ritual. The formula which provides the magic word. The '*verbum dimissum*' or whatever it might be."

"And then the Devil will put in an appearance."

"In theory."

"What language is this spell in? Latin, Hebrew or Greek?"

"I don't know."

"And where's the fault Madame de Montespan mentions?"

"As I said, I don't know that either. All I've been able to establish is that the celebrant must construct a magic territory in which to place the words obtained, having arranged them in sequence. I don't know the order of that sequence, but the text on pages 158 and 159 of *The Nine Doors* may give an indication. Look."

She showed him the text in abbreviated Latin. There was a card covered in the Baroness's small, spiky handwriting marking the page.

"Have you managed to work out what it says?" asked Corso.

"Yes. At least, I think so." She handed him the card. "There you are." Corso read:

It is the animal with the tail in its mouth that encircles the
   labyrinth
where you will go through eight doors before the dragon
which comes to the enigma of the word.
Each door has two keys:
one is air and the other matter,
but both are the same thing.
You will place matter on the serpent's skin
in the direction of the rising sun,
and on its belly the seal of Saturn.
You will break the seal nine times,
and when the reflection in the mirror shows the way
you will find the lost word
which brings light from the darkness.

"What do you think?" asked the Baroness.

"It's disturbing, I suppose. But I don't understand a word. Do you?"

"As I said, not much." She turned the pages of the book, preoccupied. "It provides a method, a formula. But there's something in it which isn't as it should be. And I ought to know what that is."

Corso lit another cigarette but said nothing. He already knew the answer to the question: the hermits' keys, the hourglass, the exit from the labyrinth, the board, the aureole . . . And other things. While Frieda Ungern was explaining the meaning of the pictures, he had discovered more differences, confirming his theory: each book differed from the other two. The game of errors continued, and he needed to set to work urgently. But not like that, not with the Baroness breathing down his neck.

"I'd like to take a good, long look at all of this," he said.

"Of course. I've got plenty of time. I'd like to see how you work."

Corso cleared his throat, embarrassed. They'd reached the point he'd worried about: the unpleasantness.

"I work better on my own."

It sounded false. Frieda Ungern frowned.

"I'm afraid I don't understand." She glanced at Corso's canvas bag suspiciously. "Are you hinting that you want me to leave you alone?"

"If you wouldn't mind." Corso swallowed, trying to hold her gaze as long as possible. "What I'm doing is confidential."

The Baroness blinked lightly. Her frown became more threatening and Corso knew that everything could go out of the window at any moment.

"You're free to do as you like, of course." Frieda Ungern's tone could have frozen all the plants in the room. "But this is my book and my house."

At that point anyone else would have apologized and beat a retreat, but not Corso. He remained seated, smoking, his eyes fixed on the Baroness. At last, he smiled cautiously, like a rabbit playing blackjack about to ask for another card.

"I don't think I've explained myself fully." He smiled slightly as he took a well-wrapped object from his canvas bag. "I just need to spend some time here with the book and my notes." He gently tapped the bag as he held out the package with his other hand. "As you can see, I've brought all I need."

The Baroness undid the wrapping and looked at its contents in silence. It was a book in German – Berlin, September 1943 – a thick brochure entitled *Iden*, a monthly publication from the Idus group, a circle of devotees of magic and astrology which was very close to the leaders of Nazi Germany. Corso had put in a marker at a page with a photograph. It showed a young and very pretty Frieda Ungern smiling at the photographer. She had a man on each arm (for she still had them both). One of the men was in civilian clothes and the caption named him as the Fürher's personal astrologer. She was mentioned as his assistant, the distinguished Miss Frieda Wender. The man on the left was wearing steel-rimmed glasses and had a timid expression. He was wearing a black SS uniform. One didn't need to read the caption to recognize the *Reichsführer* Heinrich Himmler.

When Frieda Ungern, née Wender, looked up and her eyes met Corso's, she no longer seemed like a sweet little old lady. But it only lasted a moment. Then she nodded slowly and carefully tore out the page with the photo, ripping it into tiny pieces. And Corso reflected that witches and baronesses and little old ladies working surrounded by books and pot plants, had their price, just like anyone else. '*Victa iacet Virtus.*' And he didn't see why it should be any other way.

* * *

Once he was alone he took the folder from his bag and set to work. He sat at a table by the window, with *The Nine Doors* open at the frontispiece. Before starting he parted the net curtains and glanced out. A grey BMW was parked across the street. The tenacious Rochefort was at his post. Corso couldn't see the girl at the bar on the corner.

He turned his attention to the book: the type of paper, the pressure of the engravings, any flaws or misprints. Now he knew that the three copies were only outwardly identical: the same black leather binding with no lettering on the outside, five raised bands, a pentacle on the cover, the same number of pages and location of the engravings . . . With great patience, page by page, he gradually completed the comparative tables he'd begun with Book Number One. On page 81, at the blank page on the reverse side of engraving V, he found another of the Baroness's cards. It was the translation of a paragraph on the page.

You will accept the pact of alliance that I offer you, surrendering myself to you. And you will promise me the love of women and the flower of the maidens, the honour of nuns, the rank, pleasures and riches of the powerful, princes and ecclesiastics. I will fornicate every three days and the intoxication will be pleasing to me. Once a year I will pay homage to you in confirmation of this contract signed with my blood. I will tread upon the sacraments of the Church and I will address prayers to you. I will fear neither rope, nor sword, nor poison. I will pass amongst the plague-ridden and the lepers without sullying my flesh. But above all I will possess the Knowledge, for which my first parents renounced Paradise. By virtue of this pact you will erase me from the book of life and enter me in the black book of death. And from now I will live for twenty happy years on man's earth. But then I will go with you to your kingdom and curse God.

There was another note on the back of the card, relating to a paragraph deciphered on another page:

I will recognize your servants, my brothers, by the sign impressed on some part of their body, here or there, a scar or your mark . . .

Corso cursed emphatically under his breath, as if he were muttering a prayer. Then he looked round at the books on the walls, at their dark, worn spines, and he seemed to hear a strange, distant murmur coming from them. Each one of the closed books was a door and behind it stirred shadows, voices, sounds, heading towards him from a deep, dark place.

He came out in goose bumps. Just like a vulgar fan.

It was night by the time he left. He paused in the doorway a moment and glanced to left and right, but saw nothing to worry him. The grey BMW had disappeared. A low mist was rising from the river, flowing over the stone parapet and sliding along the damp paving stones. The yellowish glow of the street lamps, illuminating successive stretches of the embankment, was reflected on the ground, lighting up the empty bench were the girl had been sitting.

He went to the bar. He searched for her face amongst the people standing at the bar or sitting at the narrow tables at the back but couldn't find her. He sensed that a piece of the jigsaw was out of place, something that had been setting off alarm signals intermittently in his brain ever since her call to warn him of Rochefort's reappearance. Corso, whose instincts had become a great deal sharper recently, could smell danger in the deserted street, in the damp vapour rising from the river and trailing to the door of the bar where he was standing. He shook his shoulders to try to rid himself of the feeling. He bought a packet of Gauloises and gulped down two gins one after the other. They made his nostrils dilate, and everything fell slowly into place, like a picture coming into focus. The alarms faded in the distance, and echoes from the outside world were now comfortably softened. Holding a third gin he went to sit down at an empty table by the slightly misted window. He looked out at the street, the quayside and the mist sliding over the parapet and across the paving stones, swirling up as the wheels of a car cut through it. He sat there for a quarter of an hour looking out for any unusual signs, his canvas bag on the floor by his feet. In it were most of the answers to the mystery posed by Varo Borja. The bookdealer wasn't wasting his money.

In the first place, Corso had now solved the problem of the differences between eight of the nine engravings. Book Number Three differed from the other two copies in engravings I, III and VI. In engraving I, the walled city with the horseman riding towards it had only three towers instead of four. In engraving III there was an arrow in the archer's quiver, while in the Toledo and Sintra copies the quiver was empty. And in engraving VI, the hanged man was hanging by his right foot, but the figures in Books One and Two were hanging by their left. He could now fill in the comparative table he'd started in Sintra.

	I	II	III	IIII	V	VI	VII	VIII	VIIII
ONE	Four towers	Left hand	No arrow	No exit	Sand down	Left foot	White board	No aureole	No dif.
TWO	Four towers	Right hand	No arrow	Exit	Sand up	Left foot	Black board	Aureole	No dif
THREE	Three towers	Right hand	Arrow	No exit	Sand up	Right foot	White board	No aureole	No dif.

NEM. PERV.T QVI N.N LEG. CERT. RIT

CLAVS. PAT.T

VERB. D.SVM C.S.T ARCAN.

FOR. N.N OMN. A.QVE

FR. ST. A

DIT.SCO M.R.

DIS.S P.TI.R M.

VIC. I.T VIR.

N.NC SC.O TEN.BR. LVX

As a conclusion, this meant that although the engravings appeared identical, one of the three was always different, with the exception of engraving number VIIII. And the differences were distributed over the three books. But the apparently arbitrary distribution acquired some meaning on examining these differences alongside those between the printer's marks for the signatures of the *inventor* (the original creator of the pictures) and of the *sculptor* (the artist who made the engravings), *A.T.* and *L.F.*

	I	II	III	IIII	V	VI	VII	VIII	VIIII
ONE	AT(s) AT(i)	AT(s) LF(i)	AT(s) AT(i)	AT(s) AT(i)	AT(s) LF(i)	AT(s) AT(i)	AT(s) AT(i)	AT(s) AT(i)	AT(s) AT(i)
TWO	AT(s) AT(i)	AT(s) AT(i)	AT(s) AT(i)	AT(s) LF(i)	AT(s) AT(i)	AT(s) AT(i)	AT(s) LF(i)	AT(s) LF(i)	AT(s) AT(i)
THREE	AT(s) LF(i)	AT(s) AT(s)	AT(s) LF(i)	AT(s) AT(i)	AT(s) AT(i)	AT(s) LF(i)	AT(s) AT(s)	AT(s) AT(s)	AT(s) AT(s)

If he superimposed the two tables he found a coincidence: in each of the engravings which differed from the other, supposedly identical, two, the initials of the *inventor* were also different. This meant that Aristide Torchia, as the *sculptor,* had made all the woodcuts for the prints in the book. But he was only identified as the *inventor* of the original drawing or works in nineteen of the twenty-seven engravings contained in total in the three books. The other eight, distributed over the three copies – two engravings in Book One, three in Book Two and the same number in Book Three – had been created by somebody else, somebody with the initials *L.F.* Phonetically very close to the name Lucifer.

Towers. Hand. Arrow. Exit from the labyrinth. Sand. Hanged man's foot. Board. Aureole. This was where the errors lay. Eight differences, eight correct engravings, no doubt copied from the original, the obscure *Delomelanicon,* and nineteen altered, unusable engravings, distributed over the pages of the three copies, only identical in text and outward appearance. This meant that none of the three books was a forgery, but it wasn't entirely authentic either. Aristide Torchia had confessed the truth to his executioners, but not the entire truth. There did indeed only remain one book. Hidden and as safe from the flames as it was forbidden to the unworthy. And the engravings were the key. There remained a single book, hidden within the three copies. For the disciple to surpass the master he had to reconstruct the book using the codes, the rules of the Art.

	I	II	III	IIII	V	VI	VII	VIII	VIIII
ONE	Four towers	Left hand	No arrow	No exit	Sand down	Left foot	White board	No aureole	No dif.
TWO	Four towers	Right hand	No arrow	Exit	Sand up	Left foot	Black board	Aureole	No dif.
THREE	Three towers	Right hand	Arrow	No exit	Sand up	Right foot	White board	No aureole	No dif.

	I	II	III	IIII	V	VI	VII	VIII	VIIII
ONE	AT(s) AT(i)	AT(s) LF(i)	AT(s) AT(i)	AT(s) AT(i)	AT(s) LF(i)	AT(s) AT(i)	AT(s) AT(i)	AT(s) AT(i)	AT(s) AT(i)
TWO	AT(s) AT(i)	AT(s) AT(i)	AT(s) AT(i)	AT(s) LF(i)	AT(s) AT(i)	AT(s) AT(i)	AT(s) LF(i)	AT(s) LF(i)	AT(s) AT(i)
THREE	AT(s) LF(i)	AT(s) AT(s)	AT(s) LF(i)	AT(s) AT(i)	AT(s) AT(i)	AT(s) LF(i)	AT(s) AT(s)	AT(s) AT(s)	AT(s) AT(s)

He sipped his gin and looked out at the darkness over the Seine, beyond the street lights that lit up part of the quayside and threw deep shadows beneath the bare trees. But he didn't feel euphoric at his victory, nor even simply satisfied at finishing a difficult job. He knew the mood well: the cold, lucid calm when he finally got hold of a book he'd been chasing for a long time. When he managed to cut in front of a competitor, nail a book after a delicate negotiation, or dig up a gem in a pile of old papers and rubbish. He remembered Nikon in another time and place sticking labels on video tapes, sitting on the floor by the television, rocking gently in time to the music – Audrey Hepburn in love with a journalist in Rome – keeping her big dark eyes that constantly expressed her wonder at life fixed on Corso. By then, they already hinted at the hardness and reproach, premonitions of the loneliness closing in on them like an inexorable, fixed-term debt. The hunter with his prey, Nikon had whispered, amazed at her discovery, because maybe seeing him like that for the first time. Corso recovering his breath, like a hostile wolf rejecting his catch after a long chase. A predator feeling no hunger or passion, no horror at the sight of blood or flesh. With no aim other than the hunt itself. You're as dead as your prey, Lucas Corso. Like the dry, brittle paper that has become your flag.

Dusty corpses that you don't love either, that don't even belong to you, and that you don't give a damn about.

For a moment he wondered what Nikon would think of him, the tingling in his groin, the dryness of his mouth despite the gin, as he sat at the narrow table in the bar, watching the street and unable to leave because there, in the warmth and light, surrounded by cigarette smoke and the murmur of conversation, he felt temporarily safe from the dark premonition, from the danger without name or shape that he sensed approaching him through the deadening thickness of the gin in his blood, with the sinister low mist rising from the river. As on that English moor, in black and white. Nikon would have understood. Basil Rathbone, alert, listening to the hound of the Baskervilles howling in the distance.

At last he made up his mind. He finished his gin and left some coins on the table. Then he put the canvas bag over his shoulder and went out into the street, turning up his coat collar. As he crossed he looked in both directions and, when he reached the stone bench where the girl had been reading, he turned and walked along the parapet on the left bank. The yellow lights of a barge on the river lit him from below as he passed a bridge, surrounding him with a halo of dirty mist.

The street and the riverside seemed deserted, with few cars passing. By the narrow passageway of the Rue Mazarin he hailed a taxi, but it didn't stop. He walked on to the Rue Guénégaud, intending to cross the Pont Neuf to the Louvre. The mist and dark buildings gave the scene a sombre, timeless appearance. Like a wolf sensing danger, sniffing the air to left and right, Corso felt unusually anxious. He moved the bag to his other shoulder so as to free his right hand and stopped to look round, perplexed. In that precise spot – Chapter XI: The plot thickens, d'Artagnan saw Constance Bonacieux emerge from the Rue Dauphine, also on her way towards the Louvre and the same bridge. She was accompanied by a gentleman who turned out to be the Duke of Buckingham, whose nocturnal adventure almost earned him a thrust of d'Artagnan's sword through his body:

I loved her, Milord, and I was jealous . . .

Maybe the feeling of danger was false, the perverse effect of reading too many novels and the strange atmosphere. But the girl's telephone call and the grey BMW at the door hadn't been figments of his imagination. A clock struck the hour in the distance and Corso breathed out. This was all absurd.

Then Rochefort jumped him. He seemed to emerge from the river, materializing from the shadows. In fact he had followed him along the riverside below the parapet, and then climbed a flight of stone steps to reach him. Corso found out about the steps when he found himself rolling down them. He'd never fallen down steps before and he thought it would go on for longer, one step at a time or something, like in films. But it was all over very quickly. A very professional first punch behind the ear and the night became a blur. The outside world seemed very distant, as if he'd drunk a whole bottle of gin. Thanks to this he didn't feel much pain as he rolled down the steps, hitting the stone edges. He reached the bottom bruised but conscious. Possibly a little surprised not to hear the "splash" – a Conradian onomatopoeia, he thought incongruously – of his body hitting the water. From the ground, his head on damp paving stones and his legs on the bottom steps, he looked up, confused, and saw Rochefort's black outline descending the steps three by three and jump on top of him.

You're buggered, Corso. This was all he had time to think. Then he did two things. First he tried to kick as Rochefort jumped over him. But his weak attempt hit only air. So all he had left was the old, familiar reflex of forming a square and letting the gunfire fade away into the dusk. What with the damp from the river and his own private darkness – he'd lost his glasses in the scuffle – he winced. The Guard dies but falls down the stairs too. So he formed a square, curled into a ball to protect the bag, still hanging, or rather tangled round his shoulder. Maybe his great-great-grandfather Corso from the other shore of Lethe would have appreciated his move. It was difficult to tell what Rochefort thought of it. Like Wellington, he rose to the occasion with traditional British efficiency: Corso heard a distant cry of pain, which he suspected came from his own mouth, as Rochefort dealt him a clean, precise kick in the back.

Nothing good was going to come of this, so he closed his eyes and waited, resigned, for someone to turn the page. He could feel Rochefort's breathing very near, leaning over him, searching inside the bag. Then Rochefort yanked violently at the strap. This made Corso open his eyes again, just enough to make out the flight of steps in his field of vision. But as his face was pressed down against the paving stones, it appeared horizontal, crooked and slightly out of focus. So at first he didn't really understand whether the girl was going up or down. He just saw her move incredibly fast, from right to left, her long legs jumping from one step to another. Her duffle coat which she had just taken off, spread out in the air, or rather moved towards a corner of the screen surrounded by swirls of mist, like the cape of the Phantom of the Opera.

He blinked with interest, in an attempt to focus, and moved his head slightly to keep the scene in the frame. Out of the corner of his eye he saw Rochefort, his image inverted, give a start as the girl jumped down the last few steps. She fell on top of him with a brief, sharp cry, harder and more piercing than broken glass. He heard a thick sound – a thump – and Rochefort disappeared from Corso's field of vision as suddenly as if he'd been on springs. Now all Corso could see was the empty flight of steps. So, with difficulty, he turned his head towards the river and laid his other cheek on the paving stones. The image was still crooked: the ground on one side, the black sky on the other, the bridge below and the river above. But now at least it contained Rochefort and the girl. For a split second Corso saw her silhouetted against the hazy lights of the bridge. She was standing, her legs apart and her hands out in front of her, as if asking for a moment of calm to listen to some distant tune. Rochefort was facing her, with a knee and a hand on the ground, like a boxer who can't quite get up while the referee counts to ten. His scar was visible in the light from the bridge. Corso just had time to see his look of amazement before the girl again gave a piercing cry. She balanced on one leg and, raising the other in a semi-circular movement that seemed quite effortless, she kicked Rochefort sharply in the face.

XII

Buckingham and Milady

The crime was committed with the help of a woman.
E. de Queiroz: *The Mystery of the Sintra Road*

Corso sat on the bottom step attempting to light a cigarette. He was still too stunned to have recovered his spatial awareness so he couldn't get the match in the same plane as the tip of the cigarette. Also one of the lenses in his glasses was cracked and he had to squint with one eye to see with the other. Once the flame reached his fingers he dropped the match between his feet and kept the cigarette in his mouth. The girl, who had been collecting the contents of the bag strewn over the ground, came and handed it to him.

"Are you all right?"

Her tone was neutral, without concern or worry. She was probably annoyed at the stupid way that Corso had been taken by surprise in spite of her warning on the phone. He nodded, humiliated and confused. But he was comforted when he remembered the look on Rochefort's face just before he got kicked. The girl had struck him precisely and cruelly but she didn't follow up as he lay sprawled on his back. He turned over in pain, but didn't challenge her or try to retaliate. He dragged himself away, while she lost interest in him and went to pick up the bag. If it had been up to Corso he would have gone after him and, without a second thought, wrung his neck until he'd extracted everything from him. But he wasn't sure whether the girl would have let him, and anyway he was too weak even to stand. Now she'd dealt with Rochefort all she was concerned with was Corso and the bag.

"Why did you let him go?"

They could make him out in the distance, a staggering figure just disappearing into the darkness round a bend of the riverbank, among moored barges that looked like ghost ships in the low mist. Corso pictured Rochefort retreating, humiliated, his face smashed to a pulp, wondering how on earth the girl could have done so much damage. Corso felt jubilant at his revenge.

"We should have questioned the bastard," he complained.

She'd gone to find her duffle coat. She came back and sat next to him, but didn't answer immediately. She seemed tired.

"He'll come after us again," she said. She glanced at Corso before looking out at the river. "Make sure you're more careful next time."

He took the damp cigarette from his mouth and started turning it over in his fingers, which made it fall apart.

"I thought that . . ."

"All men think that. Until they get their faces smashed in."

Then he saw that the girl was wounded. It wasn't much: blood was trickling from her nose to her lip, and then down her chin.

"Your nose is bleeding," he said stupidly.

"I know," she answered calmly. She touched her face and then looked at the blood on her fingers.

"How did he do that to you?"

"It was my fault really." She wiped her fingers on her jeans. "I fell on top of him at the beginning. We collided."

"Where did you learn to do that kind of thing?"

"What kind of thing?"

"I saw you, down by the water." Corso moved his hands in a clumsy imitation of her movement. "Giving him what he deserved."

She smiled gently and stood up, brushing the back of her jeans.

"I once fought with an archangel. He won, but it taught me a thing or two."

With the blood running from her nose she looked impossibly young. She put the bag over her shoulder and held out her hand to help him. He was surprised by her firm grip. When he stood up all his bones ached.

"I thought archangels fought with lances and swords."

She was sniffing and holding her head back to stop the blood running from her nose. She looked at him sideways, annoyed.

"You've looked at too many Dürer engravings, Corso. And see where that's got you."

They returned to the hotel via the Pont Neuf and the passageway alongside the Louvre, without any more incidents. By the light of a street lamp he saw that the girl was still bleeding. He took his handkerchief from his pocket but when he tried to help her she took it from him and held it to her nose herself. She walked along absorbed in her own thoughts. Corso glanced at her sideways: her long, bare neck and perfect profile, her matt skin in the hazy light from the lamps of the Louvre. He couldn't tell what she was thinking. She walked with the bag on her shoulder, and leaned her head slightly forward, which made her look determined, stubborn. Occasionally, when they turned a dark corner her eyes darted to right and left, and she put the hand holding the handkerchief to her nose down by her side, tense and alert. Then under the archways of the Rue de Rivoli where there was more light she seemed to relax. Her nose was no longer bleeding and she returned his handkerchief stained with dry blood. Even her mood improved. She didn't seem to find it so reprehensible that Corso let himself be caught like a fool. She put her hand on his shoulder a couple of times, as if they were two old friends returning from a walk. It was a spontaneous, natural gesture. But maybe she was also tired and needed support. Corso, his head clearing with the walk, found it pleasant at first. Then it began to trouble him slightly. The feel of her hand on his shoulder awakened a strange feeling in him, not entirely disagreeable but unexpected. He felt tender, like the soft centre of a sweet.

Gruber was on duty that evening. He allowed himself a brief, inquisitive glance at the pair – Corso in his damp, dirty coat, his glasses cracked, the girl with her face stained with blood – but otherwise remained expressionless. He raised an eyebrow courteously and nodded, indicating that he was at Corso's disposal but Corso gestured that he didn't need anything. Gruber handed him a sealed envelope with the two room keys. They stepped into the lift and he was about to open the envelope when he saw that the girl's nose was bleeding again. He put the message in his pocket and gave her his handkerchief again. The lift stopped at her floor. Corso said she should call a doctor, but the girl shook her head and got out of the lift. After hesitating for a moment he went after her. She had dripped some blood on the carpet. Once in the room he made her sit on the bed. Then he went to the bathroom and soaked a towel in water.

"Put it against the nape of your neck and lean your head back."

She obeyed without a word. All the energy she'd shown down by the river seemed to have evaporated. Maybe because of the nosebleed. He took off her coat and shoes and laid her on the bed, folding the pillow behind her back. Like an exhausted little girl, she let him. Before turning off all the lights except for the one in the bathroom, Corso glanced round. Other than a toothbrush, toothpaste and shampoo above the washbasin, the only belongings he could see were her duffle coat, the rucksack open on the sofa, the postcards bought the day before together with *The Three Musketeers*, a grey sweater, a couple of cotton T-shirts and some white panties drying on the radiator. He looked at the girl, embarrassed. He wasn't sure whether he ought to sit on the edge of the bed or elsewhere. His feeling in the Rue de Rivoli was still there in his stomach, or wherever. But he couldn't leave. Not until she felt better. In the end he decided to remain standing. He had his hands in his coat pockets, and with one of them he could feel the empty flask of gin. He glanced greedily at the drinks cabinet, which still had the unopened seal of the hotel. He was dying for a drink.

"You were great down there by the river," he said for the sake of it. "I haven't thanked you."

She smiled sleepily. But her eyes, with pupils dilated in the darkness, followed Corso's every move.

"What's going on?" he asked.

She looked back at him slightly ironically, implying that his question was absurd.

"They obviously want something you've got."

"The Dumas manuscript? Or *The Nine Doors?*"

The girl sighed gently. Maybe none of this is terribly important, she seemed to be saying.

"You're clever, Corso," she said at last. "You ought to have a theory."

"I've got too many. What I don't have is any proof."

"You don't always need proof."

"That's only in crime novels. All Sherlock Holmes or Poirot have to do is imagine who the murderer is and how he committed the crime. They invent the rest and tell it as if they knew it was a fact. Then Watson or Hastings congratulate them admiringly and say, "Well done, sir, that's exactly how it happened." And the murderer confesses. The idiot."

"I'd congratulate you."

This time there was no irony in her voice. She was watching him intently, waiting for him to say or do something.

He shifted uneasily.

"I know," he said. The girl still held his gaze, as if she truly had nothing to hide. "But I wonder why."

He was about to add, "This is real life, not a crime novel," but didn't. At this stage in the story, the line between fantasy and reality appeared rather blurred. The flesh and blood Corso, identity-card holder with a known place of residence, with – following the episode on the stone steps – a physical presence of which his aching bones were proof, was increasingly tempted to see himself as a real character in an imaginary world. But that wasn't much good. It was only a small step away from believing he was an imaginary character who sees himself as real in an imaginary world. Only a small step away from going nuts. And he wondered whether someone, some twisted novelist or drunken writer of cheap screenplays, at that very moment saw him as an *imaginary* character who considered himself *imaginary* in an *imaginary* world. That really would be too much.

These thoughts had made his mouth quite dry. He stood in front of the girl, his hands in his pockets, his tongue feeling like sandpaper. If I was imaginary, he thought with relief, my hair would stand on end, I'd exclaim "Woe is me!" and my face would be beaded with sweat. But I wouldn't be this thirsty. I drink, therefore I am. So he lunged at the drinks cabinet, broke the seal and gulped down a miniature bottle of gin in one go, neat. He was almost smiling when he stood up, shutting the cabinet like someone closing a reliquary. Things gradually assumed their proper place.

The room was fairly dark. The dim light from the bathroom slanted across the bed where the girl was still lying. He looked at her bare feet, her legs, the T-shirt spattered with dry blood. Then his gaze lingered over her long, tanned, bare neck. The half-open mouth showing the tips of her white teeth in the gloom. Her eyes still watching him intently. He touched the key to his room inside his coat pocket and swallowed. He ought to leave.

"Are you feeling better?"

She nodded. Corso looked at his watch, although he didn't really care about the time. He didn't remember having switched on the radio as they came into the room, but there was music playing somewhere. A melancholy song, in French. A waitress in a bar, in a port, in love with a sailor.

"Right. I've got to go."

The woman on the radio went on singing. The sailor, predictably, had gone for good, and the girl in the bar gazed at his empty chair and the wet ring left by his glass on the table. Corso went to the bedside table to get his handkerchief and used the cleanest part to wipe his undamaged lens. Then he saw that the girl's nose had once more started to bleed.

"It's started again."

Blood was running down to her mouth again. She put her hand to her face and smiled stoically, looking at her bloodstained fingers.

"It doesn't matter."

"You ought to see a doctor."

She half-closed her eyes and shook her head, gently. She looked helpless in the dim light of the room, dark spots of blood staining the pillow. Still holding his glasses, he sat down on the edge of the bed and leant over to hold the handkerchief to her nose. As he did so, his shadow, outlined on the wall by the slanting light from the bathroom, seemed to hesitate a moment between light and darkness before disappearing into the corner.

Then the girl did something strange, unexpected. She ignored the handkerchief he was offering her and stretched out her bloody hand towards Corso. She touched his face and drew four red lines with her fingers, from his forehead to his chin. Instead of moving her hand away after this singular caress she kept it there, damp and warm, while he felt the drops of blood running down the four lines on his face. Her luminous irises reflected the light from the half-open door, and Corso shuddered as in each he saw the image of his lost shadow.

Another song was playing on the radio but neither of them was listening. The girl smelt of heat and fever, a gentle pulse throbbing under the skin of her bare neck. The room was light and dark, and things became lost in the deep shadows. She whispered something unintelligible, very low, and light glinted in her eyes as she slipped her hand round Corso's neck, spreading the trail of warm blood. With the taste of blood on his tongue he leant towards her, towards her soft, half-open mouth. She gave a gentle moan which seemed to come from far away, slow and monotonous, centuries-old. For a brief moment, in the pulse of her flesh all Lucas Corso's previous deaths came to life, as if brought by the current of a dark, slow river whose waters were as thick as varnish. He regretted that she didn't have a name that he could carve in his memory with that moment.

It only lasted a second. Then, recovering his clear-headedness, Corso saw his other self sitting on the edge of the bed, still in his coat, mesmerized as she moved back slightly and undid her jeans, arching her back like a beautiful young animal. He watched her with a kind of internal, benevolent wink, with a familiar indulgence both weary and sceptical. With more curiosity than desire. As she slid her zipper down the girl uncovered a dark triangle of skin contrasting with her white cotton panties that came down with her jeans. Her long, tanned legs, stretched out on the bed, took Corso's – both the Corsos' – breath away, just as they had kicked in Rochefort's teeth. Then she lifted up her arms and took off her T-shirt. She did it completely naturally, neither flirtatious nor indifferent. She kept her calm, sweet eyes on him until her T-shirt covered her face. Then the contrast was even greater – more white cotton, this time sliding upwards over her tanned skin, her firm, warm flesh, her slender waist, her heavy, perfect breasts, outlined against the light in the darkness, her neck, her half-open mouth and once again her eyes, with all the light robbed from the sky in them. With Corso's shadow in them, like a soul locked in the bottom of a double crystal ball or emerald.

From that moment on, he knew with absolute certainty that he wouldn't be able to do it. He sensed it with the lugubrious intuition that precedes certain events and marks them, even before they have taken place, with intimations of inevitable disaster. To be prosaic, Corso realized, as he threw the rest of his clothes on top of his coat at the foot of the bed, that the initial erection caused by the circumstances was now in visible retreat. Cut down in his prime. Or as his Bonapartist great-great-grandfather would have said, "*La Garde recule.*" Totally. It made him suddenly anxious, although he hoped that, as he was standing against the light, his unfortunate flaccid state wouldn't be noticed. Very carefully he lay face down next to her tanned, warm body waiting in the dark, and used what the Emperor, out on the muddy fields of Flanders, would have called an indirect approach tactic – sizing up the terrain from the middle distance and making no contact in the critical zone. From a prudent distance he tried to play for time in case Grouchy arrived with reinforcements, caressing the girl and kissing her unhurriedly on the mouth and neck. But no luck. Grouchy was nowhere to be seen. The old fool was chasing Prussians miles from the battlefield. Corso's anxiety turned to panic as the girl moved nearer to him and slipped her firm, warm thigh between his. She must have become aware of the scale of the disaster. He saw her smile, slightly disconcerted. An encouraging smile which said something like, "I know you can do it!" Then she kissed him with extreme tenderness and put out her hand, ready to help things along. And just when he felt her hand at the very epicentre of the drama, Corso went down completely. Like the *Titanic*. Straight to the bottom, no half measures. The orchestra playing on deck, women and children first. The next twenty minutes were agony, atonement for all his sins. Heroic attacks meeting the immovable barrier of the Scottish fusiliers. The infantry on the attack glimpsing only the slightest chance of victory. Improvised incursions by the light infantry, in the vain hope of taking the enemy by surprise. Skirmishes of hussars and heavy charges by cuirassiers. But all attempts met with the same results – Wellington was messing around in a remote Belgian village, while his pipers were playing the march of the Scots Greys in Corso's face. The Old Guard, or what remained of it, was glancing desperately to left and right, teeth clenched and face against the sheets, twenty minutes by the watch which, for his sins, he hadn't removed. Drops of sweat the size of fists ran from the roots of his hair down his neck. He looked round with wide staring eyes over the girl's shoulder, desperately wishing for a gun to shoot himself.

She was asleep. He stretched out an arm, carefully so as not to wake her, and searched for a cigarette inside his coat. Once it was lit he raised himself up on his elbow and stared at her. She was on her back, naked, her head tilted back on the pillow spotted with dry blood, breathing gently through her half-open mouth. She still smelt of fever and warm flesh. In the glow from the bathroom which traced her outline in light and shadow, Corso admired her perfect body. This, he told himself, is a masterpiece of genetic engineering. And he wondered what mixture of blood, or mysteries, saliva, skin, flesh, semen and chance had commingled to create her. All women, all females produced by the human species were there, summed up in her eighteen- or twenty-year-old body. He saw the pulse at her neck, the almost imperceptible beat of her heart, the gentle curve from her back to her waist, widening out at the hips. He put out his hand and stroked the small curly triangle down where the skin was slightly lighter, between her thighs where he'd been unable to bivouac in the classic manner. The girl had taken the situation with perfect good humour. She'd made light of it and they'd drifted into a light-hearted, friendly game once she understood that on Corso's part and in that particular bout, there wasn't going to be any more action. This eased the tension. And, lacking a gun – they shoot horses, don't they – at least it stopped him dashing his head against the corner of the bedside table in an attempt to crack his skull. He'd considered it in his blind rage but discounted it, and ended up discreetly punching the wall, almost breaking his hand. Surprised by his abrupt move and the sudden tensing of his body, she looked at him, startled. Corso's effort not to shout out in pain slightly calmed him. He even managed to smile rather tensely and tell the girl it tended only to happen to him the first thirty times or so. She laughed, her arms around him, and kissed his eyes and mouth, amused and tender. You idiot, Corso. I don't mind at all. Even so, he did the only thing he could at that point – a meticulous play of fingers in the right place, with results that were, if not glorious, at least satisfactory. As she caught her breath, the girl stared at him for a long time in silence before kissing him slowly, conscientiously, until the pressure of her lips diminished and she fell asleep.

The burning tip of his cigarette lit up Corso's fingers in the darkness. He kept the smoke in his lungs as long as he could and then exhaled it in one go, watching the patterns it made in the segment of light above the bed. He felt the girl's breathing falter for a moment and he looked at her sharply. She was frowning and moaning quietly, like a little girl having a nightmare. Then, still asleep, she half-turned towards him, her arm under her bare breasts and her hand under her face. Who the bloody hell are you, he asked her soundlessly once again, bad-temperedly, although he then leaned over to kiss her. He stroked her short hair, the curve of her waist and hips now sharply silhouetted against the light. There was more beauty in that gentle line than in a melody, a sculpture, a poem or a picture. He moved closer and smelt her warm neck, and at that instant his own pulse started to hammer more strongly, awakening his flesh. Keep calm now, he said to himself. Keep cool and don't panic this time. Let's continue. He didn't know how long he could keep it up, so he hurriedly stubbed out his cigarette and pressed himself against the girl. His body seemed to respond in a satisfactory manner. Then he parted her legs and at last, bewildered, entered a moist, welcoming paradise, of warm cream and honey. He felt the girl shift, sleepily, and put her arms round him although she wasn't quite awake. He kissed her on the neck and mouth. She was moaning gently, and he realized that she was moving her hips in time with him. And when he sank right to the root of the flesh and himself, making his way easily to a place lost in his memory, she opened her eyes and looked at him, surprised and happy, green reflections through her long damp eyelashes. I love you, Corso. IloveyouIloveyouIloveyouIloveyou. I love you. Later he had to bite his tongue so as not to say something equally stupid. Amazed and incredulous, he watched from a distance and barely recognized himself. He was attentive to her, watching her beats, movements, anticipating her desires and discovering her secret springs, the intimate key to the soft yet tense body wound firmly round his own. They went on like that for about an hour. Afterwards Corso asked the girl if there was any risk of pregnancy, and she told him not to worry, that she had everything under control. Then he put it all away deep inside him, next to his heart.

He woke at daybreak. The girl was sleeping pressed against him. For some time Corso didn't move in order not to wake her. He stopped himself thinking about what had happened or might be about to happen. He closed his eyes and drifted, enjoying the peace of the moment. He could feel her breath on his skin. Irene Adler, 223b Baker Street. The Devil in love. The outline in the mist, facing Rochefort. The blue duffle coat falling slowly, unfolding, on to the quayside. And Corso's shadow in her eyes. She slept, relaxed and tranquil, aware of nothing. He couldn't link the images in his mind logically. At that moment logic had no appeal. He felt lazy and content. He put his hand between the girl's warm thighs and kept it there, very still. Her naked body, at least, was real.

Later he got out of bed carefully and went to the bathroom. In the mirror he saw that he still had traces of dried blood on his face, and also, as the result of his encounter with Rochefort and the stone steps, a bluish bruise on his left shoulder, and another across a couple of ribs which hurt when he pressed it. He had a quick wash and then went to look for a cigarette. As he was searching in his coat he found the note Gruber had handed him.

He cursed under his breath for having forgotten it, but there was nothing he could do about that now. So he opened the envelope and went back to the light in the bathroom to read the note inside. It was brief and its contents – two names, a number and an address – made him smile malevolently. He glanced at himself again in the mirror. His hair was matted and he needed a shave. He put on his glasses as if arming himself, a mean wolf off to hunt. He picked up his clothes and canvas bag quietly, and gave the sleeping girl a last glance. Maybe it was going to be a beautiful day after all. Buckingham and Milady were about to choke on their breakfast.

The Hotel Crillon was too expensive for Flavio La Ponte. Enrique Taillefer's widow must have been paying the bill. Corso reflected on this as he paid his taxi on the Place de la Concorde and crossed the marble lobby towards the stairs and Room 206. There was a "Do not disturb" sign on the door and no sound when he rapped loudly on it three times.

Three punctures were made in the heathen flesh, and the White Whale's barbs were then tempered.

The Brotherhood of Nantucket Harpooneers was about to be dissolved. Corso didn't know if he was sorry or not. He and La Ponte had once imagined an alternative version of *Moby Dick*. Ishmael writes the story, places the manuscript in the caulked coffin and drowns with the rest of the crew of the *Pequod*. Queequeg is the only survivor, the wild harpooneer with no intellectual pretensions. In time he learns to read. One day he reads his friend's novel and discovers that Ishmael's version and his own memories of what happened are completely different. So he writes his own version of the story. "Call me Queequeg" the story begins, and he calls it *A Whale*. From the harpooneer's professional point of view Ishmael was a pedantic scholar who blew things out of all proportion. Moby Dick wasn't to blame, he was just a whale like any other. It was all a matter of an incompetent captain wanting to settle a personal score instead of filling barrels with oil. "What does it matter who tore his leg off?" writes Queequeg. Corso could remember the scene around the table in Makarova's bar. Makarova, with her masculine, Nordic reserve, listening carefully to La Ponte explaining the use of the caulking on the carpenter's coffin while Zizi looked on jealously from the other side of the bar. In those days, if Corso dialled his own number, Nikon – he always pictured her emerging from the darkroom, hands wet with fixative – would answer. That's what happened the night they rewrote *Moby Dick*. They all ended up at Corso's place, emptied more bottles and watched a John Huston movie on the video. They drank a toast to old Melville when the *Rachel*, searching the seas for her lost sons, at last finds another orphan.

That's how it was. But now, standing outside Room 206, Corso couldn't feel the anger of one about to confront another with his treachery. Maybe because, deep down, he believed that in politics, business and sex, betrayal was only a question of timing. Politics aside, he didn't know whether his friend was in Paris because of business or sex. Maybe it was both, because even Corso, in his cynicism, couldn't imagine La Ponte getting into trouble for money alone. He remembered Liana Taillefer during their brief skirmish at his flat, beautiful and sensual, wide hips, smooth pale skin, a wholesome Kim Novak playing the femme fatale. He arched an eyebrow – friendship consisted of that kind of detail – he could well understand La Ponte's motives. Maybe this was why, when he opened the door, La Ponte found no hostility in Corso's expression. He was barefoot and in pyjamas. He just had time to open his mouth before Corso gave him a punch that sent him staggering across the room.

In other circumstances Corso might have relished the scene. A luxury suite, with a view of the obelisk in the Place de la Concorde, thick pile carpet and a huge bathroom. La Ponte on the floor, rubbing his jaw, trying to focus after the punch. A huge bed, with two breakfast trays. And Liana Taillefer sitting on it, blonde and stunned, holding a half-eaten piece of toast, and one voluminous white breast peeping out of the plunging neckline of her silk nightdress. With a nipple two inches wide, noted Corso dispassionately as he shut the door behind him. Better late than never.

"Good morning," he said.

Then he walked to the bed. Liana Taillefer, motionless, still holding her toast, stared as he sat next to her. Having put the canvas bag down on the floor and glanced at the breakfast tray, he poured himself a cup of coffee. For nearly half a minute nobody said a word. At last, Corso took a sip and smiled at Liana Taillefer.

"I seem to remember that the last time we met I was somewhat abrupt . . ." The stubble on his chin seemed to emphasize his features. His smile was as sharp as a razor blade.

She didn't answer. She had put the toast on the tray and hidden her generous figure inside her nightdress. She stared at Corso inscrutably. There was neither fear nor arrogance nor rancour in it. She looked almost indifferent. After the scene at his flat, Corso would have expected to see hatred in her eyes. "They'll kill you for this," etc. . . . And they'd almost succeeded. But Liana Taillefer's steely blue eyes had the same expression as a puddle of icy water, and this worried Corso more than an explosion of fury. He pictured her staring impassively at her husband's corpse hanging from the light fitting in his room. He remembered the photo of the poor bastard in his leather apron holding a plate, about to dismember a roast sucking-pig. This was some serial they'd all written him.

"Bastard," muttered La Ponte from the floor. He seemed to have managed to focus on Corso at last. He started to get up, still dazed, hanging on to the furniture. Corso watched him with interest.

"You don't look very pleased to see me, Flavio."

"Pleased?" La Ponte was rubbing his beard and looking at the palm of his hand from time to time as if he was worried he was going to find a tooth there. "You've gone nuts. Completely bloody nuts."

"Not yet. But you've nearly managed it. You and your henchmen." He pointed at Liana Taillefer. "Including the grieving widow there."

La Ponte moved slightly closer, but kept at a cautious distance.

"Would you mind explaining what on earth you're talking about?" Corso raised his hand and began counting.

"I'm talking about the Dumas manuscript and *The Nine Doors*. About Victor Fargas drowned in Sintra. About Rochefort, who's like my shadow. He attacked me a week ago in Toledo, and last night here in Paris." He pointed at Liana Taillefer again. "And about Milady. And about you, whatever your part is in all this."

La Ponte had watched as Corso counted, and blinked five times in a row, once for each finger. When Corso finished, he rubbed his beard again, but this time not from pain but confusion. He started to say something but thought better of it. When at last he made up his mind to speak, he addressed Liana Taillefer.

"What have we got to do with all this?"

She shrugged contemptuously. She wasn't interested in possible explanations and she wasn't prepared to co-operate. She was still reclining against the pillows with the breakfast tray beside her. Her red polished nails were tearing apart one of the pieces of toast. Her only other noticeable movement was her breathing, which made her ample bosom move up and down inside her plunging nightdress. Otherwise she just stared at Corso like someone waiting for the other to show their hand at cards, as unmoved by it all as a sirloin steak.

La Ponte scratched his bald spot. He didn't look too dignified, standing in the middle of the room in crumpled stripey pyjamas, his cheek swollen from the punch. He gazed disconcertedly at Corso, then at Liana Taillefer, and back again.

"I demand an explanation," he said.

"That's a coincidence. That's exactly what I came here to get from you."

La Ponte again glanced anxiously at Liana Taillefer. He looked humiliated, and with good reason. He glanced down at his pyjamas and then at his bare feet. To be dealing with a crisis in such an outfit really was laughable. At last he gestured towards the bathroom.

"Let's go in there." He was trying to sound dignified but his swollen cheek made his speech unintelligible. "You and me."

Liana Taillefer remained inscrutable, motionless, calm. She looked at them with the bored expression of someone watching a quiz on TV. Corso thought to himself that he'd have to do something about her, but for the time being he couldn't think what. After a brief moment's hesitation he picked up his canvas bag from the floor and went into the bathroom. La Ponte followed and shut the door behind him.

"Can you tell me why you hit me?"

He spoke quietly, worried the widow would hear them. Corso put his bag on the bidet, noticed the whiteness of the towels and rummaged around on the bathroom shelf before turning back calmly to La Ponte.

"Because you're a liar and a traitor," he answered. "You didn't tell me you were mixed up in all this. You've let them trick me, follow me and beat me up."

"I'm not mixed up in anything. And I'm the only one who's been beaten up here." La Ponte was examining his face in the mirror. "God! Look what you've done to me! I'm disfigured."

"I'll disfigure you even more if you don't tell what this is all about."

"What all what is about?" La Ponte was prodding his swollen cheek, looking at Corso sideways as if he'd gone completely nuts. "It's no secret. Liana and I have . . ." He broke off, searching for the appropriate words. "Hm. We've . . . Well, you saw yourself."

"You've become intimate."

"That's right."

"When?"

"The day you left for Portugal."

"Who approached who?"

"I did. Virtually."

"What do you mean, virtually?"

"More or less. I went to see her."

"What for?"

"To make an offer for her husband's collection."

"The idea just suddenly popped into your head, did it?"

"Well, no. She phoned me first. I told you about it at the time."

"That's true."

"She wanted the manuscript her late husband sold me."

"Did she give any explanation?"

"Sentimental reasons."

"And you believed her."

"Yes."

"Or rather, it was all the same to you."

"Really . . ."

"Yeah, I know. What you really wanted was to screw her."

"That too."

"And she fell into your arms."

"Like a stone."

"Of course. And you came to Paris on your honeymoon."

"Not exactly. She had things to do here."

"And she asked you to come with her."

"That's right."

"Quite casually? All expenses paid, so you could continue the romance."

"Something like that."

Corso frowned.

"Love is a beautiful thing, Flavio. When you really are in love."

"Don't be such a cynic. She's extraordinary. You can't imagine . . ."

"Yes, I can."

"No, you can't."

"I said I can."

"I'd bet you'd like to. She's quite a woman."

"We're going off the subject, Flavio. We were here, in Paris."

"Yes."

"What were you planning to do with me?"

"We weren't planning anything. We were thinking of finding you today or tomorrow. To get the manuscript back."

"Just like that."

"Of course. How else?"

"You didn't think I might refuse?"

"Liana had her doubts."

"What about you?"

"I didn't."

"You didn't what?"

"I didn't think it would be a problem. We're friends, after all. And 'The Anjou Wine' is mine."

"I see. You were her second choice."

"I don't know what you mean. Liana's wonderful. And she adores me."

"Yes. She seems very much in love."

"Do you think so?"

"You're a fool, Flavio. They've pulled the wool over your eyes as well as mine."

He'd had a sudden intuition as piercing as a fire alarm. Corso pushed La Ponte abruptly aside and ran into the bedroom to find Liana Taillefer out of bed, half-dressed and packing a suitcase. For a second he saw her icy eyes – the eyes of Milady de Winter – fixed on him, and he realized that all the while he was shooting his mouth off like an idiot, she'd been waiting for something, a sound or a signal. Like a spider in its web.

"Goodbye, Mr Corso."

He heard the words. He could well remember her deep, slightly husky voice. But he didn't know what she meant, other than that she was about to leave. He took another step towards her, not knowing what he would do when he reached her, before realizing there was someone else in the room. A shadow behind him to his left by the door. He went to turn round, to face the danger. He knew he'd made another mistake but it was too late. He heard Liana Taillefer laughing, like the wicked blonde vamp in a film. And he felt the blow – his second in less than twelve hours – in the same spot as before, behind the ear. And he just had time to see Rochefort fading before his blurry eyes.

He was out cold before he hit the floor.

XIII

The Plot Thickens

*At this moment you're trembling because of the situation
and the prospect of the hunt. Where would the tremor be
if I were as precise as a railway timetable?*

A. Conan Doyle: *The Valley of Fear*

First he heard a voice in the distance, an unintelligible murmur. He made
an effort, sensing he was being spoken to. Something about his appearance. Corso had no idea what he looked like at that moment and couldn't
have cared less. He was comfortable there, wherever he was, lying on his
back. He didn't want to open his eyes and make his head hurt even more.

Somebody was gently slapping his face so he reluctantly opened one
eye. Flavio La Ponte was leaning over him, looking worried. He was
still wearing pyjamas.

"Get your hands off me," Corso said grumpily.

La Ponte sighed with relief.

"I thought you were dead," he said.

Corso opened the other eye and started to sit up. He immediately
felt his brain moving around inside his skull like jelly on a plate.

"They really gave it to you," La Ponte informed him unnecessarily as
he helped him up. Corso leant on his shoulder and glanced round the
room. Liana Taillefer and Rochefort had disappeared.

"Did you see who hit me?"

"Of course I did. A tall, dark guy with a scar on his face."

"Have you ever seen him before?"

"No." La Ponte frowned indignantly. "Seemed like she knew him
well, though . . . She must have let him in while we were arguing in the
bathroom . . . By the way, he had a split lip, it was all swollen. He'd had
a couple of stitches." He prodded his own cheek. The swelling was
going down. He gave a spiteful little laugh. "Seems like everyone
round here's got what they deserve."

Corso, searching unsuccessfully for his glasses, glanced at him resentfully.

"What I don't understand," he said, "is why they didn't clobber you too."

"They intended to. But I told them it wasn't necessary. They could just go about their business. I was an accidental tourist."

"You could have done something."

"Me? You must be joking. That punch you gave me was quite enough. I held up my hands like this . . . Peace signs. I just sat on the toilet seat nice and quiet until they left."

"My hero."

"I'd rather be safe than sorry. Hey, look at this." He handed him a folded piece of paper. "They left this behind, under an ashtray with a Montecristo cigar end in it."

Corso had trouble focusing on the handwriting. The note was written in ink, in an attractive copperplate hand with complicated flourishes on the capitals:

It is by my order and for the benefit of the State that the bearer of this note has done what he has done.

3 December 1627
Richelieu

Despite the situation, he almost burst out laughing. It was the safe-conduct granted at the siege of La Rochelle when Milady demanded d'Artagnan's head, later stolen at gunpoint by Athos ('Bite if you can, viper') and used to justify the woman's execution to Richelieu at the end of the novel . . . In short, too much for a single chapter. Corso staggered to the bathroom, turned on the tap and held his head under the stream of cold water. Then he looked at himself: puffy eyes, unshaven, and dripping with water. Not a pretty sight. And his head was buzzing like a wasps' nest. What a way to start the day.

La Ponte appeared in the mirror, beside him, handing him a towel and his glasses.

"By the way," he said, "they took your bag."

"Son of a bitch."

"Hey, I don't know why you're taking it out on me. All I did was get laid."

*   *   *

Anxious, Corso crossed the hotel lobby, trying to think quickly. But with every passing minute it became more unlikely that he would catch the fugitives. All was lost except for a single link in the chain, Book Number Three. They still had to get hold of it, and that offered, at least, the possibility of getting to them, as long as he moved quickly. While La Ponte paid for the room he went to the phone and dialled Frieda Ungern's number. But the line was engaged. He hesitated a moment and then rang the Louvre Concorde. He asked for Irene Adler's room. He wasn't sure how things stood on that front, but he calmed down slightly when he heard the girl's voice. He let her know the situation in a few words and asked her to meet him at the Ungern Foundation. He hung up as La Ponte was coming towards him, very depressed, putting his credit card back in his wallet.

"The bitch. She left without paying the bill."

"Serves you right."

"I'll kill her, with my own hands, I swear."

The hotel was extremely expensive and La Ponte was outraged at her treachery. He had a clearer idea of what was going on, but he was now gloomy as Ahab bent on revenge. They climbed into a taxi and Corso gave the driver Baroness Ungern's address. En route he told La Ponte the rest of the story – the train, the girl, Sintra, Paris, the three copies of *The Nine Doors*, Fargas's death, the incident beside the river . . . La Ponte listened and nodded, incredulous at first and then stunned.

"I've been living with a viper," he moaned, shuddering.

Corso was in a bad mood. He remarked that vipers very rarely bit cretins. La Ponte thought about it. He didn't seem offended.

"She's a determined woman," he said. "And what a body!"

In spite of his resentment at the recent dent in his finances, his eyes shone lecherously as he stroked his beard.

"What a body!" he repeated with a silly little smile.

Corso was staring out the window.

"That's exactly what the Duke of Buckingham said."

"Who's the Duke of Buckingham?"

"In *The Three Musketeers*. After the episode with the diamond tags, Richelieu entrusts Milady with the Duke's murder. But the Duke imprisons her when she returns to London. There she seduces her gaoler, Felton, an idiot like you but in a more puritanical, fanatical guise. She persuades him to help her escape, and while they're at it, to murder the Duke."

"I don't remember that episode. So what happened to Felton?"

"He stabs the Duke. He's later executed. I don't know whether for the murder or just for being stupid."

"At least he didn't have to pay the hotel bill."

They were driving along the Quai de Conti, near where Corso had had his last-but-one encounter with Rochefort. Just then La Ponte remembered something.

"Doesn't Milady have a mark on her shoulder?"

Corso nodded. They were passing the stone steps he'd fallen down the night before.

"Yes," he answered. "Branded by the executioner with a red-hot iron. The mark of criminals. She already has it when she's married to Athos . . . D'Artagnan discovers it when he sleeps with her, and it almost gets him killed."

"It's odd. Liana has a mark too, you know."

"On her shoulder?"

"No. On her hip. A small tattoo. Very pretty, in the shape of a fleur-de-lis."

"I don't believe it."

"I swear."

Corso didn't remember seeing a tattoo. He'd hardly had time to notice that kind of thing during the brief encounter with Liana Taillefer at his flat. It seemed like years ago. One way or another, things were getting out of control. This was more than a matter of quaint coincidences. It was a premeditated plan, too complex and dangerous for the performances of Liana Taillefer and her henchman to be dismissed as mere parody. Here was a plot with all the classic ingredients of the genre, and somebody – aptly, an *Eminence Grise* – must be pulling the strings. He felt Richelieu's note in his pocket. It was too much. And yet, the key to the mystery must lie in its very strangeness and novelesque nature. He remembered something he'd read once, in Edgar Allan Poe or Conan Doyle. "This mystery seems insoluble for the very same reasons that make it solvable: the excessive, *outré* nature of the circumstances."

"I'm still not sure whether this is one big hoax, or an elaborate plot," he said aloud.

La Ponte had found a hole in the plastic seat and was nervously tugging at it.

"Whatever it is, I don't like it." He whispered even though there was a pane of safety glass between them and the driver. "I hope you know what you're doing."

"That's the problem. I'm not sure."

"Why don't we go to the police?"

"And say what? That Milady and Rochefort, Cardinal Richelieu's agents, have stolen from us a chapter of *The Three Musketeers* and a book for summoning Lucifer? That the Devil has fallen in love with me and been incarnated as a twenty-year-old girl who now acts as my bodyguard? What would you do if you were Inspector Maigret and I came and told you all that?"

"I'd assume you were drunk."

"There you are."

"What about Varo Borja?"

"That's another thing." Corso moaned anxiously. "I don't even want to think about it, when he finds out I've lost his book . . ."

The taxi was making its way slowly through the morning traffic. Corso looked at his watch impatiently. At last they reached the bar where he'd sat the night before. There were people hanging around on the pavement and "No entry" signs on the corner. As he got out of the taxi, Corso saw a police van and a fire engine. He clenched his teeth and swore loudly, making La Ponte start. Book Number Three had got away too.

The girl came towards them through the crowd, the small rucksack on her back and her hands in her coat pockets. There were still faint traces of smoke coming from the roofs.

"The fire started at three a.m.," she said, taking no notice of La Ponte, as if he didn't exist. "The firemen are still inside."

"What about Baroness Ungern?" She made a vague gesture, not exactly indifferent, but resigned, fatalistic. As if it had been pre-ordained. "Her charred remains were found in the study. That's where the fire started. The neighbours say it must have been an accident. A cigarette not properly stubbed out."

"The Baroness didn't smoke," said Corso.

"She did last night."

Corso glanced over the heads of the crowd gathered in front of the police cordon. He couldn't see much – the top of a ladder leaning against the building, intermittent flashing from the ambulance at the door, and the tops of lots of policemen's and firemen's helmets. The air smelt of burnt wood and plastic. Amongst the onlookers, a couple of

American tourists were photographing each other posing next to the policemen by the cordon. Somewhere a siren sounded and suddenly stopped. Somebody in the crowd said they were bringing out the corpse, but it was impossible to see anything. Not that there would be much to see anyway, thought Corso.

He met the girl's gaze fixed on him. There was no sign of the night before. Her expression was attentive, practical, that of a soldier approaching the battlefield.

"What's happened?" she asked.

"I was hoping you'd tell me."

"I don't mean this." She seemed to notice La Ponte for the first time. "Who's he?"

Corso told her. Then after a moment's hesitation, wondering whether La Ponte would catch on, he said, "The girl I told you about. Irene Adler."

La Ponte didn't catch on at all. He just gave them a slightly disconcerted look, first the girl, then his friend, and finally put out his hand. She didn't notice, or pretended not to. She was looking at Corso.

"You haven't got your bag," she said.

"No. Rochefort got it at last. He went off with Liana Taillefer."

"Who's Liana Taillefer?"

Corso gave her a hard look, but she looked back at him calmly.

"Don't you know the grieving widow?"

"No."

Unruffled, she met his look without anxiety or surprise. In spite of himself, Corso almost believed her.

"It doesn't matter," he said at last. "The fact is, they've gone."

"Where?"

"I've no idea." He grimaced with desperation and suspicion, showing his teeth. "I thought you'd know something."

"I don't know anything about Rochefort. Or that woman." She sounded indifferent, implying it was none of her business. This confused Corso even more. He'd expected some emotion from her. Amongst other things, she had set herself up as his protector. He thought she'd at least reproach him, something like, Serves you right for thinking you're so clever. But she said nothing. She looked around as if searching for a familiar face in the crowd. He had no idea whether she was thinking about what had just happened, or whether her mind was far away on other things.

"What can we do?" he asked no one in particular. He was bewildered. Attacks aside, he'd seen the three copies of *The Nine Doors* and the Dumas manuscript disappear one after the other. He had three corpses in his wake, if he counted Enrique Taillefer, and he'd spent a huge amount of money that wasn't his but Varo Borja's . . . Varus, Varus, give me back my legions. Damn his luck! At that instant he would have liked to be thirty-five years younger so he could sit down on the kerb and burst into tears.

"We could go and have a coffee," suggested La Ponte.

He said it jokily, as if to imply "Come on, guys, things aren't that bad," and Corso realized that the poor sod had no idea of the enormous mess they were in. Still, it didn't seem such a bad idea. In the circumstances he couldn't think of anything better.

"Let's see if I've understood." Coffee ran down La Ponte's beard as he dunked his croissant in his cup. "In 1666 Aristide Torchia hid a special book. A kind of safety copy distributed over three copies. Is that it? With differences in eight of the nine engravings. And the three original copies have to be brought together for the spell to work." He took a bite of croissant and wiped his mouth on his serviette. "How am I doing?"

The three of them were sitting on a terrace opposite Saint-Germain-des-Prés. He was making up for his interrupted breakfast at the Crillon. The girl, still slightly aloof, was sipping an orangeade through a straw and listening in silence. She had *The Three Musketeers* open in front of her on the table and was reading distractedly, turning a page from time to time, and then looking up and listening again. As for Corso, events had knotted his stomach, he couldn't swallow a thing.

"Pretty good," he told La Ponte. He was leaning back in his chair, hands in his coat pockets and staring blankly at the church tower. "Although it's possible that the complete work, the one burnt by the Holy Office, also consisted of three books with illustrations altered so that only those who were truly expert on the subject, the initiated, would be able to combine the three copies correctly . . ." He arched his eyebrows, frowning wearily. "But now we'll never know."

"Who says there were only three? Maybe he printed four, or nine different versions."

"In that case all this would be pointless. There are only three known copies."

"Whatever the case, somebody wants to piece together the original book. And is getting hold of the authentic engravings . . ." La Ponte spoke with his mouth full. He continued to eat his breakfast with a hearty appetite. "But he couldn't give a damn about the market value. Once he has the correct engravings he destroys the rest. And murders the owner. Victor Fargas in Sintra. Baroness Ungern here in Paris. And Varo Borja in Toledo . . ." He broke off and looked at Corso with disappointment. "This theory doesn't work. Varo Borja's still alive."

"I've got his copy. And they've certainly tried to set me up, first last night and then this morning."

La Ponte didn't look too convinced.

"If they set you up, why didn't Rochefort kill you?"

"I don't know." He shrugged. He'd asked himself the same question. "He had the chance twice but didn't do it . . . As for Varo Borja still being alive, I wouldn't know what to say. He hasn't answered my calls."

"That makes him another potential corpse. Or suspect."

"Varo Borja is a suspect by definition, and he's got the means to have organized the whole thing." He pointed at the girl. She was still reading and appeared not to be following the conversation. "I'm sure she could shed some light on it all, if she wanted to."

"And she doesn't?"

"No."

"So, turn her in. When people are getting murdered, there's a name for it: accomplice."

"How can I turn her in? I'm up to my neck in this, Flavio. And so are you."

The girl had stopped reading and held both their gazes placidly. She said nothing, just sipped her drink. Her eyes went from one to the other, reflecting them each in turn. Finally they rested on Corso.

"Do you really trust her?" asked La Ponte.

"Depends what for. Last night she fought off Rochefort and made a pretty good job of it."

La Ponte frowned, perplexed, and stared at the girl. He must be trying to imagine her as a bodyguard. He must also have been wondering how far things had gone between Corso and her. Corso saw him stroke his beard and cast an expert eye over the parts of her body visible beneath the duffle coat. Even if he did suspect her, there was no doubt how far La Ponte himself would take things if the girl gave him the chance. Even at times like these, the ex-chairman of the Brotherhood of Nantucket Harpooners always wanted to return to the womb. To any womb.

"She's too pretty." La Ponte shook his head. "And too young. Too young for you that is."

Corso smiled.

"You'd be surprised how old she sometimes seems."

La Ponte tutted dubiously.

"Gifts like this don't just fall from Heaven."

The girl had followed the conversation in silence. Now, they saw her smile for the first time that day, as if she'd just heard a funny joke.

"You talk too much, Flavio Whatever-your-name-is," she said to La Ponte, who blinked nervously. She grinned, like a naughty little child. "Anyway, whatever there is between me and Corso is none of your business."

It was the first time she'd said anything to La Ponte. He was disconcerted for a moment and then, embarrassed, turned in vain to his friend for support. But Corso just smiled again.

"I think I'm in the way here." La Ponte made as if to stand up but he hesitated and didn't quite make his move. He stayed like that until Corso tapped him on the arm. A dry, friendly little tap.

"Don't be stupid. She's on our side."

La Ponte relaxed slightly, but he still didn't look entirely convinced.

"Well, let her prove it. She can tell us what she knows."

Corso turned to the girl and looked at her half-open mouth, her warm, comfortable neck. He wondered if she still smelt of heat and fever, and became lost in the memory for an instant. Her limpid green eyes, full of the morning light, as always met his gaze, unflinching, lazy and calm. Her smile, full of contempt for La Ponte a second before, now changed. Once again it was like an imperceptible breath, a silent conspiratorial word.

"We were talking about Varo Borja," said Corso. "Do you know him?"

She stopped smiling and again looked like a tired, indifferent soldier. But just before, for a split second, Corso thought he saw a glint of contempt in her expression. Corso leant his hand on the marble-topped table.

"He may have been using me," he added. "And put you on my trail." It seemed absurd all of a sudden. He couldn't picture the millionaire bookdealer resorting to a young girl to set him a trap. "Or maybe Rochefort and Milady are working for him."

She went back to reading *The Three Musketeers* and didn't answer. But the mention of Milady had reminded La Ponte of his wounded pride. He finished his coffee and raised a finger.

"That's the part I don't understand," he said. "The link with Dumas . . . What's my 'Anjou Wine' got to do with any of this?"

" 'The Anjou Wine' is only yours by accident." Corso had taken off his glasses and was peering at them against the light, wondering if the cracked lens would hold up with all the goings-on. "It's what I find most puzzling. But there are several intriguing coincidences. Cardinal Richelieu, the wicked character in *The Three Musketeers,* was interested in books on the occult. Pacts with the Devil give power, and Richelieu was the most powerful man in France. And to complete the cast, it turns out that in Dumas's novel, the Cardinal has two faithful agents who carry out his orders – the Count of Rochefort and Milady de Winter. She is blonde, evil, and has been branded by the executioner with a fleur-de-lis. He's dark and has a scar on his face . . . Do you see what I'm saying. They both have some sort of mark. And if we're going to look for links, according to Revelations, the servants of the Devil can be recognized by the mark of the Beast."

The girl took another sip of her orangeade but didn't look up from her book. La Ponte shuddered as if a ghost had just walked over his grave. He clearly felt it was one thing getting involved with a statuesque blonde and quite another for his groin to take part in a witches' sabbath. He fidgeted.

"Shit. I hope it's not contagious."

Corso looked at him unsympathetically.

"There are too many coincidences, aren't there? Well, there's more." He breathed on his lenses and wiped them on a napkin. "In *The Three Musketeers* it turns out that Milady has been married to Athos, d'Artagnan's friend. When Athos discovers that his wife bears the executioner's mark, he decides to carry out the sentence himself. He hangs her and leaves her for dead, but she survives, etc." He put his glasses back on. "Somebody must be having a lot of fun with all this."

"I can sympathize with Athos hanging his wife," said La Ponte frowning, no doubt remembering the hotel bill. "I'd like to get hold of her and do the same myself."

"Or like Liana Taillefer did to her husband. I'm sorry to hurt your pride, Flavio, but she was never interested in you in the slightest. She just wanted to get the manuscript her late husband sold you."

"The bitch," muttered La Ponte bitterly. "I bet she did him in. Helped by our friend with the moustache and the scar on his face."

"What I still don't understand," Corso went on, "is the link between *The Three Musketeers* and *The Nine Doors*. All I can think is that Alexandre Dumas was on top of the world. He had success and the kind of power he wanted – fame, wealth and women. Everything went swimmingly for him, as if he was privileged or had made some special pact. And when he died, his son, the other Dumas, wrote a strange epitaph for him: 'He died as he lived – unaware.'"

La Ponte looked sceptical.

"Are you insinuating that Alexandre Dumas sold his soul to the Devil?"

"I'm not insinuating anything. I'm just trying to work out the serial that somebody's writing at my expense. It obviously all started when Enrique Taillefer decided to sell the Dumas manuscript. The mystery began there. His presumed suicide, my visit to his widow, my first encounter with Rochefort . . . And the job Varo Borja gave me."

"What's so special about the manuscript? Why is it important and to whom?"

"I've no idea." Corso glanced at the girl. "Unless she can explain any of it."

She shrugged indifferently and didn't look up from her book.

"This is your story, Corso," she said. "I understand you're getting paid for it."

"You're involved too."

"Up to a certain point." She made a vague, non-committal gesture and turned the page. "Only up to a certain point."

Annoyed, La Ponte leaned over towards Corso.

"Have you tried giving her a couple of slaps?"

"Shut up, Flavio."

"Yes, shut up," echoed the girl.

"This is ridiculous," complained La Ponte. "Who does she think she is, talking like that? And instead of giving her the third degree you just leave her alone. This isn't like you, Corso. However cute this little girl is I don't think . . ." He spluttered searching for the words. "How did she get so cheeky?"

"She once fought an archangel," explained Corso. "And last night I saw her kick Rochefort's teeth in, remember? The same guy who clobbered me this morning while you sat safely out of the way on the bidet."

"On the toilet."

"Makes no difference. You, in your pyjamas, looking like Prince Danilo in *Imperial Violets*. I didn't know you wore pyjamas when you slept with your conquests."

"What do you care?" La Ponte glanced at the girl, embarrassed, and backed off, annoyed. "I get cold at night, if you must know. Anyway," he said, changing the subject, "we were talking about 'The Anjou Wine'. How's the report going?"

"We know that it's authentic, and in two different hands – Dumas's and his collaborator's, Auguste Maquet."

"What have you found out about him?"

"Maquet? There's not much to find out. He ended up on bad terms with Dumas with all sorts of lawsuits and claims for money. There is one strange thing – Dumas spent everything during his lifetime, he died without a penny. But Maquet was wealthy in his old age and even owned a castle. Each in his own way, things went well for them."

"What about the half-written chapter?"

"Maquet wrote the original story, a simple first draft, and Dumas added to it, giving it style and quality. You're familiar with the subject – Milady trying to poison d'Artagnan."

La Ponte peered anxiously into his empty coffee cup.

"To conclude . . ."

"Well, I'd say someone who believes he's Richelieu's reincarnation has managed to collect all the original engravings from the *Delomelanicon*. Also the Dumas chapter. For some unknown reason, they seem to hold the key to what's going on. This person may be trying to summon Lucifer as we speak. Meanwhile, you no longer have your manuscript and Varo Borja doesn't have his book. I've really screwed up."

He took Richelieu's note out of his pocket and read it again. La Ponte seemed to agree with him.

"The loss of the manuscript isn't serious," he said. "I paid Taillefer for it. But not that much." He gave a cunning little laugh. "At least with Liana I got paid in kind. But you really are in a mess."

Corso looked at the girl, who was still reading in silence.

"Maybe she could tell us what kind of mess I'm in."

He frowned and then banged the table with his knuckles like a resigned player throwing in the towel. But she didn't answer this time either. La Ponte grunted reprovingly.

"I still don't understand why you trust her."

"He's already told you," the girl answered at last, reluctantly. She put the straw from her drink in between the pages of her book as a marker. "I look after him."

Corso nodded, looking amused, although there wasn't much in his situation to be amused about.

"You heard her. She's my guardian angel."

"Really? Well, she should take better care of you. Where was she when Rochefort stole your bag?"

"You were there."

"That's different. I'm just a cowardly bookseller. Peace-loving. The exact opposite to a man of action. If I entered a coward competition, I'm sure I'd be disqualified, for being too cowardly."

Corso wasn't listening because he'd just made a discovery. The shadow of the church tower was being thrown on the ground near them. The wide, dark shape had been gradually moving in the opposite direction to the sun. He noticed that the cross on the top was at the girl's feet, very near but never actually touching her. The shadow of the cross maintained a prudent distance.

He phoned Lisbon from a post office to find out how the investigation into Victor Fargas's death was going. The news wasn't encouraging. Pinto had seen the forensic report: death by forced immersion in the pond. The police in Sintra had accepted that the robbery was the motive. Perpetrator or perpetrators unknown. The good news was that, for the time being, nobody had linked Corso with the murder. Pinto added that he had put out the description of the man with the scar, just in case. Corso told him to forget about Rochefort, the bird had flown.

It didn't seem that the situation could get any worse. But at midday it became even more complicated. As soon as he entered the hotel lobby with La Ponte and the girl, he knew something was wrong. Gruber was at the reception desk and beneath his usual imperturbable expression there was a warning. As they approached, Corso saw that the concierge turned to look round casually at the pigeonhole with his room key and then gave his lapel a slight tug, in a gesture recognized throughout the world.

"Keep going," Corso told the others.

He almost had to drag the disconcerted La Ponte away. The girl walked ahead of them down the narrow corridor that led to the restaurant-bar looking out onto the Place du Palais Royal. Corso looked back at Gruber and saw him place his hand on the telephone.

They were back out in the street, La Ponte glancing nervously behind him.

"What's the matter?"

"Police," explained Corso. "In my room."

"How do you know?"

The girl didn't ask any questions. She just looked at Corso, waiting for instructions. He took out the envelope that Gruber had handed him the night before, removed the note informing him of La Ponte's and Liana Taillefer's whereabouts, and put a five-hundred franc bill inside instead. He did it slowly, trying to remain calm and make sure the others didn't notice that his hands were trembling. He sealed the envelope, crossed out his own name and wrote Gruber's on it, and then handed it to the girl.

"Give this to one of the waiters in the restaurant." The palms of his hands were sweating. He wiped them on the insides of his pockets, and then pointed at a phone booth across the square. "Meet me over there."

"What about me?" asked La Ponte.

In spite of the seriousness of the situation Corso almost laughed in La Ponte's face. He just looked at him mockingly instead.

"You can do what you like. Although I think you might have just gone underground, Flavio."

He crossed the square through the traffic, heading towards the phone booth without waiting to see whether La Ponte was following. When he closed the door and inserted the card in the slot Corso saw him a few metres away, gazing round anxious and defenceless.

He dialled the hotel number and asked for Reception.

"What's going on, Gruber?"

"Two policemen came, Mr Corso." The former SS officer had lowered his tone but he sounded calm and in control. "They're still up in your room."

"Did they give any explanation?"

"No. They wanted to know the date you checked in and asked whether we knew what your movements had been up till two a.m. I said I didn't and passed them on to my colleague who was on night duty. They also wanted a description because they don't know what you look like. We left it that I would get in touch with them when you got back. I'm about to do so now."

"What are you going to tell them?"

"The truth, of course. That you came into the lobby for a moment and went straight out again accompanied by an unknown bearded man. As for the young lady, they didn't ask about her, so I see no reason to mention her."

"Thanks, Gruber." He paused and added with a smile, "I'm innocent."

"Of course you are, Mr Corso. All our guests at this hotel are." There was a sound of paper being torn. "Ah. I've just been handed your envelope."

"Be seeing you, Gruber. Keep my room for a couple of days. I'm hoping to come back for my things. If there's any problem charge it to my credit card. And thanks again."

"At your service."

Corso hung up. The girl was back, standing next to La Ponte. Corso came out of the cabin.

"The police have got my name. That means somebody must have given it to them."

"Don't look at me," said La Ponte. "This whole thing has been beyond me for some time."

Corso thought bitterly that it was beyond him too. Everything had got out of control, the boat tossed about with no one at the helm.

"Can you think of anything?" he asked the girl. She was the last strand of the mystery still in his hands. His final hope.

She looked over Corso's shoulder at the traffic and the nearby railings of the Palais Royal. She had taken off her rucksack and put it down by her feet. She was frowning slightly, silent as usual, absorbed in her own thoughts. She looked obstinate, like a little boy refusing to do what he's told. Corso smiled like a tired wolf.

"I don't know what to do," he said.

He saw her nod slowly, possibly as a conclusion to her secret reflections. Or maybe she was just agreeing that, indeed, he didn't know what to do.

"You're your own worst enemy," she said at last, distantly. She looked tired now too, as she had the night before when they returned to the hotel. "Your imagination." She tapped her forehead. "You can't see the wood for the trees."

La Ponte grunted. "Let's leave the botany for later, shall we?" He was becoming increasingly worried, glancing round anxiously in case the *gendarmes* pounced. "We should get out of here. I can hire a car. If we hurry we can be over the border by tomorrow. Which is April 1st by the way."

"Shut up, Flavio." Corso was looking into the girl's eyes, searching for an answer. All he saw were reflections – the light of the square, the passing traffic, his own image, misshapen and grotesque. The defeated soldier. But defeat was no longer heroic. It hadn't been for a long time.

The girl's expression had changed. She stared at La Ponte now as if he was worth it for the first time.

"Say that again," she ordered.

La Ponte stuttered, surprised.

"The bit about hiring a car?" He looked at them open-mouthed. "It's obvious. On planes they've got passenger lists. And they can look at your passport on the train . . ."

"I didn't mean that. Tell us what date it is tomorrow."

"The first of April. Monday." La Ponte fiddled with his tie, confused. "My birthday."

But the girl was no longer paying attention. She'd leant over her rucksack and was searching for something inside it. When she straightened up she was holding *The Three Musketeers*.

"You haven't paid enough attention to your reading," she said to Corso, handing it to him. "Chapter One, first line."

Corso, who hadn't been expecting this, took the book and glanced at it. 'The Three Gifts of Monsieur d'Artagnan the Elder'. As soon as he read the first line he knew where they had to go to find Milady.

XIV
The Cellars of Meung

It was a dismal night.
P. du Terrail: *Rocambole*

It was a dismal night. The Loire was flowing turbulently and rising, threatening to flood the old dykes in the small town of Meung. The storm had been raging since late afternoon. Occasionally a flash of lightning lit up the black mass of the castle, and bright zigzags cracked like whips on the deserted wet pavements of the medieval town. Across the river, in the distance, amidst the wind, the rain and the leaves torn from the trees, as if the gale drew a line between the recent past and a distant present, the headlights of cars could be seen moving silently along the motorway from Tours to Orleans.

At the Auberge Saint-Jacques, the only hotel in Meung, a window was lit. It gave onto a small terrace which could be reached from the street. Inside the room, a tall, attractive blonde, her hair tied back, was dressing in front of the mirror. She had just zipped up her skirt, covering the small tattoo of a fleur-de-lis on her hip. She stood up straight, her hands behind her back to fasten the bra supporting her pale, voluminous bust which shook gently as she moved. Then she put on a silk blouse. As she buttoned it she smiled slightly to herself in the mirror, no doubt finding herself beautiful. She must have been thinking about a date, because nobody gets dressed at eleven at night unless they're going to meet someone. Although maybe the smile, with its hint of cruelty, was due to the new leather folder lying on the bed containing the pages of the manuscript of 'The Anjou Wine' by Alexandre Dumas, père.

A flash of lightning lit up the small terrace outside. There, under the dripping eaves, Lucas Corso finished his damp cigarette and threw it on the ground. He turned up his collar against the wind and rain. During the next bolt of lightning, as intense as a giant camera flash, he saw Flavio La Ponte's deathly-pale face, drawn in light and dark, his hair and beard dripping wet. He resembled a tormented monk, or maybe Athos, taciturn as desperation, sombre as punishment. There were no more flashes for a time, but Corso could distinguish, in the third shadow, crouching beside them beneath the eaves, the slender shape of Irene Adler wrapped up in her duffle coat. And when at last another flash of lightning tore diagonally across the night sky, and thunder rolled amidst the slate roofs, her bright green eyes were suddenly lit up beneath the hood of her coat.

The journey to Meung had been quick and tense. A single stint in appalling visibility, in a car hired by La Ponte: motorway from Paris to Orleans, then 16 kilometres on towards Tours. La Ponte sat in the passenger seat and, by the flame of a cigarette lighter, studied the Michelin map they'd bought at a petrol station. La Ponte was in a mess. Not far to go now, I think we're on the right road. Yes, I'm sure we are. The girl was in the back, silent. She stared at Corso intently and he met her eyes in the mirror every time they were passed by the dazzling lights of an oncoming car. La Ponte got it wrong, of course. They missed the turn and headed off in the direction of Blois. When they realized their mistake they had to drive back up the motorway in the wrong direction to get off it. Corso gripped the steering-wheel, praying that the storm was keeping all the *gendarmes* indoors. Beaugency. La Ponte insisted they should cross the river and turn left but luckily they ignored him. They retraced their steps, this time on the Nationale 152 – the same route d'Artagnan took in Chapter One – amidst gusts of wind and rain, the black, roaring expanse of the Loire running to their right, the windscreen wipers working furiously and hundreds of little black dots, the shadows of raindrops, dancing in front of Corso's eyes as they passed other cars. At last they were driving through deserted streets, an old district of medieval rooftops, façades with thick beams in the shape of crosses: Meung-sur-Loire. Journey's end.

"She's about to leave," whispered La Ponte. He was soaked through and his voice trembled from the cold. "Why don't we go in now?"

Corso leaned over to take another look. Liana Taillefer had put on a tight-fitting sweater over her blouse, emphasizing her spectacular figure, and, from the wardrobe, she took a long, dark cape fit for a masked ball. She hesitated a moment and looked round. Then she put the cape over her shoulders and picked up the folder with the manuscript from the bed. At that instant she noticed the open window and went to close it.

Corso put out his hand to stop her. There was a flash of lightning almost above his head and his dripping face was lit up. He was framed in the window, his hand held out as if accusingly at the woman standing paralysed with surprise. Milady screamed wildly in unprecedented terror, as if she had just seen the Devil.

Corso jumped over the ledge and hit her so hard with the back of his hand that she stopped screaming and fell on the bed, scattering the pages of 'The Anjou Wine'. The change in temperature misted Corso's glasses, so he took them off quickly, threw them on the bedside table and then flung himself at Liana Taillefer who was trying to get up and head for the door. He grabbed her first by her leg and then pinned her down to the bed by the waist, while she struggled and kicked. She was strong, and he wondered where the hell La Ponte and the girl could be. While he waited for them to help he tried to hold her down by her wrists, keeping his face away from her nails as she tried to scratch him. Entwined, they rolled on the bedcover and Corso ended up with his leg between hers, his face buried in her large, firm breasts. Up so close, through her fine wool sweater, he thought again how incredibly springy they were. He felt an unmistakable erection and cursed in exasperation, while he struggled with this Milady with the physique of a champion swimmer. Where are you when I need you, he thought bitterly. Then La Ponte arrived, shaking himself like a wet dog, seeking revenge for his wounded pride, and, above all, for the hotel bill burning a hole in his wallet. It was beginning to resemble a lynching.

"I presume you're not going to rape her," said the girl.

She was sitting on the window ledge, still wearing her hood, watching the scene. Liana Taillefer had stopped struggling and was now motionless. Corso was on top of her and La Ponte was holding her down by one arm and one leg.

"Pigs," she said loudly and clearly.

"Whore," grunted La Ponte, out of breath from the struggle.

After this brief exchange they all calmed down slightly. Certain that she could not escape, they let her sit up. She was still beside herself with fury and flashed venomous looks at both Corso and La Ponte as she rubbed her wrists. Corso stood between her and the door. The girl was still at the window, now closed. She had lowered her hood and was staring at Liana Taillefer with blatant curiosity. La Ponte, after drying his hair and beard on the bedcover, started to gather the pages of the manuscript spread around the room.

"We need to have a little talk," said Corso. "Like reasonable people."

Liana Taillefer gave him a searing look.

"We don't have anything to talk about."

"That's where you're wrong, beautiful lady. Now that we've got you I don't mind going to the police. Either you talk to us or you'll have to explain things to a *gendarme*. Your choice."

She frowned. She looked round like a hounded animal searching for any way out of a trap.

"Careful," said La Ponte. "She's up to something."

Her eyes shot glances as sharp as steel needles. Corso twisted his mouth theatrically.

"Liana Taillefer," he said. "Or maybe we should call you Anne de Breuil, Comtesse de la Fère. You also go by the names of Charlotte Backson, Baroness Sheffield, and Lady de Winter. And betray your husbands and your lovers. A murderess and poisoner, as well as Richelieu's agent. Better known by your alias –" he paused dramatically: "Milady."

He stopped because he'd just tripped on the strap of his bag which was protruding from under the bed. He pulled it out, not taking his eyes off Liana Taillefer or the door. She obviously intended to escape at the slightest opportunity. He checked the contents of the bag and his sigh of relief made all of them, including Liana Taillefer, look at him in surprise. Varo Borja's copy of *The Nine Doors* was there, intact.

"Bingo," he said, showing it to the others. La Ponte looked triumphant, as if Queequeg had just harpooned the whale. But the girl didn't move or show any emotion, an indifferent spectator.

Corso returned the book to the bag. The wind whistled at the window where the girl was still standing. At intervals she was silhouetted by a flash of lightning, followed by a rumble of thunder, dull and muffled, which made the rain-spattered glass vibrate.

"Fitting weather," said Corso, and looked at the woman. "As you can see, Milady, we didn't want to miss our appointment. We've come prepared to do justice."

"As a group and at night, like cowards," she answered, spitting out the words contemptuously. "Just as they did to the other Milady. The only one missing is the executioner of Lille."

"All in good time," said La Ponte.

The woman was gradually recovering her confidence. Her own mention of the executioner didn't seem to have cowed her. She stared back at La Ponte defiantly.

"I see that you've all got into your respective parts," she added.

"You shouldn't be surprised," answered Corso. "You and your accomplices have made sure of that." His face twisted into a cruel wolf-like smile, without humour or pity. "We've all had such fun."

The woman tensed her lips. She slid one of her blood-red nails across the bedcover. Corso followed it with his eyes, fascinated, as if it were a blade and he shuddered when he thought how close it had come to his face during their struggle.

"You have no right to do this," she said at last. "You're intruders."

"You're wrong. We're part of the game, just as you are."

"But you don't know the rules."

"Wrong again, Milady. The proof is, we're here." Corso looked round for his glasses and saw them on the bedside table. He put them on and pushed them up with his finger. "That's precisely what was tricky about it – accepting the nature of the game. To accept the fiction by entering the story and following the logic required by the text, not that of the outside world . . . After that it's easy. In the real world many things happen by chance but in fiction nearly everything is logical."

Liana Taillefer's red fingernail stopped moving.

"In novels?"

"Especially in novels. If the protagonist follows the internal logic of the criminal, he'll obviously arrive at the same point. That's why the hero and the villain, the detective and the murderer always meet in the end." He smiled, pleased with his reasoning. "What do you think?"

"Brilliant," said Liana Taillefer sarcastically. La Ponte was staring at Corso open-mouthed, but in his case the admiration was sincere. "Brother William Baskerville, I presume."

"Don't be superficial, Milady. You're forgetting Conan Doyle and Edgar Allan Poe. And Dumas himself . . . I thought you were better read."

The woman stared intently at Corso.

"As you can see, you're wasting your talent on me," she said contemptuously. "I'm not the right audience."

"I know. That's exactly why I've come here – for you to take us to him." He looked at his watch. "In a little over an hour it'll be the first Monday in April."

"I'd like to know how you guessed that, too."

"I didn't guess." He turned to the girl who was still by the window. "She put the book under my nose. And in an investigation a book is more helpful than the outside world. It's self-contained, with no annoying interruptions. Like Sherlock Holmes's laboratory."

"Stop showing off, Corso," said the girl, annoyed. "You've impressed her quite enough."

The woman arched one eyebrow and looked at the girl as if she were seeing her for the first time.

"Who's she?"

"Don't tell me you don't know. Haven't you ever seen her before?"

"No. They mentioned a young girl, but not where she came from."

"Who mentioned her?"

"A friend."

"Tall, dark, with a moustache and a scar on his face? And a split lip? Our good friend Rochefort! I'd really like to know where he is. Not far away, I assume. The two of you chose worthy characters, didn't you?"

For some reason, at this Liana Taillefer lost her cool. She dug her blood-red nail into the bedcover as if it were Corso's flesh and her eyes glinted with fury.

"Are any of the other characters in the novel any better?" There was disdain and an insulting arrogance in the way Milady threw back her head and stared at them one after another. "Athos, a drunk. Porthos, an idiot. Aramis, a hypocritical conspirator . . ."

"That's one way of looking at it," said Corso.

"Shut up. What do you know?" Liana Taillefer paused, jutting out her chin, her eyes fixed on Corso as if it were now his turn. "And as for d'Artagnan, he's the worst of all of them. A swordsman? He only has four duels in *The Three Musketeers*. He only wins because in one, Jussac is getting to his feet, and in another Bernajoux, in a blind attack, impales himself on d'Artagnan's sword. In the attack on the Englishmen all he does is disarm the Baron. And it takes three sword thrusts to bring down the Comte de Wardes . . . As far as generosity goes –" she jerked her chin contemptuously in La Ponte's direction – "d'Artagnan is even more of a miser than your friend here. He pays for a round for his friends for the first time in England, after the Monk affair. Thirty years later."

"I see you're an expert, although I should have guessed you would be. All those serials you claimed to hate so much . . . Congratulations.

You played the part of the widow sick of her husband's extravagances perfectly."

"I wasn't pretending in the slightest. Most of it was mediocre – useless old paper. Like Enrique himself. My husband was a fool. He never knew how to read between the lines, or appreciate quality. He was one of those idiots who go round collecting postcards of monuments and just don't have a clue."

"Unlike you."

"Of course. Do you know which were the first two books I ever read? *Little Women* and *The Three Musketeers*. Each one, in a different way, made a deep impression."

"How moving."

"Don't be stupid. You asked questions and I'm giving you some answers. There are unsophisticated readers, like poor Enrique, and readers who go into things in more depth, looking beyond stereotypes: the brave d'Artagnan, chivalrous Athos, kind-hearted Porthos, faithful Aramis . . . It makes me laugh!" And her laughter did actually ring out, as dramatic and sinister as Milady's. "Nobody has any idea. Do you know what my most enduring image is, the one I've always admired most? The woman fighting alone, faithful to an idea of herself and to the man she's chosen as her master, relying only on herself, ignominiously murdered by four heroes who are no more than cardboard cut-outs . . . And what about her long-lost son, an orphan, who appears twenty years later!" She bowed her head, sombre, and there was so much hatred in her eyes that Corso almost took a step back. "I can picture the engraving as if I had it in front of me now – the river at night, the four scoundrels kneeling, but without mercy. And on the other side, the executioner raising his sword above the woman's bare neck . . ."

A flash of lightning suddenly cast its brutal light across her distorted face – the delicate white flesh of her neck, her eyes full of the tragic scenes she described as vividly as if she had experienced them herself. Then the window-panes shook as the thunder rumbled.

"Bastards," she whispered, absorbed, and Corso didn't know whether she meant him and his companions, or d'Artagnan and his friends.

Still at the window, the girl rummaged in her rucksack and pulled out *The Three Musketeers*. Like a neutral spectator, she searched calmly for a page. When she found it she threw the book on the bed without a word. It was the engraving described by Liana Taillefer.

. . . And on the other side, the executioner raising his sword

"'*Victa iacet Virtus*,'" murmured Corso, shivering at the similarity of the scene with the eighth illustration in *The Nine Doors*.

The woman had calmed down again on seeing the engraving. She arched an eyebrow, cold and imperious once again. Sarcastic.

"It's true," she admitted. "You can't tell me d'Artagnan symbolizes virtue. He's just an opportunist. And don't mention his skills as a seducer. In the entire novel he only conquers three women, two of them through deceit. His great love is a little *bourgeoise* with big feet, lady-in-waiting to the Queen. The other is an English maid of whom he ignominiously takes advantage." Liana Taillefer's laughter rang out like an insult. "And what about his love-life in *Twenty Years After*? Living with the landlady of a guesthouse to save himself the rent . . . Very fine affairs he went in for! Maids, landladies and servants!"

"But d'Artagnan does seduce Milady," Corso pointed out mischievously.

A flash of anger once again cracked the ice in Liana Taillefer's eyes. If looks could kill, Corso would have died at her feet that instant.

"He doesn't get her," answered the woman. "The bastard gets into her bed through deceit, passing himself off as another man." Her manner was cold again, her ice-blue eyes piercing Corso like daggers. "You and he would have made a famous pair."

La Ponte was listening attentively. One could almost hear his brain working. Then he frowned.

"You don't mean to say that you two . . ."

He turned to the girl for support. He was always the last to find out what was going on. But she remained impassive, watching them as if they had nothing to do with her.

"I'm an idiot," concluded La Ponte. Then he went up to the window-frame and started to bang his head against it.

Liana Taillefer looked at him contemptuously and then said to Corso:

"Did you have to bring him?"

La Ponte was repeating, "I'm an idiot," banging his head hard.

"He thinks he's Athos," explained Corso.

"Or rather Aramis. Fatuous and conceited. Do you know he admires his shadow on the wall while he's making love?"

"I don't believe it."

"I can assure you he does."

La Ponte decided to forget about the window.

"We've gone off the subject," he said, embarrassed.

"True," said Corso. "We were talking about virtue, Milady. You were giving us lessons on the subject with regard to d'Artagnan and his friends."

"And why not? Why should a bunch of show-offs who use women, accept money from them, and only think of getting ahead and making their fortune, be more virtuous than Milady who is intelligent and courageous, who chooses to work for Richelieu and serve him faithfully, and risk her life for him?"

"And commit murder for him."

"You said it yourself a moment ago – the internal logic of the narrative."

"Internal? It depends on your point of view. Your husband's murder happened *outside* the novel, not in it. His death was real."

"You're mad, Corso. Nobody murdered Enrique. He hanged himself."

"I suppose Victor Fargas drowned himself? And last night Baroness Ungern got carried away with the microwave, did she?"

Liana Taillefer turned towards La Ponte and then to the girl, waiting for someone to confirm what she'd just heard. She looked disconcerted for the first time since they'd got in through the window.

"What are you talking about?"

"The nine correct engravings," said Corso. "From *The Nine Doors of the Kingdom of Shadows.*"

A striking clock could be heard out in the wind and rain beyond the closed window. Almost simultaneously a clock inside the building, downstairs, struck eleven times.

"I see there are more madmen in this affair," said Liana Taillefer.

She was still watching the door. There had been a noise behind it as the final chime struck, and a glint of triumph flashed across the woman's eyes.

"Careful," whispered La Ponte with a start. Corso knew what was going to happen. Out of the corner of his eye he saw the girl stand up straight, tense and alert, and he felt a sudden rush of adrenaline through his veins.

They all looked at the door handle. It was turning very slowly, like in the movies.

"Good evening," said Rochefort.

He was wearing a raincoat buttoned to the neck, shiny with rain. His dark eyes shone intensely beneath his felt hat. The pale zigzag of the scar stood out against his dark face. The bushy black moustache accentuated his southern looks. He stood motionless at the door for some fifteen seconds, his hands in his coat pockets, a puddle forming around his wet shoes. Nobody said a word.

"I'm glad you're here," said Liana Taillefer at last. Rochefort nodded briefly, but didn't answer. Still sitting on the bed, the woman pointed at Corso. "They were getting rather impertinent."

"Not too much, I hope," said Rochefort. His voice was pleasant, educated, with no definite accent, as Corso remembered it from the Sintra road. He didn't move from the doorway, his eyes fixed on Corso, as if La Ponte and the girl didn't exist. His lower lip still looked swollen, with traces of mercurochrome, two stitches holding the recent wound together. Souvenir from the banks of the Seine, thought Corso malevolently. Then he looked with interest to see the girl's reaction. But after her initial surprise, she had resumed the role of a detached spectator.

Without taking his eyes off Corso, Rochefort spoke to Milady.

"How did they get here?"

The woman gestured vaguely.

"They're pretty smart." She quickly looked over La Ponte and then stopped at Corso. "One of them anyway."

Rochefort nodded again. His eyes half-closed, he seemed to be analyzing the situation.

"It complicates things," he said at last. He took off his hat and threw it on the bed. "Really complicates things."

Liana Taillefer agreed. She smoothed down her skirt and stood up with a deep sigh. This made Corso turn slightly towards her, tense and hesitant. Then Rochefort took his hand out of his coat pocket and Corso worked out he must be left-handed. The discovery didn't do him much good – it was his left hand and in it he was holding a short-barrelled revolver, small and dark-blue, almost black. Meanwhile, Liana Taillefer went over to La Ponte and took the Dumas manuscript from his hands.

"Now try calling me a whore again." She was so close and staring at him with such contempt that she almost spat in his face. "If you've got the guts."

La Ponte hadn't. He was a born survivor. His "intrepid harpooneer" act was reserved for moments of alcohol-induced euphoria. So he made sure he said nothing at all.

"I was just passing," he said placatingly, hoping to wash his hands of the whole business.

"What would I do without you, Flavio?" said Corso, resigned.

La Ponte looked apologetic.

"You're being unfair," he said, looking offended. He went and stood nearer to the girl. It must have seemed the safest place in the room. "From a certain point of view, this is your adventure, Corso. And what's death to a guy like you? Nothing. A formality. Anyway you're getting paid a fortune. And life is basically unpleasant." He ended up looking down the barrel of Rochefort's revolver. Then he put his arm round the girl's shoulder and gave a melancholy sigh. "I hope nothing happens to you. But if it does, it'll be hardest for us: we'll have to go on living."

"Bastard. Traitor."

La Ponte looked saddened.

"My friend, I'll ignore that last remark. You're very tense."

"Of course I'm tense, you sewer rat."

"I'll ignore that too."

"Son of a bitch."

"I get the message, old buddy. Friendship is made up of little touches like that."

"Nice to see you've kept your team spirit," said Milady caustically.

Corso was thinking fast, even though there was nothing he could do. No amount of thinking could get the gun out of Rochefort's hand, although he wasn't pointing it at anyone in particular. He seemed rather half-hearted, as if he just needed to show it to get the desired effect. On the other hand, however intense his desire to settle a few outstanding scores with the man with the scar, Corso didn't possess the necessary technical skill to do so. With La Ponte not in the running, the girl was his only hope of shifting the balance of power. But unless she was an extremely accomplished actress he saw at first glance that he couldn't hope for anything on that flank. The supposed Irene Adler had shaken herself free of La Ponte's arm and had sat down on the window-ledge, from where she observed them with inexplicable detachment. She seemed absurdly determined to stay on the sidelines.

Liana Taillefer went over to Rochefort holding the Dumas manuscript, delighted to have retrieved it so quickly. Corso found it strange that she showed no similar interest in *The Nine Doors* which was still inside the canvas bag at the foot of the bed.

"What do we do now?" he heard her whisper to Rochefort.

To Corso's surprise Rochefort looked unsure. He was moving the revolver from one side to the other as if he didn't quite know where to point it. Then, exchanging a long and meaningful look with Milady, he took his right hand out of his pocket and passed it over his face, hesitant.

"We can't leave them here," he said at last.

"But we can't take them with us either," she said.

He nodded slowly. Judging by his renewed grip on the revolver, his indecision vanished. Corso felt his abdominal muscles tense as Rochefort pointed the gun at him. At the same time he tried to make some sort of syntactically coherent protest. All he managed was an indistinct, guttural sound.

"You're not going to kill him, are you?" asked La Ponte, trying to deflect attention from himself.

"Flavio," Corso managed to say in spite of the dryness in his mouth, "if I get out of this I swear I'll smash your face in. Right in."

"I was just trying to help."

"Better help your mother get off the streets."

"OK, OK, I'll shut up."

"Yeah, shut it," interrupted Rochefort menacingly. He'd exchanged a final glance with Liana Taillefer and seemed to have reached a decision. He locked the door behind him, still pointing the revolver at Corso, and put the key in his raincoat pocket. What have I got to lose, thought Corso, his pulse throbbing at his temples and wrists. The drums of Waterloo rolled somewhere in his memory when, in the final moment of clarity before desperation set in, he found himself working out the distance between him and the gun, and how long it would take him to cross it. He wondered when the first shot would ring out and in what position he'd be when it hit him. The chances of getting out of there unscathed were minimal, but maybe if he left it five seconds longer he would have no chance at all. So the bugle sounded. The last charge with Ney at the head, the bravest of the brave, before the Emperor's weary eyes. With Rochefort instead of the Scots Guards, but a bullet was still a bullet. This is ridiculous, he told himself just before he went into action. And he wondered if, in this context, the death blow about to strike him in the chest was going to be real or imaginary, and if he'd find himself floating in the void or in the Valhalla for fictional heroes. If only the luminous eyes he felt staring intently at his back – the Emperor? The Devil in love? – were waiting for him in the darkness to guide him to the other side.

Then Rochefort did something very odd. He raised his free hand, as if to say, "Give me time", rather an absurd gesture at this stage, and went to put the revolver back in his pocket. His movement only lasted a moment and he pointed it at Corso once again, but without too much conviction. And Corso, his pulse racing, his muscles taut, about to leap blindly forward, held back, bewildered, realizing it wasn't his time to die.

Still stunned, he watched Rochefort cross the room, press the number for an outside line and then dial a longer number. From where he was he could hear the sound of the phone ringing on the line and then a click.

"I've got Corso here," said Rochefort, and then he was quiet, waiting, as if there was a silence at the other end of the line. He was still lazily pointing the gun at a vague point in space. The man with the scar said "yes" twice. Then he listened, motionless, and muttered "OK" before finally hanging up.

"He wants to see him," he said to Milady. They both turned to look at Corso. Milady looked annoyed, Rochefort looked anxious.

"This is ridiculous," she complained.

"He wants to see him," Rochefort said again.

Milady shrugged. She took a few steps and angrily turned a few pages of 'The Anjou Wine'.

"As for us . . ." La Ponte started to say.

"You're staying here," said Rochefort, pointing the gun at him. Then he felt the wound on his lip. "The girl too."

In spite of his split lip he didn't seem to bear the girl much of a grudge. Corso even thought he saw a hint of curiosity as he looked at her. Then he turned to Liana Taillefer and handed her the revolver.

"Make sure they don't get out."

"Why don't you stay here?"

"He wants me to take him. It's safer."

Milady nodded sullenly. She'd obviously imagined herself playing a different part that evening. But like her fictional namesake she was a disciplined hired assassin. In exchange for the weapon she handed Rochefort the Dumas manuscript. Then she scrutinized Corso anxiously.

"I hope he won't give you any trouble."

Rochefort smiled calmly and confidently. He took a large switchblade from his pocket and stared at it thoughtfully, as if he'd only just remembered it was there. His white teeth looked bright against his dark, scarred face.

"I don't think he will," he answered, putting back the knife unopened, and gesturing to Corso in a way that was both friendly and sinister. Then he took his hat from the bed, turned the key in the lock and motioned towards the corridor with an exaggerated bow as if he was holding a large plumed hat.

"His Eminence awaits, sir," he said. And then he gave a short, dry laugh, perfectly befitting a skilled henchman.

Before leaving the room Corso looked at the girl. Milady was pointing the gun at her and La Ponte, but she had turned her back and was taking no notice of what was going on. She leant against the window and looked out, watching the wind and the rain, silhouetted against the night sky illuminated by flashes of lightning.

They went out into the storm. Rochefort was holding the folder with the Dumas manuscript under his raincoat to protect it from the rain. He led Corso through the narrow streets to the old part of the town. Blasts of rain shook the branches of the trees and splashed noisily in the puddles and on the paving stones. Large drops poured through Corso's hair and down his face. He turned up his collar. The town was in darkness and there was not a soul to be seen. Only the brightness of the storm lit up the streets intermittently, showing the medieval roofs, Rochefort's dark profile beneath his dripping hat, the shadows of the two men on the wet ground. The electrical discharges, like thunder from Hell, struck the turbulent current of the river Loire with a sound like the cracking of whips.

"Wonderful evening," said Rochefort turning towards Corso to make himself heard above the roar.

He seemed to know his way. He walked along confidently, turning occasionally to make sure his companion was still there. He didn't need to, because at that moment Corso would have followed him to the very gates of Hell. And he didn't discount the possibility that this might be their ultimate destination. With each flash of lightning he saw first a medieval archway, then a bridge over an ancient moat, a sign saying *Boulangerie-Patisserie*, a deserted square, a conical tower and finally, an iron gate with the sign: *Château de Meung-sur-Loire. XIIème-XIIIème siècle.*

A window was lit up in the distance, beyond the gate, but Rochefort turned right and Corso followed. They walked along a stretch of ivy-clad wall until they reached a half-hidden door in the wall. Rochefort took out a huge, ancient iron key and put it in the lock.

"Joan of Arc came through this door," he told Corso as he turned the key. One final flash of lightning revealed steps descending into darkness. In the momentary brightness Corso also saw Rochefort's smile, his dark eyes shining beneath the hat, the livid scar on his cheek. At least he was a worthy opponent, he thought. Nobody could have any complaints about the impeccable staging. In spite of himself he was beginning to feel a kind of twisted sympathy for the man – whoever he was – capable of playing the part of such a villain so conscientiously. Alexandre Dumas would have enjoyed it all hugely.

Rochefort was holding a small torch, lighting up the long, narrow staircase disappearing down to the cellar.

"You go in front," he said.

Their steps echoed round the turns of the passageway. After a moment, Corso shivered inside his damp coat. Cold, musty air, smelling of the damp of centuries, rose towards them. The torch beam lit worn steps, water stains on the vaulted ceiling. The staircase ended in a narrow corridor with rusty railings. Rochefort shone the torch for a moment on a circular pit to their left.

"These are the ancient dungeons of Bishop Thibault D'Aussigny," he told Corso. "From there they threw the corpses into the Loire. François Villon was a prisoner here."

And he muttered the following line melodramatically:

"Ayez pitié, ayez pitié de moi . . ."

Definitely a well-educated villain. Self-assured and with a hint of didacticism. Corso couldn't decide whether this made the situation better or worse. But he had an idea that had been going round in his head since they entered the passageway. If all is lost we may as well jump in the river, he thought. But he didn't find his joke funny.

The underground passageway was now rising beneath the dripping arches. The bright eyes of a rat shone for a moment at the end of the gallery and then disappeared with a cry. The torch lit up the passageway which widened into a circular room. Its ceiling, supported by pointed ribs, rested on a thick central column.

"The crypt," said Rochefort, moving the torch beam around. He was becoming more and more talkative. "Twelfth century. The women and children hid here when the castle was attacked."

Very interesting. But Corso wasn't in the mood to appreciate the information provided by his outlandish guide. He was tense and alert, waiting for the right moment. They were now climbing a spiral staircase, light from the storm still booming beyond the castle walls filtered through the slot windows.

"Only a few metres more and we're there," said Rochefort from behind, slightly lower down. He sounded quite conciliatory. The light from his torch shone between Corso's legs. "Now all this business is nearly over," he added, "I must tell you something. In spite of everything, you did very well. The proof is that you got this far . . . I hope you don't bear me too much of a grudge over the business by the Seine and at the Hotel Crillon. Occupational hazards."

He didn't say which occupation, but it didn't matter. Corso had already turned casually and stopped, as if to answer or ask him a question. It didn't look in the least suspicious, so in all fairness Rochefort couldn't object in any way. Maybe this was why he didn't react when, as a continuation of the same move, Corso fell on top of him, his arms and legs stretched out towards the wall so he wouldn't be dragged down the stairs. Rochefort's position was different – the steps were narrow, the wall smooth and without handholds, and in addition he wasn't expecting the attack. The torch, miraculously intact, illuminated the scene for several moments as it rolled down the staircase: Rochefort with his eyes wide open and a stunned look on his face; Rochefort flailing wildly, trying desperately to grab hold of something, disappearing down the spiral staircase, his hat rolling down until it came to a halt on one of the steps . . . And then, six or seven metres further down, a muffled sound, something like "thump", or maybe "splat". Corso, who was still gripping the walls with his arms and legs outstretched so as not to accompany his opponent on his uncomfortable journey, suddenly sprang into action. His heart was pounding uncontrollably as he leapt down the stairs three by three. He leant down for a moment to pick up the torch and then reached the bottom of the stairs where Rochefort, rolled into a ball, was moving weakly, in pain and in a bad way.

"Occupational hazard," said Corso, shining the torch on his face so that, from the floor, Rochefort could see his friendly smile. Then he kicked him in the head and heard it slam hard against the bottom step. He raised his foot to kick him again, just to make sure, but one look told him he didn't need to – Rochefort was lying with his mouth open and blood was trickling from his ear. He leant over to see if he was breathing and saw that he was. Then he opened his raincoat and rifled through his pockets. He took the switchblade, a wallet full of money, a French identity card and the folder with the Dumas manuscript, which he put under his coat, between his belt and his shirt. Then he pointed the torch beam at the spiral staircase and climbed right to the top this time. He reached a landing with a door with thick iron hinges and hexagonal nails. A crack of light filtered from beneath it. He stood motionless for some thirty seconds, trying to catch his breath and calm the beating of his heart. The solution to the mystery lay on the other side and he prepared to face it with his teeth clenched, the torch in one hand and Rochefort's knife, which opened with a menacing click, in the other.

And that's how, knife in hand, his hair soaked and dishevelled, and his eyes shining with homicidal determination, I saw Corso enter the library.

XV

Corso and Richelieu

*And I, who had created a short novel around him, had
been completely mistaken.*

Souvestre et Allain: *Fantomas*

The time has come to identify the viewpoint of the narrator. Faithful to
the tradition that the reader of mystery novels must have the same
information as the protagonist, I have tried to present the facts only
from Lucas Corso's perspective, except on two occasions: chapters
one and five of this story, when I had no choice but to appear myself.
In both these cases, and as now for the third and final time, I used the
first person for the sake of coherence. It would have been absurd to
refer to myself as "he", a publicity stunt that may have yielded
dividends for Julius Caesar in his campaign in Gaul but would, in my
case, have been judged, entirely reasonably, as unpardonable pedantry.
There is another, fairly perverse reason: telling the story as if I were
Dr Sheppard addressing Poirot struck me as, if not ingenious (everybody does that sort of thing now), then an amusing device. After all,
people write for amusement, or excitement, or out of self-love, or to
have others love them. I write for some of the same reasons. To quote
Eugène Sue, villains who are all of a piece, if you'll permit me the
expression, are very rare phenomena. Assuming – and it may be too
much to assume – that I really am a villain.

The fact is that I the undersigned, Boris Balkan, was there in the
library, awaiting our guest. Corso entered suddenly, knife in hand
and a dangerous avenging gleam in his eye. I noticed that he had
no escort, which worried me slightly, although I tried to retain my
mask of imperturbability. Otherwise I had planned the effect well:
the library in darkness, candelabra burning on the desk before me,
a copy of *The Three Musketeers* in my hands . . . I was even wearing a

red velvet jacket – which must have seemed like pure coincidence to Corso, but was in fact nothing of the sort – strongly reminiscent of cardinal's purple.

My big advantage was that I was expecting Corso, with or without escort, but he wasn't expecting me. So I decided to make the most of his surprise. I found the knife he was holding, together with the menacing look in his eyes, worrying. I opted to speak to forestall any move from him.

"Congratulations," I said, closing the book as if his arrival had interrupted my reading. "You've managed to play the game right to the end."

He stood staring at me from the other side of the room, and I have to say that I found his look of disbelief highly amusing.

"Game?" he managed to say hoarsely.

"Yes, game. Tension, uncertainty, a high level of skill . . . The possibility of acting freely, but according to obligatory rules, as an end in itself. Together with a sense of tension and pleasure at the difference from ordinary life . . ." These were not my own words, but Corso wasn't to know that. "Do you think that's an adequate definition? As the Second Book of Samuel says: 'Let the young men now arise, and play before us . . .' Children are the perfect players and readers: they do everything with the utmost seriousness. In essence, games are the only universally serious activity. They leave no room for scepticism, wouldn't you agree? However incredulous or doubting one might be, if one wants to play one has no choice but to follow the rules. Only the person who respects the rules, or at least knows and applies them, can win . . . Reading a book is the same: one has to accept the plot and the characters to enjoy the story." I paused, assuming that my flow of words would have had a sufficiently calming effect. "By the way, you didn't get here on your own. Where is he?"

"Rochefort?" Corso was grimacing in a very unpleasant way. "He had an accident."

"You call him Rochefort, do you? How amusing and appropriate. I see you've obviously followed the rules. I don't know why it should surprise me."

Corso treated me to a rather unnerving smile.

"He certainly looked surprised the last time I saw him."

"That sounds rather alarming." I smiled coolly, although I actually was alarmed. "I hope nothing serious has happened."

"He fell down the stairs."

"What?"

"You heard me. But don't worry. Your henchman was still breathing when I left him."

"Thank God." I managed to smile again and hide my unease. This went way beyond what I'd planned. "So you've done a touch of cheating, have you? Well," I said, spreading my hands magnanimously, "no need to worry about it."

"I'm not. You're the one who should be worried."

I pretended not to hear this.

"The important thing is you've arrived," I went on, although I'd lost the thread momentarily. "As far as cheating goes, you have illustrious predecessors . . . Theseus escaped from the labyrinth thanks to Ariadne's thread, Jason stole the Golden Fleece with Medea's help . . . The Kaurabas used subterfuge to win at dice in the Mahabharata, and the Achæans checkmated the Trojans by moving a wooden horse . . . Your conscience is clear."

"Thanks. But my conscience is my business."

From his pocket he took Milady's letter, folded in four, and threw it down on the table. I immediately recognized my own handwriting, with the slightly affected capitals. It is by my order and for the benefit of the State that the bearer of this note, etc.

"I hope, at least, that the game was enjoyable," I said holding the paper in the candle flame.

"At times."

"I'm glad." I dropped the letter in the ashtray and we both watched it burn. "In matters of literature, the intelligent reader may even enjoy the strategy used to turn him into the victim. I believe that enjoyment is an excellent reason for playing. Or reading a story, or writing one."

I stood up, holding *The Three Musketeers*, and paced around the room, glancing discreetly at the clock on the wall. There were still twenty long minutes to go before twelve. The gilding gleamed on the spines of the ancient books lined up on their shelves. I looked at them a moment, having seemingly forgotten Corso, and then turned towards him.

"There they are." I made a sweeping gesture to include the whole library. "They look still and silent but they talk amongst themselves, even though they seem to ignore each other. They communicate through their authors, just as the egg uses the hen to produce another egg."

I put *The Three Musketeers* back on its shelf. Dumas was in good company: between *Los Pardellanes* by Zevaco and *The Knight with the*

Yellow Doublet by Lucus de René. As there was time to spare, I opened it at the first page and began to read aloud:

"As Saint Germain l'Auxerrois struck twelve, three horsemen descended the Rue des Astruces each wrapped in a cape, seemingly as sure as the stride of their horses . . .

"The first lines," I said. "Always those extraordinary first lines. Do you remember our conversation about Scaramouche? 'He was born with the gift of laughter . . .'. Some opening sentences leave their mark a whole lifetime, don't you agree? 'I sing of arms and the man.' Have you never played this game with someone you trust? 'A modest young man headed in midsummer . . .', or that other one, 'For a long time I used to go to bed early . . .'. And of course, 'On the 15th of May 1796 General Bonaparte entered Milan.'"

Corso frowned.

"You're forgetting the one which brought me here: 'On the first Monday of April 1625, the market town of Meung, the birthplace of the author of the *Roman de la Rose*, was in a state of commotion.'"

"Indeed, Chapter One," I said. "You have done very well."

"That's what Rochefort said before he fell down the stairs."

There was silence, broken only by the clock striking a quarter to twelve. Corso pointed at the clockface.

"Fifteen minutes to go, Balkan."

"Yes," I said. The man was devilishly intuitive. "Fifteen minutes till the first Monday in April."

I put *The Knight with the Yellow Doublet* back on the shelf and paced around the room. Corso stood watching me, still holding the knife.

"You could put that away," I ventured.

He hesitated a moment before shutting the blade and putting it away in his pocket, still watching me. I smiled approvingly and again indicated the library.

"One is never alone with a book nearby, don't you agree?" I said to be conversational. "Every page reminds one of a day that has passed and makes one relive the emotions that filled it. Happy hours underlined in chalk, dark ones in pencil . . . Where was I then? What prince called me his friend, what beggar called me his brother?" I hesitated a moment, searching for more phrases with which to round off my speech.

"What son of a bitch called you his buddy?" suggested Corso.

I looked at him reprovingly. The wet blanket insisted on bringing down the tone.

"No need to be unpleasant."

"I'll do what I please. Your Eminence."

"I detect a hint of sarcasm," I said, truly offended. "From that I deduce that you have given in to prejudice, Mr Corso. It was Dumas who made Richelieu a villain when he wasn't one, and falsified reality for the sake of literary expediency. I thought I'd explained that during our last meeting at the café in Madrid."

"A dirty trick," said Corso, not specifying whether he was referring to Dumas or to me.

I raised a finger, ready to state my case vigorously.

"A legitimate device," I objected, "inspired by the shrewdness and genius of the greatest novelist who ever lived. And yet . . ." at this point I smiled bitterly – "Sainte-Beuve respected him but didn't accept him as a man of letters. His friend, Victor Hugo, merely praised Dumas's capacity for dramatic action, but nothing more. Prolific, long-winded, they said. With little style. They accused him of not delving into the anxieties of human beings, of lacking subtlety . . . Lacking subtlety!" I touched the volumes of *The Three Musketeers* lined up on the shelf. "I agree with our good father Stevenson – there is no pæan to friendship as long, eventful or beautiful. In *Twenty Years After*, when the protagonists reappear they are distanced at first. They are now men of mature years, selfish, with all the pettiness that life imposes. They're even fighting in opposing camps . . . Aramis and d'Artagnan lie and dissemble, Porthos fears being asked for money . . . When they agree to meet in the Place Royale they come armed and almost fight. And in England, when Athos's imprudence puts them all in danger, d'Artagnan refuses to shake his hand . . . In *The Vicomte de Bragelonne*, with the mystery of the iron mask, Aramis and Porthos stand against their old comrades. This happens because they're alive, because they're human, full of contradictions. But always, at the moment of truth, friendship wins out. A great thing, friendship! Do you have friends, Corso?"

"That's a good question."

"For me, Porthos in the cave at Locmaria has always embodied friendship: the giant struggling beneath a rock to save his friends . . . Do you remember his last words?"

"It's too heavy?"

"Exactly!"

I confess I felt almost moved. Like the young man in a cloud of pipe smoke described by Captain Marlow, Corso was one of us. But he was also a bitter, stubborn man determined not to feel.

"You're Liana Taillefer's lover," he said.

"Yes," I admitted, reluctantly leaving thoughts of good Porthos aside. "Isn't she a splendid woman? With her own particular obsessions . . . Beautiful and loyal, like Milady in the novel. It's strange. There are fictional characters in literature who have a life of their own, familiar to millions of people who haven't even read the books in which they feature. In English literature there are three: Sherlock Holmes, Romeo, and Robinson Crusoe. In Spanish, two: Don Quixote and Don Juan. And in French literature, there is one: d'Artagnan. But you see I . . ."

"Let's not go off at a tangent again, Balkan."

"I'm not. I was about to add the name of Milady to d'Artagnan's. An extraordinary woman. Like Liana, in her own way. Her husband never measured up to her."

"Do you mean Athos?"

"No, I mean poor old Enrique Taillefer."

"Was that why you murdered him?"

My amazement must have looked sincere. It *was* sincere.

"Enrique murdered? Don't be ridiculous. He hanged himself. He committed suicide. I should imagine that, with his way of looking at the world, he thought it a heroic gesture. Very regrettable."

"I don't believe you."

"Please yourself. But his death was the starting point for this entire story and, indirectly, the reason you're here."

"Explain it to me then. Nice and slowly."

He had certainly earned it. As I said earlier, Corso was one of us, although he didn't know it. And anyway – I looked at the clock – it was almost twelve.

"Do you have 'The Anjou Wine' with you?"

He looked at me alertly, trying to guess my intentions. Then I saw him give in. Reluctantly, he took the folder from under his coat, then hid it again.

"Excellent," I said. "And now follow me."

* * *

He must have been expecting a secret passage leading from the library, some sort of diabolical trap. I saw him put his hand in his pocket in search of the knife.

"You won't be needing that," I assured him.

He didn't look too convinced, but he said nothing. I held one of the candelabra up high and we walked down the Louis XIII-style corridor. A magnificent tapestry hung on one of the walls: Ulysses, bow in hand, recently returned to Ithaca, Penelope and the dog rejoicing, the suitors drinking wine in the background, unaware of what awaits them.

"This is a very ancient castle, full of history," I said. "It has been plundered by the English, by the Huguenots, by revolutionaries . . . Even the Germans set up a command post here during the war. It was very dilapidated when the present owner – a British millionaire, a charming man and a gentleman – acquired it. He restored and furnished it with extraordinary good taste. He even agreed to open it to the public."

"So what are you doing here out of visiting hours?"

As I passed a leaded window I glanced out. The storm was dying down at last, the glow of lightning fading beyond the Loire, to the north.

"An exception is made once a year," I explained. "After all, Meung is a special place. A novel like *The Three Musketeers* doesn't open just anywhere."

The wooden floors creaked beneath our feet. A suit of armour – genuine sixteenth-century – stood in a bend in the corridor. The light from the candelabra was reflected in the smooth, polished surfaces of the cuirass. Corso glanced at it as he walked past, as if there might be someone hidden inside.

"I'm going to tell you a long story which began ten years ago," I said, "at an auction in Paris of a lot of uncatalogued documents . . . I was writing a book on the nineteenth-century popular novel in France, and the dusty packages fell into my hands quite by chance. When I went through them I saw they were from the old archives of *Le Siècle*. Almost all consisted of printing proofs of little value, but one package of blue and white sheets attracted my attention. It was the original text, handwritten by Dumas and Maquet, of *The Three Musketeers*. All sixty-seven chapters, just as they were sent to the printers. Someone, possibly Baudry, the editor of the newspaper, had kept them after composing the galley proofs, and then forgotten all about them . . ."

I slowed down and stopped in the middle of the corridor. Corso was very still and the light from the candelabra I was holding lit up his face from below, making shadows dance in his eye sockets. He seemed to be listening intently to my story, unaware of anything else. Solving the mystery that had brought him there was the only thing that mattered to him. But he still kept his hand on the knife in his pocket.

"My discovery," I went on, pretending not to notice this, "was of extraordinary importance. We knew of a few fragments of the original draft from Dumas's and Maquet's notes and papers, but we were unaware of the existence of the complete manuscript. At first I thought I would make my finding public, in the form of an annotated facsimile edition. But then I came across a serious moral obstacle."

The light and shadow on Corso's face moved and a dark line crossed his mouth. He was smiling.

"I don't believe it. A moral obstacle, after all this."

I moved the candelabra to remove the sceptical smile from his face, unsuccessfully.

"I'm quite serious," I protested as we moved on. "On examining the manuscript I concluded that the real creator of the story was Auguste Maquet . . . He had done all the research and outlined the story in broad strokes. Dumas, with his enormous talent, his genius, had then brought the raw material to life and turned it into a masterpiece. Although obvious to me, it might not have been quite so evident to detractors of the author and his work." I gestured with my free hand as if to sweep them all aside. "But I had no intention of throwing stones at my hero. Even less so now, in these times of mediocrity and lack of imagination . . . Times in which people no longer admire marvels, as theatre audiences and the readers of serials used to. They hissed at the villains and cheered on the heroes with no inhibitions." I shook my head sadly. "Applause which unfortunately can no longer be heard. It's become the exclusive domain of innocents and children."

Corso was listening with an insolent, mocking expression. I don't know whether he agreed with me, but he was the grudge-bearing type and refused to accept that my explanation granted me any sort of moral alibi.

"To sum up," he said, "you decided to destroy the manuscript."

I smiled smugly. He was trying to be too clever.

"Don't be ridiculous. I decided to do something better: to make a dream come true."

We had stopped in front of the closed door to the reception room. Through it the muffled sound of music and voices could be heard. I put the candelabra down on a console table while Corso watched me, again suspicious. He was probably wondering what new trick was hidden there. I realized he didn't understand that we really had reached the solution to the mystery.

"Please allow me to introduce you," I said, opening the door, "to the members of the Dumas Club."

Almost everyone was there. Through the French windows opening onto the castle terrace, late arrivals entered the room full of people, cigarette smoke and the murmur of conversation above a background of gentle music. On the central table, covered with a white linen table-cloth, there was a cold buffet: bottles of Anjou wine, sausages and hams from Amiens, oysters from La Rochelle, boxes of Montecristo cigars. Groups of guests, around fifty men and women, were drinking, and conversing in several languages. Many of them were well-known faces from the press, cinema and television. I saw Corso check he had his glasses on.

"Surprised?" I asked, looking to see his reaction.

He nodded, surly and disconcerted. Several guests came to greet me, so I shook hands, exchanged pleasantries and jokes. The atmosphere was agreeably cordial. Corso looked like someone about to fall out of bed and wake up. I was highly amused. I introduced him to some of the guests and watched with perverse satisfaction as he greeted them, confused and unsure of the terrain he was crossing. His customary composure was in shreds, and this was my small revenge. After all, it was he who had first come to me with 'The Anjou Wine' under his arm, determined to complicate things.

"Please allow me to introduce Mr Corso . . . Bruno Lostia, an antique dealer from Milan. Permit me. Yes, indeed. Thomas Harvey, of Harvey's, Jewellers: New York–London–Paris–Rome . . . And Count von Schlossberg, owner of the most famous collection of paintings in Europe. As you can see, we have something of everything here: a Venezuelan Nobel prize winner, an Argentine ex-President, the Crown Prince of Morocco . . . Do you know, his father is an avid reader of Alexandre Dumas? Look who's arrived. You know him, don't you? Professor of Semiotics in Bologna . . . The blonde lady talking to him is Petra Neustadt, the most influential literary critic in Central Europe. In that group, next to the Duchess of Alba, there's the financier Rudolf Villefoz and the English writer Harold Burgess. Amaya Euskal, of the Alpha Press group, with the most powerful publisher in the USA, Johan Cross, of O&O Papers, New York . . . And I assume you remember Achille Replinger, the bookdealer, from Paris."

This was the last straw. I savoured Corso's shaken expression, almost pitying him. Replinger was holding an empty glass and smiling pleasantly beneath his musketeer's moustache, just as he had when identifying the Dumas manuscript at his shop on the Rue Bonaparte. He greeted me with a huge bear hug and then warmly patted Corso on the back before going off in search of another drink, puffing away like a jovial, rosy-cheeked Porthos.

"Damn this," muttered Corso, drawing me aside. "What's going on here?"

"I already told you, it's a long story."

"Well, finish telling it, will you?"

We had moved close to the table. I poured us a couple of glasses of wine, but he refused with a shake of his head.

"Gin," he muttered. "Haven't you got any gin?"

I indicated the drinks cabinet at the other end of the room. We walked over to it, stopping three or four times on the way to exchange more greetings: a well-known film director, a Lebanese millionaire, a Spanish Minister of the Interior . . . Corso grabbed a bottle of Beefeater gin and filled a glass to the brim, swallowing half of it in a single gulp. He shuddered slightly and his eyes shone behind his glasses (one lens was broken, the other was intact). He held the bottle to his chest as if afraid to lose it.

"You were going to tell me something," he said.

I suggested we go out on to the terrace beyond the French windows, where we could talk without interruption. Corso filled his glass up again before following me. The storm had died down. Stars shone above us.

"I'm all ears," he announced after another large gulp.

I leaned on the balustrade, still damp from the rain, and took a sip from my glass of Anjou wine.

"Owning the manuscript of *The Three Musketeers* gave me the idea," I said. "Why not form a literary society, a sort of club for devoted admirers of the novels of Alexandre Dumas and the classic adventure serial? Through my work I already had contact with several ideal candidates . . ." I gestured towards the brightly-lit salon. Through the tall French windows the guests could be seen coming and going, chatting animatedly. It was proof of my success and I didn't conceal my authorial pride. "A society dedicated to studying novels of that kind, rediscovering writers and forgotten works, promoting their republication and sale under an imprint with which you may be familiar: Dumas & Co."

"I know it," confirmed Corso. "They're based in Paris and have just published the entire works of Ponson du Terrail. Last year it was *Fantomas* . . . I didn't know you had a part in it."

I smiled.

"That's the rule: no names, no starring roles . . . As you can see, the matter is scholarly and slightly childish at the same time. A nostalgic literary game which rediscovers long-lost novels and returns us to our innocence, to how we used to be. As one matures, one becomes a fan of Flaubert or Stendhal, favours Faulkner, Lampedusa, García Marquez, Durrell and Kafka . . . We become different from each other, opponents even. But we all share a conspiratorial wink when we talk about certain magical authors and books. Those that made us discover literature without weighing us down with dogma or teaching us bad rules. This is our true common heritage: stories faithful not to what people see, but to what they dream."

I left the words hanging and paused, awaiting their effect. But Corso just raised his glass to look at it against the light. His homeland was in there.

"That was before," he answered. "Now, neither children nor young people nor anyone else has a spiritual home. They just watch bloody TV."

I shook my head confidently. I had written something on that very subject for the literary supplement of the *Abc* newspaper a couple of weeks before.

"I don't agree. Even then they're treading, unknowingly, in old footsteps. Films on television, for instance, maintain the link. Those old movies. Even Indiana Jones is the direct descendant of all that."

Corso grimaced in the direction of the brightly-lit French windows.

"It's possible. But you were telling me about these people. I'd like to know how you . . . recruited them."

"It's no secret," I answered. "I've been running this select society, the Dumas Club, for ten years now. It holds its annual meeting here in

Meung. As you can see, the members arrive punctually from all corners of the globe. Every last one of them is a first-class reader . . ."

"Of serials? Don't make me laugh."

"I don't have the slightest intention of making you laugh, Corso. Why are you looking at me like that? You know yourself that a novel, or a film made for pure consumption, can turn into an exquisite work, from *The Pickwick Papers* to *Casablanca* and *Goldfinger* . . . Audiences turn to these stories full of archetypes to enjoy, whether consciously or unconsciously, the device of repeated story lines with small variations. *Dispositio* rather than *elocutio* . . . That's why the serial, even the most trite television serial, can become a cult both for a naïve audience and for a more demanding one. There are people who look for excitement in Sherlock Holmes risking his life, and others go for the pipe, the magnifying glass and the "Elementary, my dear Watson" which, by the way, Conan Doyle never actually wrote. The plot devices, the variations and repetition, are so old that they're mentioned in Aristotle's *Poetics*. And what is a television serial if not an updated version of a classic tragedy, a great romantic drama or the Dumas novel? That's why an intelligent reader can obtain a lot of enjoyment from all this, by way of exception. For there are exceptions based on rules."

I thought Corso was interested in what I was saying, but then he shook his head. A gladiator refusing to accept the dangerous terrain offered by his opponent.

"Stop the literature lecture and get back to your Dumas Club, will you?" he said impatiently. "To that loose chapter that was floating around . . . Where's the rest?"

"In there," I answered, looking at the salon. "I based the organization of the society on the sixty-seven chapters of the manuscript – a maximum of sixty-seven members, each having a chapter as a registered share. Allocation is strictly based on a list of applicants, and changes in holding require the approval of the executive board, which I chair . . . Each applicant is discussed in depth before his admission is approved."

"How are shares transferred?"

"On no account are the shares to be transferred. If a club member dies, or wishes to leave the society, their chapter must be returned. The board then allocates it to another applicant. A member may never freely dispose of it."

"Is that what Enrique Taillefer tried to do?"

"In a way. In theory he was an ideal applicant. He was a model member of the Dumas Club until he broke the rules."

Corso finished his gin. He put the glass down on the mossy balustrade and said nothing for a moment, staring intently at the lights of the reception room. Then he shook his head.

"That's not a reason for murdering someone," he said quietly, as if talking to himself. "I can't believe that all these people . . ." He looked at me stubbornly. "They're all well-known and respectable, in theory. They'd never get mixed up in something like this."

I suppressed another impatient gesture.

"I think you're blowing things up out of all proportion . . . Enrique and I were friends for some time. We shared a fascination for this kind of fiction, although his taste in literature wasn't on a level with his enthusiasm . . . The fact is his success as a publisher of bestselling cookery books meant he could spend time and money on his hobby. And to be fair, if anybody deserved to be a member of the club it was Enrique. That's why I recommended his admission. As I said, we shared, if not the same tastes, at least the enthusiasm."

"You shared more than that, I seem to remember."

Corso's sarcastic smile had returned and I found it highly irritating.

"I could tell you that it's none of your business," I retorted uneasily. "But I want to explain everything . . . Liana has always been very special, as well as very beautiful. She was a precocious reader. Do you know that at sixteen she had a fleur-de-lis tattooed on her hip? She didn't have it done on the shoulder, like her idol, Milady de Winter, so that her family and the nuns at her boarding-school shouldn't find out . . . What about that?"

"Very moving."

"You don't seem very moved. But I assure you she's an admirable person . . . The fact is that, well . . . we became intimate. You'll recall that earlier I mentioned the homeland that is the lost paradise of childhood. Well Liana's homeland is *The Three Musketeers*. She was fascinated by the world depicted in its pages. She decided to marry Enrique after meeting him by chance at a party where they spent the evening exchanging quotes from the novel. He was already a very wealthy publisher."

"So it was love at first sight," said Corso.

"I don't know why you say it like that. They married for the most sincere reasons. The thing is that, in the long run, even for someone as good-natured as his wife, Enrique could be tiresome . . . We were good friends and I often visited them. Liana . . ." I put my glass on the balustrade next to his empty one. "Anyway. You can imagine the rest."

"Yes, I can. Very clearly."

"I wasn't talking about that. She became an excellent collaborator. So much so that, four years ago, I sponsored her entry to the society. She owns Chapter Thirty-Seven, *Milady's Secret*. She chose it herself."

"Why did you put her on my trail?"

"Let's take this one bit at a time. Lately Enrique had become a problem. Instead of limiting himself to the very profitable business of cookery books he was determined to write a serial. But the fact was the novel was awful. Absolutely dreadful, believe me. He had brazenly plagiarized all the plots of the genre. It was called . . ."

"*The Dead Man's Hand*."

"Exactly. Even the title wasn't his. And what's worse, unbelievably, he wanted Dumas & Co. to publish it. I refused, of course. His monstrous creation would never have been approved by the board. Anyway, Enrique had more than enough money to publish it himself, and I told him so."

"I assume he took it badly. I saw his library."

"Badly? That is something of an understatement. The argument took place in his study. I can still picture him, small and chubby, standing very straight, on tiptoes, staring at me with wild eyes. He looked as if he might burst a blood vessel. All very unpleasant. He said he'd decided to devote his whole life to it. And who was I to judge his writing. That was up to posterity. I was a biased critic and an insufferable pedant. And on top of everything I was involved with his wife . . . This left me absolutely stunned – I didn't realize he knew. But it seems that Liana talks in her sleep, and between cursing d'Artagnan and his friends (who, by the way, she hates as if she had known them personally) she'd been broadcasting the whole affair to her husband . . . You can imagine my predicament."

"Very difficult for you."

"Extremely. Although the worst was yet to come. Enrique was in full flow. He said that if he himself was mediocre, Dumas wasn't much of a writer either. Where would he have been without Auguste Maquet, whom he wretchedly exploited? The proof lay in the white and blue pages of 'The Anjou Wine', which he kept in his safe . . . The argument became more heated. He called me an adulterer – rather an old-fashioned insult – and I called him a moron, adding a few snide comments about his latest cookery book successes. I ended up comparing him to the baker in *Cyrano* . . . 'I'll get my revenge,' he said, sounding rather like the Count of Monte Cristo. 'I'm going to publicize the fact that your beloved Dumas was a big cheat who appropriated other people's work. I'll make the manuscript public, and everyone will see how the old fraud produced his serials. I don't give a damn about the rules of the society. That chapter's mine and I'll sell it to whoever I like. So go to hell.'"

"He got pretty nasty."

"You don't know how spiteful a spurned author can get. My objections were to no avail. He threw me out. Later I found out through Liana that he'd called that bookseller, La Ponte, to offer him the manuscript. He must have thought himself very clever and devious, like Edmundo Dantés. He wanted to create a scandal without being directly implicated and keep his reputation intact. That's how you became involved. You can understand my surprise when you came to see me with 'The Anjou Wine'."

"You certainly didn't show it."

"I had my reasons. With Enrique dead, Liana and I had assumed the manuscript was lost."

I saw Corso search his coat for one of his crumpled cigarettes. He put it in his mouth but didn't light it. He paced around the terrace.

"Your story's ridiculous," he said at last. "No Edmundo Dantés would commit suicide before savouring his revenge."

I nodded, although he had his back to me and couldn't see my gesture.

"Well, other things happened," I said. "The day after our conversation Enrique came to my house in a final attempt to convince me. I'd had enough. And I won't put up with blackmail. So, not quite realizing what I was doing, I dealt him the death blow. His serial, in spite of being very bad, felt very familiar. So, when Enrique made a scene for the second time, I went to my library, searched for an ancient edition of *The Popular Illustrated Novel*, a little-known late nineteenth-century publication, and opened it at the first page of a story signed by a certain Amaury de Verona entitled: *Angeline de Gravaillac, or Unsullied Virtue*. Well, you can imagine the sort of thing. As I read out the first paragraph Enrique went pale, as if the ghost of Angeline had risen from the grave. Which is more or less what happened. He'd assumed nobody would remember the story and had plagiarized it. He copied it almost word for word, all except for a chapter he took whole from Fernandez y Gonzalez, in fact the best part of the story . . . I was sorry I didn't have my camera to take a picture of him. He put his hand on his forehead as if to exclaim, 'Damnation!' but he couldn't actually get the word out. He just made a kind of gurgling sound, as if he was about to suffocate. Then he turned, went home and hanged himself from the light fitting."

Corso turned towards me. He still had his forgotten cigarette in his mouth, unlit.

"Then things became more complicated," I went on, sure that he was now starting to believe me. "You already had the manuscript and your friend La Ponte wasn't willing, at first, to part with it. I couldn't go round playing Arsène Lupin, I've got a reputation to protect. That's why I gave Liana the task of retrieving the chapter. The date of the annual meeting was approaching and we had to find a new member to replace Enrique. I admit, Liana did make a few mistakes. Firstly, she went to see you . . ." I cleared my throat, embarrassed. I didn't want to go into any detail. "Then she tried to get La Ponte on her side, for him to get 'The Anjou Wine' back. But I didn't know how tenacious you could be . . . The problem is she had always dreamt of an adventure similar to her heroine's, full of deception, love affairs and persecution. And this episode, based on the stuff of her dreams, gave her a great opportunity. So she set off on your trail enthusiastically. 'I'll bring you the manuscript bound in the skin of that Corso,' she promised. I told her not to get carried away. But now I recognize that the mistake was mine: I encouraged her in her fantasy, releasing the Milady that had been inside her ever since she first read *The Three Musketeers*."

"Well, I wish she'd read something else. Like *Gone with the Wind*. She could have identified with Scarlett O'Hara and gone around pestering Clark Gable and not me."

"I do admit she went slightly over the top. It's a pity you should have taken it so seriously."

Corso rubbed the spot behind his ear. I could imagine what he was thinking: the one who must really have taken it seriously was the man with the scar.

"Who's Rochefort?"

"His name is Laszlo Nicolavic. He's an actor who specializes in supporting roles. He played Rochefort in the series Andreas Frey made for British television a couple of years ago. He's actually played almost all the well-known villains: Gonzaga in *Lagardère,* Levasseur in *Captain Blood,* La Tour d'Azyr in *Scaramouche,* Rupert of Hentzau in *The Prisoner of Zenda* . . . He's fascinated by the genre, and has applied to join the Dumas Club. Liana was quite taken with him, and insisted he should work with her on this matter."

"Well, old Laszlo certainly took his part seriously . . ."

"I'm afraid he did. I suspect he's trying to gain points so his admission is approved quickly. I also suspect that he serves as her occasional lover." I smiled like a man of the world, hoping that I'd be convincing. "Liana is young, beautiful and passionate. Let's say I encourage her intellectual side with calm romantic ardour, and Laszlo Nicolavic presumably takes care of the more down-to-earth side of her impetuous nature."

"What else?"

"That's almost all. Nicolavic, or Rochefort, took charge of getting the Dumas manuscript from you. That's why he followed you from Madrid to Toledo and Sintra, while Liana headed for Paris, taking La Ponte with her as a back-up in case their original plan failed and you didn't see reason. You know the rest: you didn't let them snatch the manuscript from you, Milady and Rochefort got slightly carried away, and that brought you here." I reflected on the events. "Do you know something? I wonder whether instead of Laszlo Nicolavic I shouldn't propose you as a member of the club."

He didn't even ask whether I was being sarcastic or really meant it. He removed his battered glasses and cleaned them mechanically, absorbed in his thoughts.

"Is that all?" he said at last.

"Of course." I pointed to the reception room. "There's your proof."

He put his glasses on and took a deep breath. I didn't like the look on his face at all.

"What about the *Delomelanicon?* And Richelieu's connection with *The Nine Doors of the Kingdom of Shadows?*" He came closer, tapping me on the chest until I had to take a step back. "Do you take me for a fool? You're not going to tell me that you knew nothing about the link between Dumas and that book, his pact with the Devil and all the rest of it – Victor Fargas's murder in Sintra, and the fire at Baroness Ungern's flat in Paris. Did you give my name to the police yourself? And what about the book hidden in the three copies? Or the nine prints engraved by Lucifer, reprinted by Aristide Torchia on his return from Prague 'by authority and permission of the superiors', and the whole damn business . . ."

He said it all in a fast torrent, sticking out his chin aggressively, his eyes piercing into me. I took another step back and stood looking at him open-mouthed.

"You've gone mad!" I protested indignantly. "Can you tell me what you're talking about?"

He took out a box of matches and lit his cigarette, cupping a hand round the flame. Through the glare reflected in his glasses he kept his eyes fixed on me. Then he told me his version of events.

When he finished we both fell silent. We were leaning on the damp balustrade, next to each other, watching the lights of the reception room. Corso's story had lasted for the duration of the cigarette and he now stubbed it out on the ground.

"I suppose," I said, "I should now confess and say, 'Yes, it's true,' and then hold out my hands for you to handcuff them. Is that really what you're expecting?"

He took a moment to answer. Having recounted the story aloud didn't seem to have made him confident of his conclusions.

"But there is a link," he muttered.

I looked at his narrow shadow on the terrace floor, dark against the rectangles of light from the reception room cast on the marble flagstones and stretched beyond the steps into the darkness of the garden.

"I fear," I concluded, "that your imagination has played tricks on you."

He shook his head slowly.

"I didn't imagine that Victor Fargas was drowned in the pond, or that Baroness Ungern was burnt with her books. Those things happened. They were real. The two stories are mixed up."

"You've just said it yourself – there are two stories. Maybe all that links them is your own intertextual reading."

"Please leave out the technical jargon. The Dumas chapter triggered everything." He looked at me resentfully. "Your bloody club and all your little games."

"Don't lay all the blame on me. Games are perfectly valid. If this was a work of fiction and not a real story, as the reader you would be principally responsible."

"Don't be absurd."

"I'm not. From what you've just told me I deduce that, playing with the facts and your own personal literary references, you constructed a theory and drew erroneous conclusions. But the facts are objective and you can't overlay them with your personal errors. The story of 'The Anjou Wine' and the one about this mysterious book, *The Nine Doors*, are completely unrelated."

"You all led me to believe . . ."

"We, and by that I mean Liana Taillefer, Laszlo Nicolavic and myself, did nothing of the sort. It was you who filled in the blanks on your own, as if it was a novel based on trickery and Lucas Corso a reader being too clever for his own good. Nobody ever told you that events were actually happening as you thought. So the responsibility is entirely yours, my friend. The real culprit is your excessive intertextual reading and linking of literary references."

"What else could I do? In order to take action I needed some sort of strategy, and I couldn't just sit there waiting. In any strategy you build up a picture of your opponent and this influences your next move . . . Wellington did such-and-such, thinking that Napoleon was thinking of doing such-and-such. And Napoleon . . ."

"Napoleon made the mistake of confusing Blücher with Grouchy. Military strategy is as risky as literary strategy. Listen, Corso, there are no innocent readers any more. Each overlays the text with his own perverse view. A reader is all that he's read before, in addition to all the films and TV that he's seen. To the information supplied by the author, he'll always add his own. And that's where the danger lies: an excess of references may have caused you to create the wrong opponent, or an imaginary opponent."

"The information was false."

"Don't insist. The information a book provides tends to be objective. It may be set out by a malevolent author who wishes to mislead, but it is never false. It's you who makes a false reading."

He seemed to be thinking carefully. He had moved slightly and was again leaning on the balustrade, facing the garden in darkness.

"Then there must be another author," he said very quietly.

He stood motionless. After a time he took the folder with 'The Anjou Wine' from under his coat and put it to one side, on the moss-covered stone.

"This story has two authors," he insisted.

"That's possible," I said and took the Dumas manuscript. "And maybe one is more malevolent than the other. My story was the serial. You'll have to look for the crime novel elsewhere."

XVI

A Device Worthy of a Gothic Novel

"Here is the vexing part of the matter," said Porthos. "In the old days one didn't have to explain anything. One just fought because one fought."

A. Dumas: *The Vicomte de Bragelonne*

Leaning his head against the driver's seat, Lucas Corso looked at the view. He had parked the car in a small lay-by on the final bend of the road before it dipped down into the town. Surrounded by ancient walls, the old quarter floated in mist from the river, suspended in the air like a ghostly blue island. It was a hazy world without light or shadow. A cold, hesitant dawn over Castille, with the first glimmer of light showing roofs, chimneys and bell towers to the east.

He wanted to look at the time, but his watch had let in water during the storm in Meung. The glass was misted and the dial was illegible. Corso caught sight of his exhausted eyes in the rear-view mirror. Meung-sur-Loire, on the eve of the first Monday in April. They were now very far away, and it was Tuesday. It had been a long return journey and they all seemed to fade into the distance: Balkan, the Dumas Club, Rochefort, Milady, La Ponte. The echoes of a story concluded with the turning of a page. The author striking the final key – Qwerty keyboard, bottom row, second from the right – or the final blow. So with one arbitrary action it became no more than pages of type, strange, inert paper. Lives suddenly alien.

On that dawn so similar to the awakening from a dream, Corso sat, dirty and unshaven, with reddened eyes. All that remained was his old canvas bag containing the remaining copy of *The Nine Doors*. And the girl. That was all that was left on the shore after the tide had gone out. She moaned gently at his side and he turned to look at her. She was sleeping in the seat next to him, under her duffle coat, her head resting on Corso's right shoulder. She was breathing gently, her lips parted, occasionally shaken by small shivers which made her start. Then she'd moan again very quietly. A small vertical crease between her eyebrows made her look like an upset little girl. One hand protruded from under her coat. It was turned palm up, her fingers half-open as if she had just let something slip from them, or as if she were waiting.

Corso thought again about Meung, and about the journey. And Boris Balkan two nights earlier, standing next to him on the terrace which was still damp from the rain. Holding the pages of 'The Anjou Wine', Richelieu had smiled like an old opponent, both admiring and sympathetic. "You're very special, my friend." He had offered these final words as consolation, or as a farewell; they were the only ones with any meaning. The rest – an invitation to join the other guests – was uttered with little conviction. Not that Balkan wanted to get rid of him – he had in fact seemed disappointed when Corso left – but because he knew that Corso would refuse to come inside and would stay on the terrace, which he did. He stood for some time alone, leaning on the balustrade, listening to the echo of his own defeat. He slowly came to and looked round, remembering where he was. Then he walked away from the brightly-lit windows and returned unhurriedly to the hotel, wandering through the dark streets. He didn't come across Rochefort again, and at the Auberge Saint-Jacques he was told that Milady too had left. They both departed from his life and returned to the nebulous regions from which they had come, fictional characters once more, as unaccountable as chess pieces. He found La Ponte and the girl without difficulty. He hadn't worried about La Ponte, but he was reassured when he saw that she was still there. He'd thought – feared – that he would lose her along with the other characters in the story. He took her quickly by the hand before she too vanished in the dust of the library of the castle of Meung. He led her to the car, as La Ponte watched, disconcerted. Corso saw him receding in the rear-view mirror, looking lost, calling on their long, much-abused friendship. He didn't understand what was going on or even dare ask. Like a discredited, useless harpooneer, not to be trusted, abandoned with some bread and three days' supply of water, left to drift: "Try to reach Batavia, Mr Bligh." But then, at the end of the street, Corso stopped the car and sat with his hands on the wheel, looking at the road ahead, the girl staring, curious, at his profile. La Ponte wasn't a real character either. With a sigh, Corso reversed the car and went back to collect him. For the rest of the following day and night, until they left him at some traffic lights in a Madrid street, La Ponte said not one word. He didn't even protest when Corso told him he'd have to say goodbye to the Dumas manuscript. There wasn't much he could say.

He glanced at the canvas bag by the sleeping girl's feet. The sense of defeat was painful, of course, like a knife wound in his memory. He knew he'd played according to the rules – '*legitime certaverit*' – but had gone in the wrong direction. At the very moment of victory, even if only a partial and incomplete one, any pleasure at winning had been snatched from him. It had been imaginary. It was like defeating imaginary ghosts, or punching into the wind, or shouting at silence. Maybe that's why Corso had been staring suspiciously for some time at the city suspended in the mist, waiting to make sure that its foundations were firmly rooted in the ground before entering it.

He could hear the girl's gentle, rhythmic breathing, at his shoulder. He stared at her bare neck between the folds of the duffle coat. Then he moved his hand closer until he could feel the heat of her warm flesh throbbing in his fingers. As always, her skin smelt of youth and fever. In his imagination and in his memory he could easily follow the long, curving lines of her slender body, down to her bare feet by her plimsolls and the bag. Irene Adler. He still didn't know what to call her. But he could remember her naked body in the shadows, the curve of her hips traced by the light, her parted lips. Impossibly beautiful and silent, absorbed in her own youth and at the same time as serene as tranquil waters, with the wisdom of ages. And in the luminous eyes watching him intently from the shadows, the reflection, the dark image of Corso himself amongst all the light snatched from the sky.

She was watching him now, her emerald green eyes framed by long lashes. She had woken and was moving sleepily, rubbing against his shoulder. Then she sat up, alert. She looked round and then at him.

"Hello, Corso." Her duffle coat slid to her feet. Her white T-shirt clung to her perfect torso, as supple as a beautiful young animal's. "What are we doing here?"

"Waiting." He gestured towards the town which seemed to be floating in the mist from the river. "For it to become real."

She looked, not understanding at first. Then she smiled slowly.

"Maybe it never will," she said.

"Then we'll stay here. It's not such a bad place . . . Up here, with the strange unreal world at our feet." He turned towards the girl and waited before going on. "'I'll give you everything, if you prostrate yourself and adore me . . .' Isn't that the kind of offer you're going to make me?"

The girl's smile was full of tenderness. She bowed her head, thoughtful, and then looked up and held Corso's gaze.

"No, I'm poor."

"Yes, I know." It was true. Corso knew it, he didn't have to read it in the clarity of her eyes. "Your luggage, and the train compartment . . . It's strange. I always thought you all had unlimited wealth, out there, at the end of the rainbow." His smile was as sharp as the knife he still had in his pocket. "Peter Schlehmil's bag of gold and all that."

"Well, you're wrong." Now she was pursing her lips obstinately. "I'm all I have."

This was true too, and Corso had known it from the start. She had never lied. Both innocent and wise, she was faithful and in love, chasing after a shadow.

"I see." He made a gesture in the air, as if wielding an imaginary pen. "Aren't you going to give me a document to sign?"

"A document?"

"Yes. It used to be called a pact. Now it would be a contract with lots of small print, wouldn't it? 'In the event of litigation, the parties are to submit to the jurisdiction of the courts of . . .' That's a funny thing. I wonder which court covers all of this."

"Don't be silly."

"Why did you choose me?"

"I'm free," she sighed sadly, as if she'd paid the price for her right to say it. "I can choose. Anyone can."

Corso searched in his coat for his crumpled packet of cigarettes. There was only one left. He took it out and stared, undecided as to whether to put it in his mouth or not, before finally putting it back in the packet. Maybe he'd need a smoke later. He was sure he would.

"You knew everything right from the beginning," he said. "That there were two completely unrelated stories. That's why you never cared about the Dumas strand . . . Milady, Rochefort, Richelieu – they were nothing but film extras to you. Now I understand why you were so disconcertingly passive. You must have been horribly bored. You just flicked the pages of your *Musketeers,* watching me make all the wrong moves . . ."

She was staring through the windscreen at the town veiled in blue mist. She started to raise her hand to add emphasis to her answer, but then just let it drop, as if what she was about to say was pointless.

"All I could do was go with you," she answered at last. "Everyone has to walk certain paths alone. Haven't you heard of free will?" She smiled sadly. "Some of us have paid a very high price for it."

"But you didn't always stay on the sidelines. That night, by the Seine . . . Why did you help me against Rochefort?"

She touched the canvas bag with her bare foot.

"He was after the Dumas manuscript. But *The Nine Doors* was in there too. I just wanted to avoid any stupid interferences." She shrugged. "And I didn't want him to hit you."

"What about Sintra? You warned me about the Fargas business."

"Of course. The book was tied up with it."

"And then the key to the meeting in Meung . . ."

"I didn't know about it. I just worked it out from the novel."

Corso made a face.

"I thought all of you were omniscient."

"Well, you were wrong." Now she was looking at him, annoyed. "And I don't know why you keep talking to me as if I was one of many. I've been alone for a long time."

Centuries, Corso was sure. Centuries of solitude. He couldn't deceive himself about that. He had embraced her naked body, drowned in the clarity of her eyes. He had been inside her, tasted her skin, felt the gentle throbbing of her neck against his lips. He'd heard her moan quietly, like a frightened child, or a lonely fallen angel in search of warmth. He'd watched her sleep with her fists clenched, tormented by nightmares of gleaming, blond archangels, implacable in their armour, as dogmatic as the God who made them march in time.

Now, thanks to her, although too late, he understood Nikon and her ghosts and the desperate way she clung to life. Her fear, her black-and-white photographs, her vain attempt to exorcise memories transmitted through genes that survived Auschwitz, the number tattooed on her father's skin, the Black Order which had never been anything new but as old as the spirit and the curse of man. Because God and the Devil could be one and the same thing, and everybody understood it in their own way.

But just as with Nikon, Corso was still cruel. It was too heavy a burden for him and he didn't have Porthos's noble heart.

"Was that your mission?" he asked the girl. "Protecting *The Nine Doors*? I don't think you'll get a medal for it."

"That's unfair, Corso."

Almost the same words. Once again, Nikon left to drift, small and fragile. Who did she cling to now, to escape her nightmares?

He looked at the girl. Maybe Nikon's memory was his penance. But he was no longer prepared to accept it with resignation. He glimpsed his face in the rear-view mirror: it was contracted into a lost, bitter expression.

"Is it? We've lost two out of the three books. And what about the pointless deaths of Fargas and the Baroness?" They mattered little to him but he continued to look bitter. "You could have prevented them."

She shook her head, very serious, her eyes fixed on his.

"Some things can't be avoided, Corso. Some castles have to burn and some men must hang. There are dogs destined to tear each other to pieces, virtuous people to be beheaded, doors to be opened for others to enter . . ." She frowned and bowed her head. "My mission, as you call it, was to make sure you reached the end of the journey safely."

"Well, it's been a long journey, only to end up at the starting-point." Corso indicated the town suspended in the mist. "And now I've got to go down there."

"You don't *have* to. Nobody's forcing you. You could just forget about it and leave."

"Without finding out the answer?"

"Without undergoing the test. You have the answer within you."

"That's a pretty sentence. Put it on my headstone when I'm burning in Hell."

She gave him a gentle, almost friendly tap on the knee.

"Don't be an idiot, Corso. Things are as one wants them to be more often than people think. Even the Devil can adopt different guises. Or essences."

"Remorse, for instance."

"Yes. But also knowledge and beauty." She again looked anxiously at the town. "Or power and wealth."

"But the end result is the same: damnation." He repeated his gesture of signing an imaginary contract. "You have to pay with the innocence of your soul."

She sighed again.

"You paid long ago, Corso. You're still paying. It's a strange habit, postponing it all till the end. Like the final act of a tragedy . . .

Everyone drags their own damnation with them from the beginning. As for the Devil, he is no more than God's pain; the wrath of a dictator caught in his own trap. The story told by the winners."

"When did it happen?"

"A longer time ago than you can conceive. It was very hard. I fought for a hundred days and a hundred nights without hope or refuge." A gentle, almost imperceptible smile appeared on her lips. "That's the only thing I'm proud of – having fought to the end. I retreated but didn't turn my back, surrounded by others also falling from on high. I was hoarse from shouting out my fury, my fear and exhaustion . . . After the battle I walked across a desolate plateau, as lonely as eternity is cold . . . I still sometimes come across a trace of the battle, or an old comrade who passes by without daring to look up."

"Why me, then? Why didn't you look for someone on the side of the winners? I only win battles on a scale of 1:5,000."

The girl turned to look into the distance. The sun was rising, and the first horizontal ray of light cut the morning air with a fine, reddish line that directly intersected her gaze. When she looked back at Corso he felt vertigo as he peered into all the light reflected in her green eyes.

"Because lucidity never wins. And seducing an idiot has never been worth the trouble."

Then she leant over and kissed him very slowly, with infinite tenderness. As if she had had to wait an eternity to do so.

The mist slowly began to clear. It was as if the town, suspended in mid-air, had decided to sink its foundations in the earth. The dawn shone on the grey and ochre mass of the Alcázar palace, the cathedral bell tower, and the stone bridge with its pillars in the dark waters of the river, resembling a sinister hand stretched between the two banks.

Corso started the engine. He let the car slide gently down the deserted road. As they descended, the light of the rising sun was left behind, held above them. The town gradually moved closer and they slowly entered the world of cold tones and immense solitude which persisted in the remnants of blue mist.

He hesitated before crossing the bridge, stopping the car beneath the stone arch which led onto it; his hands on the steering-wheel, head slightly bowed and his chin jutting out: the profile of a tense, alert hunter. He took off his glasses and cleaned them though they didn't need it. He took his time, staring intently at the bridge which had now become a vague path with disturbingly imprecise outlines. He didn't look at the girl but he knew that she was watching his every move. He put on his glasses, adjusting them on the bridge of his nose, and the landscape recovered its sharp lines, but became no more reassuring. The other bank looked dark and distant. The current flowing between the pillars resembled the black waters of time and of Lethe. In the remnants of the night which refused to die, his sense of danger was tangible, acute, like a steel needle. Corso could feel the pulse beating in his wrist when he grasped the gear lever. You can still turn back, he told himself. In that way, none of what has happened had ever happened, and none of what was to take place would ever take place. As to the practical value of '*Nunc scio*': 'Now I know', coined by God or by the Devil, it was highly dubious. He frowned. Anyway, they were nothing but words. He knew that a few minutes later he would be on the other side of the bridge and river. '*Verbum dimissum custodiat arcanum.*' He gazed up at the sky, looking for an archer with or without arrows in his quiver, before putting the car into gear and gently moving off.

It was cold outside the car so he turned up his collar. He could feel the girl's intent gaze upon him as he crossed the street without looking back, holding *The Nine Doors* under his arm. She hadn't offered to go with him, and for some obscure reason he knew that it was better that way. As for the house, it occupied almost an entire block and its grey stone bulk presided over a narrow square, amongst medieval buildings whose closed windows and doors made them look like motionless film extras, blind and mute. The façade was of grey stone with four gargoyles on the eaves: a billy goat, a crocodile, a gorgon and a serpent. There was a star of David on the Moorish arch above the wrought-iron gate that lead to the interior courtyard with two Venetian marble lions and a well. It was all familiar to Corso but he had never been so apprehensive upon entering the house. He remembered an old quotation: 'Perhaps men who have been caressed by many women cross the valley of shadows with less remorse, or less fear . . ." It went something like that. Maybe he hadn't been caressed enough because his mouth was dry and he would have sold his soul for half a bottle of Bols. And *The Nine Doors* felt as if it contained nine lead plates instead of prints.

He pushed open the gate but the silence remained unbroken. Not even his shoes caused the slightest echo as he crossed the courtyard, its paving stones worn down by ancient footsteps and centuries of rain. An archway led to the steep, narrow staircase. At the top he could see the dark, heavy door decorated with thick nails. It was closed: the last door. For an instant, Corso winked privately, sarcastically at empty space, baring his teeth. He was both involuntary author and victim of his own joke or his own error. An error, carefully planned by an unscrupulous hand, and full of serpentine, illusory invitations to participate that had led him to certain conclusions, only for them to be refuted. But in the end he'd had them confirmed by the text itself as if it had been a damned novel, which it wasn't. Or what if it was? The fact is, the last thing he saw in the polished metal plate nailed to the door was his own, very real face. A distorted image that contained the name on the plate, as well as his own shape against the light behind him in the archway over the stairs, leading down to the courtyard and the street. The last stop on a strange journey to the other side of the shadows.

He rang. Once, twice, three times. No answer. The brass bellpush lay dead, and there had been no sound inside when he pressed it. In his pocket he felt the crumpled packet containing his last cigarette. Again he decided against lighting it. He rang the bell a fourth time. And a fifth. He clenched his fist and knocked hard, twice. Then the door opened. Not with a sinister creak, but smoothly, on greased hinges. And without any dramatic effects, quite casually, Varo Borja stood in the doorway.

"Hello, Corso."

Varo Borja didn't seem surprised to see him. There were beads of sweat all over his head and he was unshaven. His shirtsleeves were rolled up and his waistcoat undone. He looked tired, with dark rings under his eyes from a sleepless night. But his eyes shone feverishly. He didn't ask what Corso was doing there at such an hour, and he seemed barely to notice the book under his arm. He stood there without moving for a moment, as if he had just been interrupted during some meticulous job, or dream, and just wanted to get back to it.

Here was the man responsible, Corso knew it, seeing his own stupidity materialize before him. Of course. Varo Borja – millionaire, international bookdealer, famous collector and methodical murderer.

With an almost scientific curiosity, Corso scrutinized the face before him. He tried now to isolate the features, the clues that should have alerted him so much earlier. Signs overlooked, angles of madness, horror or shadow in the familiar, vulgar features. But he couldn't see anything. Just a feverish, distant expression, devoid of curiosity or passion, lost in images far removed from the man now ringing at the door. But Corso was holding his copy of the cursed book. It had been he, Varo Borja, in the shadow of that same book, following Corso's footsteps like an evil snake, who had killed Victor Fargas and Baroness Ungern. Not only to reunite the twenty-seven engravings and combine the nine correct ones, but also to cover any trails and make sure that nobody else should resolve the riddle set by Torchia, the printer. For the entire plot, Corso had been a tool for confirming a theory which proved correct – that the real book was distributed over three copies. He was also the victim of any repercussions involving the police. Now, paying twisted homage to his own instincts, he remembered how he felt looking up at the paintings on the ceiling of the Quinta da Soledade. Abraham's sacrifice with no alternative victim: he was the scapegoat. And Varo Borja, of course, was the dealer who went to see Victor Fargas to purchase one of his treasures every six months. That day, while Corso was visiting Fargas, Borja was in Sintra, finalizing the details of his plan, waiting for confirmation of his theory that all three copies were needed to resolve Torchia's riddle. Fargas's half-written receipt was intended for him. That's why Corso hadn't been able to get hold of Borja when he phoned his house in Toledo. Then later that same evening, before going to his final appointment with Fargas, he had called Corso at the hotel pretending he was making an international call. Corso had not only confirmed Borja's suspicions about the book, but also the very key to the mystery, thus condemning Fargas and the Baroness. With bitter certainty Corso could see the pieces of the puzzle falling into place. Apart from the false clues by chance linking the Dumas Club, Varo Borja was the key to all the inexplicable events of that other, diabolic, strand of the plot. It was enough to make one laugh out loud. If the whole damn business had been at all funny that is.

"I've brought the book," he said showing him *The Nine Doors*.

Varo Borja nodded vaguely and took the book, barely glancing at it. He had his head slightly turned to the side, as if listening out for a sound behind him, inside the house. After a moment he noticed Corso again and blinked, surprised that he was still there.

"You've given me the book. What else do you want?"

"To be paid for the job."

Varo Borja stood staring at him uncomprehendingly. It was obvious that his thoughts were miles away. At last, he shrugged, as if to say it had nothing to do with him. Then he went into the house, leaving it up to Corso whether he shut the door, stayed where he was or turned back the way he'd come.

Corso followed him through a safety door into the room leading off the corridor and the vestibule. The shutters were closed so no light could enter, and the furniture had been pushed to the far end, leaving the black marble floor empty. Some of the glass bookcases were open. The room was lit by dozens of candles that had almost burnt down. The wax was dripping everywhere: on the mantelpiece above the empty fireplace, on to the floor, the furniture and objects in the room. They gave off a tremulous, reddish light which danced about with any draught or movement. It smelt like a church, or a crypt.

Still taking no notice of Corso, Varo Borja stopped in the middle of the room. There, at his feet, a circle of approximately three feet in diameter was marked out in chalk, with a square divided into nine boxes. It was surrounded by Roman numerals and strange objects: a piece of string, a waterclock, a rusty knife, a dragon-shaped silver bracelet, a gold ring, a small metal brazier full of burning charcoal, a glass vial, a small pile of earth, a stone. But Corso winced when he saw the other things strewn on the floor. Many of the books he'd admired lined up on shelves a few days earlier were now lying ruined, dirty, with pages torn out, covered with drawings and underlinings, and full of strange marks. Candles burnt on top of several of the books and thick drops of wax were dripping onto their covers or open pages. Some had burnt down and singed the paper. Amongst the wreckage he recognized the engravings from the copies of *The Nine Doors* belonging to Victor Fargas and Baroness Ungern. They were mixed up with the others on the floor and also covered in wax drips and mysterious annotations.

Corso bent down to look more closely at the remains, not quite able to believe the magnitude of the disaster. One engraving from *The Nine Doors*, number VI, the man hanging by his right foot instead of his left, had been half burnt away by the flickering flame of a candle. Two copies of engraving number VII, one with a white chessboard and the other with a black one, lay beside the remains of a 1512 *Theatrum diabolicum* torn from its binding. Another engraving, number I, was protruding from the pages of a *De magna imperfectaque opera* by Valerio Lorena, an extremely rare incunabulum that Borja had shown Corso a few days earlier, barely allowing him to touch it. It now lay on the floor, battered and torn.

"Don't touch anything," he heard Varo Borja say. He was standing before the circle, leafing through his copy of *The Nine Doors*, engrossed. He seemed to see not the pages themselves but something beyond them, inside the square and circle on the floor, or even farther away still: in the depths of the earth.

Motionless, Corso looked at him for a moment as if seeing him for the first time. Then he stood up slowly. As he did so the candle flames around him flickered.

"It makes no difference if I touch anything," he said gesturing towards the books and papers lying scattered over the floor. "After what you've done."

"You don't know anything, Corso. You think you do, but you don't. You're ignorant and very stupid. The kind who believes chaos is random and ignores the existence of a hidden order."

"Don't talk rubbish. You've destroyed everything and you had no right to. Nobody has."

"You're wrong. In the first place they're *my* books. And what's more important their purpose is to be used. They had practical, rather than artistic or aesthetic value. As one travels along the path one must ensure that no one else can follow. These books have now served their purpose."

"You bloody madman. You deceived me right from the start."

Varo Borja didn't seem to be listening. He stood motionless, holding the remaining copy of *The Nine Doors*, scrutinizing engraving number I.

"Deceived?" He kept his eyes fixed on the book as he spoke, which underlined his contempt for Corso. "You do yourself too much honour. I hired you without telling you my reasons or my intentions. A servant has no reason to participate in the decisions of whoever is paying him. You were to steal the items I wanted to collect, and at the same time incur the technical consequences of certain unavoidable actions. I should imagine that as we speak the police in both Portugal and France are on your tail."

"What about you?"

"I'm very far removed from all that, and quite safe. In a little while nothing will matter."

Then, to Corso's horror, he tore the page with the engraving from *The Nine Doors*.

"What are you doing?"

Varo Borja was calmly tearing out more pages.

"I'm burning my boats, destroying any bridges behind me. And moving into *terra incognita*." He'd torn the engravings from the book, one by one, until he had all nine, and was looking at them closely. "It's a pity you can't follow me where I'm going. As the fourth engraving states, fate is not the same for all."

"Where do you believe you're going?"

Borja dropped his mutilated copy on the floor with the other remains. He was looking at the nine engravings and at the circle, checking strange correspondences between them.

"To meet someone," was his enigmatic answer. "To search for the stone that the Great Architect rejected, the philosopher's stone, the basis of the philosophical work. Of power. The Devil likes metamorphoses, Corso. From Faust's black dog, to the false angel of light who tried to break down St Anthony's resistance. But most of all, stupidity bores him and he hates monotony . . . If I had the time and inclination I'd invite you to take a look at some of the books at your feet. Several of them mention an ancient tradition: the advent of the Antichrist will occur in the Iberian peninsula, in a city with three superimposed cultures, on the banks of a river as deep as an axe cut, the Tagus."

"Is that what you're trying to do?"

"It's what I'm about to achieve. Brother Torchia showed me the way: '*Tenebris Lux.*'"

He was bending over the circle on the floor, laying some of the engravings round it and removing others, which he threw away from him, crumpled or torn. The candles illuminated his face from below, making him look ghostly, with deep shadows for eyes.

"I hope it all fits together," he muttered after a moment. His mouth was a line of shadow. "The ancient masters of the black art who taught the printer Torchia the most terrible and valuable mysteries, knew the path leading to the kingdom of night. 'It is the animal with its tail in its mouth that encircles the place.' Do you understand? The *ourobouros* of the Greek alchemists: the serpent on the frontispiece, the magic circle, the source of wisdom. The circle in which everything is written."

"I want my money."

Varo Borja didn't seem to have heard Corso.

"Have you never been curious about these things?" he went on, peering out from shadowed eyes. "To investigate, for instance, the Devil-serpent-dragon constant which has reappeared suspiciously in all the texts on the subject since Antiquity?"

He had picked up a glass object next to the circle, a goblet with handles in the shape of two linked serpents, and he raised it to his mouth and took a few sips. It held some dark liquid, Corso noticed, almost black, like very strong tea.

"'*Serpens aut draco qui caudam devoravit.*'" Varo Borja smiled into empty space, wiping his mouth. He left a dark smear on the back of his hand and his left cheek. "They guard the treasures: the tree of knowledge in the Garden of Eden, the Hesperides' apples, the Golden Fleece . . ." As he talked he looked absent, insane, as if describing a dream from the inside. "They're the serpents or dragons that the ancient Egyptians painted in a circle, with their tail in their mouth to indicate that they came from a single thing, and were self-sufficient . . . Sleepless guardians, proud and wise. Hermetic dragons that kill the unworthy and only allow themselves to be seduced by one who has fought according to the rules. Guardians of the lost word: the magic formula which opens eyes and makes one the equal of God."

Corso stuck out his jaw. He was standing, still and thin in his coat, with the shadows of the candles dancing between his half-closed eyelids, making his unshaven cheeks look sunken. He had his hands in his pockets, one touching the packet with its remaining cigarette, the other round the closed switchblade, next to his flask of gin.

"I said give me my money. I want to get out of here."

There was a slight threat in his voice, but Corso couldn't tell if Varo Borja had noticed it. He saw him come to unwillingly, slowly.

"Money?" He was looking at him with renewed contempt. "What are you talking about, Corso? Don't you understand what's about to happen? You have before you the mystery that men throughout the centuries have dreamt of . . . Do you know how many have been burnt, tortured and torn to pieces just for a glimpse of what you are about to witness? You can't come with me, of course. You will just stay still and watch. But even the most vile mercenary can share in his master's triumph."

"Pay me once and for all. Then you can go to the Devil."

Varo Borja didn't even look at him. He was moving round the circle and touching some of the objects laid next to the numbers.

"How appropriate that you should send me to the Devil. So typical of your down-to-earth style. I'd even honour you with a smile if I wasn't so busy. Although your remark was ignorant and imprecise: it will be the Devil who comes to me." He paused and turned his head as if he could already hear distant footsteps. "And I feel him coming."

He muttered, his speech interspersed with strange guttural exclamations, or words that sometimes seemed addressed to Corso and at others to a third dark presence near them, in the shadows:

"'You will go through eight doors before the dragon . . .' Do you see? Eight doors come before the beast who guards the word, number nine, which possesses the final secret . . . The dragon sleeps with its eye open and it is the Mirror of Knowledge . . . Eight engravings plus one. Or one plus eight. Which coincides with the number that St John of Patmos attributed to the Beast: 666."

Corso saw him kneel and write out numbers in chalk on the marble floor:

$$666$$
$$6 + 6 + 6 = 18$$
$$1\text{-}8$$
$$1 + 8 = 9$$

Then he stood up, triumphant. For a moment the candles lit up his eyes. He must have swallowed some kind of drug with the dark liquid. His pupils were so dilated that almost none of the iris was visible, and the whites had taken on a reddish tinge from the light in the room.

"Nine engravings, or nine doors." Shadow once again covered his face like a mask. "They can't be opened by just anyone . . . 'Each door has two keys.' Each engraving provides a number, a magic element and a key word, if it's all studied in the light of reason, the Cabbala, the occult, the true philosophy . . . Of Latin and its combination with Greek and Hebrew." He showed Corso a piece of paper covered in signs and strange links. "You can take a look, if you like. You'll never understand it:

Aleph	Eis	I	ONMA	Air
Beth	Duo	II	CIS	Earth
Gimel	Treis	III	EM	Water
Daleth	Tessares	IIII	EM	Gold
He	Pente	V	OEXE	String
Vau	Es	VI	CIS	Silver
Zayin	Epta	VII	CIS	Stone
Cheth	Octo	VIII	EM	Iron
Teth	Ennea	VIIII	ODED	Fire

There were beads of sweat on his forehead and round his mouth, as if the flame of the candles were also burning inside his body. He began to walk round the circle slowly and carefully. He stopped a couple of times and bent over to adjust the position of some object: the rusty knife, the silver bracelet.

"'You will place the elements on the serpent's skin . . .'" he recited without looking at Corso. He was following the circle with his finger but not quite touching it. "The nine elements are to be placed around it 'in the direction of the rising sun': from right to left."

Corso took a step towards him.

"Once more. Give me my money."

Varo Borja took no notice. He had his back to him, and was pointing to the square drawn inside the circle.

"'The serpent will swallow the seal of Saturn . . .' The seal of Saturn is the most ancient and simple of the magic squares: the first nine numbers placed inside nine boxes, set out so that each row, whether down, across, or diagonally, adds up to the same number."

He bent down and wrote out nine numbers inside the box in chalk:

4	9	2
3	5	7
8	1	6

Corso took another step. As he did so he trod on a piece of paper covered in numbers:

$$4+9+2=15 \qquad 4+3+8=15 \qquad 4+5+6=15$$
$$3+5+7=15 \qquad 9+5+1=15 \qquad 2+5+8=15$$
$$8+1+6=15 \qquad 2+7+6=15$$

A candle went out with a hiss, having burnt down onto the charred frontispiece of a *De occulta philosophia* by Cornelius Agrippa. Varo Borja's attention was still on the circle and the square. He stared at them intently, his arms folded on his chest and his head bowed. He looked like a player before a strange board, pondering his next move.

"There's one thing," he said, now no longer addressing Corso but talking to himself. It seemed that hearing his own voice helped him to think. "Something that the ancients didn't foresee, at least not expressly . . . Added together in any direction, from up to down, down to up, left to right, or right to left, you get 15. But applying the codes of the Cabbalists it also becomes a 1 and a 5, which, added together, make six . . . And that surrounds each side of the magical square with the serpent, the dragon or the Beast, or whatever you want to call it."

Corso didn't even have to work it out for himself. It was set out on another piece of paper on the floor:

	6	6	6	
6	4	9	2	6
6	3	5	7	6
6	8	1	6	6
	6	6	6	

Varo Borja knelt before the circle, his head bowed. The sweat on his face gleamed in the candlelight. He was holding another piece of paper and reading out the strange words written on it.

"'You will open the seal nine times,' says Torchia's text . . . That means the key words obtained must be placed in the box that corresponds to its number. In that way we get the following sequence:

1	2	3	4	5	6	7	8	9
ONMAD	CIS	EM	EM	OEXE	CIS	CIS	EM	ODED

" . . . Written on the serpent, or the dragon." He rubbed out the numbers in the boxes and inserted the corresponding words in their place. "This is how it looks, to God's shame:"

EM	ODED	CIS
EM	OEXE	CIS
EM	ONMAD	CIS

"It has all been carried out," muttered Varo Borja as he wrote out the final letters. His hand was trembling, and one of the drops of sweat slid from his forehead down his nose and onto the chalk-covered floor. "According to Torchia's text, it is sufficient for 'the mirror to reflect the path' to pronounce the lost word which brings the light from the darkness . . . These phrases are in Latin. They mean nothing on their own. But inside they contain the exact essence of the '*Verbum dimissum*', the formula which makes Satan, our forebear, our mirror and our accomplice, appear."

He was kneeling in the centre of the circle, surrounded by all the signs, objects and words written in the square. His hands were shaking so violently that he clasped them together, claw-like, his fingers covered in chalk, ink and wax. Proud and sure of himself, he started to laugh like a madman, under his breath. But Corso was sure he wasn't insane. He looked around, aware that he was running out of time, and he started to cross the distance between him and the bookdealer. But he couldn't make up his mind to cross the line and stand with him inside the circle.

Varo Borja looked at him malevolently, guessing his fears.

"Come on, Corso. Don't you want to read it with me? Are you scared, or have you forgotten your Latin?" Light and shadow alternated with increasing speed on his face, as if the room around him were starting to spin. But the room was still. "Don't you want to know what these words contain? On the back of that engraving poking from between the pages of the Valerio Lorena, you'll find the translation into Spanish. Place them before the mirror, as the masters of the art ordered. At least then you will know what Fargas and Baroness Ungern died for."

Corso looked at the book, an incunabulum with a very old and worn parchment binding. Then he bent over cautiously, as if the pages contained a dangerous trap, and pulled out the engraving poking from between the pages. It was engraving I of Book Number Three, Baroness Ungern's copy, with three towers instead of four. On the reverse Varo Borja had written nine words:

> OGERTNE EM ISA
>
> OREBIL EM ISA
>
> OREDNOC EM ISA

"Courage, Corso," said the bookdealer's sour, disagreeable voice. "You have nothing to lose . . . Hold the words to the mirror."

There was, indeed, a mirror very near on the floor, amongst the melted wax from candles about to burn themselves out. It was silver, old and stained, with a baroque worked handle. It lay face up and Corso's image appeared in it, tiny and distorted, as if at the end of a long tunnel of trembling red light. The image and its double, the hero and his infinite weariness, Bonaparte chained in agony to his rock on Saint Helena. Nothing to lose, Varo Borja had said. A cold, desolate world, where the solitary skeletons of Waterloo grenadiers stood guard along dark, forgotten paths. He saw himself before the final door, holding the key like the hermit in engraving II, the letter Teth coiled round his shoulder like a serpent.

He stepped on the mirror and crushed it with his heel, slowly, without violence. The mirror shattered with a cracking sound. The fragments now multiplied Corso's image in countless tunnels of shadow at the end of which countless replicas of himself stood motionless, too small and indistinct to concern him.

"Black is the school of the night," he heard Varo Borja say. He was still kneeling in the centre of the circle with his back to Corso, leaving him to his fate. Corso leant over one of the candles and held a corner of engraving I, with the nine inverted words on the reverse, to the flame. He watched the castle towers, the horse, the horseman turned towards the viewer advising silence, burn between his fingers. At last he dropped the remaining piece, which turned to ash a second later and floated on the hot air of the candles lit around the room. Then he entered the circle and moved towards Varo Borja.

"I want my money. Now."

Lost ever deeper in darkness, Borja took no notice. Then, anxiously, as if the objects on the floor suddenly appeared incorrectly laid out, he crouched and altered the position of some of them. After a brief hesitation, he began intoning a sinister prayer:

"'Admai, Aday, Eloy, Agla . . .'"

Corso grabbed him by the shoulder and shook him violently. But Varo Borja showed no emotion or fear. Nor did he try to defend himself. He continued to recite as if he were in a trance, a martyr praying unaware of the roar of the lions or the executioner's sword.

"For the last time. Give me my money."

It was no good. All he saw before him were Borja's empty eyes looking through him, wells of darkness, blank, intent on the chasms of the kingdom of shadows.

"'Zatel, Gebel, Elimi . . .'"

He was summoning the devils, Corso realized in disbelief. Standing inside the circle, aware of nothing, neither Corso's presence nor even his threats, the man was invoking devils regardless, by their first names.

"'Gamael, Bilet . . .'"

Borja only stopped when Corso struck him for the first time, a blow with the back of his hand that sent his head over to one side. His eyes rolled and then fixed on a vague point in space.

"'Zaquel, Astarot . . .'"

By the time he received the second blow, blood was already trickling from a corner of his mouth. With revulsion Corso pulled his hand away, stained with red. He'd felt he was striking something damp, viscous. He took a couple of breaths and then counted ten beats of his heart before clenching his teeth, then his fists, and striking again. Blood was now flowing from the bookdealer's twisted mouth. He was still muttering his prayer, a disturbing, delirious smile of absurd joy on his swollen lips. Corso grabbed him by his shirt collar and dragged him brutally outside the circle before hitting him again. Only then did Varo Borja cry out like an animal, in pain and anguish, struggling free with unexpected energy and dragging himself back to the circle. Corso pushed him from it three times, and three times he returned to it, obstinately. By then a trail of blood was smeared over the signs and letters written on the seal of Saturn.

"'*Sic dedo me . . .*'"

Something was wrong. In the trembling candlelight, Corso saw him hesitate, perplexed, and check the arrangement of the objects in the magic circle. But the last few drops were draining from the waterclock. Varo Borja seemed to have little time left. He repeated his last words with greater emphasis, touching three of the nine boxes:

"'*Sic dedo me . . .*'"

An acrid taste in his mouth, Corso looked round hopelessly, wiping his bloodstained hand on his coat. Yet more candles had burnt right down and went out with a hiss. Spirals of smoke rose from their charred wicks in the reddish gloom. Like serpents, he thought with bitter irony. Then he went to the desk that had been pushed into a corner with the rest of the furniture, and searched through the drawers. There was no money. Not even a cheque-book. Nothing.

"'*Sic exeo me . . .*'"

The bookdealer continued to intone his litany. Corso glanced at him, at the magic circle one last time. Kneeling within it, leaning his distorted, fervent face towards the floor, Varo Borja was opening the last of the nine doors with a smile of insane joy; his bleeding mouth, a black, demonic line across his face, like a cut from a knife made of night and shadow.

"Son of a bitch," said Corso. And with that he took his contract to be terminated.

He headed towards the grey light at the foot of the steps, beneath the arch leading to the courtyard. There, by the well and the marble lions, before the gate leading to the street, he stopped and breathed deeply, savouring the fresh, clean morning air. Then he searched in his coat until he found the crumpled packet with one remaining cigarette. He put it in his mouth but didn't light it. He stood there a moment while, red and slanting, the first ray of the sun which he'd left behind on entering the city, reached him. It slipped between the grey stone façades of the square, projecting the shadow of the wrought-iron gate on his face, and making him half-close his sleepless, weary eyes. Then the light grew, spreading slowly to fill the entire patio with the Venetian lions, who bowed their marble manes as if receiving a caress. The same glow, first red, then luminous as a suspension of gold dust, enveloped Corso. And at that instant, at the top of the stairs, beyond the last door of the kingdom of the shadows, where the calm light of dawn would never reach, there was a cry. A piercing, inhuman scream, full of horror and despair, in which he could only just recognize the voice of Varo Borja.

Without turning round, Corso pushed the gate and went out into the street. With each step he seemed to move a great distance away from what he was leaving behind, as if, in only a few seconds, he had retraced his steps on a journey that had taken him too long.

He stopped in the middle of the square, dazzled, enveloped in blinding sunlight. The girl was still in the car, and Corso shivered with deep, selfish delight when he saw that she hadn't disappeared with the remnants of the night. She smiled tenderly, looking impossibly young and beautiful, with her hair cut short like a boy's, her tanned skin, her tranquil eyes fixed on him, waiting. And all the golden, perfect light reflected in the liquid green of her eyes – the light driving back the dark angles of the ancient city, the shadow of the bell towers and the pointed arches of the square – seemed to radiate from her smile as Corso went to meet her. He looked down at the ground as he walked, resigned, ready to bid his own shadow farewell. But there was no shadow at his feet.

Behind him, in the house guarded by four gargoyles beneath the eaves, Varo Borja was no longer screaming. Or perhaps he was doing so from some dark place, too far away to be heard from the street. "*Nunc scio*": now I know. Corso wondered if the Ceniza brothers had used resin or wood to forge the illustration, lost through the whim of a child or the barbarity of a collector, in Book Number One. Although, as he thought of their pale, skilled hands, he inclined to think they had carved it in wood, basing it on Mateu's *Bibliography*. That's why things didn't tally for Varo Borja: in the three copies, the final engraving was a forgery. "*Ceniza sculpsit*." For love of their art.

He was laughing under his breath, like a cruel wolf, as he leant over to light his last cigarette. Books play that kind of trick, he thought. And everyone gets the Devil he deserves.

La Navata. April 1993

To join the mailing list and for a full list of titles please write to

THE HARVILL PRESS
84 THORNHILL ROAD
LONDON N1 1RD, UK

enclosing a stamped-addressed envelope